"Rhiannon, you must listen to me!" He shook her. "If you die bound to Pryderi your spirit will never know the presence of your goddess again. You will never know light or joy again. You will spend eternity blanketed in the night of the dark god and the despair that taints all he touches."

"I know," she whispered. "But I am finished fighting. It seems all I've done for as long as I can remember is fight. I've been too selfish, caused too much pain. Done too much harm. Perhaps it is time for me to pay for that."

"Perhaps it is, but should your daughter pay for your mistakes, too?"

His words jolted her, and she blinked back the encroaching darkness in her eyes. "Of course she shouldn't. What are you saying, old man?"

"You did not pledge her to him, but Pryderi desires a priestess with the blood of Epona's Chosen in her veins. With you dead, who do you think will be his next victim?"

"No!" But she knew he was right.

Divine by Blood

P.C. CAST

**Book Three of the
GODDESS OF PARTHOLON
series**

MIRA

All the characters in this book have no existence outside the imagination
of the author, and have no relation whatsoever to anyone bearing the
same name or names. They are not even distantly inspired by any
individual known or unknown to the author, and all the incidents are
pure invention.

First published in Great Britain 2010.
MIRA Books, Eton House, 18-24 Paradise Road,
Richmond, Surrey, TW9 1SR

ISBN 978 0 7783 0363 3

59-0110

MIRA's policy is to use papers that are natural, renewable and
recyclable products and made from wood grown in sustainable forests.
The logging and manufacturing processes conform to the legal
environmental regulations of the country of origin.

Printed in Great Britain
by Clays Ltd, St Ives plc

Dear Lovely Reader,

Divine by Blood may very well be the most difficult book I've ever written. And that's not because I had to complete Shannon's story – explain about Rhiannon – and tell the daughters' stories, too. All in one book!

The reason this book was tough for me was that in finishing it I felt as if I was saying goodbye to my family. It's no secret (sometimes much to my embarrassment) that I peopled the Divine books with characters based on friends and family. One character in particular is so close to the living man that it makes me smile just thinking about him. Unquestionably, Richard Parker was fashioned after my dad. And while he and/or his ghost show up in all the Partholon books, it is in *Divine by Blood* that his character's words and actions hold particularly true to my dad, Dick Cast. So while I poured a lot of love, and maybe even a piece of my heart, into the Divine trilogy, this last book will always be special to me – so special that it was difficult to see it end. I hope the spirit of it touches you, as it did me.

And who knows – Partholon is a big world. Perhaps there are more stories there just waiting for me to tell...

Wishing you happy reading and the brightest of blessings.

P.C. Cast

ACKNOWLEDGEMENTS

Thank you to my publishing team, Mary-Theresa Hussey and Adam Wilson, for being so great to work with – as usual!

As always, I am thankful for my agent and friend, Meredith Bernstein.

Thanks, Dad, for the ecosystem information, finding a feline basis for my lovely fictional species of cave cats, and for making the research trip to Oklahoma's fabulous Alabaster Caverns and Great Salt Plains so much fun (Mama Cast and Lainee Ann, too!).

I'd like to acknowledge the Alabaster Caverns State Park and thank the people there for being so gracious and helping with my research. The Alabaster Caverns State Park is located in northwestern Oklahoma and is well worth the trip. The Oklahoma Great Salt Plains of north central Oklahoma is also an amazing place. Yes, there are selenite crystals on the plains, but you have to dig for them, versus how I fictionalised them. What I didn't fictionalise is the magic I found in both places. For more information you can contact Alabastercaverns@OklahomaParks.com, and the Salt Plains National Wildlife Refuge at 580-626-4794. Explore Oklahoma and see for yourself!

Divine by Blood

For my stepmom and dad, Mama Cast and the Old Coach,
aka Mama Parker and Richard Parker.
With much love from Bugs.

PROLOGUE

She wasn't dead.

She wasn't alive, either.

In truth, she might have passed countless years simply dwelling in the outlands of existence. Not dying—not living. Just being. If it hadn't been for the life that stirred within her womb, and the anger that stirred within her breast. Before she remembered who she was, she remembered that she had been betrayed.

Yes, anger is good…

The voice in her mind was not her own, but it felt familiar, and she grasped it as she sought to find herself again. Who was she? Where was she? How had this happened to her?

She opened her eyes. Blackness surrounded her. Blackness and weight, as if she had been submerged in a warm pool. For a moment panic overwhelmed her. If she was underwater how could she breathe? Surley she must be dead. Dead and entombed an eternity for crimes she couldn't remember committing.

Then the child within her fluttered again.

The dead did not bring forth life.

She commanded her panic to recede, and it obeyed. Panic never helped. Cold, logical thought. Meticulous planning and precise execution of those plans. That was the way to triumph. That was the way she had always triumphed.

Until now.

But she had been betrayed. By whom? Her anger built and she fed it, channeling her frustration and fear.

Yes...allow anger to purify you...

Her self-awareness increased. Her mind was less sluggish. Her body tingled. Her anger continued to build until she could actually feel its warmth surrounding her. It energized her.

She had been betrayed...she had been betrayed...she had been betrayed...

The words circled through her mind, causing memories to leak from the dark barriers behind which they had been hidden.

A castle at the edge of the sea.

Dreams that were glimpses of reality.

A marble-walled temple of exquisite beauty and strength.

The call of a goddess.

That was it! She was divine! She was the Chosen of a Great Goddess!

Rhiannon...

The name burst through her mind, and with that knowledge the dams that blocked her memory broke, and the past shattered through her.

She had been betrayed by her goddess!

Rhiannon remembered everything. The willful choices she'd made during her life that constantly had her at odds with the Great Goddess Epona. The rape that had been her ascension ritual. The fact that Epona had never been content with her. The realization that no one in Partholon truly loved her— that they only worshipped her as an extension of the Goddess. The Magic Sleep vision wherein she had glimpsed the Fomorian demons infiltrating Guardian Castle and plotting the destruction of Partholon. The whisperings from the darkness that told her there was another way...another world...another choice. The vision of that other world she had been given through the power of that dark voice. And her decision to exchange herself for Shannon Parker, the mundane woman from that world whose physical appearance was so like hers that they could have been born from the same womb.

Rhiannon's body trembled as she remembered the rest of it. How Clint, the Shaman she had found in this world, the mirror image of Partholon's High Shaman ClanFintan, had refused to help her harness the power in this odd world where technology was magic and magic was an almost entirely untapped resource. So she had been forced to use dark powers to call forth a servant to aid her.

But something had gone terribly wrong. Clint had summoned Shannon from Partholon, and the two of them had joined to use their powers to defeat her.

The trees had named Shannon, not Rhiannon, as Epona's Chosen, Beloved of the Goddess.

Epona no longer spoke Rhiannon's name. The Goddess did not acknowledge her as Chosen. When Rhiannon had realized this, something within her had broken. Rhiannon felt sick remembering how lost and afraid she had felt. But the wound was not so fresh now.

Epona had betrayed her and allowed her to be entombed, while the usurper, Shannon, returned triumphant to Partholon and the life that should have been hers. And her child's.

You haven't been betrayed by everyone…

She now knew to whom the voice in her head belonged. The Triple-Faced God, Pryderi.

Pryderi…

The name moved through her mind, not as the explosion her own naming had been. Instead it was an alluring whisper.

I am still here with you. It is, after all, women who have always betrayed you. Your mother died and left you. Shannon stole what was yours by right. Epona turned from you simply because you would not be her puppet.

The dark god was right. Women had always betrayed her.

If you give yourself and your daughter to me I will never betray you. In return for your obedience, I will give you Partholon.

Rhiannon wanted to close her mind to the small voice within her that warned against allying herself with darkness. She wanted to give in and accept Pryderi's offer instantly, but she could not ignore the sense of desolation the thought of embracing another god gave her. Logically, she knew that Epona's favor had left her—that the Goddess had turned from her forever. But even though Rhiannon had looked to other gods...other powers...she had never taken that final step. The irretraceable step of rejecting Epona and giving herself completely to another god.

If she did that she would never be able to stand before Epona again. And what if the Goddess decided she'd made a mistake? If Rhiannon could free herself from this horrid imprisonment and return to Partholon, was there not a chance that Epona might, once again, recognize her as Chosen? Especially after she gave birth to her daughter, whose blood would be rich with the legacy of generation after generation of Partholon's priestesses?

What say you, Rhiannon? Will you pledge yourself to me?

Rhiannon could feel the edge in the god's voice. She had left him waiting for an answer too long. Hastily, she collected herself and sent her thoughts out to him.

You are wise, Pryderi. I am well and truly tired of being betrayed. Rhiannon formed her response carefully. *But how can I pledge myself to any god while I am still imprisoned? You know a priestess must be free to perform the ascension ritual that will bind her to a god as Chosen.*

Pryderi remained silent for so long that Rhiannon began to

fear she had pushed too hard. She should have just pledged herself to him! What if he left her now? She might be trapped for eternity.

It is true that a priestess must freely give herself to a god. Then we shall simply free you so that you can pledge yourself and your daughter to my service.

The tree that was her living tomb shuddered, and Rhiannon's heartbeat quickened. She'd gambled and won! Pryderi was going to free her! She strained against the weight that pressed all around her...trapping her...suffocating her.

That is not the way to freedom. You must be patient, my Precious One.

Rhiannon bit back an automatic retort. No. She must learn from the past. Confronting a god openly was not wise...

What shall I do? She sent the thought out, tempering her frustration and making sure her question felt obedient and eager.

Use your earth affinity. Not even Epona can take that gift away from you. It is a part of your soul—of the very blood that runs in your veins. Only this time you will not bother with the Goddess's trees. Seek the dark places. Sense the shadows within shadow. Call their power to you, Precious One. The time of your child's birth draws near. With her birth, you will be reborn to the earth. And to a new era in the service of a god.

I understand. Rhiannon centered herself. She was no novice priestess. She knew how to wield great power and channel the magic of the earth. Looking to the darkness was no different from tapping into the hidden power of the trees. She refused to think about what Shannon had said— that the trees willingly aided her and called her Epona's Chosen. Instead she concentrated on the darkness—on night and shadow and the cloak of blackness that monthly covers the new moon.

She felt the power. It wasn't the heady rush she'd known in

Partholon when Epona's blessing had touched her, but power was there and it was drawn to her.

Like a vessel slowly being filled, Rhiannon waited and the child within her grew.

PART I

1

Oklahoma

"Astorm comes." John Peace Eagle squinted into the southwest sky.

His grandson barely glanced up from his portable Playstation. "Grandpa, if you'd get cable out here you wouldn't have to do all that sky watching. You could check out the Weather Channel instead, or watch it on the news like everyone else."

"This storm could not be predicted by mundane means." The old Choctaw Wisdom Keeper spoke without turning from his study of the sky. "Go now. Take the truck and return to your mother's house."

This did make the teenager look. "Really? I can take your truck?"

Peace Eagle nodded. "I'll get a ride into town sometime this week and pick it up."

"Cool!" The boy grabbed his backpack and gave his grandpa a quick hug. "See ya, Grandpa."

It was only after Peace Eagle heard the engine roar and then fade as the boy drove down the dirt road that led to the two-lane highway to town that he began to prepare.

Rhythmically the Wisdom Keeper beat the drum. It did not take long. Soon shapes began stirring between the trees. They entered the clearing beside the cabin as if they had been carried there by the growing violence of the wind. In the fading daylight they looked like ancient ghosts. John Peace Eagle knew better. He knew the difference between spirit and flesh. When all six of them had joined him he spoke.

"It is good you have answered my call. The storm that comes tonight is not only of this world."

"Has the Chosen of the Goddess returned?" one of the Elders asked.

"No. This is a dark storm. An evil one stirs."

"What is it you would have us do?"

"We must go to the sacred grove and contain what is struggling to be free," Peace Eagle said.

"But we defeated evil there not long ago," said the youngest of the tribal Elders.

Peace Eagle's smile was grim. "Evil can never be truly defeated. As long as the gods give world dwellers freedom of choice, there will be those who choose evil."

"The Great Balance," the youngest Elder said thoughtfully. Peace Eagle nodded. "The Great Balance. Without light there would not be dark. Without evil, good would have no balance."

The Elders grunted wordless agreement.

"Now let us work on the side of good."

Rhiannon welcomed the pain. It meant that it was time for her to live again. Time for her to return to Partholon and take back what was hers by right. She used the pain to focus. She thought of it as purification. Ascending to Epona's service had not been a painless ritual. She expected no less from what Pryderi must have planned for her.

The labor was long and difficult. For a body she'd been detached from for so long, it was a shock to suddenly be aware of muscles and nerves and the cascade of cramping pain that radiated like drowning waves from her core.

Rhiannon tried not to dwell on thoughts of how this birth should have been. She should have been surrounded by her handmaidens and servants. She should have been bathed and cosseted and pampered—given ancient herbal infusions that would dull her pain and fear. Her women would never have left her alone to face the birth by herself. And her daughter's entry into Partholon would have been met by joyous celebrations, as well as a sign from Epona that the Goddess was pleased by the birth of her Chosen's daughter.

No, she couldn't dwell on those thoughts, even though she secretly hoped that when this child was finally born Epona would return to her and show her some sign—any sign, even though she wasn't in Partholon and this child wasn't her first. Somewhere in the blackness between the seemingly endless surges of pain Rhiannon had time to think about that other child. The infant she had aborted. Did she regret what she had done? What good did regret ever do? It had been a choice she had made in her youth. A choice she could not undo.

She must focus on the daughter she was giving birth to now, not mistakes in her past.

When the next spasm of contractions seized her she opened her mouth to scream, even though she knew that entombed as she was, her pain and aloneness would be given no voice.

You are wrong, Precious One. You are not alone. Behold the power of your new god!

With a deafening crack, her living tomb was suddenly split open, and in a rush of fluid, Rhiannon was expelled from the womb of the ancient tree. She lay gasping and shivering on the carpet of grass. Wrenching coughs shook her. She blinked her eyes wildly, trying to clear her blurry vision. Her first thought was of the man whose sacrifice had entombed her. With a shudder, she looked over her shoulder at the gaping hole in the tree, expecting to see Clint's body. She braced herself for the horror of it, but all she saw was a faint sapphire glow that faded slowly, like it was being absorbed into the bowels of the wounded tree.

Yes, her memory was intact, as was her mind. She knew where she was—the sacred grove, in the modern state of Oklahoma. And, as expected, she had been expelled from her prison inside one of the twin oaks. The other stood, unchanged, beside the shallow stream that ran between the trees. It was twilight. The wind whined fretfully around her. The bruised sky rumbled dangerously with thunder, and was answered by shards of lightning.

Lightning...that must have been what freed her.

I am what freed you.

The voice was no longer in her head, but it still had a disembodied, otherworldly tone. It was coming from under the twin tree to her oak, where the shadows were the deepest.

"Pryderi?" Rhiannon's voice sounded too raspy and weak to be her own.

Of course, Precious One, whom did you expect? The Goddess who betrayed you? His laughter brushed against her skin, and Rhiannon wondered how anything that sounded so beautiful could also feel so cruel.

"I—I cannot see you," she gasped as another contraction engulfed her.

The god waited until the pain receded again, and then the shadows under the tree stirred. A form moved slightly, so that it could be more easily seen in the fading daylight.

Rhiannon felt her breath catch at his beauty. Though his body was not fully materialized in this world and had the transparent look of a spirit, letting her see through it to the shadows beyond, the sight of him made her forget that she was swollen with impending birth. Tall and strongly built, he was imposing even in spirit form. His mane of dark hair framed a face that should have inspired poets and artists, and not the terrible stories whispered about him in Partholon. His eyes smiled at her and his face was suffused with love and warmth.

I greet you, my priestess, my Precious One. Can you see me now?

"Yes," she whispered in awe. "Yes, I see you, but only as a spirit." Rhiannon felt dizzied by such an obvious show of the god's favor. He was absolutely magnificent—everything a god should be. And suddenly she could not believe she had wasted all her life worshipping Epona, when she should have been kneeling in supplication at this wondrous god's feet.

It is difficult for me to hold corporeal form. In order for me to truly exist in the flesh, I must be worshipped. There must be sacrifices made in my name. I must be loved and obeyed. That is what you and your daughter will do for me—you will lead the people to find me again, and then I will return you to your rightful place in Partholon.

"I understand," she said, ashamed that her voice was so weak between her panting breaths. "I will—"

But before she could finish her words, two things happened simultaneously, both effectively silencing her. The night was suddenly filled with the sonorous sound of drumbeats. Rhythmically, like a heart pulsing blood through a body, the glade was wrapped in a deep, vibrating pulse. At the same moment Rhiannon was gripped by the overwhelming need to push.

Her back bowed and her legs automatically came up. She gripped the gnarled roots, trying to find something, anything that would anchor her straining body. Her wild eyes searched the shadows where Pryderi had materialized. Faintly, she could see his spectral form.

"Help me," she moaned.

The beating drums were getting louder. Within the resonant sound, she could now hear chanting, though she could not make out the words. Pryderi's form flickered and, with a horror that mirrored the pain that threatened to tear apart her body, she watched his beautiful face ripple and re-form. His sensuous mouth was seared shut. His nose became a grotesque hole. His eyes were no longer smiling and kind. They glowed with an inhuman yellow light. Then, before she could take another sobbing breath, the apparition changed again. The eyes became dark, empty caverns and the mouth ripped open to show bloody fangs and a slavering maw.

Rhiannon screamed in fear and rage and pain.

The drumbeat and chanting got louder and closer.

Pryderi's image shifted and he was, once more, the inhumanly beautiful god, only this time he was barely visible.

I cannot always be beautiful, even for you, Precious One.

"Are you leaving me?" she cried as the terrible pushing urge abated for a moment. Though his changing visage terrified her, she was even more afraid to face birth alone.

Those who approach are forcing me to leave. I cannot battle them tonight. I do not have the strength in this world. Then his eyes blazed into hers and his body almost solidified. *Rhiannon MacCallan, I have sought you for decades. I have watched your unhappiness multiply as you were shackled to Epona. You must make your choice now, Rhiannon! You have seen all of my forms. Will you renounce the Goddess and give yourself to me as my priestess, my Chosen and Incarnate?*

Rhiannon felt light-headed with pain and fear. Her eyes flicked wildly around the grove, searching for some sign of Epona, but she saw nothing of her divine light. She had been abandoned to the darkness—a darkness that had been pursuing her for years. What choice did she have? She could not imagine existing were she not the Chosen of a deity. How would she live if she did not have the power such status afforded her? But even as she made her decision, Rhiannon could not bring herself to openly renounce Epona. She would accept Pryderi. That would have to be enough for the god.

"Yes. I will still give myself to you," she said faintly.

And your daughter? Do you pledge your daughter to me, as well?

Rhiannon rejected the warning that whispered through her soul.

"I give—"

Her words were broken off by the high-pitched battle cry of seven tribal Elders as the men entered the grove, tightening a circle around the two oaks. With a roar that made Rhiannon's heart tremble, Pryderi's spirit dissolved into the shadows.

Pain bowed her body again and all Rhiannon knew was that she must push. Then strong hands were supporting her. She gasped and opened her eyes. The man was ancient. His face was deeply furrowed and his long hair was white. There was an eagle feather tied within its length. His eyes...Rhiannon focused on the kindness in his brown eyes.

"Help me," she whispered.

"We are here. The darkness is gone. It is safe for your child to enter the world now."

Rhiannon gripped the stranger's hands. She pushed with everything within her pain-racked body. Then to the beat of the ancient drums her daughter slid from her womb.

And as she was born, it was Epona and not Pryderi to whom Rhiannon cried.

The old man used his knife to cut the cord that linked daughter to mother. Then he wrapped the infant in a home-woven blanket and gave her to Rhiannon. When she looked into her daughter's eyes, it seemed to Rhiannon that the world shifted irrevocably. Deep within her soul she felt the change. She had never seen anything so miraculous. She hadn't felt like this ever before in her life. Not when she'd first heard Epona's voice—not when she'd experienced for the first time the power of being a Goddess's Chosen—and not when she'd seen Pryderi's terrible beauty.

This, Rhiannon thought with wonder, touching her daughter's impossibly soft cheek, *is true magic.*

Another round of contractions wracked her, and Rhiannon gasped. She held her child close to her breast and tried to concentrate on nothing but her while she expelled the afterbirth. Somewhere Rhiannon heard the old man calling orders to another, and understood the urgency in his voice. But the drums continued to beat their ancient rhythm, and her daughter felt so right in her arms…

Rhiannon couldn't stop staring at her. The child gazed back with wide, dark eyes that continued to touch her mother's soul.

"I have been so very wrong."

"Yes," the old man murmured. "Yes, Rhiannon, you have been wrong."

Rhiannon looked up from her daughter. With a strangely detached observation she realized that he had knelt beside her and was holding a bundle of cloth firmly between her legs. How odd that she hadn't felt him do that. Actually, she could feel very little of her body, and was relieved that the pain had stopped. Then her thoughts focused on what he had said.

"You know my name."

He nodded. "I was here the day the White Shaman sacrificed his life to entomb you within the sacred tree."

With a jolt Rhiannon recognized him as the leader of the Natives who had vanquished the demonic Nuada.

"Why are you helping me now?"

"It is never too late for an earth dweller to change their chosen path." He paused, studying her silently before continuing. "You were broken then, but I believe this child has healed your spirit." He smiled kindly. "She must be a great force for good if her birth was able to mend so much."

Rhiannon cradled her daughter, keeping her close to her breast. "Morrigan. Her name is Morrigan, granddaughter of The MacCallan."

"Morrigan, granddaughter of The MacCallan. I will remember her name and speak it truly." His eyes held hers and Rhiannon felt a chill of foreboding, even before she heard his next words. "Something within your body is torn. There is too much bleeding, and it does not stop. I have sent someone for my truck, but it will be hours before we can reach a doctor."

She met his eyes and read the truth there. "I'm dying."

He nodded. "I believe you are. Your spirit has been healed, but your body is broken beyond repair."

Rhiannon didn't feel fear or panic, and she certainly experienced no pain. She only knew a terrible sense of loss. She looked down at her newborn daughter who gazed back at her with such trust, and traced the soft face with her fingertip. She would not see Morrigan grow. She would not be there to watch over her and be sure she was safe and… "Oh, Goddess! What have I done?"

The old man did not attempt to placate her. His eyes were sharp and wise. "Tell me, Rhiannon."

"I pledged myself to Pryderi. He also wanted me to pledge my daughter to his service, but your presence drove him away before I could give her to him."

"Pryderi is an evil one? A god of darkness?" he said quickly. "Yes!"

"You must renounce him. For yourself and for Morrigan."

Rhiannon looked down at Morrigan. If she renounced Pryderi for both of them, in all probability her daughter would be trapped in this world. She might even be unable to tap into the small threads of power Rhiannon had discovered. Morrigan would never return to Partholon.

But if she did not renounce Pryderi, her daughter would be destined to serve the same darkness Rhiannon now recognized had been shadowing her entire life, whispering discontent, echoing anger and selfishness and hatred, and, most destructive of all, twisting love into something unrecognizable.

Rhiannon could not bear the thought that her daughter's life might be as tainted as her own had become. If Morrigan was trapped in this world, then so be it. At least she would not be trapped by the lies of evil, too.

"I renounce Pryderi, the Triple-Faced God, and I reject his hold on me—and my daughter, Morrigan MacCallan," Rhiannon said. Then she waited. She had been the priestess and Chosen of a powerful goddess since she was a girl. She knew how serious it was to renounce a deity. There should be a sign, be it internal or external, that would show Destiny had been altered. Gods did not bear rejection well, especially not dark gods.

"The dark one knows you are near death and very close to the realm of spirits. His hold on you is tight. He is not releasing you."

The old man's words were softly spoken, but Rhiannon felt them as if he had sliced into her heart. Even though she was growing weaker, she forced her arms to tighten around her daughter's tiny body.

"I did not pledge Morrigan to him. Pryderi has no hold over her."

"But you are still bound to him," the old man said gravely.

Rhiannon was finding it difficult to fight against the exhaustion that was graying the edges of her vision. She was cold. She wished the old shaman would leave her alone and let her stare at her daughter until...

"Rhiannon, you must listen to me!" He shook her. "If you die bound to Pryderi your spirit will never know the presence of your goddess again. You will never know light or joy again. You will spend eternity blanketed in the night of the dark god and the despair that taints all he touches."

"I know," she whispered. "But I am finished fighting. It seems all I've done for as long as I can remember is fight. I've been too selfish, caused too much pain. Done too much harm. Perhaps it is time for me to pay for that."

"Perhaps it is, but should your daughter pay for your mistakes, too?"

His words jolted her, and she blinked back the encroaching darkness in her eyes. "Of course she shouldn't. What are you saying, old man?"

"You did not pledge her to him, but Pryderi desires a priestess with the blood of Epona's Chosen in her veins. With you dead, who do you think will be his next victim?"

"No!" But she knew he was right. Pryderi had admitted to shadowing her for decades. He wouldn't do any less to her daughter. Rhiannon shuddered. Morrigan would not be haunted by the darkness she had allowed to whisper and beguile her—and twist her love for her goddess into something ugly. "No," she repeated. "Morrigan will not be his next choice."

"Then you must call upon your goddess to force Pryderi to relinquish his hold on you."

Rhiannon felt a surge of despair. "Epona has turned her face from me."

"But have you renounced your bond to her?"

"I have done things abhorrent to her." And for the first time in her life Rhiannon admitted that it had been she who had betrayed her goddess's faith long before Epona had stopped speaking to her. "She no longer hears me."

"Perhaps the Goddess has been waiting to hear the right words from you."

Rhiannon stared into the shaman's eyes. If there was just the slightest possibility that he might be right she would try. She would call upon Epona. She was close to death—perhaps her goddess would take pity on her. She could feel the misty veil already shrouding her body and numbing her to this world. Surely even from Partholon Epona knew what had befallen her. Rhiannon closed her eyes and centered herself.

"Epona, Great Goddess of Partholon—goddess of my youth—goddess of my heart. Please hear me one last time. Forgive me for my selfish mistakes. Forgive me for allowing darkness to taint your light. Forgive me for the pain I caused you and others." Rhiannon paused, struggling to focus her thoughts and to stave off the cloying numbness that was traveling throughout her body. "I know I do not deserve your favor, but I ask that you stop Pryderi from claiming my soul and my daughter's."

The wind picked up her words and rattled and shook them until they sounded like rain sloughing through autumn leaves. Rhiannon opened her eyes. The shadows beneath the giant sacred oak, the twin to the destroyed tree under which she lay, began to stir and her heart fluttered in panic. Had Pryderi returned to claim her, despite the presence of the shaman and the power of their ancient drums? Then a ball of light burst into being, chasing away the darkness. From the center of the light a figure began to form. Rhiannon's breath caught and tears filled her eyes. The old shaman bowed his head respectfully.

"Welcome, Great Goddess," he said.

Epona smiled at the old man. *John Peace Eagle, know that for your actions tonight you have my gratitude and my blessing.*

"Thank you, Goddess," he said solemnly.

Then Epona turned her gaze to Rhiannon. With a trembling hand, she wiped the tears from her eyes so that she could see the Goddess more clearly. In her childhood Epona had materialized for her several times, but as she had entered her rebellious teenage years, and then become a selfish, indulged adult, the Goddess had quit visiting her, quit speaking to her, and eventually, had quit hearing her. Now Rhiannon felt her soul quicken at the sight of her goddess.

"Forgive me, Epona!" she cried.

I forgive you, Rhiannon. I forgave you before you asked it of me. I, too, have been at fault. I saw your weakness and knew your soul was being courted by darkness. My love for you blinded me to the level of your self-destruction.

Rhiannon bit back the excuses that always so readily came to her tongue. "I was wrong," was all she said. Then she drew a deep breath, fighting against the numbness that sought to steal away her words. "Epona, I ask that you break the bonds Pryderi has on me. I have renounced him, but as you know, I am near death. His hold on my soul is strong."

Epona studied her fallen priestess carefully before asking, *Why do you ask such a thing of me, Rhiannon? Is it because you fear what will happen to your spirit after death?*

"Goddess, I find now that death is near many things in my life have become clear." She glanced down at the child she still held in her weakening arms. "Or perhaps it is the presence of my daughter that has allowed the scales to fall from my eyes." She looked up at the Goddess. "The truth is that, yes, I am afraid to spend eternity in despair and darkness, but I would not have called upon you to save me from the fate I know I deserve." Rhiannon choked, coughed, and took several gasping breaths before she could continue. "I called upon you because I could not bear the thought that my daughter would be claimed by the same darkness that has poisoned so much of my life. If you break the bonds Pryderi has upon my soul I do not ask that I be allowed to enter your meadows. I ask that you allow me to exist in the Otherworld, where I can keep watch on her and try to whisper good when the dark god whispers evil."

Eternity in the Otherworld is not an easy fate. There is no rest to be found there—no meadows of light and laughter to succor your world-weary soul.

"I do not wish to rest while my daughter is in danger. I do not want her to follow my path."

The years of your daughter's life will be only a tiny ripple in the pond of eternity. Do you truly ask an interminable fate for something that is in essence so transient?

Rhiannon leaned her pale cheek against her daughter's soft head. "I do, Epona."

The Goddess smiled and, even so near death, Rhiannon was filled with a rush of indescribable joy.

Finally, my Beloved, you have conquered the selfishness in your spirit and followed your heart. The Goddess stretched her arms over her head. *Pryderi, god of darkness and lies, I do not relinquish my rightful hold on this priestess! You shall not claim her soul without first vanquishing me!* Light shot from the Goddess's palms, splintering the shadows that had skittered to the edges of the clearing. With a terrible shriek, the unnatural darkness dissipated completely, leaving what Rhiannon now recognized as only the normal and comforting darkness that twilight foretold.

"My spirit feels light," she whispered to her daughter.

That is because for the first time since you were a child your spirit is free of the influence of darkness.

"I should have taken this path long ago," Rhiannon said faintly.

Epona's smile was, once again, filled with limitless kindness. *It is not too late, my Beloved.*

Rhiannon closed her eyes against a wash of emotions that drained her of the last of her waning strength. "Epona, I know this isn't Partholon, and I am no longer your Chosen One, but would you greet my daughter?" Her voice was almost inaudible.

Yes, Beloved. For the sake of my love for you, I greet Morrigan, granddaughter of The MacCallan, and I bestow upon her my blessing.

Rhiannon opened her eyes at the sound of the whir of wings. Epona had disappeared, but the sacred grove had been filled with thousands upon thousands of fireflies that dipped and dived and soared all around her and the infant who rested in her arms. In the fading light they illuminated the air around them as if the stars had temporarily taken leave of the night sky just to dance about the glade in celebration of the birth of her child.

"The Goddess heard your plea," the old man said reverently. "She did not forget you. She will not forget your child."

Rhiannon glanced at him, and had to blink hard to focus on his face. "Shaman, you must take me home."

His eyes met hers. "I do not have the power to return you to the Otherworld, Rhiannon."

"I know that," she said weakly. "Take me back to the only home I have known in this world—to Richard Parker, who is the mirror image of my father, The MacCallan." Rhiannon grimaced and pushed back the memory of Shannon Parker's voice telling her that in Partholon her father was dead. "Take my body there and present Morrigan to him as his granddaughter. Tell him…" She hesitated, trying to speak through the numbness that was quickly enclosing her. "Tell him…that I believe in his love and know he will do the right thing."

The shaman nodded solemnly. "How do I find Richard Parker?"

Rhiannon managed to gasp simple directions to Richard Parker's small ranch outside Broken Arrow. Thankfully, the old man questioned her little and seemed to understand the words she whispered between gasps.

"I will do this for you, Rhiannon. I will also offer prayers for your spirit in the Otherworld. May you watch over your child and keep her safe."

"My child…Morrigan MacCallan…blessed by Epona…" Rhiannon whispered. She found that she could not fight against the numbness any longer. Still holding her daughter to her breast, she allowed her head to fall back so that it rested on a gnarled root. And while firefly lights played all around them to the tune of ancient drums, Rhiannon, Priestess of Epona, died.

3

Partholon

"Okay, so here's the absolute friggin truth. If it was fun, they wouldn't call it labor." I grimaced and tried to find a more comfortable position on the huge down-filled mattress I'd dubbed the marshmallow, but I was so damn tired and my body was sore in so many intimate places that I gave up and settled for sipping more of the mulled wine a helpful nymphet offered me. "They'd call it something like *party*," I continued. "Women would say, 'Oh, boy! I'm going into party now and having a baby. Yippie!' Nope. It's definitely not called party."

Alanna and her husband, Carolan (who had just delivered my daughter), glanced over their shoulders at me. Both of them laughed, as did several of the nymphlike handmaidens who were clustered around the room, tidying, fussing, basically doing the handmaiden stuff they loved to do (and, quite frankly, I adored their abject adoration).

"I don't know what you're laughing at. In a couple months you're going to know exactly what I'm talking about," I reminded Alanna.

"And I will count on you to hold my hand through every moment of it," Alanna told me happily, and then kissed her husband's cheek.

"That's fine with me. I'll look forward to being on the hand-holding end of the childbirth thing."

"I thought women quickly forgot the pain of the birth."

I looked up at my husband, the centaur High Shaman Clan-Fintan, whose strength and stamina surpassed a man's, but who at that moment appeared uncharacteristically worn and bedraggled, as if he had fought his way through hell and back instead of standing by his wife's side as she labored (for a friggin day) and gave birth to their daughter.

"Are you going to forget it soon?" I asked him with a knowing smile.

"Not likely," he said solemnly, and for the seemingly thousandth time in the past day he bent to brush the sweat-damp hair from my face and kiss me softly on the forehead.

"Yeah, me neither. I think that whole 'women don't remember the pain of childbirth' thing is a big lie started by freaked-out husbands."

Carolan's deep chuckle rolled across the chamber. "I would have to agree with your theory, Rhea," he said.

I frowned at his back. "Great. My doctor didn't think to mention that to me *before* I went into labor?"

"No, my Lady." I could hear the thinly veiled humor in his voice. "Little good it would have done then. If I would have mentioned it, it should have been *before* you bedded the centaur."

"Hrumph!" I said, purposefully sounding like my husband, which caused Carolan to chuckle again.

"Ah, but Rhea, wasn't it all worth it?" Finally finished swaddling my newborn daughter, Alanna, smiling like she was Santa Claus, brought the baby back to my waiting arms. I took her eagerly from my best friend and all-around girl Friday, executive assistant and expert on everything-Partholon-that-I-didn't-know.

"Yes." I breathed the word, overwhelmed by the not-yet-familiar rush of love and tenderness holding my daughter evoked. "Yes, she is worth every bit."

ClanFintan knelt beside our mattress with the fluid grace with which centaurs moved. "There is nothing she is not worth," he said reverently. Then he touched the down of curly auburn hair that capped her perfect head. "What shall we call her, my love?"

I didn't hesitate. I'd had months to think about this, and during that time only one name kept circling around and around in my mind. I'd asked Alanna about it when I first heard it echoing through my head, and when she told me its meaning, I knew it had to be my daughter's name.

"Myrna. Her name is Myrna."

ClanFintan smiled and circled us with his strong arms. "Myrna, the word in the old language for *beloved*. It is as it should be, for she is truly our beloved." Then he leaned closer to me and for my ears alone murmured, "I love you, Shannon Parker. Thank you for the gift of our daughter."

I nestled against him and kissed the strong line of his jaw, holding our sleeping daughter close to us. He rarely used the name I'd been born with—and never when he could be overheard by the general populace. There were only three people who knew I was not Rhiannon, daughter of The MacCallan—ClanFintan, Alanna and Carolan. The rest of Partholon had no idea that almost one year ago I had been "accidentally" exchanged for the real Rhiannon, with whom I looked almost identical. But our physical likeness is where our similarities ended. Rhiannon had been a selfish, hateful bitch who'd abandoned her world. I liked to think that I was just mildly selfish, and only a bitch when absolutely necessary. I knew I would never abandon Partholon, or the people and goddess I had come to love there. I'd fought to stay—and stay I would.

There was no doubt that I belonged in Partholon. Epona had made it clear to me that I had become her Chosen, and that it had never been an accident or a mistake that I'd been exchanged for Rhiannon. Epona *chose* me, and therefore I belonged to this world.

Sublimely happy, I nuzzled the top of my daughter's soft head, "Happy birthday, Mama's precious."

ClanFintan's arm was warm and strong around me. He squeezed gently, and I could hear the smile in his voice. "Happy birthday to both of my girls."

I blinked in surprise and laughed. "That's right! Today's April thirtieth. It *is* my birthday. I'd totally forgotten."

"You've been busy," ClanFintan said.

"I definitely have." I smiled up at the amazing centaur with whom I was so completely in love. "I think that we should thank Epona for our magical daughter who was born on her mother's birthday."

He kissed me gently. "Epona has my eternal thanks for Myrna and for you." He drew a deep breath, and then in his resonant voice with which he called ancient shamanistic magic to him so that he could shape-shift into human form and make love to me, he shouted, "Hail, Epona!"

"Hail, Epona!" His cry was gladly taken up by Alanna and my handmaidens.

Suddenly the gauzy drapes that covered the floor-to-ceiling windows on the far wall of my chamber began to billow up like rolling clouds, and on the fragrant breeze into the room floated hundreds of rose petals. The handmaidens made happy little exclamations and began twirling around with the petals. Then the voice that I had been waiting to hear filled the room as my goddess, Epona, spoke.

My Beloved has given birth to her beloved. It is with great gladness that I welcome Myrna, daughter of my Chosen One, to Partholon. Let us greet her with joy, magic, laughter and the blessings of her goddess!

With a pop and sizzle that reminded me of Fourth of July sparklers, the rose petals exploded into little balls of glitter and became hundreds of butterflies. Then there was another popping sound and the butterflies became jewel-colored hummingbirds that swooped and dived and circled my laughing, dancing maidens.

My eyes filled with tears of happiness and relief. My daughter had been born safely, and my goddess had attended her birth. I relaxed in the warmth of my husband's arms, thoroughly and utterly content, and gazed down at the miracle that was our daughter, Myrna...

"This is true magic," I whispered.

A mother's love is the most sacred magic of all. Epona's familiar voice drifted through my mind. *In the future remember that, Beloved. A mother's love has the power to heal and to redeem.*

I was suddenly chilled. What did Epona mean? Was something going to harm Myrna?

Rest easy, Beloved. Your child is safe.

I felt a wash of relief so strong that it made my body tremble. And then I felt something else and the trembling became a shudder.

"Rhea? Are you well?" ClanFintan asked, instantly sensing the change in me.

"I'm tired," I prevaricated, surprised at how weak my voice sounded.

"You should rest." He kissed our daughter's forehead and then mine before he caught Alanna's eye. She quit dancing with the hummingbirds and handmaidens, and hurried to our side. "Rhea must rest," he told her.

"Of course she must," Alanna said a little breathlessly, her hand rubbing her protruding abdomen. Then she clapped her hands and the frolicking handmaidens looked her way. But before she could announce that it was time for them to depart, the hummingbirds, as a group, circled the air above where I lay and then, in a flurry of wings and glittering colors, they exploded and were once more rose petals, which rained on the floor of my chamber so that the rich marble was carpeted in Epona's magic. "The Goddess knows her Beloved must now sleep," Alanna said, smiling in delight at Epona's show of favor.

"Thank you for being here. Thank you for singing my child into the world." I somehow made my voice sound normal even though normal was far from what I was feeling.

"It was our honor, Beloved of the Goddess!" several of the handmaidens said together. Then, laughing, clapping and calling blessings to us, they scampered merrily out of my chamber.

I could feel ClanFintan's gaze and knew better than to try to hide what was going on from him. I looked into his dark, almond-shaped eyes.

"Rhiannon is dead," I said.

Alanna gasped, but ClanFintan grew very still. His jaw clenched and his classically handsome face seemed to turn to stone. To an outsider, his voice would sound calm, almost gentle. But I knew it for what it was—it was the way he cleared his mind and readied himself for battle.

"How do you know this, Rhea?" he asked.

I tightened my grip on Myrna's small, perfect body. "I felt her die."

"But I thought she was killed months ago, when the shaman from your old world entombed her in the sacred tree," Carolan said.

I swallowed. My lips felt cold and numb. "I thought she was, too. She should have died then, but all this time she hasn't been dead. All this time she's been trapped inside the tree…alive." I shuddered. Rhiannon was a hateful bitch. She'd caused me countless problems. Hell, she'd even tried to kill me. But I'd come to understand that she was just a broken version of myself, and I couldn't help pitying her. Thinking about her being entombed alive made me feel sick and sad.

Two hard, quick knocks sounded against the door.

"Come!" ClanFintan ordered.

One of my palace guards entered the chamber and saluted me briskly.

"What is it…" I paused, trying to remember which guard he was. I mean, they all looked so much alike. Muscular. Tall. Scantily dressed. Muscular. Something about this one's very blue eyes jogged my memory. "…Gillean?" I expected he'd come to pay homage to Myrna, but the grim set of his face had my heart beating faster.

"It is the tree in the Sacred Grove, my Lady. The one around which you pour libations every full moon. It has been destroyed."

My gut wrenched with a pain that had nothing to do with childbirth. "What do you mean destroyed? How?"

"It appears to have been struck by lightning, but the evening is clear. There is no hint of storm in the sky."

The bitterness of fear filled the back of my throat, making my voice sound rough. "Did anything come out of the tree?"

The guard didn't as much as blink at my weird question. This was Partholon, where magic was as real as the Goddess who reigned here. Weird was this world's normal.

"Nothing came out of the tree, my Lady."

"There were no bodies?" I made myself ask, trying to push away the mental image of Clint's decomposing corpse.

"No, my Lady. There were no bodies."

"Are you sure? Did you see for yourself?" ClanFintan fired the questions.

"I am positive, my Lord. And, yes, I examined the tree for myself. I had just been relieved from the northern watch outside the temple grounds. I was returning when I heard a great cracking noise coming from the grove. I wasn't far from it, and I know the Sacred Grove is important to Lady Rhiannon, so I went there immediately. The tree was still smoldering when I came upon it."

"You have to go look," I said to ClanFintan.

His nod was a tense jerk. "Get Dougal," he told the guard. "Tell him to meet me at the north gate."

"Yes, my Lord. My Lady." He bowed formally to me and then hurried out.

"I will come with you," Carolan said grimly. Then he and Alanna moved across the chamber, obviously allowing me some privacy with ClanFintan.

"If she's here, she's dead," I said, sounding much calmer than I felt.

"Yes, but I wish to be sure that if she brought anything into Partholon with her reentry, it is dead, too."

I nodded and looked down at Myrna's sleeping face. Vulnerable. I felt so damn uncharacteristically vulnerable knowing that I couldn't bear it if anything happened to my daughter…

"I will never allow anything to harm either of you." ClanFintan's voice was low and dangerous.

I met his steady gaze. "I know." But it was clear in both of our eyes that we were remembering a few months ago. I had been pulled through that very tree and taken to Oklahoma, along with a resurrected evil we had all believed we had vanquished forever. And that had happened while ClanFintan watched, powerless to save me. I had only been able to return to Partholon through the sacrifice of ClanFintan's human mirror, Clint Freeman, and the power that was in the ancient trees. "Be careful," I said.

"Always," he said. He kissed me and then Myrna. "Rest. I will not be gone long."

He and Carolan rushed out of the chamber. I could hear him calling orders for the guards to double their watch on me and on the palace, which should have made me feel safe, but all it did was send a terrible wash of cold fear through my body. Myrna began to make restless noises, and I whispered reassurance to her.

"She's probably hungry, Rhea."

Thankfully, Alanna was at my side helping to arrange my soft nightdress so that Myrna could find my breast. I tried to relax and concentrate on the sublimely intimate act of nursing my daughter, but my thoughts wouldn't be still. I had known the exact moment of Rhiannon's death. The sacred tree that had imprisoned her had been destroyed. And then there were the Goddess's cryptic words about the power of a mother's love to heal and redeem.

Rhiannon had been pregnant when she'd been entombed.

"All will be well, Rhea." Alanna lifted the now full and sleeping Myrna from my arms and placed her in the small cradle within reaching distance of my bed.

"I'm scared, Alanna."

Alanna took the wide soft brush from my vanity and knelt behind me. Gently, she began brushing my hair in long, slow strokes.

"Epona will not allow you or Myrna to come to harm. You are her Chosen One, her Beloved. The Goddess protects her own. Rest now. You are safe here in the heart of Partholon, protected by all of us who love you. You have nothing to fear, my friend…nothing to fear…"

Alanna kept up a steady murmur of reassurance. The sweet

sound of her voice and the gentle strokes of the brush coupled with the exhaustion of twenty-four hours of laboring and childbirth worked on me like a sleeping pill. My body was aching for rest. And just before I slipped into the comforting darkness, my last thought was that if there were no bodies found in the Sacred Grove in Partholon, then they must be in the mirror version of that grove in Oklahoma. What the hell was going on over there...?

4

Oklahoma

Richard Parker knew something was wrong long before John Peace Eagle drove slowly down the lane with his grim cargo. He'd been restless all evening. Worse, all six of his dogs, greyhound and Irish wolfhound mixes, had begun to howl just moments after twilight. Despite his threats, they hadn't shut up for almost a full five minutes.

He didn't have to check the calendar to know what day it was. He'd been counting down the months and weeks and days since he'd last seen his daughter in November. Not that the exact date was important. He had no idea of her due date— just a rough estimate. Late April. Today was the thirtieth of April. Shannon's birthday. In another world, one where she was revered as a goddess's incarnate, she turned thirty-six today. But remembering the day of his daughter's birth wasn't what was giving him an eerie, walking-over-his-grave feeling.

Had Shannon given birth today in an ancient world somewhere across an unimaginable barrier of time and dimension? No matter how impossible it seemed he wasn't surprised that she would try to let him know. After all, the whole damn situation was impossible.

When Shannon had first reappeared on his doorstep in the middle of a god-awful snowstorm looking scared and bedraggled with a man he recognized as Clint Freeman, an ex–fighter pilot hero, he hadn't wanted to believe her wild story about being switched for Rhiannon, Goddess Incarnate in another world, and then being pulled back to Oklahoma by Clint. But his daughter wasn't a liar. And the woman who had been running around for the preceding several months acting like a cold, calculating bitch and alienating her friends and family had looked like his daughter, but sure as hell hadn't acted like her.

Even before the evil Nuada had almost killed him in the icy pond and he had witnessed his daughter's Goddess-given powers, he had found it easier to accept the idea of an alternate world than to accept the idea that his daughter had somehow managed a total change of personality.

He'd known when Shannon had defeated Nuada and left this world, just as surely as he knew the smell of rain and the feel of a horse's hide under his hands. It was an innate knowledge, something that rang true deep in his soul. He'd also known that Clint had been killed returning her to Partholon, and that knowledge had saddened him almost as much as the loss of his only child. At least Shannon hadn't died. Actually, it was easier for him to think of it as if she had moved to Europe, or maybe Australia, and that someday they might get to visit one another again.

Richard sighed and paced restlessly from one side of the concrete patio to the other. Shannon had had to leave. She'd been married in that other world to the father of her unborn child. She loved him. And a child, a daughter, needed her father.

"…Needs her grandpa, too," he muttered. He'd hoped that

Shannon would be able to communicate with him, even if only briefly, so that he wouldn't feel as if he'd lost his daughter forever. He did dream of her often. In his dreams she was always happy and surrounded by people who adored her. He'd even seen her centaur husband in his dreams. Richard snorted. "And that had been a damned interesting sight." He believed Shannon was behind the dreams—or maybe it would be more accurate to say that Shannon's goddess, Epona, was behind them. Either way, it was almost like getting letters from her, and he'd been content with the small glimpses he had been granted.

Tonight was different than the dreams, though. This *feeling,* this terrible foreboding was lodged so firmly in his gut he couldn't even stand still. Was Shannon trying to communicate more directly with him? It fit. It was the right time for her to be giving birth to his granddaughter, and of course she would want to share the event with him. But why then was the feeling so negative? Why did he have an itchy sense of danger? He stopped pacing as a terrible thought hit him, literally driving the breath from his lungs.

Was he feeling her death? Had she died in childbirth in that ancient world where they had no hospitals or modern medicine? Was that why he felt such weight in the air around him, such a sense of pending doom?

"Please, Epona," he told the wind. "Protect her."

"Hon, what is it?" Patricia Parker, Mama Parker to the legions of football players he'd coached, called from just inside the open screen door behind him.

"Nothin'." He realized his tone had been harsher than he'd intended and smiled an apology at her over his shoulder. "Just restless tonight."

Her kind face instantly looked worried. "It's not...not...*that* again, is it?"

Patricia had been out of town visiting her only sister in Phoenix when Shannon had returned and Nuada had attacked him, but she'd seen the aftermath. And he had, of course, told her everything. Ironically, Mama Parker had been relieved to learn about the Rhiannon/Shannon switch. It had meant that the woman she'd raised and loved as if she was really her biological daughter, hadn't turned on her. That the nasty things she'd said and done had been Rhiannon, and not Shannon.

"Nope, nope, nope," he said gruffly, sorry his imaginings had upset her. He didn't really know that anything terrible had happened. Hell, it might be that the jalapeños he'd had with dinner were disagreeing with him. "Everything's fine. I'll be in soon."

"Well, okay then, hon. I'll just finish up the dishes."

She had begun to turn away when they heard the sound of the truck start up the lane. Richard glanced at his watch. After ten-thirty. Late for a social call. Ice crawled up his spine again as he watched the old blue Chevy move slowly toward him and cough to a stop behind the other two trucks already parked in the drive. An old Indian slowly got out of the cab to face him.

"Evenin', Richard Parker." Richard automatically extended his hand. The old man met his gaze steadily and returned his handshake with a firm one of his own. "John Peace Eagle. Sorry to disturb you so late."

"No problem. What can I do for you?"

"Rhiannon asked that I bring her home."

Richard felt a jolt of surprise. "Rhiannon!" When he'd had no news of her after he felt Shannon leave this world, he had assumed that she had taken Rhiannon with her, probably so that she could face the consequences of abandoning her world and her duties as Epona's Chosen in Partholon. Now she was here? Saying this was her home? He set his broad shoulders. No matter how much she looked like his daughter, Rhiannon was not Shannon, and he would not allow her to masquerade as his daughter again. But that was not something he would discuss in front of a stranger. It would wait until they were alone. Then he'd take her to town or the airport or where-the-hell-ever. Anywhere was fine, as long as it was away from Oklahoma. "Well, where is she?" He narrowed his eyes back at the cab of the truck. Someone was sitting there, but it was too dark for him to make out her features. He snorted. She should be afraid to come out here and face him.

"She is here."

The old man didn't go to the cab, but walked around behind the truck. With the sound of complaining hinges, he yanked open the tailgate. Richard followed him and then frowned. There was only one thing in the bed of the truck. At first he thought his eyes and the dim light from the pole lamp were playing tricks on him. The thing looked like a body, wrapped head to toe in a Native American blanket. John Peace Eagle climbed into the truck bed with surprising agility. He crouched down and gently pulled the blanket free. Richard felt as if something had slammed into his gut when he saw her face.

"Shannon!" He jumped into the truck bed, ignoring the stiffness in his knees.

"Not Shannon. This is Rhiannon. It was her wish that I bring her here to you, and that I also give her child into your keeping."

There was a buzzing in his ears and it was hard for him to concentrate on what the old man was saying.

"She's dead," Richard said.

Peace Eagle nodded. "She died giving birth. But not before love for her daughter healed what was dark in her spirit."

Richard forced his gaze from the dead face that mirrored his daughter's so exactly. "You know about her? About Partholon?"

"Yes, I was there when the White Shaman vanquished the

evil one and sacrificed himself to return Shannon to that world. I was also there this evening, when evil freed Rhiannon from the sacred tree in which she had been imprisoned."

Richard's eyes peered sharply into the surrounding shadows. "Did it follow you here?"

"No evil accompanies me. The Elders and I banished the dark god from the Sacred Grove, and then Epona's appearance made the last of the lurking darkness flee, as well as severing the ties that that god had to Rhiannon's soul."

"Epona forgave Rhiannon?"

"She did. I witnessed it." In the deep, rhythmic voice of an experienced storyteller, Peace Eagle recited all that had happened with Rhiannon in the Sacred Grove.

"She finally found the good within her." Slowly, Richard brushed Rhiannon's cold, pale cheek with his hand.

"Oh, God! Shannon!"

Richard looked up to see his wife standing at the tailgate of the truck, eyes wide with shock, hand pressed against her mouth.

"No, Mama Parker, no." He scooted down so that he sat on the tailgate and took her in his arms. "It's not Shannon. It's Rhiannon. Hush, don't cry." He rubbed her back while she sobbed into his shoulder. He was too busy comforting his wife to notice when the old shaman left the bed of the truck, but he certainly noticed when he returned because in his arms he held a newborn.

"This is Morrigan. Your granddaughter."

The old man held the child out and Mama Parker automatically took the infant. With trembling hands, she opened the blanket and unwrapped the baby.

Richard Parker peered over his wife's shoulder, and fell instantly, irrevocably in love.

"She looks exactly like Shannon did when she was born,"

he said, and laughed through the unexpected tears that burned his eyes. "Just like a little bug."

"Oh, hon, how can you say that?" Mama Parker's voice was breathless with emotion. "She is too beautiful to be a bug."

Richard looked at his wife. They'd been married for almost thirty years, since Shannon was just a little girl. Patricia Parker couldn't have children of her own, but she'd loved and raised Shannon as if she had given birth to her. And now she was fifty-five and he was fifty-seven—too damn old to raise a baby.

But his eyes were drawn back to Morrigan, who was so much like his Shannon, his Bugsy.

"She has no one but you in this world," John Peace Eagle said. "Rhiannon said to tell you that she believed in you and knew you would do the right thing." He paused for an instant, as if he needed to consider his words, and then added, "I have a feeling about this child. I sense a great power within her. Whether that will be power for good or for evil is yet to be discovered. The darkness that haunted her mother will very likely stalk Morrigan, too. If you turn the child away I fear that the darkness may gain an upper hand with her."

"Turn her away!" Richard felt his wife's arms tighten around the baby. "Oh, no. We couldn't turn her away."

"Pat, you have to be sure about this. We're not young anymore."

Smiling, she looked up into her husband's eyes. "Morrigan will keep us young. And she needs us, hon. Plus, she is all of Shannon we may ever have."

Unable to speak, Richard nodded and kissed his wife's forehead.

"My daughter, Mary, is in the cab. She brought some things for the child—diapers, formula, bottles. Such as will get you by for tonight."

"Thank you." Pat Parker turned her luminous smile on him. "We appreciate that."

"Why don't you and Mary take the baby things into the house? John and I will finish up here," Richard said.

Pat nodded, but before she walked away she gave Rhiannon's body one more look. "It's hard to believe she's not Shannon."

"She's not Shannon," Richard said with finality. "Shannon is alive and safe in another world."

The baby started to fret, and Pat's attention went instantly from the corpse to the child. Cooing to her softly, she hurried around to the cab of the truck. Richard waited until the women and the few sacks of baby supplies disappeared into the house. Then he turned to the old Indian.

"I'm not taking her into town. This is no one's business but ours."

John Peace Eagle nodded slowly. "It is good that the modern world does not touch her any longer. She belongs to a different time—a different place."

"I'd like to bury her down by the pond under the willow trees." He looked out at the dark pond. "Those trees have always seemed sad to me."

"Now it will be as if they are crying for her."

Richard grunted and nodded. "Will you help me?"

"I will." Together they started for the barn to get what they'd need. "What will you tell Morrigan of her mother?" Peace Eagle asked.

"The truth," he said automatically, and then added, "eventually." He wished he knew how the hell he was going to do that.

It was almost dawn before John Peace Eagle and his daughter left. Richard was exhausted. He rubbed his right hand slowly with his left, trying to work out the stiffness that always bothered him if he used it too much. He wondered if the injury would ever truly heal, and then reminded himself that it had been only five months since he'd split it open trying to claw his way out of a hole in the icy pond—a hole made by the evil Nuada as he tried to follow through on his threat to kill everyone Shannon loved. Richard's skin shivered and twitched, like a horse being harassed by a biting blackfly. He didn't like to remember that day.

The mewing of the baby pulled his concentration across the dimly lit bedroom. Quietly he got up, walked around to his wife's side of the bed and peered down at the wriggling bundle. The child was in the old cradle Mama Parker had managed to get from the attic. Shannon's old cradle. He'd forgotten he'd kept it. Christ, it must have been in that attic for thirty-plus years. Without hesitation, he picked up Morrigan. Patting her back only a little awkwardly, he hurried from the room before she could wake Mama Parker.

"Shh," he soothed. She was probably hungry. Newborns ate constantly—he did remember that. As he heated up a bottle of formula, the weight and scent of the baby caused even more memories to surface. He'd forgotten that holding his newborn daughter had seemed to him a religious experience. And he wasn't a religious man. He had no time for the stuffiness and hypocrisy of organized religion. All his life he'd wondered how people could so readily believe God could be contained in buildings and overly translated and dissected words. He found his god, or *goddess* he mentally corrected with a silent laugh, in rolling pastures of sweet hay, in the warm smell of a well-worked quarter horse, in the loyalty of his dogs. So when he thought of holding this new baby girl in his arms as religious, he didn't mean that it brought to mind church and such. He meant it brought to mind the perfection of beauty, of the miracle of nature at its finest. He sat down in the rocking recliner with a sigh at the cracking of his knees and the stiffness in his back and shoulders, but his gaze on the baby as she sucked at the bottle and made soft, puppy-like noises wasn't that of an old man. It was that of a man who was seeing anew the magic of life and birth and love reborn.

"I think we'll do fine together," he told the baby girl. "Mama Parker and I aren't young anymore, but we're also not stupid as damn knot-headed twenty-somethings. And I've had some practice with this father thing. I think if Shannon were here she would tell you that I did just fine with her."

Thinking of Shannon made him sad, as it always did. He missed her. But tonight, with the warm, sweet weight of the sleepy newborn in his arms he found that he felt his daughter's loss less sharply. The missing her would never go away, but maybe the pain of it could be eased by this child that was so like her.

He lifted the baby to his shoulder when she was through with the bottle, and chuckled when she belched like a little sailor. "Just like Shannon," he said. Then he nestled her securely back in the crook of his strong arm and began rocking her. And from the recesses of his memory came lines from a book he'd read to Shannon over and over again when she was a little girl. "'Johnny Go Round is a tan tom cat. Would you like to know why we called him that?'" The baby blinked up at him and smiled. Richard's heart, which had felt somehow heavier since the day his daughter disappeared from his world, lifted suddenly as if it had grown wings. He had to clear his throat and blink his eyes before he could continue the story. "'Well, Johnny goes round when…'"

5

Partholon / Oklahoma

DreamLand is my favorite place. Yeah, I like it better than Epona's Temple (which I adore), Tuscany (which I drank my way through whilst a group of my students tried, albeit unsuccessfully, to chaperon me) or even Ireland (again, students attempted to keep me in line on our educational pub tour; thankfully they failed). I've always been able to control my dreams, even before I came to Partholon and became Epona's Chosen. As a child growing up in Oklahoma, I thought it was normal to be able to control my dreams. I hadn't realized there was anything weird about it till I was in third grade and one of my friends said she'd had a terrible nightmare the night before. I'd laughed and said something like, "Well, why didn't you just tell your dreams to take you somewhere happy?" She'd looked at me like I was totally nuts and told me that people couldn't control their dreams. I'd (uncharacteristically) kept my mouth shut until I could get home and ask Dad about it. Dad had explained that people usually couldn't control their dreams and that maybe I should keep it to myself that I could.

Which I pretty much did after that, although the weirdness of my ability didn't dampen my DreamLand enjoyment.

In Partholon my dream weirdness turned to magic. Epona often communicated with her Chosen through dreams. Actually, it's more accurate to say that the Goddess's Chosen has the ability for astral projection, which Partholonian priestesses call the Magic Sleep. In other words, the Chosen's (moi's) sleeping soul projected anydamnwhere at the whim of Epona. Which is as cool *and* as disconcerting as it sounds. Epona has projected me everywhere from the middle of a bloody Fomorian battle where my bodiless spirit saved my husband's life, to a Partholon birth, attended by singing, laughing women where I witnessed the miracle of new life.

For most of my pregnancy, though, Epona had kept my Magic Sleep trips to a minimum. Well, that is after Nuada was vanquished, Rhiannon was entombed and I was returned to Partholon (where I definitely belong). So I was surprised when my dream of Hugh Jackman rubbing my feet while Brandon Routh rubbed my shoulders (both were, of course, in their full superhero costumes) and argued over which one of them was more worthy of my very personal attention that night (I was leaning toward Brandon. He is, after all, *super.*) was interrupted by my spirit suddenly popping up through the ceiling of Epona's Temple like a wine cork surfacing in a cask of my favorite red.

"Oh, jeesh." I gulped big breaths of night air (yes, I know, I didn't really have a "body" but just trust me on this—it *feels* like I still have a body). "Ugh, feeling sick…feeling dizzy…feeling…" I suddenly realized why I was feeling so discombobulated and I grinned. "Feeling not pregnant!"

Epona's silver laughter seemed to float musically in the air around me. *Did you expect to feel pregnant after you gave birth, Beloved?*

"Well, no. But it'll be awhile before I get back into those

little leather riding slacks that are so cute. So I guess I just figured I'd still feel fat and bloated the night after I gave birth."

The spirit recovers quicker than the body from childbirth. I was relaxed, loving the sound of my goddess's familiar voice in my head, but my aimless floating came to an abrupt end with Epona's next words. *And it is good that the spirit recovers quickly. Tonight you need to make a difficult journey, one that was not safe for you to attempt in the last stages of your pregnancy.*

"What is it? Not the Fomorians again?" I tried to keep my fear in check, but just the thought of those creatures abroad with my newborn daughter helpless, asleep…

It is not Fomorians.

I had a moment to feel relieved, and then I remembered what had happened just before the exhaustion of labor and birth had caused me to fall into a deep sleep. "Rhiannon."

Rhiannon, the Goddess agreed.

"But she's dead!" I blurted.

Yes, Beloved. Rhiannon is dead.

"I—I didn't know that she was alive inside that tree all this time." The thought of it still made me sick. I'd played a part in putting her there, as had Clint. His part had cost him his life.

Rhiannon's choices entombed her alive. Not you—not Clint. As usual, it seemed Epona could read my mind. *You should know, Beloved, that before she died, what was broken within Rhiannon's soul was finally healed.*

"I'm glad," I whispered, meaning it.

She was healed and her spirit rescued from the dark god, but Pryderi still lusts to control one who carries the blood of my Chosen.

"Myrna!" I gasped. "He'll go after my baby?"

He may, Beloved, just as he tried to draw you from me.

I snorted. "No damn chance of that."

With you and ClanFintan by her side, there will also be little chance Myrna will listen to Pryderi's dark whisperings.

"We sure as hell won't make the mistakes that were made raising Rhiannon," I muttered. Rhiannon had been spoiled and cosseted and basically never told no. (Note to self: remember to jump square in Myrna's butt if/when she gets mouthy.) "Myrna is going to know the meaning of 'no you may not, little girl.'"

So you see, Beloved, it is not Myrna about whom I am worried.

"Huh?" I said succinctly.

Ready yourself, Beloved. And remember, I will be with you.

I had just enough time to start to worry about where the hell Epona was taking me when the clear sky over the temple began to swirl as if a weird, inverted tornado had materialized. I blinked at the dark cone shape that shifted and opened to show me a tunnel of fire. And before I could say, "Billy Jo Bob loves his first cousin" my spirit was sucked into that roiling inferno. Knowing I was no longer physically attached to my body made no damn difference. It still felt like my heart was literally being squeezed within my chest. I couldn't breathe. In a total state of panic I opened my mouth to scream, and my spirit exploded from the tunnel. I was thoroughly disorientated. Nausea engulfed me. I gulped huge breaths of cool air, wondering (and not for the first time) at how a spirit body could come so close to projectile vomiting. But soon the familiar hovering sensation calmed me and I felt my vertigo fade. I glanced down, and realized where I was. Happiness shocked through my spirit, chasing away the last of the nausea. I was back in Oklahoma, floating over my childhood home. Slowly, my spirit body began to sink through the achingly familiar roof, and very soon I was hovering in the middle of my parents' living room.

I stayed very still, just wanting to soak in the room. Nothing had changed. It was clean, but messy. You know what I mean. My parents have a real home where people actually live and love and laugh instead of a cold, heartless showpiece. (I mean, please, even my opulent chamber in Epona's Temple gets messy sometimes!) Books were strewn all over the end tables and whatnot. (My parents read constantly. Their favorites are paranormal romances. Yes, even my dad reads them. Promise. Which is proof that men can evolve beyond the subhumanoid level of *Sports Illustrated* and *Maxim*.) There was only one small table lamp on and it was turned down so low that it actually took me a little while to realize that Dad was sitting in the chair next to the lamp. He was sound asleep.

I smiled and firmly told myself I would not cry. Just the sight of Dad made me feel warm and safe and loved. Man, I'd missed him. I felt the little shiver that told me Epona had worked some of her magic to make my spirit body visible, and glanced quickly down at myself. Thankfully this time I wasn't naked. Then I looked back at Dad and, with another grin, opened my mouth to shout a big *Surprise, Dad, it's me,* when the book in his lap moved. And kicked. And made a little cooing noise.

"Holy shit, that's not a book!"

At the sound of my voice Dad's body jerked. He blinked, squinting around the room sleepily, clearly thinking he'd been dreaming. Then he shifted the baby (BABY?!) from the crook of his arm to his shoulder, where he patted the diapered behind gently.

"Dad, where the hell did that baby come from?"

Dad's body jerked in surprise again. He followed the sound of my voice up and his eyes widened. "Shannon? Is that you, old Bugsy?"

"It's me, Dad." Then before I could say anything else he said, "Is everything all right with you? Did anything bad happen today?"

"I'm good, Dad—great, actually. I had a daughter today. Her name is Myrna and she's amazingly beautiful. You're a grandpa!"

"Bugsy old girl, that's wonderful!" He shifted the baby from his shoulder to his other arm so that he could wipe his eyes clear of tears. I glanced at the baby and felt the shock of recognition sear me like I'd just touched a hot iron.

"Whose child is that?"

I knew what his answer would be before he said it.

"Rhiannon's."

"How, Dad? She's dead."

He nodded his head slowly. "Yep, yep. She died today giving birth to her."

"Her?" I felt sick, even though I'd known the baby had to be a girl child. Epona's Chosen was always gifted with a girl child as her firstborn.

"Rhiannon named her Morrigan," Dad said.

"Did Rhiannon die here? I don't understand. How did she get out of that tree?"

Dad sighed. "I only know what happened secondhand. Rhiannon was dead when she got here. An old shaman found her and helped deliver the baby. He told me that Rhiannon had made a deal with a dark god to break free of the tree. She was to be his High Priestess—both she and Morrigan were supposed to pledge to his service—but the birth of Morrigan changed her. Or I guess *fixed* her would be a better way to put it. Rhiannon denied the dark god, but she was so near death that the god wouldn't release her. So she called on Epona, and the Goddess answered her."

"Epona forgave Rhiannon?"

"She did," Dad said.

I know it was wrong—selfish of me and more than a little hateful, but knowing that Rhiannon had reconciled with Epona made me feel ridiculously jealous.

You are now, and will forever be my Chosen One. My love for Rhiannon does not lessen my love for you, Beloved.

Epona's voice in my head made me jump guiltily.

Pay attention now, Beloved. Your father must be made aware of Pryderi's intentions.

And suddenly I knew why Epona had pulled me through the fiery tunnel that separated our worlds, and it wasn't just for me to tell Dad about Myrna or for me to understand what had happened to Rhiannon.

"Dad, are you keeping Rhiannon's baby?"

"Yep...yep..." He looked down at the child and touched her cheek gently before continuing. "It was Rhiannon's last request. But there's more to it than that, Shannon. This baby is so much like you were. I have to help her—I can't let her go to strangers." His eyes begged me to understand. And, oddly, I did.

"She looks just like Myrna. It's really weird. I suppose it makes sense. Rhiannon and I could have been twins. And Clint and ClanFintan are mirrors of each other—" I broke off abruptly with a gasp. This was Clint's daughter! Had I chosen to stay in Oklahoma and not returned to my life in Partholon, Clint would be alive today. He and I would be together. My next child would have been his... I clamped down on those thoughts, forcing myself not to cry...not to regret...

Dad looked only momentarily surprised. "Clint's daughter, huh? I'm glad to hear it. I liked that young man."

"So did I," I said quietly. "Did the shaman say anything about finding Clint's body by the tree?"

Dad met my eyes. "No. And I'm sure if his body had been there the old man would have mentioned it." He paused. "So Clint is dead."

Although it wasn't a question, I nodded. "It was the sacrifice of his life that returned me to Partholon."

"Yep...yep... He was brave. I'll be sure to tell Morrigan what a good man her father was."

Which reminded me. "Dad, I'm here because Epona wants me to warn you. That dark god that broke Rhiannon free from the tree?" Dad nodded. "His name is Pryderi. He's really bad news. They call him the Triple-Faced God, when they call him anything at all. Most people in Partholon won't even speak his name. A long time ago he was Epona's consort, but he betrayed her because he wanted her power. She banished him, but he wants to come back." I spoke the next words as the Goddess whispered them through my mind. "His power feeds on worship." I paused, sifting through the knowledge Epona was giving me. "It's like he's a vampire. He literally drains the good from those who worship him. He thrives on the ashes of their souls. And he needs a High Priestess as a go-between, so that his evil intentions are hidden from his worshippers." I drew a deep, shaky breath. "He wants to use a daughter of Epona's Chosen to win a hold on Partholon. That means even in Oklahoma Morrigan will not be safe because we all know sometimes people can travel from Oklahoma to Partholon."

I was shocked to see that Dad didn't look one bit surprised. He only nodded slowly and said, "Yep, that's basically what the shaman told me. It's why Rhiannon asked Epona to forgive her. So that her spirit could be free to watch over her daughter and try to keep her from being lured to the Dark Side."

Despite the seriousness of the situation, his wording made me smile. "The Dark Side, Dad? As in Darth Vader?"

"Seems like a reasonable comparison."

A laugh bubbled out of me. "I suppose you're right."

"So I'll just have to be sure that the Force is strong with her," he said, chuckling.

"Seriously, Dad, Pryderi is going to come after her. Raising her could put you and Mama Parker in danger."

"We know that, Shannon. This isn't our first time around

the dance floor." Then he smiled at me. "Dark gods or no dark gods, parenting is a damn tough job. You'll see."

I frowned at him. "I'm talking about an evil deity sniffing around, not about the terrible twos or an obnoxious teenager."

"Obnoxious teenager is redundant," Dad said automatically, and I had to force myself not to smile. Dad had been teaching and coaching for about a zillion years. He and I definitely saw eye to eye on teenagers.

"You know what I mean," I said.

"I do." He paused and then sighed. "What would you have me do, Bugsy, give her to the state to raise? I imagine that would be playing right into Pryderi's hands." He shook his head before I could answer. "Nope, nope. I won't do that. Mama Parker and I decided. We're going to raise her and do our best by her." He smiled at me and his eyes were shiny with familiar love. "It worked once before. You didn't go over to the Dark Side. It'll work again, Bugsy old girl." He cleared his throat and added quietly, "This little girl is all I'll ever have of you or my granddaughter. In this world, it's the closest I'll come to leaving a part of me behind. You can't really mean to ask me to give that up, can you?"

I blinked fast, trying to clear the tears from my eyes. "No, Dad. I can't ask you to give that up. I just want you to be really, really careful."

"I will. I give you my word on it. Plus—" he grinned "—Rhiannon's ghost is supposed to be around somewhere. I imagine she'll help out with the more boogerman-like aspects of parenting Morrigan."

I glanced around, almost afraid I'd see a spooky version of myself lurking about. "Dad, that's just weird."

He barked a laugh. "No weirder than your spirit floating around my living room while your body's in another world."

I shrugged. "You have a point."

Tell him he has my blessing, Beloved. You should not stay any longer. Having your spirit separated so far from your body is not healthy.

"Dad," I said hastily. "Epona says I gotta go in a second. But she wants me to tell you that you have her blessing."

Dad bowed his head respectfully. "Tell Epona I appreciate that, and I'll be sure Morrigan is raised spending plenty of time in the country around trees, and that she knows the Goddess's name."

"And horses," I added, intuitively knowing Epona would approve. "Be sure she's around horses."

"Yep, yep. Just like you," he said. "I'll be sure she has her own mare."

"It'd be cool if you could make it a gray mare. Epona's Chosen mare is always a silver-gray."

"Yep, I can do that."

I felt my spirit body begin to shiver, and I knew I would soon disappear. "I love you, Dad! Don't ever forget that. And I miss you! And remember that in Partholon there's a part of you that lives on there."

"I love you, too, Bugsy old girl. Try to come back and see me again."

"I will, Dad. Tell Mama Parker I love her, too."

"I'll tell her. Oh! And happy birthday, Shannon!"

"Thanks, Dad, and don't forget to be careful..." I called. The living room and Dad faded from my view as I lifted through the house and then, before I could steady myself, I was sucked back into the tunnel of fire.

"Oh, shit!" I sat up too fast and grimaced at the tenderness in my body.

"Rhea? What is it?" ClanFintan hurried up to our bed. He'd obviously just gotten back from the Sacred Grove. He smelled vaguely of damp earth and sweat.

Shakily, I pushed my wild hair out of my face. "The Magic

Sleep. It was just especially disconcerting tonight. Epona sent me back to Oklahoma."

Concern narrowed his dark eyes. "Why there?"

I answered him with a question of my own. "You didn't find Rhiannon's body, did you?"

"No." And then I saw understanding flash on his face. "She died in your old world."

I nodded. "But not until giving birth. Today. To a daughter my parents have decided to raise."

ClanFintan looked almost as shocked as I'd felt when I'd discovered Morrigan in my father's arms. Then my eyes followed his and we gazed at the perfect baby girl who slept so peacefully in the cradle beside our bed.

"Rhiannon's daughter looks just like Myrna," I said.

I saw ClanFintan jerk in surprise. Then his eyes found mine, and I saw they were shadowed with worry. "Why did Epona send your spirit to your father?"

"She wanted me to warn him. Pryderi freed Rhiannon from the tree. She was supposed to be his minion or whatever, but the birth of her daughter changed her…fixed her…" Emotions made my voice choke and I had to clear my throat before I could continue. "Rhiannon was forgiven by Epona before her death, and her bonds to the dark god were broken, but it seems Pryderi is still after a Chosen of Epona—or the daughter of a Chosen."

"That dark creature had better look elsewhere. He will not touch our daughter with his evil whisperings."

"Which is exactly why Epona had me warn Dad. He can't have me. He can't have Myrna or any other children we may have. So his next logical choice would be—"

"Rhiannon's daughter," he finished for me.

"Exactly," I said.

"Is your father prepared to fight a dark god for the soul of the child?"

I smiled grimly at ClanFintan. "Dad's not about to let someone he loves give in to the Dark Side." He, of course, hadn't seen the *Star Wars* movies (not even the old ones), but he totally got the gist of what I was saying.

"But can he stop her? The MacCallan wasn't able to stop Rhiannon from being seduced by darkness."

I felt cold, and shivered. "I don't know. I think all we can do is wait and see."

"And pray for Epona's aid," he said.

"And pray for Epona's aid," I echoed. Silently I added, *Please, Epona, somehow, even though that's not your world, help Dad and Mama Parker and little Morrigan.*

Then my own daughter began to stir and my attention shifted from Oklahoma and darkness to Partholon and the light of new beginnings.

PART II

Oklahoma

From her earliest thoughts Morrigan knew she was different. It wasn't just because she was being raised by her grandparents. She knew other kids whose parents were losers and their grandparents had to raise them. It wasn't just because her mom and dad were dead, even though she didn't know anyone else whose parents were *both* dead. And it wasn't because G-ma and G-pa taught her kinda weird stuff when it came to religion. Oklahoma was the Bible Belt, but even in Broken Arrow there were kids in school who believed in different stuff. Okay, not many. But still.

She was different because she heard things other people didn't hear, and because she felt things other people didn't feel.

Morrigan sighed and continued to pull the journals out of her closet and stack them neatly in storage boxes.

"And here it is. All my weirdness. Chronicled for the enjoyment of the masses." She bowed her head and waved her hands, as if accepting grateful accolades from a crowd. "No…no…your applause is too much. Really."

"Morgie! Hon! Do you need some help in there?"

"Grandma, no! I'm fine."

"Want a glass of sweet tea?"

Morrigan sighed again, but she smiled and made sure the smile touched her voice. "No, Grandma. Don't worry. I'll be done in here in a little while."

"Okay, well, your friends will be here pretty soon. So if you need me to help you—"

"Mama Parker, leave the girl alone. If she said she's fine, she's fine…"

Morrigan giggled at her grandpa's gruff voice and at her grandma's soft reply. G-pa always seemed to know when she needed some time to herself. Not that she didn't love her grandma and appreciate her. But G-ma tended to…well… hover. And an eighteen-year-old girl who was packing to go away to college didn't need hovering. Or at least not all the time.

She picked up another journal and thumbed through it restlessly. It was hard to think about going away, though. Sure, Oklahoma State University wasn't *that* far away. Only about an hour and a half. But it wasn't here. It wasn't home. And she'd have to meet new people. Make new friends. Morrigan frowned. She just wasn't good at that. New people didn't get her. She tended to be shy and quiet. People misunderstood that and assumed she was stuck up. So she felt like she always had to force herself to act against her personality—to smile and say hi when she just wanted to sit in the background and watch what was going on until she felt comfortable joining in. That's why she'd gotten into drama. She'd even been in several of the school plays. She and Grandpa had come up with the plan in middle school that she should take Intro to Drama so that she could learn to "act" in her daily life.

Okay, it sounded wrong and kinda even deceptive. But it wasn't. Morrigan had needed a way to fit in. And not just for herself. It was important to her grandparents that she had friends. That she acted normal. Even though she wasn't. *They* understood her. But no one else really did.

So she'd learned to act. And she got into dance and made the Tigette Dance Squad for all four of her high-school years. And she dated (mostly football players or wrestlers—they were the guys G-pa approved of). She gave the appearance of normal.

But inside, where it really counted, Morrigan was far from normal.

She tossed another journal in the storage box. It flipped open, and the childish handwriting caught her eye. She picked it up and read from the open page.

April 2 (28 more days till my 9th birthday!)
Dear Journal,
I really, really think G-pa and G-ma are getting me a horse for my birthday!! And not just because I've been asking and asking for one, and being sure I show them that I'm old enough to take care of one all by myself. The wind tells me. She whispers that my horse is coming and that I should always love and cherish my mare. The wind is almost always right.

I guess I should tell G-pa that the wind talks to me, but

Morrigan didn't need to flip the page to remember the rest of the long-ago entry.

She could recall all too well the little girl she used to be. The girl who'd loved, more than anything, the trees and the earth and the beautiful dappled gray mare she did get for her ninth birthday. The girl who didn't constantly look into shadows for bad things, but believed that all the voices in her imagination were good, her special friends, and that she wasn't a total and complete freak for being able to sense spirits in the land.

Not today. She wouldn't think about *that* today. She shook her head. Today she had enough to deal with as she packed to leave her home and then went on one last road trip with her friends before they scattered to different colleges. The battle between good and evil would have to wait till after she was settled in the dorm. She wasn't Buffy. Morrigan snorted. She wasn't even Eowyn, although she'd give just about anything to be a Shieldmaid of Rohan.

Was there really a battle between good and evil? Could it just be something her aging, eccentric grandparents had made up?

"No," she said firmly, shoving aside the fact that she didn't know if those last thoughts had been her own, or had been whispered to her on the wind. To distract herself she flipped the journal ahead to the April 30 listing, and let herself smile and relax as she read her childish excitement.

Dear Journal Dear Journal Dear Journal!
THEY DID GET ME A HORSE! I knew it! She's the most beautiful, amazing, incredible thing in the world! She's only a two-year-old. G-pa says that'll give us time to grow up together. (G-pa is so funny.) She's an awesome dappled gray that's so light she's almost silver. I think I'm going to call her Dove because she's so pretty and sweet. AND SHE'S MINE!

G-pa and G-ma are the best! It doesn't even matter that they're old.

Tonight while I was brushing Dove G-pa told me all about a horse goddess named Epona. She's also goddess of the earth and trees and rocks and everything. He said if I'm really happy about my new horse then maybe I should thank Epona, because she probably pays attention when someone gets her first horse of her very own. I thought that sounded like a cool idea, so after dark I snuck out to the big tree in the front yard (the one right

outside my bedroom window) and I said THANK YOU to
Epona. Because that's a really big tree and I figured if she's god-
dess of trees she probably liked that one a lot. Then I pulled one
of the lawn chairs over and stood on my tip-toes on it so that I
could reach to put my favorite shiny rock (the one I found when
I was weeding the garden last summer) as far up as I could. I
told Epona the rock was for her.

And do you know what? I swear I heard someone laughing
up in the branches of the tree! A girl someone!

"And the next day the shiny rock was gone," Morrigan
whispered. And that's when her relationship with Epona had
started. The older she got, the more often her grandparents
mentioned the Goddess. And the more often Morrigan
thought about her.

Morrigan didn't remember exactly when the woman's voice
in the wind had become that of the Goddess to her, she just
knew that soon after the rock disappeared she'd started thinking
of the voice in her mind, the one that sounded like music, as
the whisper of a goddess.

Until the day she had finally admitted to G-pa that the wind
spoke to her. She'd never forget the look on his face. He'd gone
from laughing with her about something Dove had done, to
being pale and serious within the space of just a few seconds.
Then he'd sat her down and given her The Talk.

Had The Talk been a big, embarrassing lecture about sex
and periods and that kind of stuff? Unfortunately, no. It'd been
a talk about good and evil, and how both might touch her life.

Morrigan put away the journal she'd been reading, and
sifted through the others until she found the one she wanted.
She didn't have to thumb through many pages to find the entry
she'd made after The Talk.

September 13
Dear Journal,
*I guess the whole thing about the 13th being unlucky is true. I
told G-pa about the voices in the wind today and he really
freaked. And the stuff he said kinda scared the s**t outta me.*

Morrigan closed her eyes. She didn't have to read the
childish version of the conversation. She remembered it all too
well—and without the cushion of childhood's innocence to
soften the impact of his words. The three of them had sat at
the kitchen table.

"Morrigan, I want you to listen carefully to me," G-pa had
said. She'd known he was dead serious because he'd called her
by her full name instead of Morgie or Morgie old girl. She remembered that the tone of his voice had made her stomach
hurt.

"You think I'm crazy because I hear the wind," she'd blurted.

"No, hon!" G-ma had patted her hand. "Grandpa, tell her
we believe her and don't think she's crazy."

"Nope, nope," he'd grumbled. "You're not crazy. We believe
you can hear voices in the wind." He sighed and rubbed his
eyes under his glasses. "It's like how you used to draw pictures
of rocks and trees with hearts in them when you were a little
girl. Remember what you told us about that?"

Of course she'd remembered. "I told you that I drew hearts
in them because I knew they were all alive."

"Right," Grandpa had said. "The wind talking to you is like
you knowing the trees and rocks have spirits."

"The wind is just another spirit in the world?" Morrigan
had brightened, thinking that if the voice was like the trees and
rocks then it should be okay. Maybe one of the voices, that
really pretty girl voice, was Epona!

"It's not that simple, hon," G-ma had said.

"The rocks and trees are good. But the voice you hear—"

"Voices," she'd interrupted. "It's not always the same voice, but I always think of it as wind."

G-pa gave G-ma a long look before he continued. "You know that there's good and evil in the world, right?"

"Yeah, we're studying WWII in history. Hitler was evil."

"That's right."

"And lots of kids believe in Satan. He's evil."

"Yes. But sometimes evil isn't as easy to identify as Hitler or Satan, just like not all that's good seems good at first."

Morrigan had scrunched up her nose and said, "Like brussels sprouts tasting nasty but being good for me?"

That had made him chuckle. "Just like brussels sprouts."

Morrigan remembered that she'd suddenly realized what he was trying to tell her. "You mean that the voices in the wind might be bad?"

"Not all of them, hon," G-ma had said.

G-pa had taken a deep breath, and she remembered thinking that he looked really tired. Then he'd said, "Your mom heard voices. Whispered voices. Some of them were good. She could even hear the sound of Epona's voice."

She'd sat there, awestruck that her mom had actually listened to a goddess. And if her mom had heard Epona, then maybe she could hear her, too! Then the rest of what G-pa was saying was like he'd thrown ice water on her.

"But she could also hear a voice that was evil. She listened to it, too, until after a while it changed her, and it wasn't until you were born that she realized she had made a mistake and let evil get a hold of her."

"But you said my mom was a good person." Morrigan had felt like crying.

"She was. There was a lot of good in her. For a while it just got smothered out by the whispers of evil."

"Like the voices I hear?"

"Morrigan—" G-pa had leaned forward and put his big, rough hand over mine "—I think your mom might be one of the voices you hear. She would want to watch over you. I think another voice might be that of Epona herself. The Goddess was close to your mother. But I also think that the evil that whispered to your mother might also be trying to influence you."

"We're not telling you this to scare you, hon," Grandma had said.

"Nope, nope. I wouldn't have told you about this until you were older. But you already hear the voices, so it's important you know that you have to be careful," Grandpa had said.

"And be smart." G-ma had smiled at me. "You're a smart girl. Like Grandpa says, don't be afraid, just be careful."

"But how do I know if I'm listening to the wrong voice?" Morrigan remembered exactly how confused and afraid she'd felt, despite their hands on hers and their assurance that she didn't need to be afraid.

"If it feels wrong, don't listen to it," G-pa had said firmly. "If it's selfish or mean or a lie, don't listen to it."

"And always look to the light, hon. The trees and the rocks and the spirits you feel in the earth are not evil," G-ma had added.

"And we'll be here to help you, Morgie old girl," Grandpa had said gruffly, patting my hand again.

"Always, hon. We'll always be here for you."

Morrigan smiled, remembering how G-ma had hugged her afterward and then thought that she'd totally distracted her granddaughter by asking Morrigan to help her cut a batch of fudge into squares. But she hadn't been distracted, or at least not for long. Later that night she'd gone down to the end of the east pasture to the huge willow tree and the headstone that rested under it. There was one stone for both of them that simply said:

SHANNON AND CLINT
BELOVED DAUGHTER AND
THE MAN BORN TO LOVE HER

Morrigan hadn't realized then, when she was just a little girl,
how weird the headstone was. That most gravestones had full
names and dates of death and birth carved on them. She'd
eventually asked G-pa about it and all he'd ever say was that
what the stone said was all that was important.

That day she'd stepped within the curtain of the weeping
willow that framed the grave and brushed off some dead leaves
from the top of the stone. Then Morrigan had traced her
mother's name with her finger.

"I wish you were here," she'd whispered. "Or at least I wish
I could tell for sure if one of the wind's voices is yours."
Morrigan listened hard, hoping to hear her mom tell her that
she really did talk to her daughter on the wind. But she'd heard
nothing but the rustle of the willow's hanging leaves.

It hadn't been till she was turning away from the grave that
it had happened. Morrigan remembered that the sun had gone
behind a cloud and she'd shivered as the wind whipped around
her cold and sharp. And on that wind she suddenly heard, *Listen
to your heart's desires and you will know me…*

Morrigan blinked, bringing herself back to the present. She
closed the old journal with finality and shoved it in the box.
She didn't want to remember that day. Her grandparents' words
had followed her enough in the years since. She didn't need to
relive it again today. She grabbed another journal.

"Something happy…something light…that's what I need,"
she muttered, and then with a glad little cry, she caught sight
of a bright pink leather journal and lifted it from the others.
"It's in this one. Yeah, here it is!" She smiled as she began
reading the journal entry she had made when she was thirteen.

November 4
Dear Journal,
Oh my gosh! The coolest thing happened today! Well, okay, it
was freezing out, but Dove needed to be exercised so I was rid-
ing her up Oak Grove Road so that we could gallop through
that big empty field. So in the middle of the field these stupid
wild turkeys flew up and scared the crap outta Dove and me.
She jumped forward and her hoof must have hit something be-
cause she tripped and I FELL RIGHT OFF OF HER. Can
you believe it? I never fall off. Anyways, it didn't hurt much and
even if it had I was too worried about Dove's leg to worry about
me. She was kinda limping around and I thought she'd broken
it. So I made her hold still and felt down her leg. I was scared
and shaking and crying and all of a sudden I realized MY
HANDS WERE GLOWING! Okay. Really. It was like I
made a light come out of them, like a little candle or something.
I cannot wait till G-ma and G-pa get home so I can tell them!
Oh, P.S., Dove's leg is just fine.

Morrigan smiled at her thirteen-year-old self, remembering
fondly her childhood with the sweet gray mare who was now
retired to Grandpa's greenest meadow to spend Morrigan's
college years lazing in clover, round and happy. Laughing softly,
Morrigan lifted her hand. Holding it palm up she stared at it,
concentrating hard. After what seemed like forever, a tiny flicker
of light danced around her palm, but it was gone almost before
she could be sure she saw it there. Morrigan sighed and rubbed
her hands together—her right palm still felt warm and tingly.
But nothing else. She could do it again, but only just a little.
Her grandparents had no explanation for her weird ability. Like
her, they were clueless about where it came from or what it
meant.

The wind wasn't clueless, though. Over the years it had

whispered *affinity for flame* and *you can bring light* and other equally cryptic things to her. Morrigan didn't understand what the voices were trying to tell her, and she was afraid to ask them to help her understand. What if that meant she was asking evil to help her? It was way too confusing.

"Morgie, hon, it's getting late."

Morrigan jumped away from her grandma's soft touch like her hand was a live wire. "Oh, crap, Grandma! Don't sneak up on me like that. You scared me so bad you almost made me pee my pants!"

"Watch your language, hon," G-ma said sternly, but she smiled to soften her reprimand. "And I didn't sneak up on you. I called you three times. Looks like you were busy woolgathering."

Morrigan felt silly sitting there in the middle of her journals. She shouldn't be dredging up the past and messing with a weird ability she'd need to keep hidden when she was at OSU. What she should be doing was focusing on the future. "Sorry, G-ma," she said quickly, shoving the last of the journals into the storage box. "Guess I was daydreaming."

"Well, come on out. Your breakfast is getting cold, and those kids will be here before you know it. The Alabaster Caverns are three hours away. You need a good meal before you go." She called the last over her shoulder as she headed back to the kitchen.

Morrigan hurried to do as her grandma had asked, enticed by the smells of bacon and coffee and blueberry muffins wafting down the hall to her room. G-ma had probably packed her—and her friends—a great lunch, too. Shaking off the weird feeling calling the flame to her hands always gave her, Morrigan grabbed her shoes and a sweatshirt and headed into the familiar warmth of the kitchen.

She ignored the echo of laughter that seemed to float on the air around her.

"Mama Parker kicks ass in the kitchen," Gena said around a big mouthful of steak hoagie.

"Yeah, but if she heard you say ass she'd tell you to *watch your language, hon*." Morrigan did a more than passable imitation of Mama Parker that made the girls laugh.

"No way would I say ass around your grandma. I don't want to piss her off. She might stop cooking for us," Gena said.

"No shit," Jaime agreed.

"Mama Parker is too sweet to piss off. Plus, that wouldn't be smart," Lori said. "We might have to start eating my mom's cooking. Then we'd be saying goodbye to yummy homemade hoagies and chocolate-chip cookies and hello to mac and cheese."

"My mom's idea of cooking is to call for pizza delivery. If she's feeling extra-fancy she'll order cheese sticks and ranch dressing, too," Gena said.

"Ditto for my mom," Jaime said.

"You know, y'all could actually try learning to cook for yourselves. I mean, you're eighteen and leaving for college in a few days. What are you going to eat?" Morrigan said.

"Dorm food, of course," Jaime said.

"I'll eat anything someone else cooks. Like Mrs. Taco Bell. I love her cooking," Lori said.

"Eat?" Gena tapped her chin with one perfectly manicured French-tipped nail and looked purposefully perplexed. "For the next four years I plan on eating beer and football players."

The three of them convulsed into giggles. Morrigan gave her friends a collective eye roll. Yes, she liked them. They'd been friends since middle school, but even when they were just kids she'd always thought of herself as older and more mature. That she felt (and acted) older used to seem kinda cute to her, and they definitely needed someone to look after them. More and more it just irritated her. Would they never grow up?

"Okay, whatever. I still say I'm glad I don't have to depend on Mrs. Taco Bell or Mrs. Pizza Hut to eat when I'm away from home."

Proving Morrigan's point about immaturity, Gena stuck out her tongue at her. "Hey, someone remind me why we're here instead of browsing through the end-of-season sale at Gap?" Gena said.

"We're here because Morgie likes to do weird stuff, and this is the last time we're going to be together doing weird stuff with her probably till Christmas break," Lori said.

"I don't think the stuff I like to do is weird."

"Exhibit A—you thought it would be fun to hike the six-mile forest trail by Keystone Dam." Lori held up one finger like a baseball umpire. "If I recall correctly, which I'm sure I do, it was *not* fun. It was hot and sweaty and I found a tick crawling up my thigh trying to find its way to my vagina."

"Ticks do not go looking for your vagina," Morrigan said, trying hard not to laugh.

"No, don't even try to change my mind about that. I saw the *House* episode. The tick was hiding in the girl's vagina." Lori shivered convulsively. "It was majorly disgusting."

"That really is gross," Gena said.

"And complete fiction." Morrigan tried, unsuccessfully, to add some common sense to the conversation.

"Exhibit B." Up went Lori's second finger. "Camping."

"Oh, come on! That was way back in ninth grade."

"Time has made it no less horrifying," Lori said primly.

"And it wasn't that bad. I remember having a good time."

"Yeah, that's because *you* like playing Boy Scout, and the great outdoors, and...and...you *like* nature." Lori said the words as if they were the name of a deadly disease. "The rest of us will remember the mosquitoes."

"Size of hummingbirds," Gena piped in.

"And the chiggers," Lori continued smoothly.

"Don't talk about it. You'll make me start to itch," Jaime said.

"*And* the snakes," Lori finished with a flourish.

"There was only one snake," Morrigan said.

"As if that mattered," Gena muttered.

"It was really pretty, though," Morrigan said. She'd never admit to them that she and G-pa had gone back to the Keystone campsite often after her one failed attempt to camp with her friends. She absolutely loved camping.

"Pretty?" Lori was saying. "No. It was dirty and hot and buggy. The new Starbucks in BA is pretty. The bracelet Keith gave me is pretty." She waved her wrist around so that the delicate gold links glittered. "My great Kenneth Cole wedges—the ones you wouldn't let me wear today because we're going to be schlepping through a nasty, dark, cold, batty cave—are pretty. Camping is not pretty. See the difference?"

"Wait, there're bats in the cave?" Gena sat up straight and quit playing with her hair. "No one told me about the bats."

"Hello! It's a cave. Of course there're bats," Jaime said.

Morrigan sighed. "It's summer. You won't see the bats.

They're hiding in the darker, cooler parts of the cave. And anyway, if you see one it won't bother you."

"And finally, we come to exhibit C in proof-that-Morgie-likes-to-do-weird-stuff." Lori paused dramatically with her three fingers up in the air. "Dancing outside naked at night."

Jaime groaned.

"Do we have to talk about that?" Gena used her hand to fan herself as her face flushed hot with remembered embarrassment.

"Admit it. That wouldn't have been so bad if we had put on shoes and if disgusting Josh Riddle hadn't been watching us," Morrigan said.

"I still have nightmares about that gross kid's beady little eyes," Gena said.

"That's not the 'little' part of his anatomy I still have nightmares about," Lori said.

Gena made gagging sounds.

"Why were we out there again? I don't remember," Jaime said. "I think I've blocked it."

"We were celebrating the Esbat." Blank looks met Morrigan's matter-of-fact statement, so she added, "A celebration of the full moon. My grandma told me the story about how some pagans like to honor the full moon by dancing sky-clad, or naked, under it. We thought it sounded fun."

"No, you thought it sounded fun. We just went along with you," Lori corrected her.

"You know, it's weird that Mama Parker knows so much about bizarre religions. I mean, she's all sweet and grandma-like and looks totally normal. Then all of a sudden one night you'll drive up the lane and see her outside pouring wine and honey around a fire she's made in the middle of the patio and she'll smile at you and say something like, 'Just finishing up my offering to the Goddess at Imbolc, hon. Make yourself at home. There're cookies in the kitchen,'" Gena said.

"Doesn't seem weird to me." Morrigan's eyes began to narrow.

"Not that I don't think Mama Parker's great. She is," Gena said quickly.

"You have to admit that she's not exactly the norm for Oklahoma," Lori said.

Morrigan shrugged. "I've never understood what's so great about the norm."

"Morrigan has a point," Jaime said. "I've been going to the super-boring First Methodist Church of Broken Arrow all my life and I've never had as much fun there as I did the time we did the Easter-wishes thing with the tree."

All of the girls smiled as they remembered. "It's called an Eostre Wishes Tree," Morrigan said.

"Remember how Mama Parker planted all of those flowers around the tree?" Gena said.

Morrigan nodded. "They were daffodils, crocuses and hyacinths. I helped her plant the bulbs the winter before."

"Then when they were blooming and beautiful Mama Parker gave us silk ribbons and crystals—"

"And those cool little stars she made out of shiny foil," Lori interrupted Gena. "Then she gave us blank wildflower note cards, biodegradable of course, and told us to write our wishes on them. When we were done we tied the cards and the decorations up in the branches of the tree."

"Yeah, and Mama Parker told us it was just another way for our prayers to be heard at Easter. Well, it was for sure way more fun than waking up too early and sitting on a hard pew through boring church," Jaime said.

"It really was cool," Lori said.

"Yeah, cool," Gena echoed.

"So maybe y'all don't mind my weirdness too much?" Morrigan kept her voice light and kidding, but she knew that there was a very real part of her that was constantly waiting for her friends to someday realize that she just didn't fit in—no matter how good her acting abilities. Then they'd walk away and leave her alone with the voices in the wind and her unanswered questions.

"Morgie, baby, we like your weirdness!" Gena cried and flung an arm around her.

"That's right. Without your weirdness we wouldn't be the Core Four," Jaime said.

"Which is why we're here, following you into a batty cave when we should be shopping," Lori said.

"Okay, enough with the bats," Gena said.

A bell rang, reminding Morrigan of something that ranchers probably used a zillion years ago to call cowboys in to dinner.

"Three o'clock tour through the cave is leaving in two minutes!" a male voice bellowed over a scratchy loudspeaker system.

The girls exploded into activity as they shoved the leftovers in the picnic basket Mama Parker had packed for them and dumped the plastic plates, et cetera, in a nearby trash can. Morrigan grabbed the basket and hurried to put it in the back of Old Red, her beat-up Ford Escort station wagon. As an afterthought, she grabbed the little emergency flashlight G-pa made sure she kept with the first-aid kit, flares and blanket in the rear of her well-used car. She shoved it into her purse and jogged to catch up with the line that was already beginning to make its way around the gift shop and picnic area down some old rock stairs that would lead to the entrance of the main cave.

Morrigan felt a tremor of anticipation. This time she wasn't just going camping in a forest, or hiking in some woodsy hills. This time she was actually going *into* the earth. She could feel the draw of it as surely as she could feel the change in temperature of the air around her.

Come… The word echoed in her ears.

"Morgie! Come on—over here."

Morrigan realized she had been standing alone at the bottom of the stairs, gazing at the surprisingly ordinary-looking slash in the earth that was the entrance to the cave. She blinked and saw Gena waving at her from the shadows just inside the cave where she stood with Lori and Jaime, and the rest of the small group they'd joined. Morrigan shook herself and hurried to her friends.

Come…

The word enveloped her, as did the cool darkness of the cave. August in Oklahoma was always hot and miserable, and Morrigan instantly breathed easier, adjusting quickly to the more than thirty-degree difference. She drew another deep breath as she reached her friends and only half listened as the guide launched into a speech about the history of the cave.

It smelled incredible! Earth…rich, sweet and rocky. The scent filled her senses and made her feel excited and relaxed at the same time.

This is where you belong.

The words drifted through her mind and for once Morrigan didn't run them through a sieve of good-thought/bad-thought where she would dissect it and struggle with it and try to figure out if it was something she should ignore or not. This time the truth in the words was too powerful for such laceration.

This is where you belong.

Unable to stop herself, she moved through the little group so that she could be the first one behind the guide to enter the bowels of the cave. The first to smell and touch and see everything. Morrigan's soul seemed to quiver in excitement and she ignored the sounds of her friends trying to catch up with her.

"Okay, if we're all ready, then let's move forward as a group," the guide was saying. "Please remember that the lights are on a timer system, so you'll need to stay fairly close to me and together."

How annoying! Like she wanted to be stuck with the herd? She was dying to explore this amazing place on her own. Irritated, Morrigan pulled her eyes from staring at the recesses of the cave, meaning to shoot the pain-in-the-ass guide a dirty look. Instead she felt her heart lurch with a little stutter-beat.

The guy was f-ing drop-dead gorgeous. And he was looking right at her like he could read her mind.

3

"Ready?" The guide spoke right to her, his brilliant blue eyes
meeting her gaze. Morrigan nodded her head. "Excellent,"
he said. "Oh, I forgot to formally introduce myself. My name
is Kyle, and I will be your guide today." Even though he seemed
to be speaking just to Morrigan, several people in the group
laughed and called, "Hello, Kyle," while he turned his back to
them and used a key to unlock a little metal box and flip a series
of switches. Instantly, the cavern was bathed in white lights.

A surge of annoyance made Morrigan forget about the hot
guide. The lighting was wrong. It was too harsh—too white—
too impersonal. The inside of the earth should be illuminated
with softness. With glowing rocks or sweetly licking flame…

"Jeesh, Morgie, quit staring and come on!" Lori grabbed
her arm and pulled as she jostled past her.

Morrigan shrugged off Lori's arm and moved ahead until
she was at the front of the group again. The guide stopped not
far inside the cave. They'd come to a room that was huge,
littered on either side of the iron-railed trail with enormous
sections of large, flat rock. Before the guide began to speak,
Morrigan knew. "This is the deepest part of the cave."

"You're absolutely right!" Kyle smiled at her. Completely

taking Morrigan off guard, she smiled nervously back at him. Until then she'd had no idea she'd spoken aloud the thought that had been whispered into her mind. Then she was further surprised to see Mr. Gorgeous Guide blush, like her smile had disarmed him, and turn hastily back to address the rest of the group. "As the young lady said, we are now at the deepest part of the cavern. From floor to ceiling it measures fifty feet, which puts us at about eighty feet under the surface."

Young lady? Morrigan thought. *He doesn't look much older than me.*

Beside her, Lori hugged herself and whispered, "It's too creepy for words thinking about being eighty feet under the ground. God, talk about a deep grave."

"No, it's not like that at all," Morrigan responded automatically, eyes scanning the magical place. "It's not creepy. It's beautiful and perfectly safe."

Safe? Why had she said that?

Lori turned her attention to Kyle the Hot Guide. "Hey, Kyle. My friend says the cave is perfectly safe. What do you say?"

"Well, it's not one hundred percent safe." All the people in the group, except for Morrigan, shifted restlessly at this, so he added hastily, "Oh, you're safe enough with me today. But the truth is that those huge slabs of gypsum that litter the floor around the entrance, and those there and there—" he pointed to giant clumps of rock off the side of the trail "—they all fell from the ceiling of the cave. The last time we had rock break loose was just this past December. Thankfully, the cave was closed for Christmas."

"How do you know none of it will fall on us today?" Lori asked.

"We have monitors checking the ceiling daily. If anything is loose, we close that area of the cave. Nothing's been loose since December."

One of the middle-aged men in the group, the one with the

big gut, snorted. "You're, what, all of eighteen? Shouldn't we check with someone else, like your boss, before we go any farther?"

Morrigan thought Kyle would blush and fidget, but was impressed when he turned a steady gaze on the old guy. "Sir, I *am* the boss, or rather the most senior member of the team here. I've been employed at the park for six years. Currently, I'm finishing up the fieldwork for my master's in geology. Don't worry, you're as safe as you can possibly be."

"Oh, well then…" The fat guy looked embarrassed and the women in the party all looked smug, clearly choosing the gorgeous young geologist over Mr. Fatty.

Morrigan wanted to say *I told ya so,* but then again Kyle hadn't agreed with her one hundred percent.

It is always safe for those who have an affinity for the earth…if the rocks speak to you and tell you when and where they will fall…

Uncharacteristically, Morrigan listened to the voice that sloughed through the winds of her mind. Here in the womb of the earth the voice seemed maternal, harmless, even nurturing. And she felt so *right* here—so like she belonged. Maybe the earth herself was insulating her from the whispers of the dark god. Maybe here she could be sure she was only hearing the sound of her mother's voice.

"Right around this corner is what we like to call the Encampment Room." The line had begun to move again and Kyle had flipped on another set of abrasive artificial lights. "It would make sense if people had used this cave as shelter— although we haven't found any evidence of ancient occupation—that they would probably have camped here. It's close enough to the entrance to be easily accessible. The floor is flat. You can see the walls have formed in such a way that they're perfect for shelves. And a stream runs here on the other side of the room, bringing in fresh water."

"Bleck. Camp here? It's way too cold." Lori shivered. "It would make something as gross as camping even grosser."

"Actually, the temperature inside the cave stays at a fairly consistent sixty degrees. It only fluctuates about five degrees either way, and that only in the middle of winter or summer," Kyle explained.

"Still means cold and creepy to me," Lori muttered.

Lori's complaint made Morrigan realize that everyone else had put on jackets or sweatshirts. Even Kyle wore a khaki-colored jacket with the Alabaster Caverns State Park logo on the pocket. She was still holding her sweatshirt. She hadn't been cold at all. As usual feeling weirdly out of sync with everyone else, Morrigan hastily tied the unneeded sweatshirt around her shoulders.

"Okay, that rock is really pretty," Gena said. "It almost makes me forget that bats live down here."

Morrigan followed Gena's pointing finger to see a huge roundish stone onto which a pink spotlight was shining. The boulder glittered in the gaudy light. Morrigan thought it looked like something that should be decorating Dollywood.

"That is the largest freestanding boulder in the cave made completely of selenite."

"It's not supposed to be pink," Morrigan heard herself say, and then she pressed her lips together. She was probably annoying the hell out of the cute guide.

Kyle gave her a surprised look that lacked any hint of irritation. "You're right, selenite isn't pink. That's just our creative lighting. If you get closer to it, or look around at the rear side, you'll see that selenite is a clear crystal, like glass. Actually, it's so clear and easy to cut that settlers used sheets of it as windows in their homesteads."

Without waiting for permission, Morrigan stepped off the well-marked pathway to look at the unlighted side of the boulder. She could easily see the clear brilliance of the glass-like stone. She touched it. The rock was soft and cool. Morrigan laid her palm flat against the surface. "You really are beautiful. You don't need that stupid pink light," she whispered.

The surface of the rock quivered like the skin of an animal.

Welcome, Light Bringer…

The words weren't in the wind around her, as were the familiar voices she'd been hearing as long as she could remember. The words somehow traveled through her palm, through her skin, soaking into her body. Morrigan let out a little yelp and stepped back so quickly that her foot slid over the damp floor and she had to windmill her arms to keep from falling on her butt.

A strong hand caught her arm, steadying her. "Careful, it's slick in here, especially if you move off the pathway."

Thoroughly shaken, Morrigan did little more than nod and mutter a belated thanks as Kyle pulled her back on the path, smiled shyly at her and then motioned for the group to follow him forward.

"Okay, that Kyle cutie is tall and blond and delicious. Excellent job of getting him to notice you by playing damsel in distress," Gena whispered to her.

Morrigan's body followed Gena but her mind was buzzing with disbelief. What was going on? She couldn't have really felt the rock move. The voice couldn't have been anything except what she'd been hearing since she was a kid. Or had she finally let all the weirdness get to her and gone totally, one hundred percent nuts? Which meant she should be packing for Laureate psycho hospital instead of OSU.

By the time Morrigan caught up with the front of the group Kyle had stopped them in a place where the cave widened out again. He waited until everyone was looking expectantly at him.

The dome…

The words flitted through Morrigan's mind just before Kyle pointed his flashlight up.

"This is the first of several domes in the cave. Notice that it is easy to see from the grooves and patterns left on the rock that the domes were created by whirlpools. At one time this cave was filled with water. Over the years it carved out the unique shape of the cave. Of course today all that is left of the once raging river is a shallow, glassy lake you'll see later in the tour and this little stream that trickles parallel to our path."

Morrigan thought the dome looked as if it had been shaped by a giant ice-cream scoop digging into the selenite-embedded alabaster ceiling. It was beautiful and mysterious, but somehow familiar. How could that be? It was like she'd known it would be there before Kyle had drawn their attention to it. But she'd never been in this cave—any cave—before now.

Staring up, Morrigan wandered to the edge of the pathway where the smooth wall was peppered with selenite crystals. She wanted to run her hand over the glistening surface. Actually, she felt compelled to touch it. But she hesitated, afraid and eager at the same time.

Discover the truth.

Morrigan was immeasurably relieved when she heard the whisper in the air around her; though she did appreciate the irony in feeling relief about something that had haunted her since she was a child. To her it still seemed the voice in the wind was more clearly maternal than usual. And she was relieved that it was in the air and not traveling through the skin of the cave. Or was she? There had been something infinitely compelling about that "other" voice—the one that had come from the selenite rock.

"This is my favorite part of the tour." The humor in Kyle's voice tugged at Morrigan's attention. She turned so that she could see him standing with the rest of the group near one of the metal light-switch boxes. "We are going to experience complete dark. It'll only last for sixty seconds, but it will be a long minute. The eye needs light to function properly. If you were to live in the dark for six weeks, you would go blind. Let's get a little taste of that now!" With a click, Kyle flipped off the lights.

The darkness was utter and impenetrable.

Little squeals of semi-pretended fear came from the group. Morrigan definitely recognized Gena's shriek. And there was the furtive rustling of people grabbing onto whoever stood beside them. Slowly, like she was moving through water, Morrigan turned blindly to the wall.

She felt no fear. In the complete dark her senses seemed to expand. Her body felt liquid, and she imagined she could be absorbed into the cave and merge with the glasslike crystals.

Morrigan realized the thought should have scared her, but it didn't. Not at all.

She reached out her hand and pressed it against the cool surface of the cave wall. She could feel the crystal selenite where it mixed with the smoother, softer alabaster, and was amazed that even though she could see absolutely nothing she could tell which rock was which. Then against her palm she felt a stirring, the same type of movement she had felt when she'd touched the crystal boulder.

Light Bringer…

The name shivered through the selenite crystals, passing into her body like a current of sound. This time she didn't pull away. Curiosity held her captive. Morrigan's hand began to feel warm, and as the lights snapped back on she was staring at her hand where it rested against the cave wall.

The selenite crystals under her palm had begun to glow.

Morrigan pulled her hand from the wall and stuffed it into

the front pocket of her jeans. The crystal flickered then went dark again.

"I told you this place was creepy," Lori said, rushing up to Morrigan. "No freaking way would I ever want to get stuck down here. I cannot believe you didn't scream your brains out when he shut off the lights and you were standing over here all by yourself."

Morrigan moved her shoulders. "No big deal. I mean, he said it was only going to last for sixty seconds." Trying to sound normal, she said, "My bikini wax last week lasted longer and was scarier."

Lori laughed and Morrigan tried to relax. Gena and Jaime joined them and the four girls followed the group continuing down the path.

"I swear to God I was sure a bat was going to fly into my hair when he turned off the lights," Gena was saying breathlessly.

"I'm cold," Jaime said. "I wonder how long this thing is."

"The path is about a quarter of a mile," Morrigan said absently, and then wondered how the hell she knew that. Thankfully, everyone else was used to her knowing stuff about the outdoors, so no one noticed her extrasensory knowledge.

"Good. Then we won't be down here too much longer," Lori said.

"Was that a bat?" Gena was squinting up at another dome formation in the ceiling. "I think I just saw a bat."

Morrigan tuned out their chatter. As often as she could she let her fingertips trail over the smooth, damp side of the cave. Whenever her skin touched selenite she felt a zap of heat. She absolutely, definitely felt something within the rock that she could only describe as sentience. The cave was alive and by some amazing miracle it recognized her. It called her Light Bringer. As she walked the rest of the path, slowly bringing up the rear, she felt as if she had left Oklahoma and entered another world—and this time it was a world in which she belonged.

But how could that be? How could she feel at home in an f-ing cave? It didn't make any sense, but then neither did hearing voices or making fire sprout from her hand. Morrigan realized it was getting warmer. They must be coming to the exit from the cave. Reluctantly, she moved up with the rest of the group where they had stopped beside Kyle.

"The modern exit from the cave is there." He pointed to where the cave path turned gently to the left. "But that's a man-made exit. Before that was built, the exit was through there." Kyle aimed his flashlight down a small tunnel that branched off from the main pathway. "To exit the old way, people had to duck and squeeze through there. They went most of the way on their hands and knees, and sometimes they even had to crawl."

"Eew," Gena said. "Talk about claustrophobia. I'd rather turn around and go out the in than do that."

Kyle chuckled. "Thanks to modern engineering, you don't have to do either."

"Can we take the old exit if we want?" This time Morrigan meant to speak aloud. Everyone turned and stared at her. The looks on her three friends' faces were predictably horrified. She didn't bother with them, though. She kept her gaze steady on Kyle's blue eyes.

"Don't you think it would be claustrophobic and tomblike in there?" He shined his flashlight down the narrow tunnel again.

"No," Morrigan said firmly. "I think it's perfect the way nature made it and I'd like to use the original exit." A quick thought made her rummage through her purse for the flashlight. "And I have this."

Kyle smiled. "Sure, go ahead. I usually take that exit when I'm not leading a group. You're small enough that you shouldn't even have to crawl—hands and knees should do it for you." He glanced at the rest of the group. "Anyone want to join Miss Adventurous?"

There were muffled laughs and lots of heads shaking. Lori started to open her mouth to protest, but Morrigan ignored her, flipping on her flashlight and striding past her gawking friends.

"Just keep your flashlight on and keep moving forward. It's really not very far. You'll meet us about twenty-five feet from here just before the rear opening." He grinned, which made him look like a really cute but mischievous twelve-year-old. "Have fun."

"Thanks, I will." Morrigan smiled back at him, wondering how old he was. At first he'd seemed way young, but he'd told the potbellied guy that he was finishing his master's. That made him twenty-something, didn't it? She hoped he was older. Young guys gave her a headache. The last guy she'd dated had been nineteen—of course, he'd acted like he was thirteen, but that had been no big surprise. If she felt years older than her girlfriends, she felt centuries older than the guys they hung out with.

"Are you changing your mind? It's okay, you know."

Morrigan jumped, realizing she'd been standing there holding her flashlight, staring into the tunnel and daydreaming about guys. No wonder she hadn't had a date in months. She was truly a dork. And an overly mature dork at that.

"Oh, no! No. I'm not changing my mind. I was just waiting for you to tell me I could go ahead."

"Oh." He blushed again, and Morrigan thought his pink cheeks made him look adorable. "You can go ahead."

"Good. Okay. See you on the other side." Morrigan got on her hands and knees and, flipping the flashlight on, crawled into the tunnel and away from the group's curious stares.

4

The tunnel turned abruptly to the right. Crawling, she followed it and the cave swallowed her. Logically, Morrigan knew she was only a few yards away from the rest of the group—that if she backed up she would pop out of the tunnel and would be on the well-marked pathway with its electric lighting system and its oh-so-safe handrails. But logic had little to do with how she'd felt since she entered the cave. The tunnel was small and smooth and pleasantly cool. She crawled on, enjoying the sense of protection the tight space gave her. When the tunnel widened just enough for her to sit on her feet, knees bent, she stopped. Morrigan spread her arms. Both hands rested on either side of the tunnel. She caressed the rock, concentrating and feeling carefully. Yes…only by touch and without looking she knew it when her palms brushed over selenite crystals embedded in the alabaster.

Light Bringer…

The name vibrated through her body and Morrigan felt an indescribable rush of excitement.

"Hello…" she whispered hesitantly.

We hear you, daughter of the Goddess.

Morrigan's heart thudded heavily. Daughter of the Goddess? The crystals thought she was the daughter of a goddess! The thrill of the thought quickly faded. What would happen when the crystals found out they were mistaken? She wasn't the daughter of any goddess. She was just an orphan kid whose family was kinda strange. Sure, like her grandparents, her mother, Shannon, had believed that trees and rocks and nature in general had souls, and that a god or goddess couldn't be confined to a building. But Shannon Parker had definitely been mortal and not a goddess. Her death was all the proof Morrigan needed of that.

Embrace your heritage.

The words didn't come from the rocks, but drifted to her familiarly through the cool air of the cave. Morrigan sighed and muttered, "It's hard to embrace my heritage when I'm not really sure what that means."

It means you are touched by the divine.

The immediate response startled Morrigan. The voices in the wind never answered her. She'd never had a conversation with them. Usually they were just random thoughts that she caught, like an overheard conversation. Sometimes she heard laughter. Sometimes she heard crying. But they'd never, ever responded to her—not even the many times she'd called out for her mother. A finger of worry shivered up her spine, but the sense of belonging and peace the cave gave her outweighed any trepidation she might have felt at the deviation from what she considered normal.

"I've been touched by the divine." Morrigan repeated the words—testing them—tasting them—trying to wrap her mind around them. "And if that's true, then the crystals really do recognize me," she reasoned aloud, the walls of the narrow tunnel absorbing the sound of her voice. Morrigan spread her fingers wide against the skin of the cave and concentrated. "Hello," she said softly. "Thank you for recognizing me."

Instantly her palms began to warm. The crystals quivered

against her skin and then the warmth intensified and the rock began to glow. Morrigan was utterly intrigued, completely absorbed in the light she was creating. It was different from the little flame that sprouted from her hands. That never lasted long and left her feeling breathless and what her grandma described as "out of sorts."

Lighting the crystals made her feel powerful.

She knew without any doubt she could turn off the flashlight and create enough light by which to guide herself. And she wasn't just making light—she was also creating warmth. If someone touched her skin it would be warm, maybe even hot. It was like she had found a power source that only she could tap into, and it lived in the crystals of the cave.

"Hey! Are you doing okay in there?"

Kyle's voice made Morrigan jump. She pulled her hands from the tunnel walls. And the crystals remained lit. Awed, she stared at them.

"Yeah! Sorry!" Morrigan yelled down the tunnel. "I just stopped to look at some of the crystals."

"Well, the group is out. We're waiting for you," he yelled back.

The internally lit selenite was incredibly beautiful. It caught the surrounding alabaster, making that section of the tunnel glow with a pure, white light.

"Morrigan?" Kyle's voice sounded closer, which jerked Morrigan out of the trancelike state in which she'd been gazing at the crystals.

"I'm coming!" She scrambled forward on her hands and knees, clutching the flashlight. Just before the tunnel took another sharp turn and opened to the larger exit, Morrigan glanced over her shoulder. The light of the crystals was fading. As she watched, it flickered...flickered...and then went dark. She hurried the rest of the way.

Kyle took her free hand and steadied her as she emerged

from the tunnel. "Wow, you must have worked up a sweat crawling through there, your hand is burning up." His brow was furrowed and he studied her carefully, as if he expected to see signs that she had had a claustrophobic fit.

Morrigan gave him her best smile. "I guess I'd better hit the gym more often." She pretended to wipe nonexistent sweat from her face and purposefully breathed heavily. "Sorry it took me so long to get through. I didn't mean to hold everyone up. It's just that those crystals caught the beam of my flashlight, and they were so beautiful I guess I got distracted."

The guide's handsome face relaxed. "I know exactly what you mean," he said as he motioned for her to follow him out of the cave. Morrigan forced herself to walk with him, but as she stepped from the mouth of the cave's exit and stood on normal ground again, with the Oklahoma heat pressing down on her and the aqua blue of the sky spreading unendingly above her, she felt the loss of being within the earth like a physical thing and she blinked her eyes hard, amazed that she felt so much like crying.

"Ohmygod! There you are!" Gena blurted as Morrigan and Kyle approached the trolleylike wagon where everyone was waiting.

"She's safe and sound," Kyle assured the group. He grinned at Morrigan. "She's just a natural spelunker, which means she has to be pried from a cave."

"Well, you and she can have it! Too dark and claustrophobic for me," called the middle-aged man. His wife nodded in such vigorous agreement that several of the group members chuckled.

Relieved that he had turned the group's attention from her, Morrigan gave Kyle a quick, grateful smile and then climbed into the trolley. Her friends made room for her and Kyle went to the cab, put it into gear and pulled them smoothly away from the cave. Morrigan wanted to scream at him to take her back. She had to grip the seat hard to make herself stay in the car. What was wrong with her? Why was she feeling like this?

Embrace your heritage… floated around her in the hot wind.

"So—" Lori leaned toward Morrigan with a knowing smile "—tell the truth. You did all of that so that hottie would be alone with you. Right?"

"Yeah, right," Morrigan said automatically.

"I'll bet he took your hand to help you out of that creepy tunnel, didn't he?" Gena said.

"Yeah."

"I think he likes you," Jaime whispered. "He kept looking at you. God, he's so damn hot. You're crazy if you don't get his number."

"I don't know if he's old enough. You know I've had it with young guys," Morrigan said.

Lori snorted. "*You're* old. You've always been old."

Morrigan met Lori's eyes. Suddenly she hated her friends with an intensity that left her breathless. She hated being surrounded by silly, stupid girls who had no damn real worries and no damn idea about what it was to feel like you never belong.

"You're right. I have always been old," she said shortly. Then she turned her head and stared back at the cave while Lori, Gena and Jaime talked endlessly about Kyle's tall blond hotness.

Morrigan needed to get home so that she could talk to the only two people on this earth who understood her. Maybe they could help her make sense out of today.

And maybe there were things about your mother they hadn't told you… whispered the wind.

This time Morrigan listened.

5

"We need to talk."

Her grandparents looked up at her from under their reading glasses. They were in their usual evening places—sitting side by side in their matching recliners reading and ignoring the TV. Grandma had poured herself a glass of red wine. Grandpa was drinking a cup of coffee (decaf, of course) and there was the crumby evidence of what had been a piece of homemade cherry pie on the whatnot table between them. Grandma glanced behind her at the empty door.

"Hon, did the girls want to come in? I have cherry pie."

"No, I sent them home. I need to talk to you guys."

Grandpa took his reading glasses off. "What is it, Morgie old girl?"

"Something happened today while I was in the cave. Something really weird." Instead of taking her usual place on the love seat, Morrigan paced. She was filled with nervous energy, and she wasn't sure why. All the way home she had been simmering. She barely spoke to her friends, and pretty soon the three of them ignored her. Shrugging off her bad mood as PMS they chattered amongst themselves about such utter nonsense that she couldn't get home and get rid of them fast enough.

"Tell us, hon," Grandma said.

"Okay. It started with the reaction I had to the cave. It was like coming home. No, no, it was more than that. It felt like I'd been there before. Only not." Morrigan puffed out a breath in frustration. "I'm not describing it right. When I entered the cave it seemed like I belonged there. You guys know how out of place I feel sometimes." Her grandparents nodded. They did understand—they'd helped her through it her whole life. "I didn't feel like that in the cave."

"Well, hon, you've always loved the outdoors. I suppose it makes sense that you would have a positive reaction to what you might think of as being embraced by the earth," Grandma said.

"That's kinda what I told myself at first. But then the other stuff happened and I knew there was more to it than just that I like the earth."

"What else happened?" She noticed G-pa's voice was guarded. He was probably worried that she'd had a fight with her girlfriends. For as long as Morrigan could remember, her grandpa had been emphasizing the importance of friends…of getting along with others…of ways that she could be a good person. Today the reminder of her G-pa's insistence that she fit in and make friends caused her to feel an unusual flash of irritation, which was reflected in the shortness of her next words.

"The crystals in the cave welcomed me as Light Bringer, and I made them glow."

No one spoke for several beats and Morrigan wanted to fidget. Instead she clasped her hands together and waited. Grandma spoke first.

"Hon, do you mean you transferred the little fire your hands make into the crystals?"

Morrigan shook her head. "No, it wasn't like that. It was

like the fire was already inside the crystals, and when I touched them I made it light."

"Did your friends see this?" Grandma asked hesitantly, as if she really didn't want to hear the answer.

"No. No one knew."

"Morrigan, when you said that the crystals welcomed you and called you Light Bringer, did you mean that you heard that in the voices of the wind?" Grandpa asked.

"No. It was way different than the voices I hear all the time. Grandpa, it was amazing!" Her temporary irritation with him forgotten, she crouched next to his chair, grabbing his big, work-roughened hand. "I touched the crystals, just like I'm touching your hand right now. And they came alive. I felt them shiver. It was like I was touching the skin of an animal. And then *through* my hand I felt them welcome me. It wasn't a voice in the wind. It was a voice in my soul. If I kept my hand on the crystals they started to get warm. That's when they glowed."

She was surprised by the sudden sadness in her grandpa's eyes. He patted her hand and turned his head to meet his wife's steady gaze.

"It's time we told her all of it," he said.

"I know," Grandma said.

Morrigan's heart squeezed and she suddenly wanted to take back everything she'd said. Grandpa's words *all of it* sounded final and scary, and she knew deep within her that after she heard what he had to say she would never be the same.

"Sit down, Morgie old girl. I have a story to tell you." Grandpa motioned to the little footstool he'd carved out of the trunk of an old oak. Morrigan sat on the stool, facing her grandparents, exactly as she had done countless times during her childhood while the three of them talked and laughed and shared their lives together. The remembrance comforted her. These were her grandparents—the people who had loved her for her entire life. She didn't need to be scared of whatever they were going to tell her.

"What is it, Grandpa?"

"Your mother wasn't Shannon."

The words were so simple. The sentence so short. But Morrigan felt as if her grandpa's voice had become a weapon, and what he had just said struck her, causing her such real physical pain that she flinched.

"Hon, it's okay. Everything is going to be okay." Grandma reacted to her hurt, as she always did, but Morrigan didn't take her eyes from her grandpa's face.

"I don't understand what you're saying. How could Shannon not be my mom?"

"Almost nineteen years ago Shannon went to an estate auction. At the auction she bought what she believed to be a reproduction of an ancient Celtic vase. It actually was a talisman from Partholon, another world—a world much like ours, where there are even people who look exactly like people from this world. Except in Partholon, magic was real and the Goddess Epona was, or rather is, that world's main deity."

"Epona…" Morrigan whispered the Goddess's name.

Her grandpa nodded. "It was Epona's High Priestess, her Chosen Incarnate, who sent the talisman here to Oklahoma like a baited fishing line to find and catch Shannon, who was her mirror image—so similar to each other that there was virtually no physical difference to tell them apart—and to change places with her. Through the vase Shannon was transported to Partholon, and Rhiannon, Epona's Chosen, came here to Oklahoma."

"But why? It doesn't make any sense. Why would the High Priestess of a goddess want to leave her world and come here?"

"Rhiannon knew an army of demons was getting ready to attack Partholon, so leaving seemed like a pretty good idea."

"That's not right. If she was a High Priestess shouldn't she have stayed to help her people?"

"Yes, she should have. But Rhiannon MacCallan was selfish and spoiled. She chose the easiest thing to do, not the right thing to do."

Her grandma leaned forward and added earnestly, "But one of the reasons Rhiannon did the things she did was because a dark god had been whispering to her and poisoning her spirit."

At the mention of the whispering, Morrigan felt a shock of understanding. That's why her grandparents had warned her so consistently not to listen to the voices she heard, even though one of them might be her mother. Her mother...

"No one warned Rhiannon about the dark god, Pryderi. She didn't realize that her unhappiness and the bad thoughts that kept going through her mind were manipulated by evil."

"No one warned her, and she became so tainted by evil that she embraced it, and was, eventually, consumed by it," Grandpa continued.

"How did you find out about all of this?" Morrigan felt cold, and wrapped her arms around herself.

Grandpa drew a deep breath and let it out with a slow sigh. "Rhiannon took over Shannon's life."

"No, she did not. Rhiannon was nothing like Shannon, and she definitely didn't take over her life," his wife said with uncharacteristic shortness.

"Your grandma's right. Rhiannon didn't step into Shannon's life, like Shannon did hers in Partholon. Rhiannon changed and twisted things, always seeking more. More power. More money. More at any cost."

"That's how she met your father."

Morrigan turned to her grandma. "So Clint Freeman really was my dad?"

"Of course, hon."

"He was a good man. He had a connection to the land."
Grandpa paused and smiled at her. "That's where I thought you
got your love of the land. He was actually physically strength-
ened by it. Shannon told us that Clint was the mirror image
of the High Shaman in Partholon she had been married to in
Rhiannon's stead."

"Wait. I don't get it. You said Rhiannon was over here and
Shannon was over there. Now you're saying that Shannon told
you things. So she talks to you from Partholon?"

"Well, she has, but not often. Mostly I dream of her, and
know that what I see is real. But that's not how I learned about
Partholon. Shannon came back to Oklahoma once, drawn
here when Clint tried to re-exchange Rhiannon for Shannon.
For a while all three of them were in Oklahoma, as was a great
evil Rhiannon had resurrected for its power and let loose in
this world."

"Is that what killed my dad?" Morrigan was amazed that her
voice sounded so normal when everything inside her was
churning around and she really wanted to jump up and cover
her ears and run from the room.

"No," Grandpa said slowly. "Your father sacrificed himself
so that he could stop Rhiannon. With his life's blood he magically imprisoned her, and at the same time sent Shannon back
to Partholon, so that she could be with his mirror image, the
father of her unborn child."

"And Rhiannon was pregnant with me?"

"Yes."

"Rhiannon is my mother, not Shannon."

She didn't speak it like a question, but her grandpa answered
her anyway. "Yes, Rhiannon is your mother."

"And you're Shannon's parents. Not Rhiannon's parents."

Instead of answering, Grandpa said, "You should know that
there was a shaman present at your birth. He brought you to

us and told us that before she died Rhiannon rejected the dark god and was reconciled with Epona."

Through the buzzing in Morrigan's head she could barely hear what he was saying. "That's why I've always felt like I don't belong. It's because I *don't* belong." She enunciated the words carefully, biting back the sickness that rose in the back of her throat. "I don't belong to this world. And I don't belong to the two of you."

"But, hon, you do belong to us! You're our child."

Morrigan felt her head shaking back and forth. "No. I'm Rhiannon MacCallan's child. And she's not your daughter. My mother wasn't Shannon, the woman whose pictures you've been showing me and who you've been telling me stories about my whole life. I'm Rhiannon's daughter." Her voice sounded weird—angry, loud, accusatory. She saw the hurt that darkened her grandma's eyes and filled them with tears, but she couldn't seem to stop herself. "I'm the kid of the woman who was so damn evil that the father of her child killed himself to keep the world safe from her." She paused, panting. Then her eyes widened as she had another, more terrible thought. "And from me. He killed himself to keep the world safe from me, too, because I'm her child. Since I came from her, I might be like her."

"No, Morrigan. You are not like her," Grandpa said firmly.

Morrigan's heart was pounding so hard that her chest hurt. "How did she get free from the magic? How was I born?" She saw the answer cross her grandpa's well-lined face and felt her stomach clench. Before he could make up something, she answered for him. "Pryderi freed her."

"The dark god freed her, but Epona forgave her."

"And that's why you warned me that some of the voices I hear on the wind might be evil. It's because my mother was evil and she listened to that awful god, so it's only logical that I might turn out like that, too."

"Hon, we wanted to be sure that you would be on your guard, that the same things that tempted and tricked Rhiannon wouldn't get to you, too," Grandma said.

"Morrigan, listen to us. You are not evil and that is not why we warned you. You're like Shannon, not Rhiannon."

"But I'm not Shannon's daughter. You said she was pregnant at the same time Rhiannon was. She has her own daughter over in Partholon, doesn't she?" When neither of her grandparents answered her, she stood up, knocking over the footstool and raising her voice. "Doesn't she!"

"Yes. Shannon has a daughter in Partholon," her grandpa finally said.

"So there are two of us, just like Shannon and Rhiannon. It's ironic, isn't it? I actually belong over there, and she should have been born here. Or no. She has a mom and they belong together. It's me who doesn't really belong anywhere."

You have the cave and you have your heritage… drifted in the air around Morrigan.

"I'm not your granddaughter. I'm not who I thought I was for my whole life." Morrigan started backing out of the room. If she stayed there much longer she was going to drown in the fear and sorrow pressing in on her.

"Of course you're our granddaughter. This doesn't change anything. The only reason we told you about all this is because you're obviously showing the powers of a priestess. That means Epona's hand must be on you, even here in Oklahoma," Grandpa said, speaking to her softly, as if she were a skittish filly.

"It's a good thing to be touched by Epona," Grandma said, smiling through her tears. "I'm sure the Goddess has a plan for you."

"What if it's not Epona who has touched me?" Morrigan's voice sounded as dead as her heart felt. "What if Pryderi has marked me as his and that's why I hear the voices and can make fire and why the crystals talk to me and glow when I touch them?"

"Pryderi has not marked you. You are not evil, Morgie old girl," Grandpa said gently.

Morrigan's eyes filled with tears. "You say that, but you don't know it for sure. And I have to know it for sure. No matter what, it's time I embrace my heritage." She whirled around and ran out of the house.

Her grandparents hurried to the door in time to see her gunning Old Red down the lane.

"She'll be all right." Mama Parker wiped the tears from her cheeks. "She'll cool off and come home and everything will be okay, won't she, hon?"

Richard put his arm around her. "I hope so. Morgie's a good girl. She's just scared and probably more than a little mad at us right now."

They returned to their chairs. Richard moved slowly, feeling his age more than usual. He tried to get back into his book, but he couldn't concentrate. He glanced at Mama Parker. She was staring out the window.

"She's a good girl," he repeated.

His wife nodded. "I know. I just… It's just a lot for her to take in, and she's so young."

Richard sighed and mumbled, "Yep…yep…yep…" And then he straightened in his chair. "Damn!"

"What is it, hon?"

"Morrigan said 'embrace my heritage.' Have you ever heard her say anything like that in the eighteen years and four months she's been alive?"

Mama Parker shook her head silently.

"But it does sound like something Rhiannon might whisper in her ear," he said.

"Or Pryderi."

He stood up and started to pull on his shoes. "No matter what that old Indian said, I still doubt there's much difference between the two."

"We're going after Morrigan?"

"Yep, we damn sure are."

"Oh, good, hon. I'm so relieved." Mama Parker hurried to grab the keys to the Dodge doolie truck. "Do you know where she went?"

Richard Parker nodded grimly. "If my guess is right, and she's listening to the damn whispers from the damn things that won't leave her alone, she's gone back to the cave."

"The place where her power is the greatest," Mama Parker said.

Richard grunted. "That's the point, isn't it? My guess is our Morrigan has power they want." As he found the old thermos in the cabinet and started to fill it with coffee, he thought wryly that where his girls were concerned his guess was usually right. Which hadn't always been a good thing.

6

Partholon

"Uh, excuse me, Myrna. What did you just say? To me it sounded like 'I'm pregnant with the troll's baby and I'm going to handfast with him, Mama.' I know I couldn't have heard you right."

Myrna tossed her auburn hair back and put her hands on her hips. I instantly recognized her "I'm ready for a fight" body language.

"You heard me right, Mama. Except for the part about Grant being a troll. You know I've asked you a thousand times to quit calling him that."

"Let's see…he's short. The top of his head is flat. He has an underbite. And a squeaky little voice. All that says troll to me."

"His voice is not squeaky."

"Fine. His voice isn't squeaky. Everything else says troll to me."

"Really? I think it says 'my daughter's soon-to-be husband and father of her child' to me."

I looked around as if I expected another person to pop up from behind one of the rosebushes in my gorgeous garden. "Do you have a grown daughter who's supposed to be away at the Temple of the Muse learning how to be well read and knowledgeable and graceful, et cetera, et cetera, but who is instead fornicating with a troll and causing you to have a giant pain in your—"

"Rhea! Myrna! There you are." Alanna (bless her heart) burst into the garden and positioned herself between my daughter and me. Before I could draw a breath to launch into another tirade, the sound of hooves pounding down the marble path told me the cavalry—aka the fornicator's father—was on his way. I turned back to (perhaps a little too vigorously) cutting my favorite violet roses for a bouquet, ignoring the rebellious fruit of my loins as well as my best friend.

I could feel Alanna glance at me, and then she hugged Myrna. "Sweet girl! Grant told me you'd arrived this morning. What a surprise. We didn't expect to see you until winter."

I snorted at the mention of the troll, but ClanFintan's arrival covered the sound. Mostly.

"Da!"

I didn't have to turn around to know that Myrna had hurled herself into her father's arms. Jeesh, she was such a daddy's girl.

As you have always been, Beloved.

I mentally rolled my eyes at my goddess and muttered, "Let's just see what her father has to say about her lovely news."

Patience, Beloved, came the entirely too familiar reply.

I turned around and crossed my arms in time to see Clan-Fintan beam a proud parental smile at our only child.

"My heart is whole once again now that my two girls are with me."

His eyes met mine and his smile included me. For a second I forgot that our daughter was driving me insane. All I could think about was how almost twenty years had only made him more handsome—and had only made me love him more completely.

Then I remembered the reason behind Myrna's surprise visit.

"Tell your father why you came home, and then my guess is he won't be quite so happy to see you," I said.

Myrna frowned at me. "You don't have to be mad at me, Mama. This really is a good thing."

"Hrumph!" I snorted, sounding purposefully like said father.

ClanFintan gave me his "let me handle her" look. I held my hands up in mock surrender, only too happy to comply. He looked down at Myrna. His tone said he was more than used to running interference between two volatile redheads. "What have you done to upset your mother, Myrna?"

I watched her turn her bright blue eyes on him and smile joyfully. "I've gotten pregnant, Da! And Grant and I are going to be handfasted!"

I heard Alanna's startled inhalation of breath. ClanFintan looked from our daughter to me.

"Told ya so," I said succinctly.

"And where would Grant be?"

I grinned at the dangerous calm in my husband's voice. Myrna, clearly recognizing her father's demeanor for what it was—the calm before the storm in which he stomped Grant's fornicating little ass to death—turned to fully face him. I watched with amusement. Usually Myrna looked so much like me that it was a little scary. I mean, she was younger and thinner and taller than me, and her hair was a darker shade of red than mine, her eyes a blue that often reminded me of my dad, where mine are a moss green, but other than that she and I looked enough alike that no one would ever doubt that we were mother and daughter. I rarely saw anything of ClanFintan in her, except when she dug in her heels about something. Then the stern, determined look that took over her face was all her father's. At that moment her face was one hundred percent bullheaded ClanFintan.

"Da, he's waiting for me to tell the two of you our news first, *then* he'll join me here."

He cocked a dark brow at her. "And why would he not come to your mother and me first and ask permission to handfast with you, as is the honorable thing to do?"

She cocked her own brow, mirroring his expression perfectly. "Because he's not stupid. Anyone with any sense would be scared of you two. But even scared to death, he wanted to come with me. I wouldn't let him. I knew I needed to talk to you alone first."

"Fine. You've talked to us. Now go get him so your daddy can stomp the crap right out of him," I said, smiling pleasantly.

"You are quite sure you're with child?" Alanna's soft voice was unnaturally sharp, catching our attention.

"I'm sure," Myrna said happily. I wanted to happily strangle her.

Alanna closed her eyes as if she was in pain. What the hell? When she opened them her gaze instantly found mine and I saw that her expression was filled with sadness, much more than what was warranted by her best friend's daughter getting knocked up when she was too friggin young by a pain-in-the-ass kid who looked like a troll.

And then it hit me and I felt all of the breath leave my body. I backed shakily up until I found the marble bench I knew was behind me. I sat down before my legs gave way completely.

"Oh, no…" was all I could say. Alanna hurried over to me and took my hand.

"Mama?"

"Myrna, we are talking about the Grant you've known since you were a child, is that right? The young man who is the only son of The McClures who own the vineyards that adjoin the temple?"

"Of course, Mama. There isn't any other Grant." I saw in

her eyes that she knew what Alanna and I had just realized. She kept on speaking, but as she did she walked over to me. "And there isn't any other man, or centaur, for me. It's Grant I love, and Grant who is the father of my child. Ask Epona, Mama, she knows."

I heard ClanFintan's sharp curse, and knew he'd just understood the full ramifications of Myrna's announcement.

"Mama..." She sat beside me and took my other hand. She spoke very gently, and I thought how old and mature she suddenly sounded. "You've known for a long time that I'm not going to be Epona's Chosen after you."

"No," I whispered through my tears. "No, I haven't."

Listen to her, Beloved. Myrna knows her heart and she accepts her destiny.

"Yes, you have. You know Epona has never spoken to me." I opened my mouth, but she hurried on. "Oh, the Goddess loves me, I know that. And I love her, too. I love the rituals you perform and I love the blessing ceremonies. But I've never had the slightest desire to lead the rituals or the ceremonies. More than that, Mama, I have no goddess-given affinity. The trees greet you. The rocks sing your name. Your spirit travels during the Magic Sleep. I don't have any of that, not even a touch of it." Myrna paused and looked down at her lap. "I love you, and I've really tried to be what you want me to be, but all I've ever wanted is to be a mother and to help Grant tend his vineyards." Her words hitched a little as she began to cry. "I'm sorry I've disappointed you and Da."

My heart hurt as I put my arms around her. "Oh, honey, you could never disappoint your father and me. We love you." Myrna clung to me, all signs of stubborn bravado gone. I could feel her shoulders shaking as she sobbed. And then ClanFintan's arms were around both of us. He kissed our daughter and then me. "If this man is what you desire, bring him here and he will receive my blessing," he said.

"Do you promise?" Myrna sniffled, pulling back so she could look into her father's face.

"You have the oath of Partholon's High Shaman," he told her solemnly.

Then she turned her gaze to me. "I really am sorry that I wasn't born to be Epona's Chosen, Mama. I know that's what you've always wanted me to be."

I looked into my daughter's eyes and knew that if I told her how desperately sad I was that she was not going to follow in Epona's service after me I would wound her irreparably. And I couldn't do that. I could never do that. So instead I smiled and used the corner of my silk robe to wipe the tears from her face.

"What I've always wanted is for you to be happy. And if the troll makes you happy, then he will have my blessing." I felt the familiar nudge in my mind and added, "And Epona's."

Myrna smiled through her tears. "Oh, thank you, Mama!" She hugged me and then jumped up. "I'm going to go get Grant right now." She started to rush away and then turned to look at me. "Mama, would you *please* stop calling him the troll?"

"I'll see what I can do," I said with forced brightness. She rolled her eyes at me and then she was gone.

"A granddaughter…" ClanFintan's deep voice sounded un-expectedly wistful. "I had not thought it would be so soon, but now that it is going to happen I cannot say that I find the idea unpleasant." His warm hand reached out and caressed my cheek. "I will pray that she looks like her grandmother."

"If it is a grand*daughter.*" Now that Myrna was gone I didn't conceal the disappointment in my voice. Had Myrna come to us and said that she was in love and pregnant with the child of one of several centaur High Shamans who had, over the years, enthusiastically attempted to court and woo her, there would be no doubt as to the sex of her firstborn. Epona's Chosen always handfasted with a centaur High Shaman the Goddess fashioned especially for her. Their firstborn was a gift from Epona, and was always a daughter. Myrna was pregnant with an ordinary human's (okay, he wasn't really a troll) child. Said child did not come with Epona's guarantee because Myrna would never be Epona's Chosen. I needed to face the awful fact that Myrna didn't have any touch of goddess gifts within her, as absolutely friggin impossible as that might seem.

Myrna will give birth to a healthy, happy girl child. And you are wrong about your daughter, my Beloved. She does carry the gifts of a goddess within her, and those gifts will be born into the daughter she carries.

My breath caught with a surge of joy at Epona's words. "Myrna will have a daughter!" I said.

Alanna clapped her hands in joy. "The line of MacCallan daughters continues. And here I am standing around as if I have nothing to do."

I raised my brows at Alanna. Jeesh, she was always so busy. "Myrna isn't even showing yet. We have plenty of time to stress about a baby's room and whatnot."

"Rhea, we have the Handfast ceremony of the only child of Epona's Chosen to plan," she said in a tone that clearly implied that while I was Beloved of the Goddess I might also be a moron. She shook her head and I swear she clucked like a hen while she muttered something about it being too late in the season for the best flowers for the most fragrant bouquets. Then, throwing me a quick, distracted smile, she hurried from the garden.

"My love, I think it would be best if we met Grant and Myrna in the Great Hall. The betrothing of our daughter should be announced with ceremony and glad tidings if we are really to give our blessing to her."

I looked up at him and sighed. "I know."

"Rhea, has Myrna's choice truly made you so distraught? You and I have spoken before about the fact that she seemed to have no desire to become Epona's Chosen."

"You're right. I can't honestly say that I'm that surprised. It just makes me wonder—" I broke off, feeling horribly disloyal to my daughter.

"You wonder about Rhiannon's child."

"It's not that I wish Myrna was different, really it isn't," I said quickly. "I adore her. She's always been a wonderful daughter. I just can't help but wonder if Morrigan is like Myrna. Epona just told me that Myrna has been gifted by her, but that those gifts are going to be born in her daughter. Does Morrigan have these hidden goddess gifts, too, or are they more tangible in her? And what if she has them, but because she's stuck in Oklahoma she's as miserable as Myrna would be if we could somehow force her into Epona's service against her will?"

"Morrigan is in Epona's hands. You must trust your goddess, and your father, to look after her."

"I do trust Epona and Dad. I just wish it was easier for me to visit him using the Magic Sleep so I could see what's going on over there with Morrigan." My spirit had only returned to Oklahoma a half-dozen times in the past eighteen years, and then I'd only stayed briefly—long enough to assure Dad that Myrna and I were okay. During those visits I had only glimpsed Morrigan three times, once had been the day she was born. The other two times I had seen her sleeping. Each time I had been amazed anew at how closely she resembled my daughter. I knew that resemblance was one reason that I felt so attached to her. How could I help caring about her? And I was totally aware, though ClanFintan and I never spoke of it, of the fact that Morrigan could have been mine (maybe even should have been mine). Had I chosen to stay in Oklahoma I would have married Clint Freeman, doubtless we would have had a child together.

"Rhea, you know the last time Epona allowed you to travel to your old world during the Magic Sleep you were ill for days afterward."

I sighed. "I know. The Goddess said traveling there is dangerous for me. It's just too far to separate my soul and body, especially the older I get. I'm supposed to be content with knowing that Epona sends dream visions to Dad so that he doesn't feel completely cut off from me."

ClanFintan smiled. "I do wish your father could cross the Divide and come to Partholon. I've missed his mirror image, The MacCallan, all these years. Having him here would be like having The MacCallan back amongst us."

"You and Dad would get along great—if you could put up with what I'm sure would be his zillions of embarrassing questions about centaur anatomy."

He chuckled. "I forget that in your old world centaurs are only myth."

"Well, Dad wouldn't let you forget it. But I wish he could come here, too."

"There might be a way to—"

"No!" I stopped him. "To change worlds requires the sacrifice of a human life. As much as we miss each other, I know there's no way Dad would be okay with someone giving his or her life so that he could join me over here. Plus—" I smiled and tried to lighten my tone "—it would have to be two sacrifices because no way he'd come without Mama Parker. Heck, make that three sacrifices. How's Morrigan supposed to stay over there alone? No. Dad will have to remain in Oklahoma."

"And you shall remain in Partholon." He didn't speak it

like a question, but I could see in his eyes the need to hear me say the words.

"I will remain in Partholon with you forever," I said. I stood up and wrapped my arms around his waist. He bent and kissed me thoroughly. I smiled coquettishly up at him. "You're pretty sexy for a grandpa."

He blinked and looked a little stunned. "We're going to have a grandchild. It is an odd yet wondrous thing to get old."

I studied him, taking in his muscular human torso that was only a little thicker than the lean, strong centaur who had handfasted with me almost twenty years ago. His dark hair was peppered with gray, but I liked it. It made him look wise and distinguished, which I didn't think was fair because the gray in my wild red hair did make me look like someone's grandma (which is why Alanna and I hennaed it regularly). He had, quite simply, aged deliciously.

"Am I passing your inspection, my love?" He cocked a brow inquisitively at me.

"Wait." I glanced pointedly behind him at the horse part of his body. "I haven't checked to see if you've become sway-backed lately."

"Hrumph!" he snorted, and grabbed me. With strength that totally did not equate to being a grandpa, he tossed me up behind him. "Swaybacked, indeed," ClanFintan muttered. "I suggest you hold on, Grandmother, or your aged husband may cause you to lose your seat."

Giggling in a very inappropriate way for a grandma, I wrapped my arms around his broad chest and bit his shoulder. He kicked into a smooth canter and we headed to the Great Hall where we would welcome our daughter's choice in husbands—whether we were particularly thrilled about it or not.

I put Morrigan out of my mind. ClanFintan was right. I had to trust that my father and my goddess would look after her.

And the simple truth was, Morrigan was not my daughter. I had my own daughter, and she wasn't a world away. I needed to concentrate on Myrna and my life in Partholon. Period.

"Hey!" I purposefully tickled his ear with my breath, and when he shivered I nipped at his lobe. "If I'm counting the months right, we should be grandparents in early fall." Just when the kids would be returning to school if I was back in Oklahoma, I added silently to myself.

"I proclaim fall an excellent time for a child to be born," he said firmly.

"Yeah…" I said, but my mind was already wandering. Fall was the time when life, and Partholon in general, prepared for winter. One usually associated spring with babies and new beginnings. Conversely, fall was a season for endings: the death of forest foliage…the last harvest of the fruits of summer…the preparation for shorter, darker days to come. I frowned and rested my chin on my husband's broad shoulder, worrying about complex symbolism in the way only an ex-English teacher could worry.

Epona, who usually spoke up, prodding my mind and telling me how silly my imaginings could be, remained uncharacteristically silent.

7

Oklahoma

Morrigan had been driving for more than an hour before she realized where she was heading. She glanced at the clock on her dashboard. It was already after ten o'clock. It would be past midnight when she got to the cave.

"That's good," she told herself, using the familiar sound of her own voice to keep herself calm. "It's not like I want an audience for what I'm going to do."

What was she going to do?

Okay, so she hadn't really thought that part through yet. Actually, she hadn't really thought through any part of what she was doing yet. She'd just known she had to get away from her grandparents, who were really not *her* grandparents. There was someone in Partholon who actually had a mom and a dad and grandparents. Her grandparents. Only they weren't hers.

The whole thing was making her head hurt almost as much as her heart and her stomach.

"So what am I going to do when I get to the cave?" Morrigan asked herself.

Embrace your heritage…

"No," she said firmly. "No, I don't want to hear anything from any of you about it." She turned up the radio so that the sounds of any wind whisperings were drowned out. Morrigan needed to think with a clear head—one that wasn't being influenced by ideas she didn't know if she could trust. If finding out who she really was, and trying to discover exactly what kind of powers she had was what the whispering meant by embracing her heritage, then she supposed that was what she was about to do.

And that maternal voice that seemed so close to her in the cave? She couldn't trust it. It wasn't Shannon, ex-high-school English teacher and daughter of Richard Parker. Morrigan bit her lip to keep herself from crying. All those pictures of the beautiful, vivacious woman who had smiled at her from cherished photographs her grandparents had shown her for as long as she could remember. Those pictures she had daydreamed about her whole life, imagining the things Shannon would have said to her if she'd lived, and the life they would have had together. That. Wasn't. Her. Mother.

Her mother had been a High Priestess from another world who had royally screwed up.

Like mother like daughter?

She seriously hoped not.

Morrigan glanced guiltily at her silent cell phone. She'd turned it off as soon as she'd gotten in her car. They'd be worried about her, and she hated that she was causing them pain. They loved her. She knew that. It wasn't her grandparents she doubted. Morrigan was already sorry for the harsh things she'd said to them. She hadn't been angry at them—or at least she hadn't been angry at them after she'd had time to calm down and think. It wasn't their fault that she wasn't Shannon Parker's daughter. She could even understand why

they hadn't told her. How could they explain to a…say…five-
or ten- or fifteen-year-old that she was really the daughter of
a priestess from another world who had turned evil, then
rejected evil, then died? It was hard enough for her to com-
prehend it and she was a supposedly mature, intelligent
eighteen-year-old.

As Morrigan drove she sifted slowly through the jumbled
sand of her thoughts. Rhiannon MacCallan. That was her
mother's name. How was she going to stop picturing Shannon Parker when she tried to get a visual image of her mother?
Even now she still envisioned the mane of curly red hair, the
bright green eyes and the full, life-loving smile. Okay, so now
she should erase the modern clothes and exchange them for
something the women on the HBO miniseries *Rome* wore. She
should also erase Shannon's smile. Her gut told her that even
if Rhiannon had smiled, it would have looked very different
from Shannon's open happiness.

Grandpa said that the shaman had told him that before
Rhiannon died she rejected Pryderi and was reconciled to
Epona. She wondered if that was really true. The shaman
probably hadn't had any reason to lie. But what about
Rhiannon? Had she lied?

And, most important to Morrigan at the present moment,
how would she know the truth about her mother? When she
was in the cave the voice that had whispered to her in the wind
had been so maternal—so loving. She had assumed it was her
mother and had felt closer to her than she'd ever felt before. After
what she'd found out today, Morrigan more than ever wanted
to know if that voice was really her mother's—really was
Rhiannon, and if it was, what was the truth behind the whispers?

So that was the real reason she was going back to the cave.
She wanted to discover the truth about her mother as much
as she wanted to discover it about herself.

★ ★ ★

Morrigan parked Old Red beside the Alabaster Caverns
State Park sign that was just inside the little road leading to the
gift shop, picnic grounds and the main cave entrance. Her
Nikes made crunching sounds against the gravel, but the sky
was so big that any noise she made was muted by the stars.
Morrigan looked up as she walked. Out there, well away from
any city, it looked like someone had spilled raw-sugar crystals
on a blanket of black velvet. The moon was a fat crescent
peeking through the leaves of the trees that lined the road. The
wind was soft and warm against her face, and she was relieved
that it carried no voices to her.

She passed the park ranger's cabin, careful to step off the road
and move silently in the spongy grass between the trees. There
was one dim light burning inside the cabin, and she wondered
briefly if Kyle was up watching TV, or maybe studying. He
really had been totally cute. And he'd definitely been interested in her. He'd even given her his card under the lame but
adorable excuse that she might want to call him sometime if
she wanted to come back and do something he called wild
caving. That's when spelunkers got together and explored the
parts of the Alabaster Caverns system that weren't developed.
She flushed with pleasure at the memory. She really would like
to do that. And, no, the fact that he was so damn hot didn't
hurt, either. When she got herself together and figured out
who she was and what she was supposed to do about it, *then*
she would call Kyle, she promised herself. Until then she
shoved him to the back of her mind. Now was not the time
to crush on a guy like a typical moronic teenage girl.

Yes, she was still a teenage girl.

Yes, she did occasionally (especially recently) feel moronic.

But, no, she was definitely not typical.

When she came to the souvenir shop, she followed the old

sidewalk around the left side of it, just like she'd done much earlier that day. The rock steps dropped down fast and she was quickly cut off from the brightness of the night sky. Morrigan groped through her purse for the flashlight that was, thankfully, still in there and aimed its beam down. Then she followed it.

She felt the opening of the cave before her flashlight illuminated it for her. Its cool breath teased her face. Morrigan breathed deeply, drawing into her lungs the earthy smell that was so welcoming. She stopped in front of the slash in the earth.

Morrigan should have been afraid. Actually, she should have been terrified. She was all alone, at night, outside, getting ready to go into a cave (with bats).

The truth was, she was exhilarated, which further proved to her just how f-ing weird she was.

Morrigan squared her shoulders and walked into the cave.

The dark really was complete. Her small flashlight made only a pinprick in the impressive blackness, illuminating no more than a tiny shard of the vast underground world. But Morrigan didn't mind the dark. It didn't scare her. She didn't think of it as mysterious or frightening or oppressive. Instead she thought of the unending blackness as soothing to her overstressed nerves.

As if she'd been coming there for years, she easily followed the path around and down into the bowels of the cave. Her footsteps were muffled. This time not by the eternal sky, but by the earth herself. Strangely, the farther into the cave she went, the more relaxed Morrigan became. The tension that had gripped her shoulders all during the return trip faded. The worry she'd felt for her grandparents dissipated. The confusion over the voices in the wind lessened.

Later she realized that this unnatural relaxation should have warned her of what was to come. Then she smiled and kept walking deeper into the cave. It wasn't until she entered the section of the cave she remembered Kyle calling the Encampment Room that she understood what was drawing her.

"The selenite boulder," Morrigan whispered as her flashlight caught the crystal-laden rock, causing it to glisten like moonlight on water. It was so much more beautiful now that the ridiculous pink light wasn't focused on it. Eagerly, she started for it. And then the whispers began.

Yes…come forward and embrace your heritage.

Morrigan stopped like she'd run into a glass wall.

She drew a deep, angry breath.

"No. Just no, dammit no. I'm so tired of being jerked around! I don't even know who I am anymore. What heritage are you talking about? And just exactly who are you?"

For the first time in your life you do know who you are, Morrigan, daughter of a Chosen High Priestess of Partholon.

Morrigan shivered as the words caressed the air around her.

Your heritage is divine, granted to you through your blood, gifted by a great goddess.

The words thrilled her, even as she struggled to maintain some degree of calm objectivity. But it was hard, so damn hard, when every particle of her soul rejoiced at the idea that she might really belong to a goddess.

"I don't know what it means," she said slowly, "to have a goddess-given heritage."

It means you are divine by blood, and have power beyond your wildest imaginings.

Morrigan bit her lip. Power beyond her wildest imaginings… Wow! That must be some power, because she definitely had an excellent imagination. It would really be nice to feel like she had the ability to control her life on her own. Wouldn't power give her that ability?

Come forward and embrace your heritage as you step into your future and accept your destiny, Light Bringer.

That title—Light Bringer—speared through her body. It was what the crystals had called her, what the very walls of the cave had named her. Unerringly, her eyes were drawn back to the selenite boulder. Morrigan couldn't stay away from it, and youthful eagerness caused her to dismiss the unanswered part of her questioning. Knowing the identity of the gentle, guiding voice in the wind seemed far less important than knowing the secrets that were hidden within herself.

Morrigan held the flashlight in her left hand. She placed her right palm against the smooth crystal skin of the boulder, trying to ignore the fact that her hand was shaking. The rock quivered and warmed. Holding her breath, Morrigan said, "Hello. It's me, Light Bringer." She tripped only briefly over the unfamiliar title. "I've come back."

Light Bringer! We welcome you!

The words rushed from the boulder, entering her body through the palm of her hand as if she held it against the jets of a whirlpool and the water was words that somehow passed through her skin.

"Oh!" she gasped.

Call forth the spirit of the crystals, as is your right, and they will answer you.

Yes! Morrigan's own spirit cried in echo to the voice in the wind. Unable to hold back the tide of curiosity any longer, she put the flashlight on the ground and placed both hands firmly against the boulder.

"Um…" She cleared her throat, all of a sudden feeling kinda foolish. The crystals weren't even beginning to glow. The rock had stopped talking to her. What if she was imagining all this weird stuff? What if she had really gone crazy and the voices in the wind were nothing more than advancing schizo-phrenia? "No." She shook her head. Years of her grandpa's firm, reassuring confidence in her overrode self-doubt. "No.

I am not crazy." Morrigan stared at the amazingly beautiful rock and drew a deep breath. Then in a rush she said, "I am Morrigan, daughter of the High Priestess Rhiannon MacCallan of Partholon, and I call forth the spirit of the crystals!"

We hear you, Light Bringer!

The surface of the boulder rippled, like an animal twitching its skin. Her palms tingled with the warmth that was flowing from the rock. Then, in a burst of sensation, the boulder blazed alight. Not like the dim glow that had begun to form under her hand during the time Kyle turned off the lights. And not like the sweet light that had shined from the selenite when she'd crawled through the tunnel. This was a brilliant light, so bright and full-moon white that it had her blinking spots from her eyes.

Eyes watering, Morrigan stared into the glowing crystal depths of the boulder, and within it she watched the stone ripple, like a wind blowing over the surface of an otherwise calm lake. She blinked hard to clear her eyes and looked through the stone to…

Her breath came out in a rush. She was seeing through the selenite boulder to another cave that looked exactly like this one. Only the walls of that other cave were covered with amazingly intricate carvings and mosaics that reminded her of the delicate silver necklace Grandpa had bought for Grandma at last year's Scottish Festival, and the room was filled with women. What was she seeing? What did it mean?

And then the power hit her and Morrigan gasped, losing her glimpse of that odd other cave. Struggling to control the white heat that surged through her she closed her eyes and took several deep breaths. It was like she was suddenly connected to more than just this awesome boulder of light—it was like she was a part of the entire cave. Calming herself, she opened her eyes again and glanced up. The selenite crystals embedded in the ceiling had begun to twinkle like a star-filled night sky. She was doing that! She was calling the crystals alive and making them shine!

Morrigan threw back her head and laughed with joy. The happy, youthful sound bounced from the cave walls like music only she could make.

Rejoice in the power of your heritage!

"It's unbelievable!" Morrigan cried, all thoughts of not fitting into her world and a possible lurking evil forgotten. Tentatively at first, she pulled one hand from the boulder. Concentrating, she stared at the glowing rock. "Stay lit." She spoke in a low, serious voice. Then, reconsidering, she repeated in a more cajoling tone, "Please stay lit." She took her other hand from the rock.

The selenite stayed lit. True, it wasn't shining with the brilliance it had when she had been touching it, but it was definitely still glowing with a pure, silver light. Morrigan whooped, and did a little twirling dance. Lifting her hands over her head she extended her fingers toward the ceiling and concentrated on the nuggets of crystal above her. "Shine for me!" she called up to them.

The ceiling responded with a blaze of sparkling and glittering that took her breath away.

"What in the hell is going on in here?"

Morrigan spun around to see Kyle—dressed in jeans and a hastily pulled on, inside-out OSU sweatshirt, thick blond hair disheveled as if he'd just woken up—standing inside the Encampment Room, staring from her to the lit crystals with wide, shocked eyes.

8

"Kyle!" Morrigan felt her cheeks flame. No one outside her grandparents knew she had weird abilities. No one. She opened her mouth to try to formulate some kind of excuse… anything…something that would begin to explain why she was there, past midnight, standing in the middle of the cave making the crystals glow…

Stop denying your heritage!

Morrigan jumped. The words crackled in the air around her. Morrigan felt their anger—felt it deep within herself—and then she realized she was angry. Why should she make excuses and deny what was hers by right—hers by blood. She lifted her chin.

"I did this. I made the crystals glow. I am the daughter of a priestess."

Kyle's head began shaking back and forth, back and forth as he stared at the glowing crystals. "I must be sleeping. This has to be a freakishly real dream."

The old Morrigan would have agreed with him and then run out, leaving him there to deal with what she assumed would be fading crystals and the possibility of a bizarre sleep-walking episode. But she wasn't the old Morrigan. She was determined never to be the old Morrigan again.

"Pinch yourself or whatever. You're not dreaming. I did this," she repeated more forcefully. "Earlier today when I went through the cave I knew I was attached to the crystals." Her hand caressed the selenite boulder fondly and it responded with a burst of light that made Kyle gasp. Morrigan looked at him. "I came back because I needed to embrace my heritage."

"My God! It's you, Morrigan," Kyle said, clearly just then recognizing her.

"Yeah, it's me." Morrigan decided she was beginning to enjoy his shell-shocked reaction. After all, he didn't look horrified, he just looked amazed. Then she thought about how he'd basically come on to her just a few hours before. And now it was like he barely recognized her? "So do you usually give women your phone number and then forget what they look like? Or is that something unique to me?"

He brushed his hand across his forehead, still looking dazed. "Of course I remember who you are. But you look different."

Morrigan snorted in disbelief (even though Grandma had told her over and over again that snorting was very unattractive). "Different? Yeah right. That sounds like a lame excuse a boy would use." She felt very superior and mature as she spoke, flinging back her hair and meeting his eyes.

"It's not an excuse. You do look different. You should see yourself." His voice had deepened; he was clearly awestruck. "Your skin is glowing." He walked toward her slowly as he spoke. "Your eyes are like blue topaz jewels lit from within." He stopped in front of her. "And your hair..." Kyle's hand reached out and Morrigan was totally shocked when he brushed back a thick strand of it that had fallen over her shoulder. "Your hair is like the rest of you—magically beautiful." Then he took her hand in his and lifted it so that she could see her arm, bare to midbiceps because she was still only wearing her OSU T-shirt.

He was right. Her skin was glowing. She pulled her hand from his and raised her other arm in front of her, spreading the fingers of both hands and turning them over and over...palm up...palm down...as she watched her skin glisten and shine with a radiance that mirrored the selenite.

"How can this be happening?" Kyle said in a low, hushed voice.

She answered automatically, without looking at him. "I'm the daughter of a High Priestess who was Chosen by the Goddess Epona." Morrigan realized there was more to her mother's history than simply being Epona's Chosen, but saying the words out loud felt good—felt more than good. It felt wonderful and right and something she should have done ages ago, *would* have done ages ago, if only she'd known. In the air around her she heard laughter. Not mocking laughter from a dark, evil god, but sweet, musical laughter that seemed to be made of pure happiness. It was her mother. It had to be her mother! With growing wonder in her voice she continued. "I have divine gifts because I carry the blood of generations of priestesses within me." She wasn't sure how, but she knew she was telling the truth.

"You're the most beautiful thing I have ever seen."

Morrigan glanced up from studying her glowing skin and was caught by the look of raw passion in Kyle's eyes.

"You're a goddess," he said.

She opened her mouth to correct him—to say no, to explain again that she wasn't a goddess, she was just the daughter of a goddess's priestess. But before she could speak, two things happened simultaneously. The wind whirled around her, carrying with it beguiling whispers that caught and echoed Kyle's words.

Yes...you are a goddess...you are beauty...

At the same time Morrigan couldn't stop staring at Kyle.

His eyes were full of adoration. He was so handsome, so desirable, so sexy!

Yes…you are a goddess…take your pleasure where you will…

Morrigan's pulse quickened. The power of the crystals still thrummed with her blood, hot and sweet and heavy through her body, boiling deep in her belly, drifting even lower to cause a rush of heat and moisture between her legs. She suddenly wanted the man who stood before her with an intensity that her very limited experience with sex left her unprepared to deal with.

Kyle moved closer to her, drawn to the open flame of her allure.

"God, you're incredible. So, so sexy. I want to touch you…"

"Then touch me," Morrigan breathed.

Without hesitation he caressed her cheek. His hand moved down to stroke the softness of the curve of her neck.

Morrigan trembled. Not from the nerves of a virgin, but from the liquid rush of sensation that was shivering its way from his fingertips through her body.

"More," she whispered.

With a moan Kyle pulled her into his arms and bent to kiss her. She met his tongue with her own, snaking it into the warmth of his mouth and swallowing his moans of desire. She wound her arms around his broad shoulders. She'd never felt like this before—strong, powerful, filled to overflowing with passion.

You are an object of desire to be worshipped and obeyed, the wind whispered.

Yes, yes I am, Morrigan thought as she sucked at Kyle's bruised lips and rubbed her breasts against him, molding her hips to his, rocking against the hot hardness in his pants. Her eyes were open and she could see the crystals sparkling all around them, blazing brilliant white light as if in response to her passion.

"God! This is all like a dream, one damn hot dream," Kyle gasped against her lips. His hands cupped her butt and pulled her more firmly against him.

Somewhere in the back of her mind Morrigan was shocked at her behavior, but she couldn't seem to stop. She didn't want to stop. Her glowing skin was burning with heat and need and lust. She was overflowing with power. She was a goddess!

"Morrigan Christine Parker, just what in the hell is going on here!"

Grandpa's voice splashed cold water all over her hot make-out scene. She jumped back and blurted, "Grandpa!" Face blazing, head spinning and blood pounding from unfulfilled lust. Over Kyle's shoulder she could see her grandpa, looking like a cross between a grizzly bear and a giant pissed-off blowfish. He was wearing a ratty old hunting jacket and holding the ultra-heavy-duty flashlight that was usually kept in the barn. And (oh, no!) Grandma was standing beside him. They were both frowning severely at Kyle.

"Young man, who are you and why did you have your hands all over my granddaughter?"

Morrigan almost laughed. Typical of G-pa, he ignored the fact that crystals were glowing with magical power all around him, the fact that she had basically run away and probably worried the hell out of him, and the fact that she'd had her hands all over Kyle, too. G-pa's narrowed eyes and dark expression said that it didn't matter that he was seventy-five. He was more than willing (and able) to kick the guy's butt who was, in his decidedly slanted opinion, taking advantage of his supposedly innocent granddaughter.

"Sir, I'm sorry." Kyle ran his hands shakily through his hair. "I—I guess I got carried away. She's just so beautiful and I…" He trailed off, looking completely embarrassed. "I didn't mean to disrespect her." Then he cleared his throat and stepped forward, offering Grandpa his hand. "Sir, my name is Kyle Cameron. I'm the head guide and curator of Alabaster Caverns State Park. I met your granddaughter earlier today when she and her friends toured the cave."

Grandpa grunted and reluctantly shook Kyle's hand, still eyeballing him narrowly. Morrigan had no doubt he was also squeezing the crap out of Kyle's hand.

"Well, Kyle Cameron, do you always maul young ladies the same day you meet them, or is this *gentlemanly*—" Grandpa laced the word heavily with sarcasm "—behavior exclusive to my granddaughter?"

"Sir, I—" he began.

"Grandpa, he—" she sputtered, finally finding her voice.

"Hon, look at the crystals. I think Morrigan is making them glow." As usual, G-ma's was the voice of reason.

Grandpa broke off (thankfully) what Morrigan was sure was going to be a severe lecture on respecting the integrity of well-raised young ladies, when his eyes finally registered something in the cave besides Kyle making out with her. She watched her grandpa look around the Encampment Room, taking in everything from the glistening crystals in the ceiling to the glowing boulder.

"Selenite," he grunted, nodding his head thoughtfully. "Settlers used slices of it for windows in their homesteads."

"Yes, sir, that's right," said Kyle eagerly.

Grandpa looked at him like he had no sense at all. "I'm a retired biology teacher, son. I know more about the ecosystems of Oklahoma than whatever Podunk high school you attended taught you in their on-level, overly crowded biology classes."

"Sir, I'm finishing up my master's."

Richard Parker raised his eyebrows at him. "Do tell. What is your field?"

"Geology."

Morrigan forced herself not to grin. Grandpa had a doctorate in zoology.

"Huh," he snorted. "You must be a damn sight older than eighteen."

"Twenty-two, sir. I tested out of most of my general college classes, so I got my B.S. early."

"Huh," Grandpa grunted. "Then you should have enough sense not to maul my granddaughter."

"Hon, Morrigan and the crystals…" Mama Parker nudged him.

He grunted again, but shifted his attention to his granddaughter. "Morgie old girl, are you doing this?"

She nodded. "Yes, Grandpa."

"Oh, so you've decided we're your grandparents again, have you?"

Morrigan looked down at her feet. "I'm sorry about that, Grandpa." She glanced sheepishly up at Mama Parker. "I'm sorry, Grandma."

"Oh, hon, that's all right! I know what you learned today has been a lot to take in."

Morrigan straightened her spine and met her grandpa's level gaze. "Yeah, it was a lot, but I shouldn't have freaked out and taken it out on you guys. You'll always be my grandparents, no matter what."

"Of course we will, Morgie old girl," Grandpa said gruffly. Then he cleared his throat. "You can make the crystals glow. What else can you do?"

"The rocks speak to me. I can hear them."

Mama Parker nodded her head thoughtfully. "An affinity for the spirits of the earth. Celtic druids, as well as Native American shamans reported such things."

"Shannon heard the spirits in the trees. They greeted her as

Epona's Chosen and lent her power when she called on them," Grandpa said.

"They call me Light Bringer," Morrigan said softly.

Her grandpa's sharp gaze bored into her. "Do they call you Goddess? Greet you as the Chosen One?"

Morrigan started to shake her head no, but Kyle interrupted her. "She is a goddess!" he blurted. "If you had seen her just a little while ago you'd understand what I mean. Her skin was literally glowing." He took a half step closer to her and raised his hand so that he brushed the hair from the side of her face. "She must be a goddess come to earth."

"Son, she isn't a goddess. She's the daughter of a goddess's priestess," Grandpa said.

Do not allow him to steal your divinity! the wind wailed around her. Morrigan tried to ignore it, but she felt a stirring of anger at her grandfather's words. No matter that her thoughts had echoed them not long before, suddenly it felt as if what he was saying was slighting her...stealing something that was, or should be, hers.

"My mother was more than a priestess." Morrigan spoke the words aloud that were moving in the wind around her. "She was Goddess Incarnate and she held the power of her goddess."

She noticed that her grandpa's forehead was furrowed with worry, but all she heard when he spoke was a denial of her heritage and a rejection of her newfound powers.

"Morrigan, your mother, Rhiannon, might have once been Epona's Chosen and her High Priestess, but she lost her position, and the powers that went with it."

"Did she lose them, or were they stolen from her?" Morrigan heard herself ask the question in a voice that sounded cold and unfamiliar.

Her grandpa paused, and then his eyes narrowed. "Who am I speaking to? Morrigan or Rhiannon?"

"Now *you* don't know whether I'm your granddaughter or

not?" Morrigan felt the hurt of his words slice through her. But instead of tears, anger and betrayal swelled within her, bubbling together in a bitter soup and making it seem there was an earthquake of emotions happening inside her.

"Ah, dammit! Of course I know you're my granddaughter! I just want you to sound like her and not some crazy-assed, power-hungry stranger."

Morrigan jerked back as if he'd slapped her. "All my life you've told me I'm not crazy. How did that change all of a sudden?"

"Morrigan Christine, I did not call you crazy."

That isn't who you are…swirled around her.

"Who gave me my middle name?"

Her grandpa blinked and looked momentarily confused.

"Well, we did, hon," Grandma supplied.

"Because it was Shannon's middle name," Morrigan said.

"Because Christine is one of my favorite girl's names," Grandpa said, sounding indignant.

"My mom didn't give it to me." Morrigan didn't let her grandpa respond, she just kept on speaking, as if a dam had broken inside her and the words couldn't help but spill out in a rush. "My name isn't Morrigan Christine Parker. I'm not that girl. Shannon Christine Parker is not my mother. My name is Morrigan MacCallan, daughter of Rhiannon MacCallan, Chosen of the Goddess Epona."

"She was the Goddess's Chosen, but she also denied and betrayed Epona, so that she lost that position," her grandpa said gruffly.

"How do we know all of that? How do we know exactly what happened?"

"We knew Rhiannon. And we knew Shannon. You'll just have to trust that we're telling you the truth."

With a groan of frustration, Morrigan whirled around and

leaned against the selenite boulder, taking comfort from the echoes of *Light Bringer* that rustled against her palm. She was completely, utterly confused. Her mind was a jumble of heat and thought and doubt. Her world was being shaken into millions of little pieces.

"Morrigan! I asked if you're doing that!"

Kyle's sharp voice intruded on her inner turmoil, and she glared up at him, wondering why his face was so colorless and his eyes so big and dark.

"Doing what?" she snapped.

"Are you making the cave rumble?"

"Wha—" Morrigan looked up just as a fist-size chunk of rock dropped from the ceiling.

Beware, Light Bringer! There is danger here. You must depart swiftly.

And through the crystals the certain knowledge came to Morrigan that unless they got out of there immediately they were all going to die.

9

"Grandpa! Grandma! Get out of here!" Morrigan yelled over her shoulder at them. Rationally, she knew she should rush out of the room, hauling her grandparents and Kyle with her, but she couldn't make herself take her hands from the selenite boulder.

"Morrigan, what's going on?" Kyle cried.

Another chunk of rock fell so close to her grandpa that Morrigan's stomach clenched painfully.

Danger, Light Bringer! screamed the crystals.

"You have to go! The ceiling's falling," she called as the rumbling that she had thought was nothing more than the turmoil inside her began to growl through the cave, vibrating up through the floor. More pieces of the ceiling came loose and fell in a deadly rain to the floor. She tore her eyes from the crystal and said, "You, too, Kyle. Get out of here!"

"Morgie?" Grandpa sounded torn and started to take a step toward her.

"Go, Grandpa! I'm coming!" she lied.

She saw him nod, take her grandma's arm and begin helping her up the pathway toward the entrance. Then he stopped and turned back toward her.

"Morrigan, come on!" he shouted above the gravelly roar.

She smiled sadly at him and thought how much she loved his craggy, weather-worn face that always reminded her of Rooster Cogburn in the old John Wayne movie *True Grit*. She didn't have to look into the boulder to know that the middle of it had rippled and changed, once again affording her a glimpse into a weird mirrorlike image of that other cave. She knew what that image had to be—in her soul she'd known it from the first. She'd known even then what she must eventually do. Morrigan pushed against the boulder and felt her palms dip into it, like it had turned from rock to half-set Jell-O.

"I love you, Grandpa! I love you, Grandma!" she yelled. "I'm sorry for this. I'm sorry for everything!"

Her grandpa's expression shifted from worry to despair.

"No, Morrigan!"

He took a step toward her, but was forced to stop when a large hunk of the ceiling just mere feet in front of him broke off and crashed to the floor, causing a cloud of dust and debris to lift and to obscure her view of him. She couldn't see him anymore, but she could still hear his words, even though they were muffled by the growing sound of the cave-in.

"Morrigan, get out of there! You don't know what you're doing. Crossing over isn't that easy."

"Morrigan, we need to go! Now!" Kyle said urgently, grabbing her arm and trying to pull her away from the boulder.

She yanked herself away from him. "No. You need to go, Kyle. I'm staying."

"That's crazy!" he yelled. Kyle pointed up at the ceiling. "It's coming down and it will kill you. I don't really know you, but I feel something for you that I've never experienced before, and I sure as hell don't want to lose you before I understand what's going on between us!"

She met his eyes and, ignoring the awful, sinking feeling it gave her, made her voice hard and cruel. "You're right. You

don't know me. Now get out of here and leave me alone!"
Morrigan pulled one hand free from the boulder with a wet,
sucking sound that made Kyle's eyes widen. "You wouldn't
believe the things I can do. I have power you can't compre-
hend." She spat the words at him. "I don't belong here. Ask
my grandparents. They'll tell you." Then, channeling heat and
power from the crystals, she pushed him. And was thoroughly
shocked when he was lifted from his feet and shoved several
yards away from her.

Wow! It was just like she was Storm from the *X-Men!*

"Leave, Kyle," she said firmly.

"Morrigan!" Her grandpa's yell was muffled.

"Get out of here!" she shouted, raising her voice above the
growling earth.

Kyle was getting to his feet as he stared at her with a mixture
of awe and fear. Still, he seemed unable to leave.

"Morrigan, don't push me away. I don't want to leave you."
He took one hesitant step toward her.

And, with a sickening crack, the ceiling above him shattered
and gave way. Morrigan watched in silent, screamless horror
as Kyle was buried beneath an avalanche of stone. Disbeliev-
ing, she stared at the huge pile of rock that covered him. She
shook her head back and forth, back and forth as her body
began to tremble. She couldn't take her eyes from the rock. In
all the dust and debris she couldn't see Kyle, but he had to be
dead. But no, maybe he wasn't. Maybe she should try to move
the stones off him. She could use the power of the crystals to
help her.

But before she could pull her other hand free of the selenite
his heart no longer beats drifted through the crystal and into her body.

Then the floor beneath her began to shake again and the
earth growled.

You are in danger, Light Bringer! the crystals told her insistently.

What had she thought she was doing? This wasn't a game she was playing. She'd caused a man's death. Morrigan had to get out of there. She pulled her other hand free from the boulder and began stumbling toward the path. And the ceiling in front of her rained death, neatly cutting off her escape. Choking and coughing from the thickening dust, she lurched backward and fell against the selenite boulder. It gave under the weight of her body.

Escape through the Divide, *child. The blood sacrifice has been made.*

Morrigan looked frantically around her. The voice in the wind seemed too real, like it belonged to someone who was standing beside her. It was a woman's voice. She'd heard it before within the host of voices that populated her imagination, though not often. It definitely wasn't the voice she'd heard exclusively since she'd entered the cave.

More of the ceiling fell around her and Morrigan wiped tears and dirt from her eyes.

You must escape now, child, the voice repeated.

"I don't know how!" she sobbed.

Yes, you do. Believe in yourself and let the crystals guide you.

Morrigan turned around and faced the boulder, embracing it as if it was the mother whose arms would never hold her.

"Take me out of here!" she cried.

We hear you, Light Bringer…

While the world trembled and fell apart around her, Morrigan felt herself falling forward into the warm, soft mass of the boulder where she was engulfed in liquid and pressure. She tried to draw a breath, and could not. She tried to scream, and could not. Frantically, Morrigan flailed about, panic overwhelming her. She was suffocating!

Believe in yourself, child…

That voice! Morrigan wrenched her eyes open and felt shock

suffuse her body. Standing in front of her, long red hair and gossamer robes suspended around her as if she was floating underwater, was the woman whose face had smiled out at her from countless photos. Morrigan realized that she had been right. This woman's smile wasn't as open and joyous as Shannon's had been, but it was kind, even if it was so obviously sad.

Come, daughter. Your destiny awaits. You have much yet to do.

Rhiannon held her hand out. Morrigan grasped it and suddenly she was being pulled through the thick, suffocating pressure and flung out onto the jarring hardness of a stone floor. She couldn't see and couldn't breathe. Then, with a painful gasp, she was choking and vomiting bitterness from her lungs.

Morrigan's final thought before unconsciousness, thick and cloying in its darkness, claimed her was that if she had just seen her mother she was probably dead...

PART III

1

Partholon

Right before my life was destroyed I was grooming Epi, thinking that the crisp fall morning would be an excellent time for us to go for a brisk ride. "We may be old," I told the mare, whose silver-gray ears tilted back to listen to me, "but we can still enjoy a nice morning canter. My thighs are up to it, how about yours, old girl?"

Epi snorted in response and reached around to lip at my leather riding pants. I laughed and gently pushed her head away. "You're so fresh! Especially for an old—"

"Rhea! You must come. Now."

Frowning, I turned from Epi to see Alanna running (running?) toward me. Her face was so unnaturally pale that I felt my stomach instantly tighten in response. Something was terribly wrong.

I handed the curry brush to the stable nymph who seemed to appear magically, and gave Epi's nose a quick kiss. I couldn't help but notice that the mare had gone still and silent and was staring at Alanna with a dark, unwavering gaze, which caused a tremor of terrible foreboding to shiver through me. I hurried out of the stall to meet Alanna. She barely waited for me to reach her before she began to quickly retrace her path out of the barn. I hurried to keep up with her as we rushed into the temple proper.

"What is it?"

"Myrna. The baby is coming."

Instantly I was thrilled and scared shitless. It was the middle of August, and I'd been visiting my very pregnant, very moody daughter almost daily at her new home on Grant's (no, I wasn't calling him the troll anymore—or at least not to his face and, well, not often) family's land which adjoined the grounds of Epona's Temple. Myrna was beyond ready to deliver my granddaughter, and I didn't blame her. I totally remembered the feeling of being too pregnant to do anything comfortably. So this should be a joyous day. I glanced sideways at Alanna's colorless face, and the first of several awful thoughts struck me. We shouldn't be hurrying into my temple. We should be rushing around, saddling Epi and various and sundry lesser horses (I don't include my husband in this group), and hotfooting or hoofing it to the McClures' vineyard to attend the birth.

"What's gone wrong?"

Alanna didn't look at me. "They brought Myrna in just a few moments ago. Carolan is with her. He sent a centaur runner to bring ClanFintan in from the archery range. I came to get you."

I grabbed her arm and forced her to look at me. "Is it bad?"

She nodded tightly and I could see that she was fighting tears. "Carolan says there's too much blood. Something..." She paused, swallowed hard, and then continued. "He said something has broken inside her."

"No..." I was barely able to whisper the word. Everything within me chilled. It was like I suddenly lost all the warmth in my own blood. Alanna took my hand and we ran through the courtyard for the part of the temple that housed the infirmary. My personal guards, silent and somber, pulled open the doors for us so that we entered the infirmary with no impediments.

"This way, my Lady," said a stone-faced young woman I recognized as one of the temple's nurses. She led us to an inner room. Just before I opened the door she touched my shoulder, respectful yet firm. "My Lady, you should prepare yourself. Your daughter will need your strength."

Automatically I narrowed my eyes, wanting to strike out at her and vent my terror and rage, to tell her she shouldn't presume anything about what my daughter needed, but what I saw in her eyes silenced my words before I could speak them.

I saw the surety of death.

I turned away from her and Alanna and leaned my forehead against the pale peach-colored wall. *Oh, Epona,* I prayed fervently, *don't let this happen! Myrna can't die. I can't lose her. I beseech you as your Beloved, as your Chosen One, if you need a life, take me! But please don't take my child.*

Epona's voice was almost unbearably kind within my mind. *Sometimes fate works in ways even a goddess cannot change, my Beloved. But know that Myrna is my child, too, daughter of my Chosen Beloved, and that she will dwell eternally within my soft meadows and—*

"No!" I cried, covering my ears like a child. "No," I sobbed brokenly. I felt Alanna's arms go around me and I allowed myself to cling to her for just a moment before I pulled away and wiped my face with the sleeve of my silk shirt. There would be time enough for tears later. The nurse was right. Myrna needed my strength, not my hysterics. I nodded at the nurse. "Okay, I'm ready."

The room was immaculate and it seemed smaller than I

knew it was because of the press of women who surrounded the narrow bed that stood in the center of it. I ignored them, though somewhere in my mind I registered that what they were humming was a variation of the Partholon birthing song I had never before heard. It was a softer, gentler version of the joyous welcome that had greeted Myrna's birth eighteen years earlier. It was still sweet, melodic and anciently rhythmic—like a heartbeat put to music—but there was no laughing and impromptu dancing. As soon as they saw me the women parted to let me near Myrna.

My daughter was between contractions. Her eyes were closed and she was breathing heavily. Instead of being flushed and pink-cheeked, Myrna's face was as colorless as Alanna's. Her lips were tinged with blue. She was naked. Her stomach was a huge, swollen mound, covered by a fine linen sheet. I glanced down toward her feet where Carolan stood looking gray and weary and stone-faced as he examined her. He handed one of his assistants a thick linen cloth that was soaked with blood. His eyes met mine and he didn't need to say anything. I already knew what was happening. Grant was standing at the head of the bed, looking as pale as his wife. When I smiled at him and moved closer to Myrna he looked as if he was going to cry with relief.

I took Myrna's hand and kissed her forehead, pressing my cheek to hers. "Hello, Mama's precious." I whispered the endearment I'd greeted her with so many times in her childhood.

Her eyes fluttered weakly and then opened to focus on my face. "Mama! I'm so glad you're here. I meant to call for you sooner, but everything happened so fast and then it—" She broke off as a contraction took control of her body. Her grip on my hand tightened, viselike, and she cried out in pain, her eyes going wide and glassy with panic.

"It's okay, sweetie. Look at Mama—breathe with me,

precious girl. Mama's right here. Everything will be okay. Look at Mama…" Myrna clung to my hand and to my voice, seeming to anchor herself to me through the wrenching pain. When the contraction finally passed, both of us were panting heavily. I took a cool, wet cloth from one of the women standing nearby and wiped Myrna's forehead, while Grant smoothed back her sweat-drenched hair and murmured endearments to her.

"I can see your daughter, Myrna." Carolan spoke in a calm, reassuring voice. "She is clearly proving how unique she is already, because she's insisting on entering this world rear-end first instead of headfirst, so this next part will be the most difficult for you, but with the next contraction I want you to center yourself and then push with all your heart and soul."

Myrna didn't open her eyes. "I don't think I can," she whispered.

"Yes, you can, my Precious One." I bent and kissed her wet forehead. "I'll help you. Hold tight to my hand and use my strength." I had the Goddess-given ability to channel earth power, but it was much more effective when I was physically in contact with an ancient tree. Frantically, I wondered if there was time to move Myrna outside. If I could get her into the forest that surrounded the temple, would that save her? Could I channel enough power through the trees to give her the energy to survive this birth?

You cannot change her destiny, Beloved. It will only cause her unneeded pain. I had to bite my lip to keep from crying out in response to Epona's words. *Please don't let her suffer,* I sent the fervent prayer to the Goddess, and her answer came swift and sure. *You have my oath, I will not allow her to suffer, Beloved.*

"I'm so glad you're here, Mama," Myrna repeated. Her voice was weak, but her grip on my hand was unnaturally strong.

"So am I, Mama's precious," I said softly.

She smiled up at me. "Mama's precious. You haven't called me that in years."

"I may have stopped calling you my precious, but that's how I've always thought of you," I told her.

"Mama," she said so softly that I had to bend close to her to hear her. "I'm afraid."

I put my arm around her, cradling her against me. "There's nothing to be frightened of, sweet girl. I'm here. Epona's here. And soon, your daughter will be here."

"Be sure you take care of her for me, Mama. And take care of Grant, too. He'll need you."

I felt her words send a physical jolt of pain through my body. "You'll be here to take care of your daughter and to take Grant's side when we argue about her bedtime and me feeding her too many sweets."

Myrna's eyes met mine steadily. "I know something's wrong, Mama."

I was saved from answering by ClanFintan bursting into the room.

"Da!" she cried.

Again, women parted so that he could stand on the other side of her bed. As I had, he bent to kiss her damp forehead. "Ah, my bonny sweet girl, how goes it with you?" He spoke to Myrna, but he looked at me. I saw the despair within his dark, almond-shaped eyes.

"It's hard, Da, and—" Myrna began, then interrupted herself with "—it's starting again!"

"You must push with this one, Myrna!" Carolan ordered.

ClanFintan, Grant and I propped up Myrna's straining body, all three of us speaking encouragement to her while she gritted her teeth and pushed with all of her failing strength. Then there was what seemed like only a second's rest, and again Carolan was calling for her to push. I did not count how many times this cycle repeated—push...a moment's rest...push... I do remember glancing down Myrna's swollen, struggling body to see Carolan take a knife from one of his silent assistants. There was an awful, ripping sound. Then before I could speak, another contraction hit Myrna and she screamed as her daughter finally slid from her body in a river of blood.

Then everything happened incredibly fast.

"Does she live? Does she live?" Myrna kept repeating over and over. I was trying to soothe her and see what was going on at the foot of the bed with Carolan and then, blessedly, the strong, distinctive cry of a newborn filled the room, echoed by a shout of joy from the watching women.

Carolan handed the swaddled, crying infant to Alanna, who had been standing silent and pale not far from him. Alanna, cooing softly, brought the baby to Myrna. Myrna's arms went eagerly around the bundle and we all peered down at the tiny, red-faced girl child who was quite obviously perfect.

"Hello, Etain," Myrna said. "I'm so happy you are finally here."

We were all crying, and Grant and Myrna were kissing their baby while ClanFintan and I touched her sweet, tiny arms and feet. I was filled with such incredible love and happiness that I had begun to believe that everything would be okay after all.

Then Myrna gasped and moaned. Her eyes flew up to mine. "Mama..."

Moving completely on instinct, I lifted Etain gently from her mother's arms, kissed her amazingly soft head and then handed her to her father. "Grant, hold her close to Myrna, so she can see her and touch her." I didn't have to add *even after she no longer has the strength to hold her*. Grant's tear-streaked face told me he understood. I took ClanFintan's hand and drew him beside me, so that he and I were pressed closely to one side of Myrna, her husband and child to the other.

A spasm rippled down through Myrna's body and the fecund, metallic scent of birthing blood mixed with fresh hemorrhaging wafted over us. At some level I was aware that Carolan was working to try to stem the seemingly endless blood that was flowing so swiftly from Myrna's body that it was spilling onto the floor and spreading in a scarlet pool. I could hear ClanFintan begin the soft chant of a High Shaman preparing to soothe the passing of a newly freed soul and to encourage it in its journey to Epona's meadows. I knew he was weeping openly, but his prayer never wavered and the ancient magic in it filled the room so completely that I could feel its power brush against my skin.

But I did not look away from my daughter's face. Her eyes locked on mine, clearly searching for reassurance. I pushed aside my bottomless sorrow and focused on Myrna. My daughter needed me once more in her life. I was Epona's Chosen, the Goddess's High Priestess. I could do this. I could bring her comfort and ease her passing.

"It's going to be okay, Mama's precious." I smiled gently at her and stroked her hair. "You have nothing to fear. Epona has known you and loved you since the moment she rejoiced at your birth."

"I—I believe you, Mama." Her voice broke. She turned her head so that she could see Etain. "Tell her I'm sorry, Mama. Tell Etain that I love her and that I'll miss her."

I nodded and struggled not to sob. *Help me, Epona!* Instantly, I was filled with a sense of calm that I knew came from my goddess.

"I will tell her, sweet girl." My voice was strong and sure. "I will tell Etain stories of her mother's beauty and wit and love."

Myrna looked from her daughter to me. "Thank you,

Mama." Another spasm shook her already exhausted body and she closed her eyes. I held tightly to her hand, willing the Goddess's comfort from me to her. Her eyes opened slowly and refocused on me. "It—it doesn't hurt, Mama. And I'm not afraid anymore." Then her gaze drifted up and over my shoulder. Her eyes widened. "Oh, Mama! It's Epona! She's so beautiful." Her face was suddenly lit by incredible joy. "She's speaking to me. Epona says that she did give me a gift of magic, and that gift is Etain. She'll be a great priestess, beloved and honored by Partholon, and her children will be great priestesses and warriors." Myrna drew in a rasping breath and her body shuddered again, but it seemed that she was already removed from the physical realm, because the joyous look on her face didn't falter. Still staring over my shoulder, she said, "I love you, Mama. I'll wait for you with Epona…" Smiling, Myrna let out a long, weary sigh, and then she breathed no more.

I kissed Myrna and bowed my head. "Go with the Goddess, Mama's precious. We'll be together again someday, in Epona's bright meadows, where there is no death or pain or sorrow. Until then, I will miss you every moment of every day, and keep you in my heart."

"My Lady."

I looked up to see Grant, tears falling down his cheeks, holding out to me the swaddled bundle that was my granddaughter.

"She looks like Myrna," he said in an utterly broken voice.

I took the baby, who did, indeed, look like a miniature version of her dead mother, and, holding her close to my heart, I wept.

Morrigan's head was killing her. She'd had headaches before, but nothing like this pounding, splintering pain that was jabbing through her skull. She thought that this must be what a migraine felt like. No wonder people who had them said they sucked royally. Great. As if she didn't have enough crap to deal with in her life—voices in the wind, the weird ability to make flames sprout from her hand, the weirder ability to hear crystals and to make them glow, the fact that her dead mom wasn't her dead mom. Actually, that reminded her. Kyle was dead and—

And Morrigan's memory slammed through the foggy curtains of pain and disorientation in her mind.

The cave-in! Kyle! Her grandparents! Moving through the crystal boulder!

Her eyes opened and she gasped in pain. Her vision was blurred and her eyes stung. Actually, her entire body hurt like she had a killer cold.

"Rest, Light Bringer. All is well."

The voice was kind and familiar. Morrigan closed her eyes, and something cool was pressed against them, helping to relieve some of the stinging burn. Then a cup was placed to her lips, and automatically she drank something that tasted like sweet cough medicine mixed with red wine.

"Sleep now. You are home," the voice said.

*Home…sleep…*the seductive voice in her mind repeated with a tantalizing whisper.

Morrigan felt as if she had little choice as the syrupy drink led her back into unconsciousness.

When she woke up again Morrigan ran her tongue around her disgustingly dry mouth. Bleck! G-pa would say her mouth tasted like the bottom of a birdcage. Oh, man, she felt terrible! Did she have to go to school today? Wait, no, it was summer. The end of summer. She was getting ready to go off to college and—

"Drink, my Lady. It will soothe your throat."

My Lady? Why was she being called that?

Because it is your right. The words weren't in the wind around her, nor coming to her through the touch of crystal. This time they echoed softly inside her head, which did nothing but add to the confusion in Morrigan's mind.

"Here, my Lady, drink."

Gentle hands helped lift her, and a cup of cool water was pressed against her lips. Morrigan drank thirstily. Then she opened her eyes. The light was dim and her vision was blurry. She blinked and rubbed her eyes. Her mind was as messed up as her vision. What was going on? Had she been at a party? She usually showed better sense than to get wasted. G-pa was going to kill her. Even though she was grown and practically on her own, he still got pissed if she—

Wait. She hadn't been at a party. She'd been at the cave with her friends.

Morrigan forced her eyes open again. Her vision swam briefly, and then, as if someone had adjusted the tracking on G-pa's ancient VCR player, everything—her vision and her memory—popped into focus. The first thing she noticed was the woman who was sitting on a fur-covered stool beside her, smiling kindly.

Morrigan's eyes went wide in surprise. "Grandma!"

The woman's smile faltered only a little. "Welcome, Light Bringer," she said in a sweet, soft voice that mirrored her grandma's completely—except it was missing its distinctive Oklahoma accent. "I am Birkita, High Priestess to Adsagsona." The woman stood, and then dropped almost to the floor in a deep, respectful curtsy. "In the name of the Goddess I welcome you home, and rejoice that we have been gifted with a Light Bringer."

Morrigan opened her mouth. Shut it. And finally opened it again to say, "You're not my grandma."

The dark-haired woman tilted her familiar face up. Her smile was kind, but her brow was wrinkled with confusion. "No, my Lady. I am of an age to be a grandmother, but I chose to swear chasteness in the Goddess's service when I was a young woman, so I have no children, nor grandchildren."

Morrigan wiped a shaky hand over her face. "I'm sorry, I'm just…" She trailed off, trying to sort through the questions in her mind. She couldn't stop staring at the woman who knelt in front of her. She looked like her grandma! Except that G-ma always kept her dark hair cut short, so that she looked like a pixie, and this woman's hair was obviously long, neatly braided in a thick plait that hung heavily down her back. Morrigan looked closer and saw that her hair was a lot grayer than G-ma's. Actually, she looked older in general than her grandma. Her face was more heavily lined, her skin more transparent. Grandma had always seemed ageless to Morrigan. Sure, she was *old,* but she was filled with energy and rarely sick. This version of her looked like her frail twin sister. She was dressed in a beautiful leather dress that reminded Morrigan of the ceremonial outfits Native American women wore to Oklahoma powwows; only, this dress wasn't decorated with fringe and feathers. Instead, between the beadwork were embroidered elaborate designs of knots that wound around and around in mazelike detail. With a little start Morrigan realized the woman was still crouching as she gawked at her like an idiot. "Oh! Get up!" she said hastily, and then added an uncomfortable, "Please."

The woman who looked like her grandma but called herself Birkita rose as gracefully as she had knelt, and resumed her place on the fur-padded stool beside Morrigan's bed. As if she was unable to control her mouth, Morrigan blurted, "Where am I?"

"You are in the Caves of the Sidetha."

Morrigan's stomach clenched, and she wasn't sure if it was with fear or excitement. "That's not in Oklahoma, is it?"

Birkita's brow furrowed again. "Oklahoma? I am sorry, my Lady, I do not know that Keep." She paused and added, "Is it in the southern Realms of Partholon? I have never traveled far from our caves, and much of Partholon is unfamiliar to me."

Morrigan gasped and she felt as if her heart was going to pound out of her body. "Partholon!" She breathed the name like a prayer, making Birkita smile. "I'm in Partholon?"

"You are, indeed, Light Bringer."

"Am I dead?"

Birkita's musical laugh mirrored her grandma's completely, making her suddenly look a decade younger, "No, my Lady. You are very much alive, though I worried for your life when you first emerged from the sacred rock."

"Sacred rock? I don't understand..." But even as Morrigan spoke she remembered how she'd glimpsed another cave through the selenite boulder. Then, with a shock, she also remembered her mother's spirit materializing within the boulder in front of her, and how Rhiannon had guided her from drowning in the quicksandlike liquid.

"The sacred crystal rock in the Usgaran."

"The huge boulder made of selenite crystal." Morrigan's voice sounded faint. "I—I escaped through it."

"Escaped, my Lady?"

"There was a cave-in. I—I would have been killed if I hadn't gone through the boulder." Kyle had been killed. The memory hit her with enough force that it made her hands shake. Birkita instantly leaned forward, patting her and making consoling, grandma noises.

"But you weren't killed, my Lady. Adsagsona's hand was upon you. The Goddess saved you and guided you home to your people." Birkita touched Morrigan's face gently, almost reverently. "The Goddess came to me in my dreams last night. Adsagsona spoke to me and told me that she had Chosen a Light Bringer, that we would know her because she would be born through the sacred crystal. I witnessed your birth myself, Daughter of the Goddess, Light Bringer, Chosen of Adsagsona."

There was a deafening hum in Morrigan's ears, like she was standing inside a giant seashell.

"I have to see the sacred rock," Morrigan said, sitting abruptly and swinging her feet from the wide, fur-lined pallet on which she lay. Birkita rushed to help her, and Morrigan was glad for the strength of her touch, as dizziness blurred her vision and jellied her knees.

"Carefully, my Lady. You are still very weak."

"I'm fine. I'm fine. I just need to see the boulder." She hadn't meant to sound so short, like she was giving orders to Birkita who looked like Grandma. It was just that she felt the sudden compulsion to be near the selenite boulder so intensely that it was almost a physical pain.

"Of course, my Lady," Birkita murmured as she took a firm hold of Morrigan's elbow, and helped support her first few awkward steps.

Morrigan was vaguely aware that Birkita was leading her from the room in which she'd awakened through a round tunnel that was somehow lit with a soft, blue-white light. In the back of her mind was the thought that she should be looking around, observing her surroundings, taking in the landscape of her new home. But she was so focused on reaching the boulder—touching the crystal—that her world had narrowed to that one driving need.

Morrigan had no idea how long they had been walking, when the tunnel emptied into an eerily familiar room. She could instantly tell it was a mirror image of the Encampment Room of Oklahoma's Alabaster Caves. It had the same low ceiling and flat floor. A stream ran though the side of the room, and the walls formed natural, shelflike ledges. But in this world, the room was draped with lush furs and filled with women who were talking and laughing—until they caught sight of Morrigan and Birkita.

Morrigan barely noticed the women and the changes in the room. Her entire being was focused on the beautiful crystal boulder that rested, like an enormous, magical egg in the center of the room. Shaking off Birkita's help, she stumbled to it, surprised and thrilled to see that her passage through the boulder hadn't ripped it in half. Actually, it looked exactly as it had in Oklahoma, minus the gaudy artificial pink lighting. With a happy cry that sounded a lot like a sob, Morrigan pressed her palms against the boulder. The response was immediate and so forceful that she felt as if she'd grabbed onto a live wire, but instead of shocking her, the current of power was filling her and making her complete.

Light Bringer!

"Yes! It's me. I—I need you," Morrigan blurted, not sure of anything except the need. Thankfully, the crystal understood.

We hear you, Light Bringer.

The flood of electric power changed, heated, increased, until little by little the tightness in Morrigan's chest began to loosen and the deafening confusion and numbing shock in her mind cleared. Her breath came slower and the pounding in her heart changed to a normal, steady beat. Logic and reason returned to her, along with the knowledge that Birkita must be her grandma's mirror image, just as Shannon and Rhiannon had been mirrors of one another.

Morrigan was in Partholon.

The knowledge thrilled her, filling her with incredible happiness as well as great sorrow. She had changed worlds, just as her mother before her had. Morrigan really had no idea how she'd managed to get there, so chances were pretty good that she would probably not know how to get back. Which meant she would never see her grandpa and grandma, her friends or the future she'd imagined for herself again. G–pa and G–ma would be devastated. Morrigan closed her eyes against the pain it caused her to think about how sad they would be without her.

They'd know she was alive and in Partholon, wouldn't they? Surely they'd figure that out when Kyle's body was the only one found in the cave-in rubble. Morrigan felt tears leak from her eyes and wash her cheeks. Maybe they'd be just a tiny bit relieved that she had finally left the world she'd never truly belonged to and found her way to the land of her mother— found her way to her destiny.

Daughter of the Goddess...Light Bringer...Chosen... The titles Birkita had named her echoed around and around her mind as the truth of what had happened settled through her.

She was in Partholon, her mother's land. She was no longer

a freak, someone who didn't belong. She had been Chosen by a goddess.

Morrigan was home.

Yes, Light Bringer! You are home!

The jubilant spirits in the crystals sang through her skin, warming her body and her soul.

"I'm home," Morrigan whispered. Then she opened her eyes and gazed in wonder at the crystal that glistened beneath her hands. "I'm home," she said more loudly. Then she drew a deep breath, and with a grin added, "I'm home, so light the place up for me!"

We hear you and we gladly do your will, Light Bringer!

The boulder blazed under her hands with a light that had the purity and beauty of a perfect diamond. With a grin, Morrigan lifted her arms and pointed at the crystal-encrusted ceiling. "Up there, too!" There was a crackle in the air and the ceiling of the room blazed into crystalline brilliance.

"Wow," Morrigan whispered, tilting her head back to gaze at the glistening stones. "It's totally amazing."

"Blessed be the Light Bringer, and blessed be Adsagsona!"

Morrigan was startled out of her reverie by her grandma's voice filled with happiness. Her eyes moved from the shining crystals to the woman who was so like her grandma—and was shocked to see that Birkita had dropped to her knees. Her face was damp with tears, but she was smiling lovingly at Morrigan. "Hail, Light Bringer!" she shouted, and the cry was taken up by the other women in the room, all of whom had also fallen to their knees.

This isn't Grandma, Morrigan told herself sternly. *And I'm not in Oklahoma anymore.*

No, you are not. You are home... the voice whispered through her mind, seductive, beguiling.

Are you my mother? Are you Rhiannon? Morrigan shot the

mental question back, but only the cryptic *Embrace your destiny*...flitted through her mind in a reply that seemed more mocking than helpful.

The glistening of the crystals in the ceiling sputtering and then going out broke Morrigan's internal questing, and brought her back to awareness of the external. She was shocked anew to be standing in the center of the room, surrounded by kneeling women who were all crying openly with happiness. She cleared her throat, completely clueless about what was expected of her.

"Er, hum. Well. Thank you for such a nice welcome." With an effort, she didn't roll her eyes at her own moronness. "Please, there's no need for you to kneel to me. You can stand up," she added quickly, but she admitted to herself that, even though it overwhelmed her, she liked the respect the women were all showing her. Then a movement caught at the corner of her eye and Morrigan turned her head to see that what she had at first glance assumed was just another fur pelt was actually an enormous cat that leaped gracefully from one of the ledges to stretch languorously while its huge amber eyes studied her with obvious intelligence.

"Holy crap, that's a big cat!" Morrigan blurted.

With soft laughter, the women rose. Grandma, *no,* Birkita, Morrigan mentally corrected herself, said, "She is Brina, a cave lynx and a familiar of Adsagsona's priestesses. She has not moved from that spot since the Goddess appeared in my dream and told me of your coming."

Entranced by the feral beauty of the big cat, Morrigan felt a rush of pleasure when Brina approached her, and then, delicately sniffed the hand she automatically offered. As if finding her acceptable, the animal began rubbing around Morrigan's legs, purring with all the subtlety of a lawn-mower engine.

"You are a pretty, pretty girl," Morrigan crooned. The cat

was so huge that she didn't have to bend down to let her fingertips caress the incredibly soft fur of her back. When Morrigan glanced up at Birkita, she saw that she, along with the rest of the half dozen or so women, were smiling in approval at her. "I think she likes me."

"She recognizes one Chosen by the Goddess," Birkita said.

Those words, Chosen by the Goddess, seemed a tangible thing. They caused the small hairs at the back of Morrigan's neck to prickle, and her eyes to unexpectedly fill with tears.

Birkita was beside her in an instant, touching her arm with grandmotherly reassurance. "You must be very hungry, Light Bringer. The workers will be returning from the tunnels, and the evening meal awaits them and us. Will you join us, or would you rather retire to your chamber to eat and regain your strength in privacy?"

Morrigan cleared her throat and got a handle on her composure. "No, I'd like to eat with you." She paused and smiled at the women standing around them. "With all of you. I'm not tired, but I am hungry." Touching the selenite boulder and being greeted as Light Bringer by the spirits of the cave had filled her with an energy that had chased away the last of the exhaustion that changing worlds had caused. Now she wanted food, and then she wanted to begin exploring her amazing new home.

"As you wish, my Lady," Birkita murmured. "This is the way to the Great Chamber." With a smile, the woman who looked like her grandma led her from the room that mirrored the Encampment Room. With the big cat padding silently by her side, Morrigan followed Birkita to dinner, and to her future.

3

The Great Chamber was carved from the room that Kyle had described on their tour as the deepest part of the cavern. Thinking about him made her heart hurt, but Morrigan pushed aside the tragedy of Kyle's death and remembered the awe she'd felt that day when she'd intuitively known, even before he'd told the group, that from floor to ceiling the room was at least fifty feet, which put it about eighty feet below the surface. When she and Birkita came to the chamber she recognized it, but only vaguely. That cavernous, rough, rock-littered room in Oklahoma was just a crude shadow of its magnificent Partholonian twin. Morrigan paused on the threshold, holding her breath with wonder.

The huge chamber was buzzing with people who flitted about with food and drink between the long rows of what looked to Morrigan like picnic tables carved from rock the color of butter. *Limestone*…the identity of the stone came to her as she brushed her fingers against the smooth side of the room's entryway. She accepted the knowledge easily, sending automatic, silent thanks to the spirits in the stone. Actually, she was too busy gawking at the room and the people in it to give much thought to the addition of yet another layer to the magic that surrounded her.

The room was surprisingly well lighted from lots of open blue-white flames burning in stone basins resting atop pedestals that were so beautifully carved with designs that they looked more like stone flowers unfolding to hold flames within their petals than containers of rock. With a little start, Morrigan realized that she'd seen those same flame holders in the Encampment Room, as well as intermittently along the tunnels, and she wondered what could possibly burn with such a bright, smokeless light. But her eyes didn't stay on the flames; they were drawn to the walls of the cavern that were encrusted with exquisite mosaics that brought alive the animals and people and landscapes they depicted.

"It's amazing…" Morrigan breathed. "So beautiful."

"Come, Light Bringer. You should take the place of honor."

Wordlessly, Morrigan let Birkita lead her into the chamber to what was obviously the head table. Behind it on the wall, polished stones the color of moonlight formed the curving figure of a woman. The figure reminded Morrigan of the silver-pendant goddess images her grandma liked to wear, only instead of having arms upraised to cup the roundness of a full moon, this image's arms were pointed downward, in a reverse V. Her palms were open outward, hands stretched down, as if she was gesturing to mysteries below her fingertips. As before when she was drawn to the selenite boulder, Morrigan felt herself pulled to the mosaic with a single-mindedness that blocked out everything around her. She approached the wall on which the female figure was encrusted, and raised her hand slowly, reverently, to touch the surface of the stones. Instantly, through the nerves in her fingertips came the whispered knowledge that the stone was polished alabaster, and the figure was the Sidetha's Goddess, Adsagsona. Morrigan had only a moment to be awed by her new way of *knowing,* and also wonder about the voice she'd heard in her head since she had entered Partholon. If she was Adsagsona's Light Bringer, and had been Chosen by the Goddess, as Birkita had said she was, then shouldn't her goddess speak to her? So was the new voice really Adsagsona, and not her mother or the dark god her grandparents had warned her about? But Morrigan had no time to ponder the details and complexities of her new position because she became aware of the excited murmur that was washing through the room behind her.

"Light Bringer…Adsagsona's Chosen…Daughter of the Goddess…"

Morrigan drew a deep, fortifying breath and turned around. The huge chamber was filled with people. With a sense of shock Morrigan wondered how long she had been standing there, oblivious to everything except the mosaic of the Goddess. Clearly it had been enough time for everyone to hear that she was there, and a shitload of people to rush in to stare at her. As if it had just been waiting for her full attention, Morrigan's innate shyness speared through her, almost paralyzing in its intensity. Years of drama class had given her the tools to act beyond her fear of crowds and her hatred of speaking in public, but it couldn't erase what she was in the core of her being—a shy young woman who had always wanted to fit in more than she wanted to stand out. And now an entire roomful of strangers from an unknown world were gawking at her…

No, Morrigan told herself severely. *Don't be so cynical. They're not gawking. They're just excited.* And the world wasn't unknown—it was really *her* world, the one in which she could fit in and finally belong.

*They worship you, as is your right…*echoed through her mind, and she tried to ignore the little thrill the words gave her.

People were actually worshipping her! That was nothing to be freaked out about—it was cool. (Wasn't it?)

It is your right...your destiny... Again, a thrill passed through Morrigan. Was that Adsagsona's voice? It seemed logical—even right, that the Goddess would be reassuring her. She'd brought her here. Home to Partholon where she belonged.

Hadn't she?

With an effort, Morrigan pulled her attention from her inner turmoil so she could focus on the introduction Birkita was making.

"Light Bringer, I would like to present to you the Sidetha's Cave Master, Perth, and his mate, Mistress Shayla," Birkita said, moving once again to her side.

Morrigan had to force herself not to automatically (and nervously) hold out her hand for the couple to shake, and was very glad she'd suppressed the notion when the man bowed to her and the woman dropped into a graceful curtsy.

"We are honored by your presence," Perth said.

"Adsagsona has blessed us greatly," Shayla said.

"Th-thank you," Morrigan managed to mumble, overwhelmed that these two people, who were old enough to be her parents and dressed so richly in fur and jewels that they must be like the king and queen of the Sidetha, were bowing to *her.*

"Please," Perth said, motioning her to the place at the head of the table. "Join us at the seat of honor."

"Which will be yours for as long as you gift us with your presence," Shayla said. Her regal smile displayed white teeth so perfect they would be envied by any twenty-first century dentist.

Morrigan muttered another thank-you, this time without stuttering, and was taking the offered seat when she noticed that, though Brina had stretched out proprietarily beside her chair, Birkita had curtsied and was gracefully backing away from the head table.

"No, Birkita, wait!" Morrigan blurted, causing conversation at the surrounding tables to stop, and the people who were already glancing at her to stare. She swallowed nervously and continued. "I don't want you to go." Then, as an afterthought, Morrigan turned to the royal-looking couple who were sitting beside her. "If that's fine with you."

"Of course, as you wish," Shayla said smoothly. "As a priestess of Adsagsona, Birkita is always welcome at our table."

Morrigan couldn't help but notice that though Shayla's words sounded welcoming, Birkita's face flushed, and as she moved hesitantly into the chair beside Morrigan, she stared down at her plate with obvious discomfort. Okay, so Birkita wasn't actually her grandma, but she looked so much like her, Morrigan couldn't help but already feel protective of her, and no-damn-body was going to upset G-ma. Morrigan's temper spiked, defensive and angry.

"Good, I'm glad Birkita's welcome at this table, because where I go, she goes." Morrigan met Shayla's cool gaze and gave her best fake smile. "She's important to Adsagsona, and she's important to me." The big cat licked Morrigan's ankle, causing her to jump and add, "The cat, too. The cat's with me, too."

It was Shayla's turn to blush, and Morrigan felt a sense of accomplishment when the beautiful, richly dressed woman nodded uncomfortably, and mumbled, "Of course, my Lady, it will be as you wish," and then got oh, so busy motioning for people to begin serving them.

"Careful," Birkita whispered under cover of the resumed conversations around them. "The Master and his mate are very powerful."

Morrigan felt her anger stir again at the worry and what

sounded like fear in Birkita's voice. "Really?" she whispered back. "Can they do this?" Abruptly, Morrigan stood, causing the conversation all around them to stop again. Without looking at anyone, or thinking too much about the impulse she was following, Morrigan hurried the few steps over to the cave wall behind them on which rested the beautiful mosaic of Adsagsona. She raised her hand, pressing it against the smooth rock, and closed her eyes, probing with her inner senses through the skin of the cave, seeking...calling...until she found a vein of selenite crystal that ran from the wall, up across the ceiling, and down the other side of the chamber. "Light for me, please," Morrigan said softly to the rock.

We hear and obey, Light Bringer!

The response was immediate and powerful. A sizzle of energy zapped from her palm into the stone and Morrigan could feel the crystals illuminating like happy grade-school kids running out to play at recess. Before she opened her eyes and turned around, the gasps of the crowd told her all she needed to know. She lifted her chin, set her face into what she hoped was a calm, goddesslike mask and faced the room. This time she expected everyone's stares. Okay, fine. It was fine. She would just pretend that she was onstage. She used her diaphragm and pitched her voice to carry, just as she had in the senior play, and using a purposeful pun on her new title said, "I thought I'd bring a little light to dinner."

Morrigan was pleased to notice Shayla's and Perth's twin expressions of shock as they, along with everyone except Birkita and the women from the Encampment Room, who were scattered about at lesser tables, gazed upward at the selenite crystals that were embedded in the distant ceiling, which now glittered and twinkled like fanciful stars. When she returned to her seat the conversations around her were hushed and the looks were less curious and more reverent.

"That should show them," she said under her breath to Birkita, and was surprised by the sad look the woman gave her. It was the same wordless, contemplative look her grandma gave her whenever Morrigan had done something to disappoint her. Not a big disappointment, like flunking a test or getting a speeding ticket, but something small and private, like forgetting to say please or thank-you, or laughing at someone else's embarrassment. Morrigan was instantly chastised, and then wondered why she should be. Birkita had obviously been upset by Shayla. Actually, the more Morrigan watched the queenly-looking woman, the more she noticed how haughty both she and Perth acted. It wasn't really anything they said. It was just an air about them—how they motioned for more food and drink, and how they seemed to hold themselves apart from everyone, even she and Birkita, who were sitting closest to the couple. The conversations that had resumed didn't touch them, and Morrigan imagined that they were somehow separated from everyone else by a transparent, but icy, wall. Clearly, they were respected, but Morrigan's gut told her that they weren't liked. So why should she feel bad about standing up to, and, yes, even intimidating them? She shouldn't. She wouldn't. She'd just eat her dinner and—

Morrigan realized that Shayla was watching her intently with those cold blue eyes. Something about the Sidetha Mistress's gaze gave her a creepy, walk-over-your-grave feeling. Morrigan made herself give Shayla a friendly smile.

"You look very familiar." Shayla spoke in a casual, conversational tone, which completely contradicted the sharp expression in her eyes. "Were you, perhaps, trained at the Temple of the Muse?"

"Our Mistress was schooled at the Temple of the Muse. It is unusual for a Sidetha to leave the caves for that long, but Shayla is an unusual woman, as is our daughter, Geally, who has followed her mother's tradition and is in her third year of being educated by the Muse," Perth said. He patted his wife's hand warmly in a gesture that would have seemed affectionate had Morrigan not been looking into Shayla's eyes at that moment, and very clearly seen the look of revulsion that passed quickly across the woman's beautiful face.

"Uh, no, I've never been to the Temple of the Muse," she said, wondering what was really going on inside that marriage (not that it was any of her business). Then added hastily, "But congratulations on being educated by the Muse." Whatever that meant.

"You are not, of course, Sidetha, but have you visited our caves before?" Shayla asked. With a fluttery little movement, she extracted her hand from under her husband's.

"No. I've never been here before." Morrigan snuck a glance at Birkita, but the older woman avoided eye contact. Surely Birkita had told people that she had appeared through the boulder, hadn't she? Morrigan didn't feel comfortable explaining that she was from a whole other world, but she certainly hadn't meant to pretend she'd just walked in through the front door of their cave. Hell! She didn't even know if the cave had a front door.

"Strange that you look so familiar…" Shayla let the sentence trail off and went back to her meal, but Morrigan could feel the looks she continued to slide her way.

"I don't like them. They make my skin crawl," she whispered to Birkita, cutting her eyes at Perth and Shayla. When the older woman paled, Morrigan lightened her tone and said, "But I do like Brina," and promptly snuck the big cat a piece of something that tasted and looked a lot like fried chicken.

Birkita looked relieved to have the subject changed and Morrigan admitted to herself that she was glad to lighten up the conversation, too. Between bites of her own chicken, Birkita said, "You probably know, my Lady, that *brina* means *protector* in the Old Language." She smiled at the cat, who was stretched out possessively at Morrigan's feet, eyes half-lidded and purring contentedly. "Brina has long protected the Usgaran, but has never been particularly fond of one priestess over another. That is, until now. Now it seems she will protect you along with the Usgaran."

"Brina is amazing," Morrigan said around a full mouth, and tickled the cat on the top of her head. She swallowed and took a quick drink. "Birkita, you mentioned an Usgaran? What is that?" She kinda remembered Birkita using the word, but she couldn't think of its meaning.

Before Birkita could respond, Shayla's voice, suddenly way too sweet and silky, replied for her. "How is it that a High Priestess of Adsagsona is unfamiliar with the Usgaran?"

Birkita surprised Morrigan by immediately speaking up. "Mistress, the Light Bringer is from afar—a Keep called Oklahoma." She tripped only slightly over the long, unfamiliar word. "Perhaps there, the room that holds the sacred crystal is called by another name?"

The table looked at her expectantly.

"The Encampment Room," Morrigan said, feeling definitely out of her element. "That's what we call it in Oklahoma."

"Oklahoma?" Perth sounded baffled. "I have never heard of such a Keep. Where is its location?"

Morrigan's palms started to sweat and she, once again, silently thanked G-pa for forcing her into all of those years of drama class. Improvisation—that's all this was. "Oklahoma is far away. In the West. Southwest actually."

Still frowning, Perth said, "The Sidetha do not make a habit of leaving our lands, but I am not totally ignorant of the rest of Partholon. There is no Oklahoma Keep in the southwest. I don't believe there is an Oklahoma Keep in all of Partholon."

"It's not in Partholon." Which definitely was not a lie, she thought smugly.

There were gasps of surprise all around her as she heard murmurs of "Not in Partholon!" and "The Light Bringer is from across the B'an Sea!"

"Yes, Oklahoma is far away from Partholon, and that's why a lot of this—" Morrigan made a dramatic, sweeping gesture "—is strange to me. So, I'll need your help learning the names of things and the way your, uh, Keep works."

Even though Shayla's laugh was humorless, several people at the closest tables echoed it. "The Caves of the Sidetha are not a mere Keep. We are a Realm of our own, ruled by our own—though we do pay homage to Epona's Chosen," she added as almost an afterthought. Then her gaze sharpened and Morrigan felt a vague but real sense of danger in the next question she asked. "Were there no cave Realms in Oklahoma?"

"Of course there were caves there," Morrigan said, sticking to the truth, which—as her grandparents had taught her—was usually the best road to take. "They're called Oklahoma's Alabaster Caverns."

"And Adsagsona? Were you the Goddess's Light Bringer in Oklahoma's Alabaster Caverns, too?" Shayla asked with a sly edge to her voice.

The truth, Morrigan reminded herself, ignoring the fluttering of anger that seemed to move through her mind, independent of her own will. *I stay with the truth as much as I possibly can.*

"The crystals spoke to me in Oklahoma, and they also lit for me, but I didn't know about Adsagsona. Until I came here, I thought…" Morrigan hesitated and then finished in a rush, "I thought I was Epona's Chosen."

Instead of freaking out the group of people, what Morrigan

finally admitted to them and to herself seemed to resonate with
the Sidetha—or maybe it was the honest emotion that filled
her voice, and the sadness that was so apparent on her face.
Whichever, the people understood. They talked in hushed
voices and nodded their heads. Even Shayla and Perth looked
mollified.

Birkita's hand covered hers briefly. "The ways of the gods
and goddesses are sometimes difficult to understand and hard
to follow. It would be unimaginable to be Chosen by Adsagsona and touched as a Light Bringer, but held apart from your
goddess. Like her people, Adsagsona is loath to leave the Caves
of the Sidetha. It shows the depth of her love for you that Adsagsona found you in Oklahoma, took you from the dark,
lonely place in which you dwelled and brought you to join
her people—*your* people." Her touch and her words were so
familiar in their kindness that Morrigan had to blink away tears
of homesickness. "Hail, Adsagsona!" Birkita said, and her
joyful cry was echoed by many of the women scattered
throughout the chamber.

Morrigan noticed that Shayla and Perth mouthed the words
but did not actually speak the Goddess's name. Weird…

The rest of the meal passed with a lot less drama. Shayla and
Perth were lost in a private conversation with one another.
Morrigan asked Birkita to tell her about the mosaics decorating the huge chamber, and she was able to relax and eat while
her grandma's voice chattered about art and stone.

She had just finished eating, and had to suppress the urge
to stretch and yawn like Brina was doing, but Birkita's keen
eyes caught hers. "My Lady, you are still weary from your
journey here," she said.

"I wanted you to show me around, but I think you're right.
I'm still a lot more tired than I thought." Then she turned to
the royal couple and forced herself to smile and not sound sar-

castic. "It was nice to meet you. Thank you for the meal, and for making me welcome."

"You said that you did not know you had been Chosen by Adsagsona when you were in Oklahoma." Morrigan had begun to stand when Shayla's cool voice stopped her.

"That's right. I didn't know about Adsagsona then." Morrigan answered the Mistress of the Sidetha warily. "But now I do. I know she brought me here, and here is where I belong."

"Well, then, if you are Adsagsona's High Priestess as well as her Light Bringer you will want to perform the Goddess's Dark Moon Ritual tomorrow night."

Having no clue about a dark moon anything Morrigan scrambled to find something to say. Thankfully, Birkita spoke into the awkward silence.

"*If* Morrigan is Adsagsona's Light Bringer and High Priestess?" There was an unexpectedly steely edge to Birkita's voice. "She traveled through the sacred crystal to arrive in the heart of the Usgaran, just as I foretold she would because the Goddess foretold her arrival through my dreams. The spirits of the cave speak to her and acknowledge her as Light Bringer. And we have all witnessed that she can call alive the light within the crystal." Birkita pointed up at the still-glowing ceiling. "I mean no disrespect to you, Mistress, but there is no question that Morrigan is High Priestess of Adsagsona."

"Of course there isn't." Shayla's tone was patronizing. "Obviously she's a Light Bringer. I didn't mean to sound like I was questioning that. Actually I was honoring her and showing proper respect for our *new* High Priestess by mentioning the ritual. I assumed that Morrigan would be taking your position, or are you still maintaining the position of High Priestess? I thought there can be only one. Or am I wrong? I certainly could be." Her laugh was high and sarcastic. "I am, after all, not as well versed in the mysteries of the gods and goddesses as are you. I'm much too busy with the more mundane job of the day-to-day business of our Realm."

Birkita hesitated. When she spoke, her soft voice was sincere. "No, Mistress, you are not wrong. There can be only one High Priestess. I willingly step down from that position. It is, indeed, the Light Bringer's role to be Adsagsona's Chosen and her High Priestess."

"Wait, no—" Morrigan began, but Birkita's insistent hand on her arm cut off her words.

"It is Adsagsona's will. I am no longer of the age of a maiden or a mother. I will be glad to take a lesser role, my Lady." Birkita smiled at Morrigan warmly.

"Good. That's settled. Then that means Morrigan will be performing the Dark Moon Ritual tomorrow night," Shayla said.

Morrigan saw Birkita stiffen. "Mistress, I'm not sure that would be—"

"Is it not the responsibility of our High Priestess to perform the Dark Moon Ritual?" Shayla snapped.

"It is," Birkita said.

"Then I'll perform the ritual," Morrigan heard herself say, and then was sorry she'd spoken so quickly when she saw a flash of triumph cross Shayla's beautiful face.

"But you were unconscious for days, and though the Goddess breathed strength into you today through the sacred stone, you have not yet recovered fully," Birkita said.

"Our Light Bringer is young and strong, and she has obviously been greatly blessed by the Goddess. Surely she will be recovered from her journey by tomorrow night," Shayla said.

Morrigan wondered how the woman could make words that should have been complimentary sound like insults.

"Yes, Mistress, our Light Bringer is, indeed, strong with the Goddess," Birkita said reluctantly, still throwing worried looks at Morrigan.

"I'll be fine. I just need a good night's sleep, that's all," Morrigan interrupted, meeting Shayla's cold blue gaze steadily.

"Excellent. Our new High Priestess will perform the ritual. It seems an auspicious omen for our goddess that her Light Bringer arrived just before the dark moon. Don't you think so, Birkita?" Perth said.

Shayla had overshadowed him so much that Morrigan had almost forgotten Perth was there. Now as she turned her attention to him she got the distinct impression that he was exactly what he seemed to be—a handsome but henpecked shell of a middle-aged guy whose wife clearly didn't like him much. But Birkita said that he was the Sidetha's Cave Master. She'd assumed that meant that Perth was touched by, or in a way special to, the Goddess. Didn't it? If so, why was hateful Shayla obviously in charge?

"Yes, Master Perth. The dark moon is auspicious for Adsagsona, so Morrigan's arrival so close to it is an excellent omen," Birkita was saying.

Morrigan refocused on the conversation, smiled perkily and wrapped her arm through Birkita's, pulling the older woman to her feet. "Then that sounds perfect. I'm sure it's different than an, um, Oklahoma Dark Moon Ritual, but Birkita can fill me in on all the details. So, thanks again for everything." Arm in arm, they walked from the huge room with Brina padding silently behind. Morrigan could feel Shayla's eyes boring into her back, but she also noticed that several women, and even a few of the men, bowed their heads respectfully as she passed their tables.

4

Birkita took the lead as soon as they left the Great Chamber. "Okay, there was a lot about that that was truly weird," Morrigan began, but Birkita shook her head and whispered, "Not here, my Lady." So Morrigan bit back her zillions of questions and let Birkita lead her down the winding tunnel.

This time she actually paid attention to her surroundings. At first they followed the same path that was mirrored in Oklahoma, which led from the deepest part of the Alabaster Caverns to the Encampment Room. Of course, in Partholon the cave wasn't the crude, undeveloped rock structure it was in Oklahoma. The pillars of smokeless flame illuminated smooth, widened walls that, every few yards, branched out to the left and right in new tunnels. The pathway was clean and even, completely free of debris, dirt and dampness. Ledges held delicate pottery and statuary. Some of the walls were decorated with intricate stone mosaics, some of them were painted with beautiful, interweaving designs within which Morrigan recognized the figure of the Goddess. In the domed part of the cave, a brazier hung from silver chains anchored on the underlip of the circular pattern, looking like a fantastic chandelier made of fire and fantasy. Awed, Morrigan tried to take in all the wonders at once until her mind was overfilled with beautiful, exotic images of the underground marvels.

It didn't take long for them to come to the Encampment Room—*no, it was called the Usgaran,* Morrigan silently corrected herself. The selenite boulder was still glowing, but only softly. As Morrigan approached it and automatically stroked her fingers across its skin, the crystals blazed into diamond brilliance again as if she had flipped on a hidden switch.

"It's so beautiful," Morrigan murmured.

"It is, indeed." Birkita paused before adding, "The High Priestess before me told stories of Light Bringers, as Adsagsona's Chosen before her had also told. We all know that the crystals can be called alive. But knowing and seeing are very different things. Until you arrived I had only imagined the beauty of the light."

"So there wasn't a Light Bringer before me, like there was a High Priestess before you?"

Birkita shook her head. "There hasn't been a Sidetha Light Bringer in more than three generations." She smiled and pointed to one of the many side tunnels that led from the large room. "Your antechamber lies through there. Though it has been many years, Adsagsona's priestesses have kept the Light Bringer's chamber ready for her. Some of us never doubted your return."

As if she understood exactly where they were going, Brina padded ahead of them through the arched tunnel way. The passage narrowed and then made a little S curve, emptying into an arched doorway covered by a large animal skin, which the cat nosed aside and disappeared behind. Morrigan paused and looked questioningly at Birkita, who brushed one side of the hide curtain aside and motioned for her to enter.

Morrigan climbed three smooth stairs up and then the tunnel widened. To her right was a small entryway that was also covered by a hide curtain. Ahead, the tunnel rounded to dead-end into an amazing room. It was lit by one small pedestal light, which licked soft shadows on the smooth walls. A wide, waist-high ledge that ran around a good length of the right side of the chamber was filled with furs and pillows and plump comforters. On the opposite side of the room, shelves were carved into the wall. They held what looked like perfume bottles and boxes brimming with ropes of semiprecious stones. A mirrored vanity sat beside an intricately carved wooden wardrobe. Two plump fur-upholstered chairs completed the opulent furnishings. Morrigan stared around her, shocked to silence by the richness of everything. Then her eyes were drawn upward and she gasped, automatically brushing her fingertips against the nearest wall. *Light Bringer*…whispered through her skin, and the crystal stalactites that hung in icicle cascades from the ceiling lit, displaying a beauty more delicate and timeless than the finest Venetian-glass chandeliers.

"It's so lovely." Birkita's voice was hushed. "We could see that the hanging rock was made of crystal, of course, but having the light called to them…" She paused, blinking hard as if she was trying not to cry. "It is simply breathtaking." She turned her bright gaze to Morrigan. "I hope the chamber pleases you. The ancient legends say that when Adsagsona formed the caves for her people she took special care to fashion a chamber for the most beloved of her priestesses. To this High Priestess the Goddess also gave the gift of hearing the spirits in the stone, as well as the ability to call light to her sacred crystals."

Morrigan walked around the room, touching the gorgeous bottles and peeking into the jewelry boxes. "This is all so amazing." She looked back at Birkita. "And so confusing. Birkita, I need you to help me understand this place."

"Of course, my Lady. I am here to serve you and the Goddess." Morrigan sat on the thick bed pallet. Brina jumped up and stretched out behind her and Morrigan stroked her soft pelt while she considered how to sift through the sandbox full of questions in her mind. *Well,* she decided, *first things first.*

"I don't want to take your job," she said miserably.

"Job?" Birkita's face was a question mark.

"Being High Priestess. I don't have any right to walk in here and take the job you've had for years and years."

Birkita smiled. "Being High Priestess is not a job, it is a calling. Do not let it distress you, darling child. This is the way of it. Each High Priestess is someday replaced by a younger woman. In truth, it will be a relief to pass my duties to you. I am old and weary, and want to retire to the outskirts of the Goddess's service."

"I don't think it'll be much of a relief for a while. I don't have a clue what I'm doing."

"Trust yourself and your goddess, Light Bringer."

"And you," Morrigan added.

Birkita inclined her head graciously. "If you wish, my Lady."

"So, tell me, what's up with Shayla and Perth? Are they in charge here?"

"They are Master and Mistress, and have been for almost two decades. Under their rule, we have prospered." Her smile turned wry. "Even more than is usual for the Sidetha, which is truly quite impressive."

Morrigan's gaze went back to the boxes of glittering stone jewelry. "Y'all are rich, aren't you?"

Birkita laughed softly at Morrigan's odd language. "If by *y'all* you mean the Sidetha, then yes, we have always been a prosperous people. The Goddess has gifted us greatly with valuable rock and precious stones found nowhere else in Partholon. Our people are talented, not simply in finding veins of hidden rock, but also in fashioning things of beauty from it. The earth outside the caves is fruitful, and though it is colder here than in the rest of the country, our crops are hardy and plentiful. We have little cause to leave our Realm. It has been a simple thing for us to acquire riches. And, of course, our reigning Master and Mistress find riches, and the acquisition of them, very important."

"You don't like Shayla and Perth, either."

Birkita hesitated, choosing her words carefully. "I have been saddened to see the focus of too many of our people change from loving the beauty they can create and praising Adsagsona for the blessing she has given us, to loving the riches those gifts can command in the outside world."

"Shayla feels wrong to me." Morrigan spoke the words aloud without really realizing what she'd said, but when she looked up from petting Brina, Birkita's eyes were sharp and knowing.

"Trust your goddess-given intuition, my Lady."

"I will." Morrigan took Birkita's hand. If she couldn't trust the woman who was her grandma's mirror image in this world, and tell her the complete truth, then she was utterly lost. "Birkita, Oklahoma is not across the B'an Sea. It's way more complicated than that."

Birkita's hold on Morrigan's hand tightened. She nodded solemnly. "You may tell me, Morrigan. I will keep your counsel."

"Oklahoma is in another world. I'm from another world," she said quickly, holding on to Birkita's hand. "I know hardly anything about goddesses and the spirits I can talk to in the rocks and being a Light Bringer."

"But you said you thought you were Epona's Chosen."

Morrigan nodded. "I do know about Epona, but only a little. See, my mom died right after I was born and I was raised by my grandparents." She smiled and added, "You look like my grandma."

"That's a lovely thing for you to say, my Lady." Birkita blinked away tears.

"No, you don't understand. I don't mean that you remind me of her. I mean you *are* her, or actually her mirror image in this world. I know it's confusing, and I don't even really understand it. I totally don't understand how these two worlds could exist. But I know they do. I know they do because my mom came from Partholon. She was trapped in Oklahoma, though, and that's why I was born there."

"But you said your grandparents raised you. Were they your father's parents?"

"No. They were the parents of my mom's mirror image."

"My Lady, this makes no sense."

Morrigan chewed her bottom lip. She'd decided to trust Birkita, so telling her parts and pieces of the truth wasn't right. *Claim your destiny*…drifted through her mind and Morrigan didn't ignore it. This time she took courage from the whispered words.

"Who is Epona's Chosen?"

Birkita looked surprised, but answered the unexpected question. "Rhiannon MacCallan is Blessed of Epona and the Goddess's Chosen."

Morrigan stared into Birkita's eyes and shook her head slowly from side to side. "No. Rhiannon MacCallan *was* Epona's Chosen. She was also my mother. She died a little over eighteen years ago after giving birth to me. The woman who has been Epona's Chosen for the past eighteen years in her place is Shannon Parker, and she's also from Oklahoma."

Birkita had gone very white. "How can this be? She has the blessing of Epona."

"I'm not saying that Shannon's not Epona's Chosen. All I'm saying is that she's not Rhiannon MacCallan. She's Rhiannon's mirror image. She exchanged places with her before I was conceived." Morrigan looked down at their joined hands and said the rest of it. "My mom, Rhiannon, made some pretty big mistakes. She started listening to a dark god and she turned her back on her people. Epona had to replace her." Still looking down, Morrigan ignored the tears that were tracking slowly down her face. "That's why I thought I might be Epona's Chosen. I thought that maybe Epona had given me special powers as kind of a way of showing that she'd really forgiven Rhiannon before she died."

"You have been Chosen, Morrigan. Not by the Great Goddess of Partholon, but by the Goddess who reigns below. Adsagsona is a loving goddess who gives the spark of her spirit to the heart of our land. You will find her easy to love and faithful to her own."

"I'm scared that because I wasn't raised here I won't recognize Adsagsona's voice. What if I listen to the wrong god?"

Birkita lifted Morrigan's chin and gently wiped away her tears. "You are not your mother."

"Sometimes I wonder," she whispered.

"Light Bringers do not traffic with evil," Birkita said firmly.

"Neither does the Chosen of a Great Goddess," Morrigan countered.

Birkita shook her head. "There is no evil in you. Of this I am certain."

"That sounds just like something Grandma would say."

Birkita smiled. "Then you should believe me." The older woman's expression sobered. "My Lady, I do not believe it is wise for us to tell anyone about this mirror world of Oklahoma, or that Epona's Chosen is not who they believe her to be. I cannot see that the knowledge would benefit you or Partholon. It could do the opposite. It could harm the very fabric of our world."

"She has a daughter who's my age, doesn't she?"

"Yes, Epona's Chosen was gifted with one child, a daughter called Myrna. Word came not long ago that the Chosen One's daughter will soon give birth."

"I might be her mirror image—or she could be mine—or however you put it." Something passed through Birkita's eyes that Morrigan couldn't identify. "What is it? Why did you look like that?"

"Shayla seemed to recognize you," Birkita said quickly, her forehead wrinkling with worry. "I wonder how close this resemblance with Myrna is."

Morrigan snorted. "If it's like Rhiannon and Shannon, then Myrna and I could be twins."

"Then it is a good thing that few of the Sidetha travel beyond our Realm. It is not a good thing that Shayla is one of those few."

You must not hide from your destiny! The words in her mind jolted Morrigan. "Well, I'm not going to make a big announcement about my real mom, but I'm also not going to hide like I've done something wrong."

"Of course you've done nothing wrong! But this is all quite a shock." Birkita passed a hand across her eyes, and Morrigan noticed that she was looking even paler than she had before.

"To me, too. I mean, I always knew I was different from other kids. None of my friends could ever understand why I loved being outside so much, and then there were the voices I've heard since I was a little girl. I've never belonged."

"You belong now, Light Bringer," Birkita said firmly.

Birkita's words settled through her body, soothing Morrigan's frayed nerves. "I just found out days ago about Partholon and my real mom. It was the same day I heard the spirits in the crystals and made them light. Then something awful happened in the cave in Oklahoma, and I was pulled here through the crystal boulder."

"Home, my Lady. Adsagsona brought you home through the Usgaran, and tomorrow you will perform your first ritual for the Goddess."

"Are you sure I should do the ritual? I don't have any idea about what goes on in any ritual, let alone a Dark Moon Ritual. I—I'm scared of saying or doing something wrong. Maybe we should just tell Shayla that I'm too tired."

"The ritual is quite simple, and you will be alone most of the time, so there is no need for you to fear saying or doing anything wrong. The other priestesses and I will bathe and anoint you, then we will take you to the Usgaran. There you will ask Adsagsona's blessing for a new cycle of the moon."

"That's it? Then why didn't you want me to perform the ritual when Shayla mentioned it?"

"I was concerned for your health, not for your ability to perform the ritual. A High Priestess must abstain from eating food before the ritual, and I know your journey here has taxed you greatly." Birkita smiled and squeezed Morrigan's hand reassuringly. "But Shayla was correct when she said that you are young and strong and blessed by the Goddess. All will be well, Light Bringer."

Morrigan thought about that and decided it shouldn't be so bad. Sure she was tired, but it didn't feel like anything a good night's sleep couldn't fix. And if she'd be alone for most of the ritual, well, how bad could she screw things up? Plus, Birkita was totally fragile-looking—if she could do it, Morrigan should be able to.

"That doesn't sound so awful," Morrigan said.

Birkita smiled seraphically. "The Dark Moon Ritual is magical. I've performed countless of them, and ever look forward to the next one. It is one of the moments the veil between the Goddess and her High Priestess is thinnest, so you will be very near Adsagsona." She patted Morrigan's cheek. "And now you must rest and prepare for the Goddess."

Birkita walked quickly to the large wardrobe and pulled out a nightdress. Returning to Morrigan she matter-of-factly helped her out of the beaded leather dress and then into the long white robe of a fabric so soft and warm it instantly made Morrigan want to snuggle down in the bedclothes and sleep.

"The door near the opening of this room is your bathing chamber," Birkita explained as she tucked Morrigan into bed. "It is for your use only, so you need not worry about anyone invading your privacy." She smiled down at Morrigan and caressed her hair. "Welcome home, Light Bringer."

"Thank you, Birkita. Thank you for everything you've done for me."

"It has, indeed, been my pleasure, child."

"You know, you look tired, too. Be sure you sleep well tonight."

"Now that you are here and well, I shall revive quickly." Birkita smiled. "I will return in the morning." She kissed Morrigan's forehead gently and then left.

Morrigan stared up at the ceiling. She was amazingly tired, but she couldn't close her eyes. The beauty of the stalactites entranced her, even after she touched the wall of the cave and whispered, "Not so bright now," and the crystals faded from brilliant stars to the elegance of a many-faceted chandelier that had been dimmed for evening ambience.

"I'm in Partholon." She spoke the words aloud, tasting and testing them. "I'm in another world." More quietly, she added, "And I don't have a clue what I'm doing."

You are living your destiny.

"Adsagsona? Is that you?" Morrigan said softly.

There was no response. Not in her mind, and not in the air around her.

She wished Grandpa was there. He could probably help her figure all this stuff out. He'd really like the way these caves looked, too. That thought made her smile, but the smile started to quiver when Morrigan realized that not only would her grandpa never see the Sidetha's caves, but he would never see her again, either.

"And I was so mean to him." Her voice caught on a sob as homesickness broke over her, making it hard to breathe. *I'm sorry, Grandpa. I'm sorry, Grandma. Please forgive me and know how much I love you. I'll miss you forever.* Brina meowed softly and nuzzled her face. Morrigan put her arms around the big cat, buried her face in her thick fur, and then she cried herself to sleep.

5

It was dark and cold in Morrigan's dream. Not the soothing cool darkness of a cave, but a frigid, pressing blackness that brought to her sleeping mind images of being buried alive. She tried to tell herself it was only a dream; she should just wake up. But it had the feel of one of those nightmares that clings like a barnacle, impossible to shake even in the currents of daylight and reality and the waking mind.

Morrigan couldn't move, and she suddenly remembered the suffocating feeling of being stuck in the middle of the selenite crystal, unable to go forward, unable to turn back. Only, in the dream she was drowning in darkness…unending, unyielding darkness. Out of the black drifted voices. First, a woman's laughter, low and mocking, her proud voice saying *Choose me* with a haughty tone that implied Morrigan had no choice at all. Next, a man, possessive and arrogantly proclaiming, *You are mine.* Then a softer, more distant woman's voice insisting she *be wise…be strong.* Morrigan could hardly hear her at all, and her sleeping mind screamed that she didn't know what to be wise about and she was too damn confused to be strong! Yet another woman's voice, this one not so distant, but no less enigmatic, telling her, *Trust yourself, child.*

Morrigan struggled against the confining blackness. Trust herself? How? She didn't know the world. She didn't understand ancient gods and goddesses. She didn't know how to wield magical powers. The dark pressed more closely as if dirt was being bulldozed over her grave. *But I'm alive down here! Don't bury me!* Her heart was beating so frantically that her chest hurt. She couldn't breathe!

Then the blackness was split, like a stage curtain being parted. A hand slid through, open and beckoning for her to take it. She did, and was pulled up out of the pit to look into Kyle's handsome, smiling face. Morrigan threw herself into his arms. He held her close, but she noticed that as soon as she relaxed in his arms he changed, hardened, felt weird and wrong against her skin. She pushed back from him to find a skeleton had taken his place—a skeleton with his warm brown eyes that looked sorrowfully at her. *It's okay,* the words rattled from his fleshless mouth. *We all have to die sometime.*

Morrigan's scream finally broke the dream and thrust her awake.

Brina was stretched out beside her and was watching her with a cocked-head, pricked-ears expression of feline interest. Morrigan sat up, wiping her eyes free of sleep and trying hard to put the dream out of her mind. In a gesture that was becoming more and more automatic, she brushed her hand against the wall of the cave and murmured, "More light, please." The hanging crystals in the ceiling instantly blazed with renewed light, chasing away the lingering darkness of her nightmare. Morrigan was just beginning to realize that she was hungry and that she definitely had to go to the bathroom, when Birkita's voice came from the other side of the hide door.

"My Lady, have you awakened?"

"Yep! I'm up," Morrigan called cheerfully, determined not to let the stupid bad dream mess up her day.

Birkita was all smiles as she entered the room and dropped to a deep, formal curtsy. "Good morning, Light Bringer."

Morrigan grinned and bowed her head. "Good morning, Birkita." Seeing her grandma's familiar face first thing in the morning was so normal, so much like how she'd been awakened for all of her life that it comforted her and helped soothe the ache of missing her grandparents. Speaking of missing someone—there was no sign of Brina. "Hey, where'd the cat go?"

Birkita glanced around the room and shrugged. "I imagine she's hunting, but you need not worry. Brina is always present during our rituals."

"Oh, good," Morrigan said. She'd grown up with G-pa's zillions of humongous dogs, and she'd liked them a lot, but she was totally drawn to Brina and already missed the big cat.

"There is so much to do today. Word came at dawn that Partholon's Stonemaster and the Master Sculptor will be arriving late today. One of the more prosperous Keeps is probably planning to commission work for a new temple. Whatever the reason, a visit from Master Kai is always an occasion, add that to the Master Sculptor, Kegan, joining him, and on the same day as the Dark Moon Ritual. The Realm will be triply busy..." Reminding Morrigan even more completely of her grandma, Birkita continued to chatter and complain about having too little time to ready everything as she herded Morrigan over to the vanity and began expertly brushing out her long auburn hair.

When Birkita finally took a breath, Morrigan said, "Um, I have to use the bathroom."

"Oh, of course you do! What am I thinking? You just go into your bathing chamber while I straighten things out here."

"Birkita," Morrigan snagged one of the older woman's hands so that she'd actually hold still and listen to her. "I can make my own bed and clean up my own room. You're a High Priestess, not a cleaning woman. You shouldn't pick up after me." Besides, this version of her grandma seemed so much frailer than the one she was used to—and she wouldn't even let G-ma wear herself out picking up after her.

"Oh, there you are wrong, my Lady. It is the old High Priestess's duty to see to the young Chosen One. Someday you will do the same for your youthful replacement. It is the way we show our respect and appreciation for Adsagsona. I will stay as near to you as if I was your servant until you feel truly comfortable as High Priestess."

"Well, I am glad you're going to stay close to me, but I want you to relax, rest. I can take care of myself."

"Do not fret, child. I enjoy puttering about. Now go on to your toilette."

Just like G-ma, Morrigan thought as she hurried out of the room. Birkita called after her, "But do not bathe yet. You must be cleansed properly and anointed for the ritual."

"Okay," Morrigan called over her shoulder. She ducked under the curtain that separated her bedroom from the tunnel that led to the Usgaran. Looking to her left she saw another, smaller hide-covered doorway and walked over to stand in front of it. She hesitated, readying herself for a crude bathroom with a round hole cut in the side of the stone or whatever, like a cave version of a Porta Potti. The hide curtain was probably what kept the smell from seeping out into the tunnel. Eeesh. Holding her breath, she pushed the curtain out of the way and entered the room.

No bad smell hit her at all. The room was bigger than even a really nice, modern master bathroom. It was lit with a couple of the smokeless pillars of fiery liquid. Along one wall, shelves had been cut, much as they had been in her bedroom. Here, thick towels were neatly folded, waiting for use. Beside the towels were beautiful glass bottles filled with all sorts of liquids. Morrigan picked one up, pulled open the stopper, sniffed and smiled at the sweet soapy fragrance. Intrigued, she noticed a huge round area that had been carved right out of the floor of the cave. Perched over it was something that looked like the old-time well-water spiggot Grandpa had had to replace a few summers ago. It had a lip and a handle. Curious, Morrigan lifted the handle and instantly a stream of clear, warm water flowed from the lip and cascaded down into the sunken bathtub.

"How cool…" she whispered. Exploring more, she discovered in the very rear of the room, behind a half wall, the toilet facilities, and was thrilled to find that though they were, indeed, holes carved in the cave, water ran constantly under them and they weren't nasty at all. "Huh," she said as she washed her hands. "Who says cavemen, or rather *cavewomen,* can't live well?"

In the little while Morrigan had been gone Birkita had made her bed and had a beaded linen dress the color of the sky with matching slippers set out for her.

"I'm absolutely starving, and you'll be happy to know that I don't feel half as tired as I did yesterday," she said as Birkita helped wrap the complicated folds of the dress around her and close them in place with pretty, silver brooches.

"I'm pleased your strength has returned, but I am sorry to remind you that you won't be able to break your fast yet. You must not eat before the Dark Moon Ritual."

"Oh, jeesh, no food? I'd forgotten about that." As if it understood perfectly, her stomach growled loudly in protest.

"Not until after the ritual. Then you may feast as you celebrate your first ritual for the Goddess. Until then you may have water, tea or wine."

"Ugh, water? For breakfast? And wine on an empty stomach? I think I'll stick with tea," Morrigan grumbled.

Birkita chuckled as she laced up the back of her dress. "The young are ever starving for everything—food, love, life. Have patience, child, and ready yourself for the Goddess's service."

Morrigan stifled a frustrated sigh. Birkita was probably right. Grandma usually was. "Well, would it be okay if I had some tea brought to the Usgaran? I should probably spend time there before the ritual starts."

"There, that sounds more like words spoken by a true High Priestess."

"I guess I need practice at this High Priestess stuff."

"No need to worry, my Lady, you shall get it," Birkita said, gave a satisfied tuck to one of the deep folds of soft material, and then they left the Light Bringer's chamber together.

Morrigan was relieved that she had no trouble remembering which turns to take to return to the Usgaran. Actually, she supposed she couldn't ever get lost in a cave. All she'd need to do was touch the wall and ask the spirits of the crystal to lead her to wherever, but the thought of having to be led around made her feel restless and uncomfortable. She wanted to find her own way—make her own place in this new world. In Partholon she didn't want to be an outsider.

The tunnel emptied into the Usgaran, but Morrigan hesitated in the shadows of the threshold of the room, taking in the scene before her. If Morrigan had imagined the place as somewhere she could sit quietly and commune with (or send silent frantic questions to) Adsagsona, she realized quickly that she had been mistaken about the purpose of the room. Yes, it housed the selenite boulder that was at the heart of the Sidetha's worship of the Goddess, but it was definitely not a dim, hushed place of meditation and prayer. It was more like the hub of a busy village. Talking women sat comfortably on the fur-lined ledges. Some of them were sewing; some had easels in front of them and were painting; a few women were carving blocks of creamy stone. Under their skilled hands Morrigan could already see the shapes and patterns taking form that had been hidden within the marble. Even more women were working pieces of glittering jewels into necklaces or bracelets. There were very few men among the women, but they, too, were busy creating beautiful pieces of art or jewelry.

Morrigan had just opened her mouth to ask Birkita why there seemed to be so many more women than men in the Usgaran, when two men suddenly entered the chamber. They were dressed like everyone else, in leather-trimmed garments with intricate patterns of interwoven semiprecious stones and fur, but they seemed somehow different to Morrigan. She concentrated on them and realized what it was that made them seem odd. It was their attitude. Silently, they radiated an arrogance that was so palpable it bordered on disdain.

Morrigan watched them closely. Each of them carried large, densely woven buckets of some kind of dark brown reed. Together they walked over to the crystal boulder and placed the buckets in front of the stone.

"Good, you're in time to bless the mixing of the alabaster sap," Birkita said and began to walk into the chamber, but Morrigan grabbed her hand and pulled her back into the shadowy entryway.

"Who are those men?"

"They are the Cave Master's apprentices. Only apprentices of the Master travel far enough in the bowels of the caves to harvest alabaster sap. Come, you can bless the mixing of it. We should hurry—we don't want to keep the apprentices waiting."

"Hang on, what do you mean? If they're only apprentices, then why should we worry about making them wait? And besides that, I don't know anything about blessing the alabaster sap. I don't even know what alabaster sap is."

Birkita's eyes widened in surprise, but she quickly explained. "In the buckets there is alabaster sap. It is collected from the deepest caves where the alabaster rock is most ancient and pure. Clefts are hewn in the stone and the sap is collected there."

"But if that stuff burns, isn't this whole cave system flammable?"

Birkita shook her head. "The sap is harmless in its raw form. It's only after it is blessed by a priestess of Adsagsona and then mixed with the distilled and purified juice of corn that it has to ability to burn with the clean light you see everywhere in the caves."

"Juice of the corn?" Morrigan was utterly, completely confused.

"Yes, in its most potent form it is colorless, like water. But it is powerful. The Healers use it to cleanse wounds."

"Alcohol!" Morrigan realized. "Well, that's definitely flammable." And, if she remembered her chemistry labs correctly, it was from the alcohol that the flame got it bluish tint. "Huh, so that's the stuff that makes the smokeless light."

"Morrigan, if you did not have alabaster sap in Oklahoma, how did you make the liquid to light caves?"

"We used something called electricity." Morrigan paused, having no clue how to describe electricity to Birkita. "It's, um, like harnessing a lightning bolt."

Birkita looked dubious. "I would like to see a lightning bolt tamed. Are you able to do it?"

"Uh, no. I only make crystals light. Electricity is a whole different kind of magic."

The older woman nodded. "I can imagine that type of goddess magic would be difficult to control." Birkita jerked her chin toward the impatiently waiting men. "Much like Cave Master apprentices, who are also difficult to control."

"But *you're* the Goddess's High Priestess. Or rather you used to be and now I am. Shouldn't those men be waiting on us? I mean, without us can the sap be turned into the stuff that keeps the caves lit?"

Birkita's face went even paler than usual. "I would never think of withholding my goddess-given gifts and leaving the people in darkness."

"I understand that would be a bad thing. All I'm saying is that we should be respected for our power, and for the Goddess we represent."

"We should be, yes. But under the reign of Shayla and Perth, power and the respect it breeds come from riches and not from Adsagsona," Birkita said softly.

"Sounds too damn much like the worst parts of the world I'm from," Morrigan muttered. "So I guess that means the sap needs to be blessed, no matter what kind of jerks those guys are."

"Jerks?"

"Arrogant know-it-alls."

Birkita's lips tilted up. "Ah, yes. Jerks. It is an appropriate naming. As you say, my Lady, shall we bless the mixing of the sap before the *jerks* become too restless?"

Morrigan's grin was short-lived. "Yeah, but can I watch you do it first?"

The old High Priestess's gaze was kind. "You must learn to believe in yourself, child. The Goddess has already Chosen you—all that is left is for you to formally begin her service."

"I want to. I really do want to."

"Part of Adsagsona's divinity already rests within you. Come, I will bless one basket, then let us see if you would like to bless the other."

Morrigan's stomach lurched nervously, but she nodded and stepped into the Usgaran at Birkita's side. The busy room hushed as soon as they caught sight of Morrigan, but she was prepared for that. *There hasn't been a Light Bringer here in three generations. They're not gawking; they're curious, that's all. Relax. Breathe. It'll be fine.* As if she was entering a stage, Morrigan straightened her spine and lifted her chin. She and Birkita walked to the two large baskets.

"Well met, Beacan and Mannix." Birkita nodded and smiled at the two men. "It is a lovely harvest of sap you have provided us."

"We aren't used to being kept waiting, Priestess," the shorter of the two men said.

Morrigan felt an instantaneous flush of rage at the man's rude tone. Without hesitating to consider the source of such unaccustomed anger, she caught the man's haughty gaze. "Birkita was with me. That's why she was late."

"You are the Light Bringer," the other man said.

His tone was curious, but almost flippantly so, as if she was one of those overachieving four-year-olds who could recite all the presidents' names, but who couldn't tie her own shoes. It pissed her off. So instead of answering him right away, Morrigan walked a couple feet to the huge selenite boulder that rested behind him. It was still glowing softly from her touch yesterday. She placed the flat of her palm against its surface and, raising her voice, said, "Yes, I am the Light Bringer. I am also the new High Priestess of Adsagsona." At the same time she spoke, Morrigan sent a silent plea to the spirits of the crystal to give her some serious brightness. The spirits answered her with a brilliant blaze that exploded in prisms of flashing light. Morrigan caressed the stone in thanks before turning to the men, who she now pointedly ignored, though she could feel their startled gazes on her. *Hmm, must not have been at dinner last night,* she thought. Then she smiled at Birkita.

"Go ahead and bless the sap now. The Usgaran isn't a place for impatience, so let's send these guys on their way." Morrigan could hear the startled intake of breath from several of the women closest to her, but she didn't care—not even when Birkita sent her a worried look as she quickly took her place in front of the first basket. There was something wrong here, Morrigan could feel it. She knew it deep within her, the same way she knew the crystals would light for her touch. She also knew she needed to do something about it, but Birkita's raised hands and the hush of the room distracted her attention from her gut feeling.

"Adsagsona, I call upon you, above—" she paused and moved her hands from over her head down, to form an openpalmed reverse V on either side of the basket "—and below." Then Birkita began swirling her hands in a graceful pattern over the top of the basket. Entranced, Morrigan watched a smoky darkness rise from the sticky, gelatinous sap as the woman who looked and sounded so much like her beloved grandma continued to speak. "From darkness comes light. From stone comes liquid. We know our Goddess hears our prayers because she nurtures us within the womb of her own body. Sidetha we are. Of the Goddess we are. And from the power of Adsagsona comes the way to see." Morrigan's hair lifted on the back of her neck as Birkita completed the blessing. "Bring us light, Goddess." There was a small sizzling sound and the black fogginess that had formed in the basket under Birkita's hand suddenly dissipated, leaving the sap clear and sparkling, like colorless Jell-O.

"It is your turn, High Priestess."

Morrigan's body jerked involuntarily at Birkita's words. She glanced up from the basket of newly blessed goo to see that everyone in the room was watching her expectantly. She opened her mouth to tell Birkita thanks, but no thanks, when the words *Embrace your destiny* slicked through her mind and, with a little start of shock, she realized that she wanted to bless the sap.

Morrigan wanted to be High Priestess.

Without giving herself a chance to chicken out, she moved over to the second bucket. Mirroring Birkita, she raised her hands over her head. For an instant her mind was absolutely blank; like the first time she'd walked out on a stage in front of a real audience, all the words left her. But in the next moment her mind was filled with the blessing and, just like that first play, Morrigan spoke in a clear voice that carried to the corners of the room.

"From darkness comes light. From stone comes liquid." She said the remembered lines quickly, and then Morrigan stopped, drew a deep breath and moved her hands to point downward. When she spoke again she recited the words that were coming from her heart instead of the by-rote words of a remembered prayer. "Hear me, Adsagsona. I am Morrigan, your Light Bringer, and your High Priestess. I ask light to come to me— impossible light from impenetrable darkness—something only a goddess could give me the power to create." Morrigan paused while she began drawing her hands back and forth, around and over the sap in the bucket. From the alabaster liquid dark fog began to rise. The smoky blackness that fanned from her palms roiled and intensified, but within that darkness she felt it. The spark of crystalline light that had already grown familiar to her, like a childhood friend, and when she completed the blessing with the words "Light for me, please, Goddess" the power that snapped under her hands wasn't a subdued sizzle. It was a clap of energy and light that made even Morrigan jump in surprise.

"Blessed be Adsagsona!" Birkita cried.

"Blessed be Adsagsona!" the room echoed.

Morrigan glanced at the two arrogant men and saw that they alone weren't calling thanks to the Goddess. Instead they were watching her with hooded, considering eyes.

Her hands still tingling with power, Morrigan lifted one eyebrow and smiled smugly at both of them.

6

The rest of the morning passed quickly, but not uneventfully. Morrigan worked off the advice her grandpa had given her over and over again. "If you keep your mouth shut and listen, you'll be surprised what you learn about the people around you." So after the arrogant apprentices left, Morrigan settled comfortably onto a fur-covered ledge. With Brina curled at her side she sipped milky, heavily sweetened tea and she listened. Naturally, G-pa had been right. If she smiled and nodded encouragingly but silently, people soon either forgot she was there or became ever so willing to chatter on and on to her. Consequently Morrigan learned several things.

First, lots of people didn't respect the priestesses of Adsagsona anymore—not since Perth and Shayla had become Master and Mistress of the Sidetha. And it was obvious that Shayla held the real power. The priestesses seriously didn't like Shayla, not that Morrigan blamed them. Her one small introduction to the woman had been enough to have her agreeing (albeit silently) with the consensus. But it was also clear that even though the current Master and Mistress weren't well liked, they were feared by the priestesses. It was also clear that the Sidetha outside the service of Adsagsona were firmly behind the current rulers, even though no one really liked them. The people were outrageously prosperous—Morrigan decided that many of them were flat-out rich. Shayla and Perth had made that happen.

The longer Morrigan listened, the more she realized that she had stepped into a major power struggle. The Master and Mistress were all for making the Sidetha, and themselves, as rich as possible. The priestesses had nothing against living well, but they believed Adsagsona was being forgotten in the midst of the people's wealth, so they wanted the people to refocus on worshipping the Goddess and following something they kept referring obscurly to as "the old ways." Whatever that meant.

This whole situation was doubly uncomfortable because it seemed Shayla had the tendency to banish from the caves anyone who pissed her off too much. The word *banish* was spoken in a whisper and was usually accompanied by a shudder.

So where did this leave Morrigan? Well, the priestesses were clearly thrilled that she had suddenly appeared, and it looked like Shayla was equally as unthrilled. Great. Just what she needed—to be caught in the middle of a political tug-of-war.

It was a little after midday, while she was contemplating how to (subtly) ask if it was possible for a Light Bringer and/or High Priestess to be banished, that her liquid diet changed from milky sweet tea to red wine, which was at first too dry and dark, but after about half a glass became amazingly easy to drink. Actually, as she started the second glass Morrigan couldn't remember why it was that in the past she hadn't really liked wine. Just then she was thinking that she felt nice and warm and not hungry at all...

"My Lady?"

Morrigan looked up from her half-full second glass of wine to see Birkita and two lesser priestesses she'd been introduced to that morning, Deidre and Raelin, standing in front of her, smiling expectantly.

"Time for more wine?"

Birkita's smile widened and the young women giggled. "No, my Lady. It is time to begin bathing and anointing you for the Dark Moon Ritual."

"Okeydokey," she said cheerfully. When Morrigan stood up she was surprised at how the room rolled gently under her feet.

"Perhaps changing to water would be a good idea," Birkita said as she took Morrigan's arm to steady her.

"I'm really not much of a drinker," Morrigan confided as the four women made their way back down the tunnel to the Light Bringer's bathing chamber.

"No one would have ever guessed that, my Lady," Birkita said, causing all of them to laugh good-naturedly.

Morrigan decided that the glass and a half of wine on an empty stomach might not have been that bad of an idea. At least it allowed her not to be so uptight about three women bathing her. Actually it was kinda fun—more like a slumber party (except that she was naked and up to her chin in hot, soapy water) than a preritual anointing.

"Is the Keep of Oklahoma much different from our Realm, my Lady?" Deidre asked as she scrubbed one of Morrigan's arms.

"Oh, yeah, lots different," Morrigan said, and then added before she really realized what she was saying, "I never felt like I belonged there."

"That is because you belong here, my Lady," Raelin said with a bright smile.

"I think you might be right about that." She turned, tilted her head back, and while they rinsed the excellent-smelling shampoo from her hair, Morrigan continued. "Even though I haven't been here very long it's like something inside of me has unwound and relaxed for the first time in my life."

"I cannot imagine the pain it would cause to be separated from Adsagsona," Birkita said. The other women nodded in solemn agreement.

"At least I understand it now. Before, I thought I was the weird one. I was constantly telling myself that it was my fault I felt like that because I wasn't trying hard enough to be like everyone else."

"Oh, no, my Lady!" Deidre said, near tears. "It was separation from your goddess that made you feel that you were an outlander."

"You will never feel so again," Birkita said, squeezing her bare, wet shoulder.

"You know, I was nervous about the ritual. But I'm really starting to look forward to it." Actually, as the women toweled her vigorously dry and began rubbing sweet, almond-scented oil into her skin, Morrigan realized she was feeling almost giddy with excitement.

She was getting ready to hear the voice of her goddess!

Wrapped in a thick towel, Morrigan, accompanied by the three women, went to her room. Spread out on her pallet was a weird-looking piece of clothing made of a material that shimmered silver white in the light of the selenite stalactites. Morrigan stroked the beautiful cloth.

"Wow, it's like silk, but it's really leather."

"It is the finest of kidskin, softened by the hands of Adsagsona's priestesses, dyed and embroidered with the finest diamonds by a High Priestess who went to spend her eternity with the Goddess decades ago. I wore it for my first Dark Moon Ritual nearly fifty years ago." Birkita's smile was wistful. "Would that I was supple and young enough to wear it again."

Morrigan studied Birkita's petite form. *Just like G-ma,* she thought, *barely over a hundred pounds soaking wet.* "Oh, please! You could still wear this."

The older woman's cheeks warmed to a blushing pink, but she smiled. "It is time for a new High Priestess. I wish you many years of joy wearing it." She motioned for Deidre and Raelin to help her, and together the three women began wrapping the supple leather around Morrigan's body.

"Oh, nuh-uh. Hang on. There must be a piece—or two or three—missing," Morrigan said when they had finally stepped back and were surveying their work while she gazed at herself in the full-length mirror. The glistening diamond-embroidered leather clung to her body, making her waist look tiny and her hips look full and curvy. There were slits on either side of it, almost up to the top of her thighs (and she didn't have a damn thing on underneath). But what was really freaking her out was the fact that the garment laced tightly up her rib cage, and stopped there, like an incomplete bustier *leaving her breasts and shoulders completely bare!*

"You are correct, Morrigan. There is more to the garment." Birkita paused as she turned to the large armoire and pulled out another beautiful piece of white leather. "This was added to the High Priestess's ritual dress during the past decade." She finished, placing the short, cape-like material around Morrigan's shoulders and lacing it up.

Wrong…it is wrong…blasphemous. The whisper in her head was angry and clipped, and it overshadowed Morrigan's embarrassment at her bare boobs. "It's not right." She spoke almost to herself as she fingered the soft material.

The two younger priestesses were visibly uncomfortable. They kept glancing furtively back and forth from each other to Birkita.

"What is it?" Morrigan's frustration at again not having a clue about what was really going on made her voice sharper than she'd intended. She drew a calming breath and said, "What don't I know?"

"For generations Adsagsona's High Priestess has bared her breasts during Dark Moon rites to the Goddess. It is only right—only logical." Birkita's voice sounded strained. "If a priestess covers her body before her goddess, what else might she be covering? Guilt? Secret desires? Dishonesty?"

"If that's what you believe, then why did you start covering yourself?" But Morrigan knew the answer before Birkita spoke it.

"Shayla decreed that it was immodest. She even used the word *vulgar*," Birkita said, disgust clear in her voice. "Oh, at first she didn't phrase it like that. At first she spoke only about my age."

"Instead of honoring our High Priestess as a woman of value, one who has passed from Maiden to Mother to Wise Woman, Shayla made small comments about how unseemly it was to see the naked breasts of a woman who was of the age of a grandmother."

Morrigan looked at Birkita and saw the hurt and embarrassment in her eyes, but the old High Priestess lifted her chin proudly. "None of the younger priestesses had been called as Chosen. There was no one else to perform the rituals. I know Adsagsona sees nothing but beauty in my body, but the people—the Mistress's people—they are not the Goddess."

"Some of them do not even know the Goddess," Deidre said angrily.

"Many of them do not know the Goddess," Raelin agreed.

"So you stopped baring your breasts?" Morrigan wasn't exactly comfortable with the idea of her grandma—or a woman who looked like G-ma's twin—going around without a top, but she was more uncomfortable with the idea that a hateful bitch had made her stop.

"Shayla had that made for me." Birkita motioned to the cape

that was now securely laced over Morrigan's bare breasts. "She gave it to me in a very public display right before a Dark Moon Ritual. She said it was a gift from the Mistress of the Sidetha to Adsagsona's High Priestess. Refusing it would have been a terrible insult."

"Wasn't wearing it a terrible insult?"

Birkita met Morrigan's eyes steadily. "That, my Lady, is something you must decide for yourself. You are now Adsagsona's High Priestess."

"Yes, I guess I am…" Morrigan murmured as she gazed at herself in the mirror.

There wasn't much dressing left to do. Birkita combed some kind of lovely product into her hair so that as it dried it didn't frizz at all. Instead the heavy waves of auburn glistened like dark water. Dangling from her ears and around her neck hung ropes of a light blue jewel Birkita said was blue topaz, because, she said, "It perfectly matches your eyes." Then Morrigan slipped her feet into soft leather shoes that reminded her of ballet flats, and the women inspected her.

"You are beautiful, my Lady," Deidre said.

"Lovely," Raelin agreed.

"Perfect," said the woman who looked so much like her grandmother.

"Nervous. Again," Morrigan said.

"Priestesses, you may leave us now. Call the people to the Usgaran. The High Priestess will be there shortly," Birkita said.

"Thank you for helping me get ready," Morrigan said as the women curtsied and left the chamber. She turned to Birkita. "Okay, tell me what I'm supposed to do."

"There are ritual words you should say, and I can easily teach you those. First I want you to tell me what you know of the dark moon. In your old world, what did it symbolize?"

"I've been thinking about this—by dark moon you mean new moon, right? The time between the waxing and waning moon when it isn't visible."

"Yes, the dark moon is as you describe."

Relieved that she understood something, Morrigan answered easily, thankful that Grandma had been way into the moon and its different phases. "The new moon, or dark moon as you call it, symbolizes new beginnings. My grandma always said it was the perfect time to start new projects, begin new relationships, start a trip. Things like that."

"Your grandmother was a wise woman. It does, indeed, symbolize new beginnings. There is also another aspect to the dark moon, just as in life good is balanced by evil. The dark moon is a time when the mystical veil between our world and the Otherworld, that world of gods and goddesses, is thinnest. Great magic can be worked during the dark moon—for good or for evil."

Morrigan felt a shiver begin at the base of her spine. "Evil?" Her voice sounded weak and strange.

Birkita took her hand. "You have nothing to fear. You have been Chosen by Adsagsona and not by another dark power."

"But how do you know for sure?" The wine buzz was gone, leaving Morrigan feeling slightly sick to her stomach and headachy.

"We spoke of this before. You are a Light Bringer. They do not traffic with evil. You must banish doubts from your mind, Morrigan. Perhaps it would help you to know that Adsagsona is an unusual goddess. She exists in the Underworld, deep in the womb of the earth. She is comfortable with darkness, as are her High Priestesses. Tell me, child, have you ever feared the darkness?"

The answer was simple. "No. I've never been afraid of the dark. I actually like it. My grandparents used to tell me if I didn't turn on a light when I got up at night to use the bathroom that I'd stub a toe or something, but I never did. I—I've worried that my being comfortable with the darkness is a bad thing," she added.

"No, child. It was an early sign of Adsagsona's favor. I, too, have always been easy with the darkness. Our goddess is a loving, nurturing mother to the Sidetha. She marks her priestesses young and cherishes them for all their lives. But you must remember that though Adsagsona prefers the dark, she also cherishes the light, which is why she created her Light Bringers with the gift to call forth light from crystals deep within the earth. Evil that lurks in the darkness shuns the light. Your light can sear that evil should it ever try to touch you."

"Did evil ever try to mess with you?"

"No, child. I never found anything in the darkness but Adsagsona's love."

"Somehow that doesn't make me feel any better," Morrigan said.

"Banish your doubts, High Priestess. Your goddess is good. She has gifted you with great power. Do not allow inexperience and youth to make you falter in her service!"

"Okay, I'll do my best," Morrigan said quickly, automatically responding to Birkita's sharp tone.

Birkita sighed, and suddenly looked very tired. "I did not mean to be harsh with you. It is just that I believe you are allowing insecurities from your old world to plague you here. Morrigan, you did not belong to that world, those people. This is the world in which you belong, and we are your people, just as Adsagsona is your goddess. All will be well here, Light Bringer."

"You're right, Birkita." Morrigan wished she felt as sure as she sounded. "All will be well now that I'm here."

Birkita smiled. "Now we should hurry. The people will be waiting for us." Her smiled widened. "You, actually."

"That's not helping my nerves."

"It is a good thing!" She laughed and gestured for Morrigan to follow her from the chamber as she continued to explain. "We will enter the Usgaran. The people will have made a large circle around the crystal stone. You will stand before it and invoke the Goddess's presence."

"How do I do that?"

"You did it earlier today when you blessed the alabaster sap."

Morrigan nodded. "Okay, I can do that. Then what?"

"Then you simply thank Adsagsona for the blessings she provided during the past phase of the moon. When your blessing is finished, say, 'Hail, Adsagsona,' and the people will echo you. Then everyone will depart, leaving you alone in the Usgaran. The last part of the ritual is personal. It is between the Goddess and her High Priestess only."

"Well, that's good."

"It has long been my favorite part of the ritual," Birkita said warmly. "There will be wine for libation in a goblet near the crystal boulder. Take it and pour it around the boulder. Then you must extinguish each of the sap flames. You must also extinguish the light you call forth from the crystals. In the womb of darkness that is Adsagsona's Realm beseech the Goddess's blessing during the coming phases of the moon—from now until the next dark moon—for the Sidetha. Thank the Goddess, relight the flames and join the other priestesses in the Great Chamber to break your fast."

"That doesn't sound so bad," Morrigan said. They'd come to the entrance to the Usgaran and they paused inside the shadowy archway. The room was packed with people. Their murmuring voices reminded Morrigan of the rustling of fall leaves in a windstorm. She took a deep breath and rested her fingertips lightly on the cave wall. "Light the stone up for me, please," she whispered. She gave Birkita a tight smile and said,

"Time to do this thing." As the selenite boulder blazed, Morrigan stepped into the room.

"Luck and the Goddess be with you, child," Birkita called after her as the older woman melted back into the shadows. No one noticed her, and no one noticed she was crying softly.

7

The talking stopped as soon as the boulder lit up. Every eye turned to bore into Morrigan as she strode forward. She felt like a tightly wound rubber band and was afraid she might break something inside herself until she heard a familiar padding sound and felt Brina's soft fur brush the side of her leg as the big cat joined her, perfectly matching her pace. When they came to the selenite boulder, Brina moved a little way off to the side, tail twitching restlessly, narrow eyes studying the large crowd.

Morrigan waited a moment, collecting her thoughts and staring into the depths of the brilliantly sparkling crystal. Then, acting on a gut impulse, Morrigan turned from the stone to face the group who circled it and her. In one quick movement she yanked open the laces that held the leather cape demurely in place around her shoulders and pulled the thing over her head. As she threw it away from her, Brina snarled a war cry that caused the flesh to rise on Morrigan's bare skin.

Yes! The word blasted through her mind, chasing away her nervous embarrassment. She saw more than heard the shocked gasps of the people, and barely spared Shayla's tight, disapproving face a glance, before she proudly tossed back her hair and lifted her arms over her head. Using her diaphragm to project her voice, the Sidetha's new High Priestess invoked her goddess's presence.

"Adsagsona, I call upon you, above!" Morrigan moved her hands from over her head down, to form an open-palmed reverse V. "And below." Staying in that position she lifted her chin and let her strong, young voice ring from the walls of her beloved cave. "Goddess, I ask that you be with me on this night that is so special to you—the night of the dark moon. I ask it as your new High Priestess, and with the asking I promise you that I swear I will do my best to do your will and make you proud of me." Morrigan closed her eyes in concentration. *Please don't disappoint me. Please don't leave me hanging here all by myself.* Aloud she said, "Come to us, Adsagsona, and let your people thank you for the blessings you have given them over the past month of moon phases!" Morrigan threw her hands up again and hoped for the best.

"Welcome, Light Bringer, in whom I am well pleased!"

Morrigan's eyes sprang open at the sound of the voice that shimmered with visible power through the air around her. All she saw was light. All she felt was an immense wash of power and warmth. She looked down at herself and could hardly believe it. Her body was on fire! No—not fire. It looked like the Goddess had turned on a switch inside her and, just like the crystals who answered her call for light so willingly, her soul had answered with a visible burning light. It was awesome! Morrigan threw back her head and laughed with pure, uninhibited joy—a sound that was echoed by each priestess of the Sidetha. Many of the watching crowd fell to their knees, weeping with joy as they thanked Adsagsona.

In decades to follow, the Sidetha composed poetry and sang ballads about how their High Priestess the Light Bringer had looked during that very first ritual, and about the events that followed her miraculous appearance to the Sidetha. Genera-

tion after generation would speak of her…sing of her…
remember her. That night strong magic was born in the form
of a young, inexperienced woman. Of Morrigan one bard
sang:

> Spirit made of shining beauty and grace
> The Goddess's Chosen, Morrigan came
> Light licked her skin, her hair and her bright face
> Sidetha's souls would never be the same.
> Breasts robed only in power she stood proud
> No humble old woman and no young fool
> Fear, greed, denial, guilt—no longer allowed
> For the Goddess had found her heart's true tool.
> Many present wondered; many there feared
> This shining star's price too rich to be paid
> Gaze at a Goddess and you may be seared
> Warriors, queens, noblemen—low have been laid.
> In Morrigan we glimpsed our souls' delight
> But could the moth survive her own bright light?

Oblivious to the awestruck crowd and unknowing that she
had just birthed a legend, Morrigan spread wide her hands and
spoke from her heart to her goddess.

"Adsagsona, I know that I'm supposed to thank you for how
rich you have made the Sidetha, but I'm a new High Priestess
so this is going to be a new kind of blessing." She paused,
focusing her eyes on the crowd until she could pick out indi-
viduals, then she spoke to each person she named. "I want to
thank you for Donnetha's ability to make beautiful jewelry."
The middle-aged woman's eyes widened when her name was
called, then she blushed happily and bowed her head. Morrigan
found another woman she recognized from her day listening
in the Usgaran. "I want to thank you for Gladys's ability to carve

life from marble." She smiled at the attractive sculptress's blank look of surprise, and continued calling out those she'd watched create beauty that day: "I want to thank you for Ahearn's ability to tool leather. I want to thank you for Kathleen's ability to paint lovely pictures. I want to thank you for Evelyn's ability to embroider. I want to thank you for the kindness of Deidre and Raelin and how they helped me this afternoon." Then Morrigan found the face that was most dear to her of all the Sidetha. She smiled warmly and said, "And, most of all, I want to thank you for and ask a special blessing on your High Priestess Birkita, who loves you and loves me with true selflessness." Morrigan pointed her hands down in the upside-down V that already felt so natural and so right, and finished the blessing. "Goddess, as your new High Priestess I want to thank you for the gifts you've given the Sidetha in the form of their talents, instead of the riches your gifts have gained. Hail, Adsagsona!"

There was only a slight pause, and then, led by the glad voices of priestesses, the people responded with the cry "Hail, Adsagsona!"

Morrigan stood there, skin glowing, breasts proudly bared, palms open and fingers pointed downward, trying to catch her breath as the completely hushed crowd filed out of the Usgaran. Her body felt as if she had just run a series of sprints, but instead of wearing her out it had invigorated her. She was sure she could climb a mountain—five mountains! The Goddess had spoken to her! Had she recognized her voice? Morrigan couldn't be sure. Aloud it had sounded so different—powerful yet kind. Well, maybe now that she had heard Adsagsona's voice, the next time there was a voice in her head or in the wind around her, she *would* be able to recognize it.

Morrigan gazed down at her body again. Her skin was flushed and still glowing with an unearthly light. She glistened with a mixture of anointing oil and a light film of sweat. And she had to admit that her breasts looked great, all shiny and bare and perky. Let that damn Shayla try and tell her that she should cover herself. The hag could go straight to hell, or wherever that would be in Partholon. It wasn't her destiny to tiptoe around some power-hungry queen wannabe. It was her destiny to be High Priestess and Light Bringer, and she would fulfill her destiny!

When she finally looked up, Morrigan was surprised to find that, except for Brina, the huge room was empty. "Okay, okay—time to settle and do what comes next," she told the cat. What was it that Birkita had told her? She thought back to the conversation that seemed to be forever ago—seemed to have happened to a totally different girl than the shining, goddess-touched woman she was now. Birkita had said that she was supposed to pour the wine around the boulder as libation for the Goddess, and then the last part of the ritual was supposed to be performed alone and in the dark.

As in Oklahoma, the selenite boulder wasn't situated in the center of the room. It rested very close to the northernmost wall. Morrigan looked at the ledge that was behind it and saw that a large goblet stood there. She lifted it, admiring its delicate design. The goblet had been carved out of a solid piece of rose-colored quartz. The red wine that filled it looked like it had made the stone blush. Hoping she was doing it right, Morrigan made her way around the boulder, carefully pouring the wine in a neat circle. It perfumed the air with the scent of grapes and spices, making her head feel nicely dizzy—kinda like she'd gulped a glass of it down herself.

Then with feet that hardly touched the ground, Morrigan went to the closest of the more than dozen open braziers that were situated around the circumference of the room, and was relieved to see a large, bowl-like thing that looked like a giant candle snuffer tucked neatly behind it. Working quickly, she put out each of the flames before returning to stand in front of the glowing selenite boulder.

Morrigan's fingers caressed the skin of the rock. "You're so beautiful, especially now that yours is the only light in here." She glanced at the skin of her hand and arm that was still shining with an amazing internal light. She laughed, "Well, except for me you're the only light in here."

We hear you, Light Bringer, Chosen of the Goddess.

The words passed through her fingers, warming and thrilling her. "Thank you. Thank you so much. But now I need you to turn off for a little while so I can finish the ritual."

It shall be as you request, Light Bringer!

Immediately the faceted white light that blazed from each of the thousands of selenite crystals in the room extinguished and Morrigan was plunged into absolute darkness. Her skin didn't even glow. Morrigan blinked hard several times, trying to acclimate herself to such complete and utter blackness. For a moment she felt a tiny needle of panic. Not because it was so dark, but because it suddenly reminded her of the suffocating trip through the boulder as she moved from one world to another.

Then she felt the soft warmth of Brina's fur rub against the side of her leg and the familiar "huh huh" sound the big cat often made. She wasn't alone and she wasn't suffocating. Brina was here. The Goddess was here. Forcing herself to take several long, slow breaths, Morrigan regained her composure. Then, once again, she lifted her arms. "Adsagsona, I call on thee above!" She moved her arms down so that her fingers pointed down, as if she was gesturing to the bowels of the cave. "And below." Holding herself in that position, she bowed her head and spoke. "It's just us now, so I don't have to pretend to know what I'm doing. I—I hope it's okay that I just talk to you like you're a normal person, even though I don't mean any disre-

spect, because I know you're not just some normal woman."
Morrigan paused and bit her lip, wishing she didn't sound so
young and stupid.

You may continue, Light Bringer.

Morrigan squelched the squeaky sound of surprise that
slipped from between her lips. The Goddess's voice wasn't as
powerful as it had been before, and it drifted in the darkness
around her, almost tangible.

"I want to ask your blessing on the Sidetha during the
coming phases of the moon."

All of the Sidetha? the disembodied voice said from the black.

"Actually, that's something I'd like to mention. I don't like
how Birkita was being treated. Some things, okay, some people
around here feel wrong to me. So I guess more specifically I'd
like to ask your blessing on those who don't feel wrong."
Morrigan chewed her lip again, unsure of what else to say.

Should the Chosen of a Goddess not pray for all of her people?

Morrigan frowned. "Probably, but I haven't been a High
Priestess very long, and as I'm sure you know, I'm not even
from this world. So there's a good chance that I might be
messing all of this up."

The Goddess's laughter caused little sparks of light to glitter
in the darkness. *Follow your instincts, child. They will not fail you.*

For a second, the Goddess sounded so human, so close to her,
that Morrigan almost asked her about the different voices she'd
heard all her life. She opened her mouth to speak, but the words
just wouldn't come. Did she have to taint this amazing experience with doubts from her past? Like Birkita said—that was a different world. She should leave all that crap back there. So instead
she said, "Thank you, Goddess. I'll try to listen to my instincts."

*Then know that you have my blessing, Morrigan MacCallan,
Light Bringer. Through you the people shall be blessed and your light
will illuminate the darkness…*

Morrigan felt a breath of wind from the darkness. It wrapped around her body, lifting her hair and gently caressing her skin, almost like a mother's embrace. She trembled from the beauty of it and whispered through tears, "Hail, Adsagsona!"

As the Goddess's presence left the chamber, every brazier lit with a sound like waves pounding on a darkened shore. Morrigan lifted her head, wiped her eyes and hugged herself with happiness.

She belonged to a goddess!

8

Morrigan almost didn't think about putting her top back on before she left the Usgaran. Almost. Thankfully the jiggling and, well, bareness of everything reminded her that she was half-naked. Now that the ritual was over and the Goddess's presence gone, walking around partially naked didn't seem like such a good idea. Though she did admit to herself, as she laced up the ties, that hurling off her top had been a very 1960s, girl-power thing for her to do. Grandma would have loved it. She hoped Birkita approved. She'd be waiting for her in the Great Chamber with Deidre and Raelin. The anticipation of seeing the women, and the fact that Morrigan was starving, had her hurrying out of the Usgaran, Brina trotting alongside.

Happily, Morrigan remembered the way to the Great Chamber. Of course, even had she not, it would have been a simple thing to follow her nose. The smell of freshly baked bread was as effective as road signs. When she and Brina entered the chamber Morrigan was surprised by the number of people who were there. They were all engaged in animated conversations, and she noticed right away there was a lot of laughing and talking going on—lots more than had been going on the night before at dinner. A woman Morrigan recognized as the sculptress Gladys looked up and caught sight of her.

"The Light Bringer comes!" she cried.

With happy little sounds, all of the women stood and then dropped into fluid curtsies while the men—there were fewer of them, but there were men present—bowed like gentlemen from back in the day. The attention brought Morrigan up short and made her stomach feel all fluttery.

And then Birkita was there, curtsying in front of her. Morrigan bent quickly, took the older woman's hands and lifted her. "Please don't," she said earnestly.

Birkita smiled through happy tears. "It is only proper to show respect to our High Priestess."

"Not you—everyone else, but not you." Morrigan threw her arms around Birkita and whispered, "How did I do?"

"You were wonderful—perfect," Birkita said.

"So the topless thing worked okay?"

Birkita pulled back a little and touched Morrigan's cheek. "It was proper, and the Goddess was pleased. But I want you to be careful, child. Arrogant disregard for authority can get even a High Priestess in trouble."

Morrigan linked her arm through Birkita's. "The Goddess is my boss, and I'm not disregarding her authority—arrogantly or otherwise."

Birkita looked like she wanted to say more, but a tide of happy, chattering women engulfed them, pulling Morrigan to the head table, which was filled with food and pitchers of wine. She noticed that Shayla and Perth were conspicuously absent, but Morrigan didn't have much time to wonder about that. She was too busy eating and talking to the women who wanted to gush about how magical her glowing skin had looked and how beautifully the crystals had shined. Everyone was excited and happy. To Morrigan it seemed the Great Chamber had been filled with the love of a goddess, and they were all basking, which was why Shayla's overly sober voice disrupted the mood like cold water dashed on someone bathing in a hot spring.

"If you are not too busy, High Priestess, it would be nice if you would accompany us to greet our guests."

Mouth stuffed full of cheese and meat, Morrigan looked up to see Shayla and Perth standing in front of the table. They were dressed in clothing as fine as her ceremonial dress. Shayla was even wearing a wide band of gold around her head that looked like a crown. Morrigan gulped, wiped her mouth and tried to answer with some measure of good humor.

"Sure, I'll come. No problem." She gave a tight-lipped smile to the people nearest to her at the table. "Excuse me, seems duty calls." Morrigan stood up, motioning at Birkita. "Calls *us,* that is."

"It is customary for the High Priestess to greet distinguished guests, not retired priestesses," Shayla said, barely sparing Birkita a glance.

Morrigan met Shayla's cold eyes squarely and said in a matter-of-fact voice. "Haven't you ever heard of on-the-job training?"

The Mistress blinked in obvious surprise, but recovered quickly. "Job training?" She laughed humorlessly. "Pardon me, *High Priestess*—" she made the title sound like a baby's nickname "—but I thought your position was a calling and not merely a job."

"Vernacular," Morrigan said shortly. "Where I'm from, a job can be a calling. Take my grandpa, for instance. He was a coach and a teacher—a man who shaped young boys and made a difference in their lives. He called it his job. It was, but it was also his calling. I'm from a different country, Shayla, but just because some of my words are different it doesn't mean the feeling behind them is wrong."

"Indeed," Shayla sniffed. "Still, it is not traditional for an *entourage* of priestesses to greet guests."

"Yes," Perth finally spoke. "They might believe some kind of religious fervor has overtaken the Sidetha."

"Ah, there you see—vernacular again. Where I'm from, religious fervor in a people would usually be considered a good thing. And tradition? I think I already messed that up once tonight. In Oklahoma during rituals the High Priestess bares herself before her goddess. So I got rid of this." Morrigan fingered the cape that was, once again, securely laced over her breasts and mentally crossed her fingers, thinking it wasn't a total lie. G-ma had told her about Wiccan friends of hers who performed rituals sky-clad—she had just stretched that truth. A little. While Shayla was glaring at her, Morrigan took Birkita's hand. "I'm ready. We probably shouldn't keep your guests waiting."

Without another word, Shayla turned her back on Morrigan and strode from the Great Chamber with Perth scrambling to keep up.

"This should be interesting," Morrigan muttered as she and Birkita followed the royal couple.

"Do not bait her so, child. Shayla is a dangerous enemy," Birkita whispered.

"Don't worry, Birkita. I'm a little dangerous myself. Plus, Adsagsona told me to follow my instincts, and my gut tells me that I need you with me."

"Perhaps you could find a way to prudently follow your instincts?"

Morrigan put her arm around Birkita and squeezed. "I'm eighteen. Nothing I do is prudent."

Birkita sighed. "That is what worries me."

Morrigan didn't reply. Too many people had joined them for a private conversation. Plus, curiosity was killing her. She recognized that they were following a gently upsloping pathway that mirrored the way she had entered the cave in Oklahoma. Of course, in Partholon the path was clean and beautifully decorated—and there were several tunnels that branched away from the main path that definitely weren't in her old world. But the general design was similar enough that Morrigan thought she could have easily found the surface by herself (without asking the spirits in the crystals for help). Sure enough, it wasn't long before she saw the rectangular-shaped opening of the mouth of the cave. Large torches and open brazier pits illuminated the area. Over the heads of the gathered men Morrigan could just glimpse the night sky, empty of a moon but overflowing with a sea of stars.

"Come," Birkita whispered to her. "You should be beside the Master and Mistress so that you may greet the guests in Adsagsona's name after Shayla and Perth greet them."

"That's all I have to do? Just greet them?"

Birkita nodded. "Make them welcome in Adsagsona's name. Tradition says that the High Priestess is also expected to break bread with them and see that they are well looked after, but Shayla has not followed that tradition in years."

"Okay, so I'll greet them and go on about my business. Now hold tight." Keeping a good grip on Birkita's hand, Morrigan tunneled her way through the crowd until the two of them popped out into the entryway like two corks surfacing in a turbulent pond. Morrigan hurried over to where Shayla and Perth were standing with Birkita close behind her. Perth was already speaking to someone who was just outside of Morrigan's line of vision.

"Stonemaster Kai, as always we are honored by your visit."

"Likewise, Kegan Dhiannon, we are pleasantly surprised as well as honored by a visit from Partholon's newly appointed Master Sculptor," Shayla said.

Morrigan forced herself not to roll her eyes at Shayla's oh-so-sickening-sweet tone. The woman definitely had issues. Recognizing her cue, Morrigan smoothed back her hair, raised her chin and stepped forward to complete her part of the greeting.

And her body froze. She couldn't breathe. She couldn't think. She couldn't move. Standing before her was a distinguished-looking middle-aged man and Kyle. Or at least the top half of Kyle. The bottom half of him was *a horse!*

A small squeak came out of her open mouth, so Morrigan quickly closed it. But the sound drew attention to her and she saw mirrored looks of shock pass over both men's faces.

"Stonemaster Kai, Master Sculptor Kegan, allow me to introduce to you our new High Priestess and Light Bringer, Morrigan." Birkita had moved swiftly up to stand beside Morrigan.

"Morrigan?"

"A Light Bringer?"

The two men spoke together. Their faces had gone utterly blank, but they were still staring at her. She could also feel Shayla's sharp gaze, along with curious looks from the Sidetha.

"Priestess?" Birkita prompted.

"Hello. Adsagsona welcomes you to the Realm of the Sidetha," Morrigan managed to say in a voice that sounded way calmer than she felt. From the corner of her eye she saw Birkita curtsy and then move to the side. Hardly conscious of feeling her body, Morrigan mimicked the old High Priestess.

For a few awful seconds Morrigan thought the two men were going to do nothing but stare at her, but Shayla's imperious voice broke the spell.

"Come, honored guests. Your journey from Epona's Temple has been long. Food and wine and soft beds await you."

"Thank you," said the man Shayla and Birkita had named

Kai. With an obvious effort, he stopped following Morrigan with his eyes and dismounted. "Sidetha's hospitality is much appreciated."

"Indeed," said Kyle the horse-man. (Who clearly didn't need to dismount because he was, well, *a horse.* The thought had Morrigan pressing her lips tightly together to ward off a hysterical bubble of laughter that threatened to escape.)

Hastily and as quietly as possible, Morrigan took several steps backward, wishing she was invisible. Kyle! How could Kyle be here? Kyle was in Oklahoma. Dead! *And how the hell could he be part horse?*

"Morrigan, you will, of course, join us," Shayla said, effectively cutting off Morrigan's retreat.

She could only nod mechanically, but she couldn't make her feet follow the group as they moved past her into the cave and headed toward the Great Chamber.

"A moment, Light Bringer. Your garment has come unlaced." Birkita stepped in front of Morrigan and pretended to relace and straighten the leather cape. "What is it?" Birkita whispered frantically. "What is the matter?"

"He's—he's half horse!" Morrigan hissed, choosing the easier of the two shocks to deal with first.

"Kegan is a centaur High Shaman of the Dhiannon herd. He has also recently been named Partholon's Master Sculptor." Birkita's brow was wrinkled with worry. "He is young, but well known to the Sidetha, as he has been traveling here since he was an adolescent to practice his vast carving skills."

"Birkita, centaurs don't exist in Oklahoma. Hell! They don't exist anywhere in my world. I'm sure he's a good guy, or whatever. But the fact that he exists is—well, it's more than a little shocking."

"A world without centaurs? That is hard to imagine, though I can understand why seeing your first centaur would be shocking, but you must control your reactions and carry out your duties." Impatiently Birkita drew Morrigan along with her back down the pathway.

"It's not just that. I know him, or at least the human part of him, from my old world."

"Are you quite sure?"

She hesitated. *Think! Don't just freak out.* "Kyle must be his mirror image, weird as it is that a guy who's half horse can have a human mirror image," Morrigan said more to herself than Birkita. Then she shook herself, reordering her thoughts. "It's like Rhiannon and Shannon are mirror images."

"And, I'm afraid, like you and Myrna are mirror images, too."

"Uh-oh," Morrigan said.

"Exactly," Birkita said.

9

"Maybe Shayla just wants to show she has control over me. She might leave me alone if I make an appearance and prove she can boss me around," Morrigan said. She and Birkita paused outside the Great Chamber.

"Let us hope…" Birkita said, but looked as doubtful as Morrigan felt.

Staying in the shadows of the entryway, they peered into the Great Chamber. Morrigan managed to stifle a groan. At the head table Shayla had seated herself between the centaur and Kai. Beside Shayla, the centaur had somehow reclined at the end of the table in place of the portion of bench usually used for seating—that is, when a person's body was person and not part horse. So actually the horse part of him was lying down, with legs tucked neatly under him, which should have looked awkward as hell, but instead seemed to work very well for him. Morrigan rubbed her temple where a tension headache was starting to pound.

"So you said Kegan—" Morrigan tripped only slightly over the name "—has visited here a lot?"

"Yes, he comes here much more often than other outsiders—well, by outsiders I'm not including Stonemaster Kai.

He has long been a visitor here. Kegan is unusual in many ways."

Morrigan snorted. "You mean other than being half horse?"

"Child, centaurs are not unusual in Partholon, though they do not visit here often. Kegan is unusual because he became a High Shaman at an unusually young age. Add to that the fact that he was recently made Partholon's Master Sculptor, an honor usually reserved for someone more than twice his age." Birkita smiled. "Kegan is unique. I quite like him, though he is somewhat of a rake."

"Rake?"

"He is very popular with the maidens."

Morrigan stared at Birkita. She was blushing! She looked back at the head table. Shayla pushed the centaur's shoulder playfully, and giggled ridiculously in response to something he said. Morrigan frowned. Jeesh, she was a hussy.

"Okay, anyway, Kegan comes here a lot and so does Kai."

"Yes, as Partholon's Stonemaster, Kai chooses which stones are to be used in all major building projects, and also for minor jobs completed for important people." Birkita lowered her voice even more before she continued. "Shayla tends to show powerful visitors *special attention*." She looked pointedly at Morrigan, leaving no doubt as to what kind of *special* attention Shayla liked to show. "And Kai has long been a favorite of the Mistress. I have often thought that she would have mated with him had he been of the Sidetha, and her desire for him is one reason she disdains Perth." Birkita shook her head. "It does not help that Kai is here so often, choosing stone for statues to honor Epona."

"Jeesh, talk about a Lifetime Movie of the Week," Morrigan muttered. Then she had another thought. "So, with all this stone-choosing-for-the-goddess stuff, Kai must know Shan—" Morrigan hesitated, stumbling over the name "—I mean Rhiannon."

Birkita nodded. "Stonemaster Kai has long lived at Epona's Temple. If Kegan hasn't moved there yet, he soon will. Epona's Temple is also where the Goddess's Chosen, Rhiannon, lives."

"Crap. Both of them must know Myrna."

"I know that Kai is very close to Rhiannon and her family. And even were Kegan not Master Sculptor, he's a High Shaman, which means he meets with Partholon's centaur High Shaman, ClanFintan, often."

Morrigan gave Birkita a blank look. Birkita sighed. "Clan-Fintan is mated with Rhiannon. Epona always fashions a centaur High Shaman as lifemate for her Chosen."

Morrigan felt her stomach lurch. "Shannon has sex with a centaur?" Then she felt another jolt of shock. "Myrna's dad is the half-horse mirror of my dad! Well, shit! No wonder Rhiannon revolted and escaped to Oklahoma."

"Quietly, child!" Birkita pulled Morrigan from the entry-way of the Great Chamber back down the deserted path. Still speaking in a hushed voice, Birkita said, "High Shamans are shape-shifters. Rhiannon would have coupled with him only after he shifted to his human form."

"Well, that's a relief." Morrigan rubbed her forehead again. "Birkita, I'm in way over my head here. I just don't know enough about Partholon. Too bad this world doesn't have the Internet."

"Internet?"

"A way of getting a lot of information about almost any-thing really fast."

"*You* have that, Light Bringer."

"Huh? The Internet? Uh, Birkita, I really don't think so."

Birkita smiled. "You have a way of getting information. Here." She touched Morrigan's head. "And here." She touched the spot over her heart. "Listen to your instincts and let the Goddess guide them."

Morrigan stopped herself from asking how she could be sure

she was listening to the right voices in her head and heart. *I need to believe in myself.* "I'll try, Birkita, I really will, but that won't help with the fact that I probably look just like Myrna, and Kegan and Kai know it." Thinking, Morrigan chewed her bottom lip. "Okay, the only thing I can do is avoid those two as much as possible. Hopefully, out of sight will mean out of mind. Plus, there are people who resemble other people. It's really not that weird."

"Perhaps a strong resemblance is all you have with Myrna."

"Yeah, so let's go in there and sit at a table away from the head table. Shayla's definitely preoccupied—she might not even notice us. We'll make an appearance, and get out of there as soon as possible."

"It is a good plan," Birkita said.

"Okay, here we go..."

Together they entered the Great Chamber. Morrigan headed straight to a table several removed from the head table, one where many of the other priestesses were sitting.

"Ah, Morrigan. There you are," Shayla called from across the room.

Morrigan stopped and made a quick curtsy in the general direction of the head table. "Sorry to make you wait. I'll just join the other priestesses at—"

Shayla made an imperious gesture. "No, no, no. You must join us." She paused, then added with a frown, "Birkita, too, of course." Then she turned her attention to Kai. "The Stonemaster and Master Sculptor steadfastly refuse to reveal to us the purpose of their unexpected visit until our new High Priestess joins us." Shayla was talking to Morrigan, but her gaze barely touched on the High Priestess. Instead she smiled back and forth from Kegan to Kai. She gave the Stonemaster a coquettish, under-her-eyelashes glance. "Tonight Kai's face is even more unreadable than usual." Then she swung her flirtatious gaze around to Kegan. "And our centaur friend is being unusually closemouthed. I cannot begin to guess what patron they are here for, which really is rather teasing of both of them." As she spoke, she gave Kai a pout and touched his arm, which made the sober-faced Stonemaster glance around nervously and look obviously uncomfortable.

When Morrigan continued to hesitate, Birkita whispered to her, "Refusal will only draw more attention to you."

Reluctantly Morrigan changed direction to the head table, and was further disconcerted to see that the only places left empty were two spots directly across from Shayla and Kegan. She sat quickly and motioned immediately for a server to bring her something to eat and drink while she kept her eyes averted and her face turned away from the way-too-familiar-looking horse-man who sat across from her.

"When did you become High Priestess, Morrigan?"

Kegan's voice—so like Kyle's that it made her stomach clench—was deep and emotionless. Morrigan looked up and the intensity with which he was staring at her completely belied his tone. Meeting his gaze, it seemed that she had somehow said or done something to upset him deeply.

"I, well. Um. I became High Priestess just—just a few days ago," she managed to stutter, completely thrown off-balance by his soul-piercing gaze.

"I was here four cycles of the moon ago. I did not see you with the other priestesses then, and no mention was made of Adsagsona choosing another High Priestess," Kai said. He too was watching Morrigan with an incredibly focused expression.

"Most especially we had no news of the coming of a Light Bringer," Kegan said.

"You didn't see her and you didn't hear about her because she wasn't here." The sultry tone had left Shayla's voice, making her annoyance at the men's interest in Morrigan obvious.

"Yes, Adsagsona gave her to us," Perth chimed in. Morrigan thought he made her sound like a crappy present given to an unwanted stepchild.

"Yes, yes, yes. Birkita foretold it. She waited in the Usgaran until Morrigan appeared. And now you know the story of our new Light Bringer and High Priestess." Shayla paused, collected herself, and then continued with a smile for Kai and Kegan, which was completely wasted on its intended victims because neither sets of eyes had left Morrigan's face. "Stonemaster, you promised you would reveal the reason for your visit when the High Priestess joined us." Shayla leaned into Kai, allowing her breast to graze his arm. "Morrigan is here, so let us not waste time with chatter."

Morrigan decided she'd seen subtler moves on MTV rap videos.

With an obvious effort, Kai took his gaze from Morrigan. Ignoring Shayla, he spoke past her to the centaur. "Kegan, will you make the announcement, or shall I?"

"I'm just the sculptor. You're the Stonemaster and messenger," the centaur said.

"Very well." Kai stood and walked up the short steps to stand in front of the mosaic of Adsagsona. He waited for the room to quiet. It wasn't until then that Morrigan noticed how tired and dirty he looked. Several strands of his long brown hair had come loose from the tie that held the rest of it back. His clothes— leather pants with a plain linen shirt tucked into them and a well-tooled leather coat—were travel-stained and rumpled. His eyes were shadowed by fatigue and his face was heavily lined. Not that he wasn't a handsome man—he definitely was, even for an older guy, with his broad shoulders, square, strong jaw and kind face. But he looked really tired and sad, and Morrigan wondered what had happened to him. Finally, the Great Chamber was silent and everyone had turned their attention to the Stonemaster.

"Your Mistress asks why the Master Sculptor and I have journeyed here today in such haste. We come because we have been commissioned with the task of choosing the marble for, and then carving the effigy of, one who was very dear to Partholon." A concerned murmur began in the crowd, but Kai's raised hand stilled it. "Seven days ago Myrna, the daughter of Epona's Beloved, Rhiannon, died giving birth to a daughter. The child lives. I believe the babe is all that keeps Rhiannon tied to this earth." He paused, clearly having to fight to control his emotions.

Morrigan felt as if someone had driven their fist into her gut. Myrna was dead. Myrna. Shannon's daughter—the person who could have, probably should have, been her. Should have lived her life. Should have grown up being loved by her grandparents. And she was dead. Then another punch hit her. Myrna had died seven days ago. It was exactly seven days ago that Morrigan had passed through the selenite boulder and entered Partholon. Suddenly cold to the bone, Morrigan wrapped her arms tightly around herself.

Kai continued. "Partholon's High Priestess is in deep mourning, and though the pyre was made and the funeral bier for Myrna burned, she asked that a likeness of her beloved only child be carved to hold her ashes and to be a memorial to her. That is our sad task." Kai paused again and bowed his head slightly to Shayla.

From his place at the table, Kegan spoke up. "The Lady Rhiannon asks that I be allowed to stay with the Sidetha until I've completed the carving of the effigy. I ask your permission to do so, Mistress Shayla—" he turned to bow slightly to Perth "—and Master Perth."

"Kegan, of course you may remain here with us until your task is complete," Shayla said before she rushed up the stairs and took Kai's hands. "I know how close you have been to

Epona's Chosen and her family. I am so very sorry for your loss."

Perth got to his feet and joined his wife's very public condolences. Then Birkita's arm slid around Morrigan's waist. "Are you well, child?"

Morrigan leaned into the older woman, needing her comfort and her warmth. "No," she whispered. "No, I'm not okay. It was the day I got here, wasn't it? That's the day she died."

"Yes, it was."

"What's going on? I don't understand what's going on," Morrigan whispered frantically.

"Not here, child."

Morrigan clamped her lips closed on the questions that were swarming through her mind. Birkita was right. She needed to keep it together.

She felt his eyes on her before he spoke.

"Perhaps you will offer prayers to your goddess asking that Myrna's spirit's journey to Epona's meadows be swift?" Kegan asked.

Morrigan looked at the bizarrely familiar centaur. "Yes, of course I will," she said.

"Thank you, High Priestess." Even though his smile was shadowed with sadness, she found herself responding to it. His human half looked so much like Kyle! With the way he was sitting, his human torso was about all Morrigan could see of him. And most of that was muscular and mostly bare since the little leather vest he wore didn't do much to cover all that golden tan skin. Like Kyle, Kegan was so blond that his thick hair was almost gold. His skin was more tanned than his human mirror's though, which made him look healthier and sexier, too.

With a start, Morrigan realized she'd been gawking at him like a kid. "You're welcome," she said quickly.

Kai, Shayla and Perth returned to the table. Shayla was still murmuring soft condolences to Kegan and Kai that Morrigan thought sounded too damn much like flirty cooing. Birkita squeezed her arm. When Morrigan glanced at her, the older woman gave her a pointed look before standing.

"Mistress, if you will excuse us, the High Priestess has said that she would like to offer prayers tomorrow for the spirit of Myrna. Indeed, all of the priestesses should join her in petitioning Adsagsona to aid Myrna's journey to the Otherworld, as well as offering prayers for Epona's Chosen. There is much to be done for such an offering." Birkita glanced over her shoulder and made a small motion, at which all of the priestesses present got to their feet, curtsied to the head table and began to leave.

Taking that as her cue, Morrigan stood. "Yes, we have a lot to do."

"Very well. You are excused," Shayla said dismissively.

"Epona's Chosen would appreciate your offer of prayers for her daughter's spirit," Kai said abruptly.

Morrigan met the Stonemaster's eyes, wondering at his weird tone. "I'm glad to do it," she told him. She'd already curtsied and had begun turning to go when Kegan's voice stopped her short.

"Where did you come from?"

She looked back at him and opened her mouth to say, *Oklahoma, which is across the B'an Sea in the southwest,* but what actually came out of her face was, "I came from the Goddess."

Kegan continued to stare at her for several heartbeats, then he bowed his head and said with a small, ironic smile, "I have no doubt of that at all, my Lady."

Thankfully, Birkita took her hand and pulled her from the Great Chamber before anything else unexpected could come out of her mouth, but as they made their way across the large room Morrigan could feel Kegan's eyes still on her.

10

There weren't a great number of Sidetha guest chambers, but the few they had were large, comfortable and private. Kegan knew them well. He also knew they were so private because the Mistress of the Sidetha preferred it so. The centaur frowned and rubbed a hand through his hair. Shayla, unfortunately, never changed. Her masque was predictably the same. She liked to seduce visitors. Not all visitors, of course. Only those who were most powerful. By the Goddess, he'd hardly been more than a pubescent colt when she'd started his seduction. Perhaps this visit she would be so focused on Kai, a longtime favorite of hers, that he could avoid her completely. Kegan knew her game; he had wearied of it years ago. At first she would offer herself, warm and seductive, pliant, even. When he rejected her she would show her true nature and turn cold and sarcastic. He didn't need to wonder about why she kept offering herself to him even though he'd been rejecting her for the past several years. He understood her well. She knew even before he knew it himself that as High Shaman and the youngest Master Sculptor in Partholon's history he would one day command a high level of respect and power. Shayla craved both.

And the unfortunate truth was that he had not always rejected her.

Kai rubbed his hand through his hair again. He needed a bath and a good night's sleep. The bath was easy enough to come by. Sleep would be more elusive. He must talk with the Stonemaster about what had happened. With a weary sigh he made his way to the next guest chamber, but he hesitated before going inside. There was little doubt that Kai would be even more shaken by her than he had been, and the Stonemaster's mood had been dark enough lately to—

"Stop lurking and come in," Kai called gruffly from the other side of the leather-curtained doorway.

Kegan pushed aside the thick drape that closed the room off from the passageway. The centaur looked around and nodded in approval. "I suppose it's only right that your chamber be more opulent than mine. You are the obvious favorite."

Kai frowned at him. "I don't think you're here to talk about the decor or my status with the Sidetha."

"It's bizarre, isn't it?" Kegan said as he crossed the chamber and filled two goblets with wine. He handed Kai one and then took a long drink from his. "She looks too much like Myrna for it to be a coincidence."

"She's not Myrna," Kai said flatly.

"Again, I say she looks too much like her for it to just be a coincidence. The goddesses are at work here, of that there is little doubt."

"People can look alike without there being divine intervention."

The centaur's brows went up and his lips quirked sardonically. "The Sidetha's new High Priestess and our dead Myrna do not simply look alike. They are mirrors of one another."

"They aren't mirrors. Myrna was big with child. Morrigan

is still as slender as—" He broke off and Kegan continued the thought for him.

"As Myrna was before she got with child. No, Morrigan doesn't look like Myrna did recently, but go back nine cycles of the moon and then tell me the two could not be mistaken for each other."

"They could," Kai said reluctantly.

"What would Lady Rhiannon do if she—"

It was Kai's turn to interrupt. "No! Neither you nor I will tell the Lady Rhiannon that there is a High Priestess of the Sidetha whose looks mimic those of her newly dead daughter."

"Perhaps it would comfort her." Kegan shrugged. "And it was whispered that Lady Rhiannon was truly disappointed when Myrna showed no sign of being touched by Epona. This Morrigan is already a High Priestess, and did they not call her Light Bringer, too?"

"They did."

Kegan knew Kai was probably unfamiliar with a Light Bringer's gifts, but the centaur High Shaman knew exactly what the title implied and how rare a manifestation of power it was. "Kai, a Light Bringer is a spectacular gift. Do you not think Epona's Chosen would want to know that Adsagsona has given her people such a rare gift?"

"Do you honestly believe that it would cause Lady Rhiannon anything but more pain to be faced with a powerful priestess who resembles her dead child!"

"Consider carefully, Kai. Clearly there is a goddess at work here."

Kai studied the handsome young centaur before he replied. "You attempted to woo Myrna, did you not?"

Kegan shrugged again. "What of it? Many centaur High Shamans courted the daughter of Epona's Chosen. Had she followed her mother and become the next Beloved of Epona, one of us would have been fashioned by the Goddess to love her."

"If I remember correctly, you more than any other centaur spent a considerable amount of time courting her."

"I did. Myrna was attractive and intelligent. It was no hardship to spend time with her. Besides—" he grinned "—I have never hidden the fact that I enjoy the attention of females, be they human or centaur."

"And had Myrna chosen you as her mate you would have been the most powerful male in Partholon."

Kegan's nonchalant attitude shifted and hardened. "Had she chosen me it would have meant that Epona had fashioned me to love her for eternity."

"Which means for this lifetime you would have been the most powerful male in Partholon."

Kegan's face relaxed and his boyish grin returned. "All of Partholon knows that. There is no shame in desiring the position of Partholon's High Shaman, especially when it comes with such a delectable mate."

"But she didn't choose a centaur High Shaman as her mate."

Kegan snorted. "No, she chose a grape grower. A *human*. And thus dashed her mother's dream of having her daughter follow her as Epona's Chosen."

"So you think this Sidetha High Priestess would be a good substitute because Lady Rhiannon obviously stopped loving her daughter when it became clear she wouldn't be Chosen by Epona?" Kai's voice was heavily sarcastic.

"I did not say Lady Rhiannon stopped loving Myrna. I simply repeated common court gossip about Epona's Chosen being disappointed in her daughter's choice."

"*Common court gossip* should be beneath you to repeat."

Frustrated at the stubborn old Stonemaster, Kegan paced while he tried to reason with Kai. "Court gossip aside, I have simply stated the obvious—that Morrigan's resemblance to Myrna is too great to be ignored. That I believe the divine is at work here."

"And you suggest we do what?"

"I only suggest that we leave ourselves open to the divine."

Kai narrowed his eyes. "Do you mean we, or you?"

"Both of us, of course."

"Well, *I* suggest that leaving ourselves open to the divine does *not* mean we need to relay hurtful news to Lady Rhiannon." Kegan started to speak, but the Stonemaster interrupted him. "Which means we also do not need to share the fact that Morrigan so closely resembles Myrna with any of the Sidetha."

Kegan raised an eyebrow. "You will have more to do with that than I. You're Shayla's favorite, and the Mistress is also one of the few Sidetha to be educated outside of their Realm. If any of them were to recognize Morrigan it would be Shayla."

Kai sighed and stared into his wine. "Her sharp eyes miss nothing," he muttered. "I suppose I will simply have to be sure the Mistress is too preoccupied to think of such things."

Kegan tried unsuccessfully to cover his knowing grin. "It's a good thing you are a man of such experience." He cleared his throat to hide a chuckle. "Well, I happen to agree with you that no one else in Partholon need know that the mirror image of Lady Rhiannon's newly dead daughter is the Sidetha's High Priestess—at least they don't need to know at this time. Perhaps my mind, or yours, will change before we return to Epona's Temple." Kegan upended his goblet, finishing off the rest of it. He wiped his mouth with the back of his hand and gave Kai a jaunty little bow. "I'll leave you to your rest, Stonemaster." Just before he ducked back through the leather curtain he grinned over his shoulder at the older man. "You should know I've decided to spend as much time with Morrigan as possible as part of how I am going to remain open to the working of the divine. I suggest you spend an equal amount of time avoiding Shayla's questions. I'm sure you'll find a way to keep her mouth busy with other duties." Laughing, Kegan left the chamber with Kai's growl of "Damn arrogant centaur!" following behind him.

Kegan was still smiling to himself as he went into his well-appointed private bathing chamber and washed the layers of travel dirt and sweat from his body. What an amazing stroke of fate—to find a powerful priestess who was the twin image of the dead, and decidedly powerless, Myrna. He'd made light of his failed attempt to woo Myrna to Kai. The truth had been that Kegan had been drawn to the daughter of Epona's Chosen from the first instant the two of them had been introduced. It had been more than a blow to his ego when she obviously felt no similar attraction to him and had completely rejected him. *For a powerless human.* It still amazed Kegan.

Perhaps the appearance of this *other* Myrna, this young woman who had been touched by a goddess and gifted with unusual power, would be a second chance for them. Epona's ways were often as mysterious as they were difficult.

And he certainly wouldn't mind the additional power gaining such a mate would accord him.

Deep in thought, Kegan returned to his chamber and, with a sigh, made himself comfortable on the thick pallet of furs that had been made up for him on the floor. He closed his eyes, trying to will himself asleep even though against his lids he saw Morrigan's face—the face that looked so much like Myrna. When he finally did sleep, his dreams were filled with the echo of a woman's weeping.

"I must look as much like Myrna as Kegan looks like Kyle," Morrigan said as Birkita helped her change into her sleeping gown. After sending the other priestesses off to braid ropes of sacred herbs for the special prayer ritual the next day, they were finally alone.

"Kyle?" Birkita said, motioning for Morrigan to sit so she could comb out her hair.

"He's the man I knew in Oklahoma who looks just like Kegan. Uh, except he's definitely not half horse."

Birkita stopped combing Morrigan's hair and studied her face. "There was something between this Kyle and you."

Morrigan sighed. "You're just like Grandma. She always knew stuff about me I wish she didn't know."

"Tell me."

"The day I came here was the first day I'd ever been in a cave."

Birkita's eyes widened in shock. "You said the Keep of Oklahoma had caves."

"It does, but people don't live in them."

"How can that be?"

"It's not like it is here. Caves in Oklahoma, well, actually, caves all over my old world are a lot rougher than the Sidetha's caves. People visit caves, but they don't live in them—at least not anymore. So that day was the first day I'd ever visited a cave. It was the first day I'd ever heard the spirits in the crystals greet me as Light Bringer. It was also the first time I'd met Kyle."

"Kyle had something to do with the cave?"

Morrigan nodded. "Yeah, his job was to guide people through it. He also lived on the grounds of the cave, but I didn't know that until I went back late that night." She stopped and swallowed hard, hating the memory of what she'd caused. "I fought with my grandparents. It was a stupid argument. *I* was stupid. I guess you could say I ran away, and I ran to the cave."

"Of course you did, child. You belong in the womb of the Goddess, and you would find comfort there."

"I didn't really understand that then. I just kinda ended up there. It was late and I thought the place was deserted. I went into the cave and called the lights of the crystals to me. It—it was amazing. Birkita, I was filled with such incredible power, and I felt *right*."

Birkita nodded in silent but complete understanding.

"Well, Kyle saw the light and followed me into the cave. We, uh…. He and I, we had a connection earlier that day, and when he saw me calling the crystals to light he…uh…"

Birkita smoothed back Morrigan's hair and smiled. "It is often an awe-inspiring experience to be touched by a goddess."

"Well, it was more than just awe-inspiring." Morrigan felt her cheeks getting hot. "It was, uh…" She paused, discarding words like *hot* and *sexy.* Finally she finished in an embarrassed rush, "It was really passionate."

Birkita's smile was knowing. "I never married, child, but that does not mean I am a stranger to passion."

Morrigan's cheeks were blazing. She really did *not* want to go into what had been happening between Kyle and her. "Anyway, my grandparents found me in the cave with Kyle, and we were in the middle of that really embarrassing scene when a cave-in happened. My grandparents got out, I'm sure they did, but Kyle wouldn't leave me. He—he was killed, and that's when I went into the crystal boulder and came here."

"And that is why Kegan's presence has affected you so."

Morrigan nodded and silently added, *And that's why Shayla's flirty crap is so damn annoying, too.* "This is all so messed up, especially because Kegan and the Stonemaster definitely recognize me," she said miserably.

"Perhaps it is not such a bad thing." Birkita spoke slowly, as if she was thinking through the situation aloud. "Partholon's Master Sculptor and Stonemaster are not going to rush back to Epona's Temple to tell the grieving Beloved of Epona that a mirror image of her newly dead daughter lives with the Sidetha. What good would that accomplish?"

"I don't know," Morrigan said, even though the thought of Shannon Parker, the woman she had believed up until a few days ago was her mother, knowing she was in Partholon made an intense thrill skitter through her body.

"It would accomplish nothing. It would only cause Lady Rhiannon pain. They will say nothing, or at least they will say nothing until more time has passed. And it seems to me that there is a reason Partholon's Master Sculptor is the mirror image of the man with whom you were connected in your old world."

Morrigan started to correct Birkita. To tell her that she really hadn't had enough time to be connected to Kyle, but then she thought about the way he had looked at her, and how his hands and lips had felt on her body, and had to suppress a shiver of remembered desire.

"Perhaps Adsagsona has brought Kegan to you. And, child, gifts from a goddess should never be ignored."

In Morrigan's dreams that night a man came to her. He had Kyle's body. His hands were Kyle's and his lips were Kyle's, but she could not see his face. While he made love to her with a passion that bordered on violence, circling around and around in her head she heard a man's mocking laughter.

11

In the morning Morrigan was awake long before Birkita came to her chamber. She'd gotten up and dressed carefully in a flowing, butter-colored dress that was made of a material that felt like a mixture of expensive linen and heavy silk. It hung beautifully around her body and was trimmed in yellow faceted stones. Then she'd curled up on her pallet, resting her back against the living stone of the cave wall, and as she petted Brina, Morrigan thought about Myrna.

Her grandparents had said that Rhiannon and Shannon looked like mirror images of one another. She'd seen Rhiannon in the selenite crystal, and so she knew that what they had said was true. Except for the sadness in her smile, Rhiannon and Shannon could have been clones. Kyle and Kegan definitely looked alike. Even with the small changes in Kegan—like the length of his hair—and the major changes— like the fact that the back half of him was a horse—the two could easily be mistaken for each other. Grandpa had said that her father had been the mirror image of Shannon's husband in Partholon, and, according to Birkita he was a centaur, too. It was no less true because it was bizarre. So, logically, she and

Myrna must look almost exactly alike, too. Only, Myrna had died the same day Morrigan had entered Partholon.

What was it her mother's spirit had said? Something about the blood sacrifice being made so she could pass through the Divide into Partholon. Morrigan had assumed Rhiannon had meant Kyle, but now she wasn't so sure.

It was disconcerting enough that Shannon's daughter had looked exactly like her, and it gave her a dull, queasy feeling to think that Myrna was now dead. *And maybe because of me.* No. Morrigan's stomach rolled, and for a second she thought that she might actually throw up. *No,* she repeated firmly to herself. She couldn't have had anything to do with Myrna's death—she'd been in Oklahoma. Until the day of that terrible cave-in Morrigan hadn't even known Partholon existed, let alone Myrna.

But the dark god Pryderi knew Partholon existed, and she would bet he also knew Myrna existed—he definitely knew Morrigan existed. According to her grandpa, Pryderi had been present at her birth.

"No!" Brina yowled a complaint as Morrigan pushed to her feet and began pacing the chamber. "Pryderi doesn't have anything to do with me. I belong to Adsagsona. I'm not like my mother. I'm not going to listen to the whispers of a dark god." Of course, her grandpa had said that Rhiannon hadn't realized she had been listening to darkness until it was too late. "It's not the same thing. Plus, I've been warned, so I know what to watch out for." She stopped pacing and stared at her reflection in the vanity mirror. "I had nothing to do with Myrna's death, but it's not a surprise that finding out about her, and the fact that she's dead, has freaked me out. Prayers for her soul—at least that's something positive I can do."

"Morrigan?" Birkita called from the other side of the leather curtain. "May I come in?"

"Yeah, yes, of course," Morrigan called quickly.

Birkita looked around as she entered the chamber. "Are you alone? I thought I heard voices within."

Morrigan pointed at her reflection and smiled sheepishly. "Just me talking to myself."

Birkita's smile looked only a little worried. "Shall we break our fast?"

"I—I think I want to say prayers for Myrna first." Morrigan stopped and drew a deep breath. "No, I don't *think*. I know I want to say prayers for Myrna before I eat. It makes sense to me. Yesterday I had to fast before the Dark Moon Ritual. This isn't any less important," she finished with a calm sense of surety that she was right to follow this intuition.

"Yes, my Lady," Birkita said with approval in her voice. "If you wait here, I will call together the priestesses."

"Let Kegan and Kai know, too."

"I will, my Lady."

After Birkita left, Morrigan continued to stare at her reflection in the mirror. "Do you have a clue what you're doing?"

You are embracing your destiny…

The words seemed to float around her in the cool, earthy air of the cave. Morrigan tried to hear the Goddess's voice in them, but all she could really be sure of was the sound of her own doubts.

Morrigan decided that she liked the solemn fuss when all of her priestesses (they called themselves *her* priestesses!) came to escort her to the Usgaran for the special prayer ritual. She also liked the sweet scent of the lavender and sage braids each of them carried. It clung to them, reminding Morrigan suddenly of fragrant Oklahoma springtime, sitting on her grandparents' patio watching hummingbirds feed from the blossoms of mimosa trees.

There were twelve priestesses, and they made a column of twos—six and six—in front of Morrigan. Brina padded beside her when they slowly moved off down the tunnel in a wave of scent and complete silence, which gave her plenty of time to wonder where Birkita was and to get an even sicker nervous stomach as they approached the Usgaran.

The large chamber was deserted except for Kegan, Kai and (thankfully) Birkita. The three of them stood in front of the selenite boulder. As the priestesses entered the chamber, Birkita met Morrigan and curtsied respectfully to her. The priestesses took their places, six on either side of the boulder. Then, as one, they turned to the burning braziers around the circumference of the room and lit the thick ropes of lavender and sage they carried. Allowing the braids of dried herbs to burn for just a moment or two, the priestesses blew them out and then repositioned themselves about the great central boulder as the incenselike smoke from the smoldering ropes wafted in gray, foggy swirls around them.

Morrigan was shocked anew at the terrible beauty of the centaur, and she had a hard time keeping her eyes from him. Kegan looked young and handsome and completely exotic, though his expression was properly sober and sad, and she wondered just how friendly he'd been with Myrna…Birkita had called him a "rake." Morrigan clamped down on that thought right away, and then told herself Myrna's relationship with Kegan was none of her damn business. She needed to focus on prayers for the dead girl's soul, not the soap-opera stuff that might have been going on with her.

Morrigan stopped looking at Kegan and walked forward until she stood directly in front of the massive selenite boulder, as she had the night before during the Dark Moon Ritual. This morning the boulder remained dark, as she had left it. She closed her eyes and concentrated. What should she say to help the soul of Myrna, and to help those she left behind? Like her mom. Shannon. The woman Morrigan had dreamed as her own mom and longed for and missed her entire life. A sudden burst of anger fueled by despair shot through her and Morrigan lifted her arms over her head and began the ritual in a voice that rang against the crystal walls of the chamber.

"Adsagsona, I call upon you above!" She paused and drew her arms down to form the open-palmed reverse V. "And below." Keeping her eyes closed, she continued while trying to wade through the complex emotions Myrna's life and death caused within her. "Visitors here, Master Sculptor Kegan and Stonemaster Kai, have brought us sad news. Myrna, the daughter of Epona's Chosen, has died. So your priestesses and I ask that you help her soul find the Realm of her goddess, and that you also help those she left behind. That somehow you ease their pain and their grief." Eyes still closed, Morrigan paused, struggling with a wave of jealousy that threatened to drown her. Right now Shannon was probably crying about the death of her daughter— the same way Morrigan had soaked her pillow endless nights during her childhood while she cried herself to sleep staring at Shannon's picture, aching for a mother she could never have. But all that time—all those nights— Shannon had been alive and happy and living in Partholon, loving her *real* daughter.

With an intensity that made her body begin to tremble, Morrigan wished that her grandparents hadn't kept the truth from her. It wasn't fair. If they had told her, maybe she could have found the way to Partholon sooner—she definitely would have looked for it—and then she could have had a mother, even if it was a mother she had to share with her mirror image. After all, Myrna was dead. Morrigan was alive. Shannon would still have her. But that choice had been taken away from her. Like a fire fueled by the old, dry deadwood of a painful past, Morrigan's frustration and anger ignited.

Birkita's voice suddenly filled in the silence that had begun to gather uncomfortably in the Usgaran. "O gracious goddess who gives rest, O Lady of the twilight realms and womb of the earth, we do thank you for helping to guide Myrna's spirit to the golden portals of the beauteous meadows of Epona. It is said that arrayed in a new flesh someday another mother will give birth, so that with sturdier body and brighter mind the old spirit will take the earthly road again. We wish that journey to be joyous for Myrna, daughter of Rhiannon MacCallan, Epona's Chosen and most Beloved of her Goddess."

At first Morrigan was relieved that Birkita had taken up the ritual, but as she listened to her, other emotions engulfed the relief. Birkita knew Rhiannon was Morrigan's mother, not Myrna's, yet she had named her specifically! Couldn't she just have called her Epona's Chosen? And why did she have to remind everyone that she was "most Beloved of her Goddess"? Her mother, the *real* Rhiannon MacCallan, had served that role for a good part of her life. Grandpa had even said that Epona had forgiven her for her mistakes right before she died. Birkita should show more respect for Rhiannon than that. Before the old High Priestess could say anything else, Morrigan spoke, and as she did she felt anger burn brightly within her.

*Yes…your anger is good…righteous…*whispered seductively through her mind.

"It's not just for Myrna or her mother that I pray today. It's for everyone who has been hurt by this death. Everyone who is saddened by the injustice of the situation." Morrigan kept her eyes squeezed shut and spoke passionately. To her the words had more than a double meaning. They had depth and layers—different levels of sadness and grief, pain and loss. "Help us to find happiness in the sadness, meaning in the unjust, light in the darkness. And maybe, just maybe, I can be a part of that light in the darkness." The anger that had been smoldering inside her for years continued to flame. She opened flashing eyes and hurled her hands out before her as if she was throwing all of the emotions inside her at the crystal boulder. "Hear me, spirits of the crystals! Let there be light!" It wasn't just the boulder that responded to her. Every piece of selenite crystal in the entire Usgaran blazed into glorious, furious light.

Morrigan lifted her arms, reveling in the passion and the power that pulsed around and through her.

Yes! Claim your power. Claim your destiny.

"I do claim what is mine. I am High Priestess and it is my light that blazes here for everyone who has been hurt or wronged." *I'm not an outsider and an orphan anymore,* she added silently to the voice in her mind.

The moment Morrigan entered the Usgaran, Kegan felt the anticipatory thrum of the crystals. It passed through him as if he was standing there naked and a lover had just blown teasing air across his sweat-dampened skin. He'd watched her approach the sacred boulder and had been surprised, as well as taken aback, by the way she had scrutinized him. When she finally began the ritual her voice was impassioned, as if Morrigan had been deeply saddened by Myrna's death. She had been so emotional that for a time she had not been able to go on, and it had appeared that Birkita was going to have to complete the prayers for her.

Then Morrigan had begun speaking again and her tone had completely changed. Her voice was filled with an anger and intensity that had more to do with battle than funerals, and when she opened her eyes and commanded the crystals to light, it was with a ferocity that blazed passion and anger and need—not lamentation and loss. But the crystals were not the only things that lit. Morrigan, too, flamed. The room was hazy with smoke from the sweet ritual herbs, and the light from the crystals caught the wispy, curling vapor, giving everything an eerie, underwater cast. Morrigan stood in the center of the sea kingdom, a magnificent goddess robed in light. Power pulsed around her, lifting her hair with its elemental strength. Kegan's breath whooshed out of his chest as, mesmerized, he watched her claim her destiny. The shaman in his spirit automatically responded to her. Morrigan was definitely not Myrna. Rhiannon's daughter had been beautiful and intelligent, sweet, even, beloved by her parents and content that her destiny was not to serve the Goddess.

The woman that blazed before him made Myrna look like an incomplete, poorly sketched copy of the original. And she drew Kegan as if her light was his guiding flame, making the attraction he had felt for Myrna seem weak and insubstantial in comparison.

Of course he had desired Myrna. She'd been attractive; they had been friends, and as Kai had so crassly noted, had she loved him he would have been the most powerful male in Partholon. Naturally, he'd been interested in her. But he'd never felt anything for her like what he was feeling for Morrigan. Watching her, Kegan's body pulsed and he had to stifle the urge to touch her—to go to her and call the Change so he could shape-shift into human form and take her there on the floor of the Usgaran. He could feel the heat and passion and power of her through the very stone that surrounded them, and he desired her with an intensity he had known for no female, woman or centaur, before her.

Kegan heard an odd, choked sound to his right and he glanced over to see Kai staring at Morrigan with a mixed expression of awe and sadness. Anger filled the centaur. He knew it was unreasonable. He knew he had no right. But he didn't want any other male to be drawn to Morrigan, even if it was only the Stonemaster and he was probably only staring at her like that because he was overwhelmed by her bizarre resemblance to Myrna.

It was then that Morrigan shouted, "Hail, Adsagsona!" The priestesses echoed her cry and the ritual was over. Morrigan lowered her hands and shook back her hair. Her body had lost most, but not all, of its glow. Kegan thought she looked slightly dazed. She just stood there, gazing at the sacred boulder while the priestesses put out the smoking herb ropes and began to quietly file out of the chamber as they gave their High Priestess furtive looks that were almost fearful.

"Incredible..." Kai said softly, still staring at Morrigan. "Have you ever seen anything like that?"

"No. No one has for three generations."

"What do you mean?"

Kegan took his gaze from Morrigan long enough to fix Kai with a hard look. "After all the years you've spent with the Sidetha, did you never study their lore?"

Kai frowned. "I have, of course, become knowledgeable about Adsagsona, and I consider myself friendly with their old High Priestess, Birkita, but the focus of their people has not exactly been on the spiritual."

Kegan snorted. "You mean Shayla's mercenary nature has tainted them."

"And I could argue that Shayla's nature has been what has brought such an era of prosperity to her people, but be that as it may, it has been my duty to act as intermediary between the reclusive Sidetha and those in Partholon who wish to purchase products found only in their Realm. It has not been my duty to study their spiritual history. You are the High Shaman, not I."

Kegan thought about mentioning the fact that Kai had become Stonemaster because of his spiritual gifts; therefore, he should at least be curious about other gifts from the

Goddess, but he decided that he was probably just being overly sensitive. Truthfully, Kai had no reason so delve into the spiritual past of the Sidetha. Kegan knew their lore only because of his training as a High Shaman.

"She's a Light Bringer, which means her powers are easily as vast as mine. If not more so," he explained.

Kai looked thoroughly shocked. "She's that powerful? Truly?"

"She is."

"Then her power might rival that of Epona's own Chosen?"

Kai's question sent a jolt of realization through Kegan. Adsagsona was not Epona, Warrior Horse Goddess and prime deity of Partholon, but she was goddess of the underrealms of the world—the womb of Partholon. He'd never thought of any other of the various gods or goddesses worshipped to a lesser extent by pockets of the different races of Partholon as being in any way comparable to the mighty Epona. But what if a priestess of Adsagsona, or at least one uniquely gifted by her goddess, could wield powers similar to Epona's Chosen?

Then wouldn't that High Priestess, that gifted Light Bringer, require an equally gifted mate? Might he have been fashioned as Morrigan's soul mate, and that was why he'd felt an instant attraction to Myrna, who'd mirrored her so completely in all ways but that of the spirit?

"Kegan? What is it?"

"It is just that I never considered what having another priestess whose powers rival Epona's Chosen might mean to Partholon."

"But now you are considering it."

Kegan's eyes met the Stonemaster's and he saw there the knowledge that he had never attempted to hide—that he enjoyed the power his unusual position as a centaur High Shaman, as well as the youngest Master Sculptor in Partholon's history, brought him. He also guessed it had been obvious—at least to Kai—that part of the enthusiasm with which he had courted Myrna had had more to do with the power that would have been his if he were to have won the love of the next Chosen of Epona. Of course, Myrna had not had the slightest touch from the Goddess. And Kegan, along with every other centaur High Shaman, had lost the chance to rule Partholon beside Myrna.

And now Kai had to be reading a kind of rekindled hope in the centaur's eyes.

"Yes," he said flatly. "I am now considering it, as are you." Kegan looked away from the Stonemaster and back at Morrigan. Birkita was talking to her. Kegan couldn't hear what the older woman was saying, but she was speaking with a controlled intensity that lined her forehead and made her look perturbed. Kegan wondered what could be wrong. Yes, Morrigan's prayer ritual had been unusual, but she was a Light Bringer. Historically they were greatly gifted, passionate women who made their own rules. Birkita had been a highly competent and knowledgeable High Priestess. Surely she knew that Light Bringers followed their own paths.

At that moment Morrigan exploded with anger, raising her voice so that it carried easily to Kegan. "I need some damn air!" She made an abrupt gesture with her hand, cutting off Birkita's next words. "No. I don't want to hear any more right now." Then the Light Bringer's eyes met his. Kegan felt the look as if a burning brand had speared through him. There was nothing else in the world except Morrigan. His thoughts, his desires, his vision—all tunneled down to only include her. Unable to stop himself, he moved quickly to her.

"My Lady, allow me to escort you to the surface," he said with a bow and a formal flourish.

Morrigan hesitated for only a moment, then she placed her

hand on his offered arm. "Fine. Whatever. I just need to get out of here for a little while."

"Your wishes shall be my commands, my Lady," Kegan said. Then he called to one of the priestesses still in the chamber, "Have a basket of food and wine brought to the surface. Your Light Bringer needs to ground herself after her ritual."

"Yes, my Lord," the priestess said, and she hurried off.

With Morrigan not speaking a word yet thrumming with energy and so tightly strung that her hand seemed to burn against the skin of his arm, Kegan escorted her from the Usgaran. He could feel Kai's considering gaze on him long after they'd left the chamber.

12

Morrigan burst from the mouth of the cave like a fading star. She dropped the centaur's arm and strode forward, only aware enough of her surroundings to stop at the edge of a drop-off. Hands on her hips, she stared into the horizon. Half blinded by the golden sunlight, she blinked hard, acclimating herself to the brightness of day. Gulping deep breaths of the warm morning air Morrigan tried to calm her tumultuous emotions and breathe through the vestiges of power and excitement that still electrified her body. The ritual had begun as her response to hurt and sadness, but her feelings had quickly morphed into anger. It was then that she had been filled with the power. Power! The way the light had rushed through her body had been even rawer and more thrilling than that time in the Oklahoma cave right before the accident when Kyle had witnessed it. Morrigan shivered as she remembered the desire that she had felt then, too.

"Your ritual moved me."

She'd forgotten the centaur was there and she jumped a little in surprise when he spoke. He was standing behind her, but she didn't turn to look at him. "Really? Well, it moved me, too."

"It wasn't like any ritual for the dead I've ever experienced."

Morrigan still didn't look at him. "Sorry about it being abnormal. Seems it freaked out Birkita, too," she snapped.

"Freaked out?"

She sighed. "Freaked out equals shock plus annoyance."

"Then, no, your ritual did not make me freaked out. I said it moved me, not shocked or annoyed me. And, quite frankly, I cannot see what Birkita would have found so shocking. Light Bringers always follow their own paths."

She steeled herself against the bizarre familiarity of his features and turned to face him. "You know about Light Bringers?"

"Historically they were passionate women greatly gifted by the gods who made their own rules." His smile was slow and warm. "But I'd never seen one perform a ritual until today. It's much more interesting in person than it is in the dry, stale pages of history."

"Kinda like centaurs," she said automatically, and then wanted to slap her hand over her stupid mouth when she realized what she'd actually said aloud.

His smile didn't waver. "Centaurs?"

Well, crap. She couldn't pretend she hadn't said anything. Okay, so she'd stick as close to the truth as possible. "You were there yesterday when Perth said that Birkita foretold my coming and that Adsagsona had brought me to the Sidetha, right?"

Kegan nodded. "I was."

"All that's true. They just left out the part about Adsagsona bringing me here from far away. Really far away."

"Where did you come from that is so far away?" Kegan looked mildly amused.

"It's a Keep called Oklahoma. It's in the Southwest. Oh, and we didn't have centaurs there—at least we didn't have living ones. Only in, let's see, how did you put it? Only in the dry, stale pages of books."

Kegan blinked several times, utter shock replacing amusement on his handsome face. "No centaurs?"

"Absolutely none."

"I'm the first centaur you've ever seen?"

"Absolutely the first."

"And were you—" he hesitated, raising his eyebrows "—*freaked out* by me."

Morrigan laughed. "Yes, I'll admit I was a little."

"So how do I compare to the pages of history?" His smile was brilliant, and it made him look even more like Kyle, if that was possible.

She took her time answering him, enjoying the excuse to study him. First she let her eyes roam from his face to his mostly bare human torso, then she studied the horse part of him. What she had thought about him earlier held true under scrutiny—he had a terrible beauty that was as alluring as it was alien. Kegan was different from Kyle. The centaur mirror of him was masculine in the extreme—a male animal barely tempered by the man. As she'd reacted in the Oklahoma cave, the arousal she still felt from the ritual's power responded to him with an elemental strength that had her stepping forward and closing the space that separated them.

"I think you are magnificent," she said.

He hadn't moved as she'd studied him, but kept his blue eyes trained on her. His expression said he enjoyed the attention and welcomed her scrutiny.

"Then we have that in common. I think you are magnificent, too." His voice had deepened and it sent electric shivers through her already sensitized body.

"May I ask you something?" she said.

"Anything, my Lady."

"Birkita told me that a centaur High Shaman can shape-shift. Is that true?"

He smiled again. "It is."

"Into anything?"

"Into any living thing," he corrected. Slowly, he reached forward and took her hand in his, lifting it to his lips. He turned it over and kissed the meaty spot under her thumb, and then, very lightly, he bit her there before saying, "Perhaps someday you will allow me to demonstrate my abilities for you."

His lips were warm, and the soft bite sent sparks of pleasure through her body. "Would you shape-shift into a human man?"

Kegan's thumb caressed a lazy circle around the spot below her thumb he had just kissed. "No matter what shape I take you should know that I will always be more than a human man."

"I can see that," she said a little breathlessly. Morrigan loved the way the teasing game between them made her feel. His alien beauty that mixed so perfectly with his similarity to Kyle excited her and she wanted to touch him, though she knew she probably shouldn't.

You are a Light Bringer! Passion and fire are your right!

The voice exploded in her head, goading her into action. She tugged her hand free from his. He let her go easily, and then she could see the surprise in his eyes when, instead of moving away from him, she stepped even closer.

"Do you mind if I touch you?"

"Not only do I not mind, I welcome your touch," he said without hesitation.

First, she reached up and placed her hand on his arm, putting it lightly on his shoulder just above the swell of his biceps. He was dressed in the same type of open leather vest he'd been wearing the night before, which left most of his torso bare. Kegan's grin was teasing. "You've already touched me there."

"I know, but I was distracted then and wasn't really thinking about you."

"And now?"

"Now I'm definitely thinking about you." She let her hand trail down his arm until it was resting on his forearm, much as it had been when he'd escorted her from the cave. "Your skin is so hot. Is it always like that?"

"Yes, a centaur's body temperature is warmer than humans'."

Completely intrigued, Morrigan placed her palm where his vest opened, against the bare skin of Kegan's chest, and splayed her fingers wide. Without taking her eyes from his, she began to move her hand down in a sweeping caress that passed over his well-defined abdominal muscles, down and around to his waist, and then past his human torso to where equine met man in a shining golden coat. She could feel his muscles tremble against her hand and reveled in knowing that one small touch from her could cause such an obvious reaction in him.

"Amazing…" She breathed the word.

"Morrigan." He moaned her name as he slid his hand around the back of her neck, bent and pressed his lips to hers.

The kiss wasn't an intrusion; it was a question. Morrigan answered it with an exclamation mark. Her arms slid up and as far around his shoulders as she could reach and she opened her mouth, meeting his tongue with her own. He was so hot! And he tasted like something wild and male and yummy. The erotic energy that had been building in her body flamed again and she pressed herself against him, wanting to drown in the heat and passion he had ignited, just as she had wanted to once before in that crystal-lit Oklahoma cave.

"Oh, excuse me, my Lady!"

Morrigan broke away from Kegan's embrace and had to stifle an urge to whirl and shriek at the wide-eyed priestess, who she recognized was Deidre.

Kegan recovered first. "Excellent, you brought the food." Smiling, he took a laden basket from Deidre.

"I—I'm sorry. I didn't mean to interrupt," Deidre stammered.

"Don't worry about it." Morrigan was definitely pissed by the interruption. Her body was on fire and she'd been totally making out with Kegan when Deidre had to come bumbling up. Great. She could only imagine the gossip that was going to spread—not to mention what Birkita would have to say about it.

Morrigan's sharp tone made the priestess flinch and repeat nervously, "I didn't mean to interrupt."

When she just stood there staring, Morrigan said with exaggerated politeness, "Thank you very much, Deidre. You can go now."

The priestess curtsied and practically ran back into the mouth of the cave. Morrigan was glaring at the cave when she heard Kegan's deep chuckle and turned her flashing eyes on him.

Still laughing, he held the basket out to her as if making an offering to an irate goddess. "I surrender! Indeed, it was me who asked the priestess to bring food and wine. Be merciful."

Kegan's amused reaction brought her up short. What was it she was so angry about, anyway? She'd got caught kissing a centaur. So what? Birkita had said that Myrna's dad had been a centaur—so clearly centaur/human kissing wasn't exactly a never-done thing. And anyway, it had been Birkita who had said that Kegan's similarity to Kyle might be a gift from the Goddess, so she shouldn't ignore it. Besides, Birkita was not her grandma, and even if she was, it was about time Morrigan took charge of her own life, which meant she shouldn't be embarrassed when she got caught kissing a guy. She definitely needed to get a grip. It was just that her emotions felt so close to the surface and so ultra-*everything:* ultrasensitive, ultra-angry, ultrahorny. She slid her eyes over to Kegan. Well, most of her friends had already lost their virginity. Why not…

"Deciding whether or not you're going to make me explode in a ball of light?" he asked with a grin.

She opened her mouth to say she couldn't do that, and then thought better of it. Maybe she actually *could* do that. Instead she smiled back at him. "It's not you I'd explode."

That made him laugh again. "Have pity on the poor priestess. You already made her freaked out."

Morrigan rolled her eyes. "Okay, enough Oklahoma words for you." She gestured at the basket, suddenly realizing she was absolutely ravenous. "Want to share what's in the basket?"

"Well, my Lady, that depends."

"Depends on?"

"I'm going to ask a price for the sharing." His eyes sparkled mischievously.

Morrigan frowned. She already wanted him; she didn't like the thought that he wanted to barter with her desire. "I don't sell myself," she said, all teasing gone from her voice.

His face sobered instantly. "You misunderstand me, Morrigan. I would never try to buy you. I was making a jest, perhaps a poor one, and was simply going to try to purchase more Oklahoma words from you."

Morrigan felt her cheeks getting warm. She really was acting like a raving bitch. "Oh, sorry about overreacting."

"You just need to eat. After a powerful ritual the body and soul need to be replenished." He held out his arm to her again. "I know a spot not far from here that would be a perfect place for us to eat."

"That sounds good." Morrigan slid her hand over the top of his forearm and let him escort her, like an old-time knight. She liked the way he felt—his strength and his heat. She liked how he shortened his incredibly long stride so that she didn't have to jog to walk beside him. She also liked that, unlike Kyle, he wasn't so shy around her.

"Are you becoming used to touching me?" He bent intimately toward her, keeping his arm close to his side so that Morrigan's body brushed against his as they walked.

She looked up at him and the passion shivered through her body again. Her smile was flirtatious. "I don't know. I might have to do it some more to see for sure."

"As I said, my Lady, your wishes shall be my commands."

13

Kegan showed her a path that ran around the side of the mouth of the cave, and then circled up and over the top of it. As she held her dress up and out of the way with one hand, and clung to the centaur's arm with the other, she realized that this was the same path that led down to the cave in Oklahoma. On top of it there had been a pretty park area built, complete with outdoor grills and picnic tables, which was where she and her girlfriends had unpacked and eaten G-ma's picnic lunch a week ago. Just a week ago! It seemed like a lifetime had passed and not seven short days.

Standing on top of the cave entrance, Morrigan was awed by the lush, untamed beauty that surrounded her. She walked over to the lip of the cave and turned slowly in a complete circle, taking in everything she could see.

"So this is Partholon." She spoke her thought aloud, glad that she'd admitted to Kegan that she was from a faraway place.

Kegan laughed. "No, Morrigan. *This* is the Realm of the Sidetha." He pointed. "Do you see the green outline there in the far south?"

"Yes."

"*That* is Partholon."

"Well, it looks pretty, but I think I'm partial to this." Morrigan threw wide her arms and spun in another slow circle. It reminded her a lot of the land around the Alabaster Caves in Oklahoma, only this place was so much bigger! The similarities were there, though. Her first impression of this part of her home state was that it looked more like what she'd imagined New Mexico to look like than Oklahoma. The mountains were rocky and scrub covered—the dirt was really red—and there were even cactuses all over. Here some of that was the same, except that she could see the land to the east had been planted with what looked like wheat and corn. The rest of it reminded her of Oklahoma, only it was more so: bigger, wilder, more like an imagined Old West. It had a beauty that was untamed and powerful. When she looked to her left the rough mountains got even bigger and they seemed to lose any vegetation and were a red that was deeper than the earthy rust color around her cave.

"The Tier Mountains," Kegan said. "The Realm of the Sidetha tunnels under the eastern half of the mountains, but the Tiers go on from here to the sea. Except for Guardian Castle, which watches the only pass through the mountains, no one claims that land. It has a dark reputation, and is better left alone."

His words gave Morrigan a little prickle of foreboding.

"To the east the Realm of the Sidetha stretches on until it meets the inhospitable Land of the Cyclops."

Morrigan's eyes widened. "Cyclops?"

Kegan grinned. "None of them in Oklahoma, either?"

"Only in books."

"You come from an odd place, my Lady."

She took up his teasing tone. "You know, I was just thinking the same thing about you." He started to protest and she waved him off. "I wish you would continue my tour, please."

His grin turned wry, and he bowed slightly, saying, "Your

wish—my command." He gestured to the land in front of them and Morrigan looked out over the top of the cave. "The Salt Plains are Sidetha land, but soon they give way to the Wastelands, which is even more uninhabitable than the Land of the Cyclops."

Morrigan took the last few steps forward. The sight made her feel breathless and small, but at the same time connected and somehow part of the vast majesty of the land. From the mountains in which the mouth of the Sidetha cave system was located, the land took an abrupt downward plunge until it met what looked to Morrigan like a huge, glassy lake. Out of the lake jutted shards of raw rock that glistened gold in the morning sun.

"The Salt Plains? But isn't that a lake?"

"I suppose you could call it that, and it appears like a lake from a distance, but it never gets any deeper than your shapely calf, and it is saltier than the sea."

"Are the rocks really gold?"

"No, they're just taking on the color of the sun right now. Actually, they're made of the same crystals as the cave."

Morrigan's eyes widened and she grabbed his arm in excitement. "The crystals! My crystals! Those huge rocks are all made of the crystals that speak to me?"

"They are. Wouldn't it be magnificent if you went out on the Plains as the sun was setting and called the light of the crystals alive?"

"I'm going to do it! Kegan, it's going to be amazing!" Impulsively she hugged him, and the heat of him against her skin had her recalling just how *amazing* his mouth had felt on hers.

His vibrant blue gaze said that he was recalling the same thing. "Then let us make it sunset tonight. Allow me to escort you there." His smile was cocky, his tone teasing. "With me, my Lady, you have a protector and a mount all in one."

Morrigan's lips tilted up. "What if I need protection against you?"

He didn't answer. Instead he bent and kissed her lightly— too lightly for Morrigan's taste. Kegan's grin said he read exactly that in her eyes. He kept an arm looped possessively around her shoulders as he guided her away from the lip of the cave back toward the semiflat boulder on which he'd deposited the basket of food. "You should eat and drink, especially if you're going to call the crystals to you again tonight."

"I *am* starving." Using the boulder as a table, Morrigan started pulling things out of the basket, only to pause her actions when Kegan folded his legs and reclined across from her.

"Different from the pages of a book?" he said, catching her curious look.

"Unimaginably different." She used a conveniently close rock for a makeshift chair, sat, and then handed Kegan a biscuit that had been filled with cold bacon and fragrant cheese. "Yum, these smell wonderful," she said before biting into her own.

They ate for a while in silence, which Morrigan was just beginning to feel might be turning awkward. Without really thinking, she blurted out the first question that came to her mind. "So, you're a High Shaman and the youngest Master Sculptor in Partholon?" She wanted to smack herself on the forehead for sounding like a fan girl, but Kegan answered her easily.

"I am. During this past moon the Lady Rhiannon named me Master Sculptor. Five full passes of the seasons ago I drank of Epona's chalice at the Goddess's well and accepted the gift of High Shaman."

Intrigued by the subject, as well as by the handsome centaur himself, Morrigan's mind bubbled with questions. "Is Epona's well in Partholon?"

"It isn't in this world at all. It is in the Otherworld—the place of gods and goddesses and spirits."

"Was it scary going there?"

Kegan smiled. "Only my spirit traveled there and, yes, some parts of a shaman's journey are scary."

"What does a High Shaman do?"

Kegan's brow wrinkled. "Do you not have High Shamans in Oklahoma?"

Her immediate response was a big No Way, and then she thought about some of her grandma's Wiccan and pagan friends, and also about the Native Americans she'd met at various powwows, and changed her answer. "We do, but everything is so different there. You know—" she grinned at him cheekily "—no centaurs."

He snorted. "Different, indeed. Well, as a centaur High Shaman I wield spiritual powers. I can walk in the Otherworld and find shattered souls. I help to nurture the good in my herd, as well as rebuke evil."

"So you're kind of like a spirit doctor?"

"I am. Though because I am the youngest male High Shaman of our herd, I chose to exercise my sword arm as much as my spiritual abilities."

"Really? I'd think you would have said that you chose to exercise your talents as a sculptor. Sculptor, High Shaman, warrior—it's the warrior part that doesn't feel right in that equation."

"Well, that's probably because I never intended to be a sculptor, Master or otherwise." He gave a little laugh and rubbed his hand through his thick, golden-blond hair. "Actually, it was because of my desire to be a warrior that my talent as a sculptor was discovered."

"Okay, you've got to explain that."

"I was young, only about ten passes of the seasons old. As

is typical with colts, I was frustrated by the speed at which my instructor was teaching me the art of swordplay. I, of course, believed I already knew everything, and was quite beyond using a wooden practice sword. So I used my position as the Herdmaster's son, albeit the youngest." Here Kegan paused and shook his head in a self-deprecating gesture. "Now I understand the smithy was only humoring me—then I believed he was acknowledging my rank."

Morrigan laughed and said, "Sounds like centaur children are a lot like Oklahoma children. My grandparents raised me, and I remember believing that all of my teachers paid extra attention to me because I was so smart and funny. Now I realize I got extra attention because Grandpa had practically been a living legend as a coach and a teacher, and they all knew him. Basically, they were just looking out for his granddaughter and humoring me."

"We definitely have that in common. So, the smithy let me fashion my own metal sword. Then I made the mistake of actually listening to what I now know are the spirits in the metal. They told me the embellishment they wanted carved on their hilt." Kegan shrugged. "So I carved it. Seemed like a ridiculously simple thing to me, but when the smithy saw the finished sword he immediately took it to my mother. It was then that my swordsmanship lessons were supplanted by instruction in carving. The rest, as they say, is history."

"You sound like you wish no one had found out about your talent for carving."

"I did then. As I matured, my feelings changed, and I appreciate my Goddess–given talent now. Then, I simply wanted to become a warrior."

"But you said you are a warrior. You must have continued your sword lessons."

"I did. Much to the irritation of my parents and my sculpting instructors. They feared I would cut off a finger."

Morrigan laughed as he held up his hands and wiggled his fingers and folded over several fingers, pretending that they had been lopped off.

He laughed with her and then sobered and said, "But today I found myself being more grateful for my talent. Were I not Partholon's Master Sculptor I would not have been asked to accompany Kai here to carve Myrna's effigy, and then I would not have met you."

Morrigan nodded absently and reached for a floppy bag that was corked. She took her time opening it, sniffing the contents, and then drinking deeply of the sweet, cool wine while she decided just exactly how to word her next question. Finally, she looked up at Kegan to find him watching her.

"How well did you know Myrna?"

"Fairly well. I courted her."

That sent a little jolt through Morrigan. "You were with Myrna?"

"Not really. It's more accurate to say that I attempted to be with her. Myrna was never interested in me, or in any of the other centaurs who wooed her. She met the human she eventually married when they were children. He won her heart early and kept it, much to Lady Rhiannon's dismay I'm sure. Though once the two were betrothed, he seemed to be well accepted."

"Wait. Myrna's parents didn't approve of the man she loved?"

Kegan popped a piece of cheese in his mouth, and continued to speak around it. "The part about Lady Rhiannon being dismayed is just my own supposition. You'd have to ask Kai for the truth. He's very close to Epona's Chosen and ClanFintan. My guess is that it was not so much that they didn't approve of Grant, but what it meant for Myrna to choose a human as a mate."

Morrigan mentally filed away what Kegan had said about

Kai. And then, remembering what Birkita had told her about centaurs and Epona's Chosen, Morrigan realized the meaning behind Kegan's words. "Myrna mating with a human man would mean she wouldn't be Epona's Chosen after her mom."

Kegan nodded, chewed another bite of food thoughtfully and finally said, "You look like her."

Morrigan had told herself to be ready for something like this, but still his words made her go numb. "I look like Myrna?" she said, trying to add nothing but the appropriate amount of curiosity to her voice.

"Yes, well, Lady Rhiannon, too. Myrna looked a lot like her mother."

"What is it, the same color hair or eyes or something like that?" she said nonchalantly.

Kegan snorted. "The same everything. You and Myrna could have been twins. You look like you were born from the same mother's womb."

Morrigan's stomach rolled. "That's impossible. My mother died giving birth to me."

"I am sorry for your loss."

"Thank you." Morrigan shook her hair back and took another drink of the wine. "Anyway, sometimes people resemble each other."

"It's decidedly more than that. Except for the difference being a Light Bringer makes in you, the two of you are almost identical."

Morrigan frowned. "What do you mean, the difference being a Light Bringer makes?"

"Surely you are aware of how it changes you when the spirits of the crystals fill you?" He reached out and stroked his thumb down Morrigan's arm. "What it does to that luscious body of yours—how it makes you shine, burn, sizzle with passion and power." She shivered under his touch. His smile was slow and knowing. "Myrna never wielded such power."

Morrigan pulled her arm back and forced herself not to rub the skin he'd caressed and where she could still feel his touch. "So there you have it. Myrna and I aren't really that alike. It's just one of those freaky coincidences."

"Freaky..." He tasted the word, and then grinned. "Which reminds me, you owe me more Oklahoma words."

Morrigan was glad to change the subject, so she raised an eyebrow playfully. "I don't know if you can be trusted to use them correctly. You know, words are powerful weapons."

"Ah, but you must remember that I am a High Shaman as well as a warrior—I'm trained to wield swords *and* words."

She tapped her chin and studied him as if she was giving his statement serious thought. "Okay, I'll give you another Oklahoma word, but only because you're a High Shaman, so you might be able to handle it."

He bowed his head graciously. "Thank you, my Lady."

"Y'all," Morrigan said.

"My Lady?"

"Yaaaa all," she repeated more slowly. "It means several people. Like, 'Y'all come back now, hear?' Understand?"

"Y'all," he said. "Like, 'Y'all have an odd way of speaking in Oklahoma.'"

"Exactly like that." They smiled at each other and Morrigan felt the sizzle of attraction that passed between them all the way down in her toes. "If you're good, tonight I may teach you an Oklahoma hello."

The centaur leaned forward and took her hand, lazily circling his thumb over her skin. "I assure you, my Lady, that I am *very* good."

Kegan was lifting her hand to his mouth and Morrigan was attempting to come up with a witty yet sexy reply when Brina chose that moment to pad up the path. The big cat took one look at Kegan touching her, and, as Morrigan later described it to Birkita, turned into psycho-freak cat. Brina's eyes narrowed to dangerous yellow slits. Her tail went straight up and her fur stood up all along her hackles. Then she bared her teeth and hissed a warning, clearly aimed at the centaur. Who, wisely, let loose Morrigan's hand.

"Brina! What's wrong with you?" Morrigan chastised her. "Come here and act right." She held out her hand to the big cat, and Brina moved to her, all the while keeping her slit-eyed glare on Kegan. "Jeesh, settle down." Morrigan stroked the cat, and Brina leaned into her, but she didn't stop glaring at Kegan. "He wasn't hurting me. He was just kissing my hand." She glanced up at Kegan. "Sorry about that."

"It's good that she is so protective of her lady."

"Well, she definitely knows how to kill a mood." Morrigan sighed, gave Brina another long caress, and then started putting the scraps of leftover food and wine back in the basket. "Actually, except for her rudeness, Brina's interruption is a good thing. I really should be getting back. There are things I need to take care of before tonight." One of those things should probably be apologizing to Birkita for how short she'd been with her after the ritual. She was starting to feel really crappy about it. Maybe Birkita didn't know as much about Light Bringers as Kegan did. Maybe she didn't know that Morrigan was supposed to do things her own way—make her own path—which was why the ritual was different from anything Birkita was used to. Morrigan shouldn't have been so pissed off. Birkita hadn't really even said much to her.

"Will your cat allow me to take your arm?"

Morrigan was a little embarrassed to see that Kegan had been watching her while she'd been standing there, full basket in her hand, staring off into the distance.

"Sorry," she said quickly. Morrigan glanced down at the cat, who was sitting on her haunches not far from their makeshift table, eyes still trained on Kegan. "Brina, behave yourself," Morrigan told the cat sharply. Brina stood up, shook herself, muttered what Morrigan thought was a very rude grumble and then trotted back down the path. Morrigan smiled and took Kegan's offered arm. "Her manners are almost as bad as mine. I didn't mean to zone out like that."

"Zone out?" He grinned at her as they navigated their way down the path. "Another Oklahoma word?"

"Very sly of you to sneak them out of me like that. I'll have to watch you."

"I will look forward to your close attention," he said, wrapping her arm more intimately through his.

She raised a brow at him, and continued. "Zone out equals me standing there staring like I have no sense."

"You didn't look as if you were lacking in sense. You looked as if you had much on your mind."

"I did. I was thinking about Birkita. I hurt her feelings and I need to find her and apologize. She really didn't say anything to deserve me snapping at her like that." Morrigan knew that was true. It hadn't been the older woman's words that had gotten to her. It had been the look she'd given Morrigan— the look that had seemed shadowed with fear. That fear had touched a live nerve of unexpected anger inside Morrigan, making her lash out at Birkita.

"A wise High Priestess knows when to apologize," Kegan said.

"A *wise* High Priestess wouldn't do things she had to apologize for," Morrigan said.

They'd come to the entrance to the cave. Morrigan was surprised to see how busy it was there. People were carrying baskets of food and other supplies back and forth from a path that looked much better used than the one they'd just climbed down. Morrigan couldn't miss the many curious glances the people were giving her, and she suddenly felt nervous about being clutched so tightly to Kegan's arm. She untangled herself from him and took a step back.

"Thank you for escorting me and making sure I was fed," she said.

Kegan didn't seem to mind her awkward, obvious withdrawal. Instead he smiled and said formally, "It would be my greatest pleasure if you would allow me to escort you to explore the Salt Plains tonight, my Lady."

"Yes, yes, I will," she said in a rush, wondering why all of that sexy, passion-filled, grown-ass woman confidence had, all of a sudden, completely and utterly left her.

Kegan bowed gallantly, looking like her suave, cool, absolute opposite. "Call for me when you are ready. And remember, your wishes shall be my commands."

"All righty, then. See you later tonight." Morrigan bobbed a ridiculous little curtsy and then hurried away toward the Usgaran before he could see how red her face had to be.

14

"So you'll forgive me?" Morrigan asked Birkita for the second time. She'd found her where she expected the ex–High Priestess would be—in the Usgaran—and she'd pulled her over to an alcove where they could have some measure of privacy.

"As I said before, of course, my Lady."

"But you're calling me 'my Lady' again with that tone."

A smile tugged at Birkita's lips. "I am simply showing you proper respect."

"Your feelings are still hurt. I know that tone. You and Grandma share it."

Birkita cupped Morrigan's cheek in her palm. "There, this is the girl I am coming to know and love. And this is also why I was so concerned for you during the ritual."

Morrigan stiffened and Birkita's hand dropped from her face. "*This* is me. *That* was me. It's all me."

Birkita's sharp gaze never wavered from Morrigan's. "Be quite certain, child. Know yourself, so that you can recognize the influence of others."

"Birkita," Morrigan said, trying hard to control her rising ir-ritation. "You have never been filled with the spirits of the crystals. And you told me that there hasn't been a Light Bringer in more than three generations, so no one for a really long time has been filled with the spirits of the crystals. It's an incredible thing."

"Yes, I am quite sure it is, but—"

"Kegan told me that historically Light Bringers have made their own paths and gone their own ways. That it's normal for me to do different things and to be filled with passion and adventure."

"Kegan told you."

Birkita hadn't said it like a question, but Morrigan answered anyway, feeling foolish and defensive. "Yes, Kegan. He is a High Shaman as well as Master Sculptor. I think that should give him some kind of authority about, well, matters of the spirits and whatnot."

Birkita's look was way too knowing. "Kegan is, indeed, a High Shaman. But he is also the mirror of one you were connected to in Oklahoma."

"Yeah, and you said he might be a gift from Adsagsona, and that I shouldn't ignore her gifts. So I'm not."

"Don't ignore them, but also don't take everything the centaur says as words from the Goddess. He is very young. Morrigan, you should understand that being a High Shaman or a High Priestess—" she paused and added gently "—or even a Light Bringer doesn't automatically mean a person is all-knowing."

"Okay, yes, I understand that. But with the same reasoning I could tell you that just because someone is young, it doesn't make him or her wrong."

"Of course it doesn't. I am not saying that you are wrong, or that Kegan is. All I'm saying is that I want you to be careful. Progress slowly as you explore your new powers. Remember that you are automatically vulnerable to Kegan because of your history with his mirror image. And, most of all, listen for the voice of Adsagsona."

"I am," Morrigan said quickly.

"Child, sometimes the Goddess's voice can be mistaken for, or drowned out by, our own. A High Priestess is special to her goddess, that is true, but it is also true that she is her goddess's conduit to her people, and the blessings she has been given should be used to help others and not for the High Priestess's own selfish desires."

Morrigan stiffened. "What do you mean? You said that I should explore this thing with Kegan."

"I'm not speaking of Kegan right now. Morrigan, the prayer ritual was supposed to be for Myrna's spirit and for healing the lamentation of those she left behind. Instead it disintegrated into a display of your power, fueled by your personal wounds. I understand how—"

"No!" Morrigan snapped at Birkita, ignoring the compassion that had filled the old woman's voice and letting the anger that had been simmering within her roil hot and thick. "You *don't* understand. You had a mother and a father. No one lied to you and pretended you were someone else. She took my place!" When Morrigan paused to draw a deep breath and try to calm herself, *claim your destiny* hissed through her mind. "Okay, here's the deal, Birkita. I don't want to hurt your feelings. I care about you, and I think you're a really nice person. But I'm going to be different from you as a High Priestess. It seems to me that your kinder, gentler way wasn't working very well for you. Shayla was walking all over you and the other priestesses. She's not going to pull that 'you can't go topless' or that 'you can't sit at the high table' crap with me. So maybe Adsagsona brought me here because her priestesses need my, what you call, *selfish desires.*"

Birkita didn't look away from Morrigan's angry glare. She simply inclined her head and said softly, "As you will, my Lady. You are now High Priestess and Light Bringer. By right it is you who are closest to the Goddess's will."

Morrigan let out a long, frustrated breath. "Okay then. At least we're straight about that. Now I think I'm going to do some exploring of the caves. Oh, and you don't need to worry about showing me around. I'll be fine on my own."

"Yes, my Lady." Birkita dropped into a curtsy.

As Birkita began to turn away, Morrigan touched the old woman's shoulder so that she paused and looked up at her. Morrigan hated how haggard Birkita looked and, no matter what, she was sorry that she might be the cause of some of the weary worry she saw in her eyes. "Don't be mad at me, okay?"

Birkita rested her hand over Morrigan's for a moment. "I could not be angry with you, child." She squeezed Morrigan's hand, and then walked back to the heart of the Usgaran and the other priestesses and craftspeople who where gathered there, already busy with the day's work.

Morrigan sighed and let her fingers play over the skin of the cave wall. "I want to get out of here," she whispered to the spirits of the crystals. "Lead me to see something amazing that's *not* under Birkita's nose."

We hear and we obey, Light Bringer! came the predictably perky reply. Instantly a series of small crystals lit along the wall at about her waist level. Like a long row of dominoes, one leading another, Morrigan began following their sepentlike pattern through the Usgaran and into a tunnel she recognized as having been the main pathway she had followed through the cave in Oklahoma. She walked close to the wall, so that her fingertips continually brushed against the smooth cave. She was amazed at how the two places, in two different worlds, could be so similar and yet so different. It was like the cave in Oklahoma was a shoddy, underdeveloped shadow of this magnificent underground creation. Which made her wonder if the same was true for the people who mirrored each other in both worlds. And if so, which was she and which had Myrna been?

The crappy, half-realized version or the amazing version? She was afraid she knew which one Birkita would say she was.

The old woman does not understand.

"Exactly!" Morrigan said in response to the whisper in her mind, drawing some odd looks from three workmen who were walking past her. She cleared her throat, coughed and hurried down the tunnel away from them, still being careful to follow her bread-crumb trail of crystals. They led her to take a smaller tunnel that arched off to the right—one that definitely wasn't there in Oklahoma. She noticed in the middle of the floor were narrow tracks, as if a miniature train traveled inside the cave, which was soon explained when a flatbed car filled with lumps of smooth, white, marble-looking stone was pulled past her by a couple of burly workmen. She returned their brief greetings with quick hellos. Huh. So that must be how the Sidetha got the rock from deep in the cave up to the surface.

The tunnel made an S curve and then took an abrupt downward turn. The alabaster floor went into a steep, ramplike descent that had her leaning backward to keep her balance. Here the open braziers that lighted the tunnel weren't pedestals placed on the floor. Instead there were flaming stone bowls set in niches carved out of the wall itself, or they hung from chains suspended from the ceiling, reminding Morrigan bizarrely of her grandma's hanging spider-plant holders. The farther she descended, the fewer and fewer people she met, and her mind wandered.

What Birkita had said to her today reminded Morrigan a lot of some of the fights she'd had growing up with grandparents as parents. Sure, they had been great. They loved her and tried their best to understand her. But in reality they'd been old. Really old. She used to try to tell Grandma that it wasn't making her look "loose" or "fresh" (Grandma's words) to wear short jean skirts—it was just the style. Sometimes Morrigan actually won the fight. Temporarily. Grandma always won the battle. Mostly because G-pa jumped in squarely on her side. Morrigan could practically hear him. "Morgie, you can act like a damn fool and look like a damn fool on your own time." And by "your own time" G-pa had meant, morbidly enough, after they were dead. Actually, the farther she traveled down into the cave, the more relaxed she felt. Morrigan smiled at the memory of her grandparents, and the last of the angry tension in her dissipated. *Please let my grandparents be okay. Let them not be too sad that I'm gone.* Morrigan sent the silent, heartfelt prayer into the body of the cave, hoping that it would reach Adsagsona, and that the Goddess would somehow be able to comfort her grandparents.

Feeling easier in her skin, Morrigan decided that the spat with Birkita was the S.O.S.—the same old shit. Basically, a generation problem. Or, more specifically, a generation-gap problem.

Then Morrigan blinked and realized that she'd walked right past the arched entryway the crystals had turned into. Shaking her head at herself, she backtracked and walked through the new doorway and then gasped at the incredible beauty into which she'd stepped. The room was big and round even though its entrance had been so small that Morrigan had had to duck her head to walk through it. The walls and ceiling were completely covered with jutting clusters of purple crystals. There was a huge brazier on a tripod in the middle of the room, and its white flames made the room glisten.

"Amethyst…" Awestruck, Morrigan breathed the word on a sigh.

"Good day, my Lady. Is there something I can do for you?"

The voice made Morrigan jump. She hadn't noticed the workman in the far end of the room. He had a delicate-looking chisel in one hand and a small hammer in the other, and had obviously been tapping a cluster of crystals loose from the encrusted wall.

"Oh, I didn't mean to interrupt. I've just been exploring."

Unlike the stuck-up men who had brought the baskets of alabaster sap to the Usgaran the day before, or even the dead-faced workmen who had been dragging the flatbed car, this man had a friendly smile. "You aren't lost, are you, my Lady?"

"No. I, uh, don't think I can get lost. I'm Morrigan, the Light Bringer, and, well—" she pointed to the lighted trail of diamondlike crystals that had led her into the room "—they show me the way."

"Oh, of course, my Lady. I know who you are," he said.

"So, is this amethyst?" Morrigan asked, to fill the awkward silence.

"It is. I am choosing six clusters for Laragon Castle. It is a special request from the Chieftain himself. This year the lavender harvest has been especially prosperous, and he wishes to reward the six lead farmers."

"They're absolutely beautiful." She smiled at him. "Well, I'll let you get back to your work. I'm sorry, I don't know your name."

"Arland, my Lady." He gave her a snappy bow.

"Well, Arland, it's nice to meet you."

"And you, Light Bringer."

She was just ducking her head to go through the small entrance when Arland called after her. "My Lady?" Morrigan looked back at him. "There are some of us who believe the Goddess has truly blessed us with your presence."

Morrigan's heart did a happy little skip. "Thank you, Arland." Then she added impulsively, "And may Adsagsona bless you for your kindness."

His head was still bowed when she left the amethyst chamber. Feeling so much better than she had when she started

on her explorations, Morrigan practically skipped after the trail
of crystals that continued leading her farther into the womb
of the caves. She was a little better prepared for the beauty in
the next chamber they took her into, but she still gawked like
a true country girl and was glad that the room was empty.

Brilliant topaz-colored crystals that faded to transparent
white at their bases encrusted the walls and ceiling. They
looked familiar, but Morrigan couldn't quite name them. "I
don't know what you are, but you are certainly beautiful," she
whispered as she caressed their shining tips.

Citrine…the name came through her fingertips and she
smiled in pleasure. "Thank you," she murmured to the glistening stones.

The next chamber she was led into had several workmen
chipping delicately away at large, lethal-looking shards of rock
that were a deep, glossy black so dark that stepping into the
room gave her the impression of entering a bottomless mouth
filled with deadly teeth. *Onyx*…the spirits in the stones told
her, and she berated herself for being so silly as to imagine
something sinister in the darkness of the beautiful rock.
Actually, Morrigan decided that she would have liked to linger
in the room, running her hands over the jagged stones and
studying the nuances of color that were apparent once she
looked deeper, but the men in that room weren't warm and
welcoming as Arland had been. Not that they were rude. Basically once they figured out she hadn't been sent with a message
for any of them and wasn't lost, they ignored her. Their attitude
might have pissed her off, but she was way too preoccupied
with checking out the wonders of the cave to let them annoy
her.

She had just made a little left turn when she stopped short.
Brina was sitting at the bottom of a short descending ramp,
looking for all the world like she'd been waiting for Morrigan

to show up. Morrigan ruffled her long, pointed ears and then gave her back a swooping caress that had the big cat arching in pleasure and purring loudly.

"What are you doing down here?" she asked as she scratched the cat, noticing just then the long, soft fur that jutted right underneath her chin. Morrigan tugged playfully on it. "This is a little devil's goatee. Very appropriate after your behavior toward Kegan this morning." Brina wound sensuously around her legs. "You were rude, you know that? You're going to have to learn to act right around him. I have a feeling he and I are going to be spending quite a bit of time together." Brina looked up at her and sneezed tremendously, making Morrigan laugh. "Oh, never mind. As G-pa used to say, cats have people— people don't have cats. I guess I'm your person, so I'm just gonna have to tolerate you." And, if she was going to really be honest with herself, Morrigan admitted that she kinda liked the fact that Brina had wanted to protect her. Kegan was cute and funny and just plain hot, but he was also a lot more cocky than his Oklahoma mirror had been. He needed to be reminded that he wasn't dealing with an ordinary, run-of-the-mill priestess chick.

With Brina close by her side, Morrigan followed the crystal trail into a chamber that was filled with smoky quartz so gorgeous that they looked like zillions of dusky diamonds, and another right after that one that had lumps of stones workmen were delicately prying loose from long troughs in the walls that she discovered were raw emeralds.

Thoroughly bedazzled, Morrigan left the emerald chamber and followed a tunnel that narrowed to her right. She was just thinking how lucky it was that she wasn't the least bit claustrophobic when the crystal trail emptied into yet another side chamber. With Brina, Morrigan ducked into the room and instantly felt the difference in the walls around it. The enormous room had a listening quality. The walls weren't encrusted with crystals or gems. Here the walls were a magnificent butter color with swirls of cream throughout. Peppering the floor of the chamber were huge lumps of the yellow stone, some taller than Morrigan and wider around than she could reach. She was just moving to put her hand against the smooth wall and ask the name of the marvelous stone when a sound drew her attention to the middle of the room.

There was a man on his knees in front of a large, shapeless column of stone. Both of his hands were pressed against the side of it, and his head was bowed as if he was in prayer. Not wanting to interrupt whatever the man was doing, Morrigan would have backed soundlessly from the room, but Brina, who had shown no interest in any of the other workmen they had encountered, trotted directly up to the man and began rubbing herself languorously against his back. Morrigan heard him make a strangled sound that was somewhere between a laugh and a sob.

"Brina, you beautiful girl, how did you know I needed company just now?"

Morrigan was suddenly riveted to the floor as, with a weary groan, Kai turned around so that he sat with his back pressed against the column. He reached out to fondle Brina's ears the exact way Morrigan knew the cat liked, and only then caught sight of Morrigan.

15

"Hi. I, uh, I didn't mean to intrude," Morrigan stuttered. Kai smiled at her, as if being caught on his knees in front of a pillar of stone doing god (or goddess) only knows what didn't embarrass him in the least.

"No, you don't intrude. As I told Brina, I needed company."

Curiosity and his obviously open attitude overcame Morrigan's hesitation and she walked across the huge chamber to join him at the pillar of stone. "What is it?"

Kai reached up over his head to caress the stone in a gesture that seemed as intimate as it was automatic. "It is the finest marble in all of Partholon. And this—" he patted the stone gently "—is the piece that Kegan will carve into Myrna's likeness for her monument."

Morrigan studied the large lump of stone. "How do you know this is the exact right piece?"

"I can answer that most easily by asking you another question. How did you find this chamber?"

"The crystals led me here. Way up in the Usgaran I asked them to, well, basically show me around. And so here I am."

Kai smiled. "And that is my answer to your question, too."

"Meaning the marble led you to it?"

"Yes. Marble speaks to me like the spirits in the crystals speak to you. The difference is that instead of calling forth light from the marble, I know what is hidden within it—shapes that are innate to it or duties it wishes to perform."

"Really? Tell me more about how it works for you." Intrigued, Morrigan circled the pillar, staring up at it.

Still seated, Kai scratched Brina's ears as he explained. "You already know the crystals are ensouled. Everything is—the earth is alive. And everything has a purpose. The spirit of a thing already knows its purpose." He made an abstract gesture. "Unlike mankind who often flounders about searching and searching but never being still enough to listen within and know its purpose."

Morrigan thought about the vast majority of her friends back in Oklahoma and decided that floundering was a good way to describe how they got through their days. "So the stones tell you their purpose."

"Yes."

"Can you hear the spirits in all stones?"

"I can connect to all stones, but the spirits in marble are most clear. How about you? Do you hear other spirits, or is it only the sacred crystal that speaks to you?"

Morrigan had come full circle around the marble pillar and was standing in front of where Kai sat again. "I don't know. I've never really thought about it until now." She smiled crookedly. "The voices of the crystals are so loud I don't know if I could hear anything else over them."

His smile mirrored hers in understanding. "The spirits of things that don't move on their own, like rocks and trees and the earth itself, can often be surprisingly exuberant."

"Yeah, that's for sure. They've been so exuberant that I haven't even thought of trying to hear any other spirits."

"I think you should try." He gave Brina one last scratch, and then stood. "The only sacred crystals in this chamber are those very near the entrance, so they shouldn't be able to shout out the voice in the marble."

"Oh, well, okay. I guess I could." Morrigan started to raise her hand, as if she was going to place it against Kai's pillar of stone, but the Stonemaster surprised her by moving quickly to block her way to the stone.

"Not this one."

"Why not?" Morrigan said, more curious than annoyed.

"The spirits in this stone are lamenting. They know that it is their destiny to be carved into the likeness of the lost daughter of Epona's Beloved."

"So they're sad about having to be a tomb for Myrna?"

"No, that's not it at all. The marble is pleased about its destiny. Once it is carved in Myrna's likeness it will comfort all who visit her monument. They mourn for the pain of Lady Rhiannon. She is not only Chosen of Epona. The lady was born under an earth sign, so she has a strong affinity to the earth, its trees and rocks. To some degree, all of Partholon feels her pain. Most especially the stone that was created to hold her daughter's likeness."

Morrigan's mouth felt dry. "Is Rhiannon's birthday April thirtieth?"

Kai didn't appear to be surprised at her question. "Yes."

"That's my birthday, too."

"It was also the day Myrna was born," Kai said, then added in a voice filled with gentle compassion, "You know, don't you?"

Morrigan couldn't look away from his eyes. They were deeply brown—intelligent and understanding. He was so easy to talk to, this wise older man who heard the spirits in stones. It was as if he was the father she never knew.

"I know that I look just like her," Morrigan whispered.

"Yes, that is true. Do you know how this happened?"

Morrigan shook her head and answered truthfully. "I don't really know how any of this happened." She hesitated. "Kegan told me you're close to Rhiannon and her family."

"I am."

"Am I a lot like her?" she asked tremulously.

Kai waited several moments before he answered. "You look as Myrna would have looked had she been touched by a goddess."

Morrigan couldn't help but find satisfaction in Kai's words. Myrna had looked like her, had her same birthday, and even had the mom Morrigan had thought was hers. But Myrna didn't have her power—she'd never had her power.

And it is your power that makes you unique…

The words inside her head were oddly faint, but still they were able to rouse a sliver of the anger that had clung to her since the prayer ritual earlier that day.

"So Myrna didn't have any goddess powers at all?"

"None that I knew of."

Morrigan opened her mouth to make a snappy comment about being sure that was a disappointment to her mama, Ms. Epona's Chosen, but the sadness in Kai's eyes changed her words. Instead she said, "Did you love her?"

Kai looked surprised. "Myrna?"

"Yes, of course Myrna."

"I watched her grow from a precocious child to an intelligent woman who knew her own mind well enough to stand up for her choice of man, and her choice of life paths, when her mother, the most powerful person in Partholon, would have chosen the direct opposite for her. I respected her and I liked her, and yes, I did love her. As a father loves a favorite daughter."

"Does my resemblance to her make it hard for you to be around me?"

"Yes, it does. But," he hurried on, "that doesn't mean I don't want to get to know you better."

"Because of my similarities to Myrna."

"No, because of your differences."

Morrigan lifted a brow. "Really?"

"Really." Kai pointed at a lump of butter-colored marble not far from where they stood. "For instance, let us see if you can hear the voices in the marble as well as the spirits of the sacred crystal."

"Okay." Morrigan walked with Kai over to the marble. It was a roughly rectangular-shaped blob about the height of her chest. If she and Kai had linked hands they could just barely circle it. "Now what?" she asked him.

"It's the same with all spirits. Just touch and ask."

Morrigan wiped her palms down her thighs and then placed them against the smooth side of the stone. Closing her eyes, she concentrated on sending her thoughts into the marble. "Hello?" she spoke hesitantly. "Are you there?"

There was a fleeting sense of movement under her hands, and Morrigan felt a little glow of warmth, like she was holding her hands up to catch the heat of a banked fire. Then she sucked in her breath as images flashed against her closed eyelids. She saw creamy buildings with beautiful domes. Incredibly attractive women were everywhere. They were engaged in a variety of tasks, everything from listening to lectures, to taking painting lessons, to studying an enormous, dark map that was covered with brilliant sparkly crystals Morrigan realized must represent stars and constellations. Finally, the images slowed to focus on one particularly lovely scene. It was a garden filled with roses in every shade of white and yellow Morrigan had ever imagined. Then, with a small pull, the heat left her hands and the images faded to the darkness of her closed eyes.

She opened her eyes to see Kai watching her. "Did the marble speak to you?"

Morrigan brushed her hair back from her face, surprised that her hand was shaking. "It didn't really speak, but wow! It was incredible."

"Did it send you feelings?"

"No, I saw things. Beautiful things."

"Describe them, Morrigan."

"I was looking at a place that was filled with amazing buildings, no, more like temples. They were a creamy white color and most of the roofs were domed. There were women everywhere—and they were all really pretty. It might have been some kind of school."

"The Temple of the Muse," Kai said, his voice edged with excitement. "Did the marble focus on any one scene in particular, or did it just give you a general vision?"

"At the end it focused on a rose garden." Kai's laugh caught her off guard. "What? Why is that funny?"

"Before Myrna died and I received this emergency commission to find the stone for her monument, I already had a journey to the Sidetha planned because Calliope's Incarnate had commissioned me to carve a new bench for her rose garden."

Morrigan didn't have a clue who Calliope was, but she did understand the gist of what Kai had said. She smiled and pointed at the formless lump of marble. "That's going to be a bench?"

"It is, indeed."

"So I helped you to find the right piece of marble."

"And I do thank you, my Lady." Grinning, he took the hand she was pointing in his, formally bowed over it and lifted it to his lips in what he obviously meant as a sweet, kidding gesture. But before his lips met her skin Morrigan felt a nasty jolt spark through her hand, like she'd just received the mother of all static-electric shocks. Quickly she pulled her hand from his and rubbed the spot. She looked apologetically at Kai, ready to make a comment about his shocking personality, when his expression registered on her. Clearly, Kai had felt something pass between them, too. His body was rigid and he was staring at her with a mixed expression of horror and disgust.

"Who are you?" Kai's voice sounded so strained he was even short of breath.

She had the sudden urge to blurt out the truth to this man who she would have liked to have had as a friend or father and who, until that moment, had been so kind to her. *Say nothing!* The voice in her mind was still faint, but Morrigan could hear the urgency in it—and the command. Obviously, the Goddess didn't want Kai to know the truth about her.

So instead Morrigan drew herself up and straightened her spine. She wasn't just some powerless kid who could be intimated by a middle-aged man gone weird. "I thought you knew me. I'm the Light Bringer, High Priestess to Adsagsona. I just helped you find the right stone for Calliope's bench. And I don't have any idea what your problem is right now, so I'm going to leave you alone to work through your issues. Oh, and if it's too hard for you to be around me because you think I look like Myrna, then feel free to avoid me. Whatever." Morrigan stuck her chin in the air, turned and left the butter-colored room with Brina scrambling to follow her.

After Morrigan left, Kai found it difficult to concentrate. He should call the Sidetha workmen to him and have them transport the stone to Kegan's chamber so that the centaur could begin carving Myrna's image. He also had several other commissions he could work on: Woulff's Chieftain wanted a piece of rare onyx from which a wolf would be carved as decoration for their Great Chamber...a centaur herd was looking for a piece of sandstone to be carved into a likeness of Epona...

But instead of his commissions, all Kai could think about was Morrigan and what he'd felt when he'd touched her hand.

It wasn't a surprise that he had been curious about her. Even had she not looked remarkably like the dead Myrna, who he'd long thought of as the child he had never had, he would have been intrigued to meet a Light Bringer, especially after witnessing her demonstration of power earlier that day. As Kegan had explained, priestesses with that gift were rare—there probably wouldn't be another one born in his lifetime. And obviously a Light Bringer's affinity was close enough to his own that he would automatically find her fascinating.

They'd been having a lovely conversation. The child really was very much like Myrna—bright and intelligent and inquisitive. It had been a stroke of luck that she had identified the spirits in the bench meant for Calliope; she'd certainly saved him some time. Then he'd touched her and had a sudden, shocking glimpse into what was hidden within her soul.

Darkness. He'd been jolted by a seething darkness that hovered just under the child's skin like an unseen fungus. She was riddled with it. He saw the light within her, too. But it was being consumed by the darkness.

How could that be? The child was a Light Bringer, Chosen of the Sidetha's goddess. Kegan had said she had been gifted with great power by the Goddess and—

Kai's thoughts jolted to a halt. What if her power wasn't a gift from a goddess? Her remarkable similarity to Myrna couldn't be an accident. What if dark powers had brought her here, with this form and these powers, at this exact moment when Rhiannon was grief stricken by the loss of Myrna? The Fomorian War had been over for almost twenty years, but it still lived in his memory all too well. The demon Fomorians had infiltrated Partholon because people—regular Partholonian people—had allowed Pryderi, the horrible three-faced god of darkness, to gain a whispering access to their spirits, and then their lives, and finally their world.

Kai shivered and felt physically ill. Could it be happening again? Could Pryderi be behind Morrigan's amazing resemblance to Myrna, as well as her miraculous powers?

He had to speak with Kegan. The centaur was young, but he was a High Shaman and his powers in the spiritual realm were vast. He would know what they should do.

First Kai would instruct the workmen which pillar of marble he had chosen, and then he would take a quick turn through the sandstone and onyx rooms—working with the spirits in the stones would calm and center him. Tonight he would speak to the centaur. Kai left the chamber with determined steps, hating the odd feeling of watching eyes that crawled across his skin.

16

Morrigan fled to familiarity—to where she'd been retreating to lick her wounds and regroup since she was a toddler. Or at least the closest thing to familiarity. Morrigan found Birkita.

"Oh, my Lady! You've been gone all day. I was beginning to worry."

"I'm so sorry I've been such a bitch!" Morrigan told Birkita and then hugged her hard, not caring how it made the priestesses in the Usgaran stare and whisper. The older woman pulled back gently and looked into Morrigan's face.

"Come, you look tired and dirty. A good soak is what you need."

Morrigan wrapped her arm through Birkita's as they walked the short way to her bathing chamber. "I knew you'd know exactly what I needed."

They didn't talk much as Birkita helped her out of her dress and filled the deep stone tub full of warm, soapy water. It was only when Morrigan was submerged up to her neck and Birkita was behind her, gently rubbing shampoo into her head that Morrigan finally started to open up to her.

"The crystals showed me some amazing things today.

Rooms totally covered with amethyst, citrine, onyx, marble and even emeralds."

"Adsagsona has gifted her people greatly. You saw only a portion of those gifts today."

"No wonder Shayla has a thing for riches. She's surrounded by them."

"That is true," Birkita said slowly, "but the Mistress should be remembering and acknowledging the source of our riches."

"Oh, I agree with you. I'm just sayin', what I saw today was pretty impressive."

"But something else happened to you today, too. And I do not mean your interlude with Kegan."

Morrigan scowled. Just like G-ma, Birkita knew everything. "So you heard about me kissing Kegan."

"What I heard was that you were kissing one another."

Morrigan could hear the smile in Birkita's voice. She glanced over her shoulder, wiping suds from her face to peer up at the old woman. Sure enough, she was smiling. "So, you're not ashamed of me or embarrassed or anything like that?"

"Of course not. You have already explained your connection with the centaur's mirror image in your old world. And, even had the two of you not had that otherworldly connection, there is nothing wrong with you being attracted to Kegan and taking your pleasure where you may. I swore chastity in the Goddess's service, but that was my own choice." Birkita paused and cupped Morrigan's chin in her soapy hand. "Was sex not a gift from the Goddess in your old world?"

Ridiculously, Morrigan felt her cheeks getting warm again. "No, not really. Or, I guess you could say that there were a lot of rules attached to it." *Like not discussing it with your grandma,* she added silently.

"Truly? How very sad. Well, in this world you will not find

such an archaic viewpoint of sex. We enjoy the sexual act. A man is honored when a woman chooses to allow him to warm her bed, and her body." Birkita grinned, suddenly looking decades younger. "Not that fidelity isn't prized. It is. But dalliances are also acceptable, especially if one is dallying with a priestess. It is considered a blessing to be chosen to be the lover of a priestess."

"Oh, well. Okay," Morrigan said lamely. She was glad Birkita was cool with her messing around with Kegan, but that didn't mean she wanted to get into a big discussion with her about it.

"But as I said, something besides your flirtation with Kegan happened to you today. Can you talk about it?"

"I want to, but I don't really understand what happened, so it's hard."

"Just tell me, child."

"I found Kai in the room with butter-colored marble."

"Yes, the Stonemaster began his search for Myrna's stone today."

"He found it. Brina and I went into the room not long after the stone spoke to him."

"And that upset you?"

"No. Yes." Morrigan sighed and started over. "Not exactly. Yes, it makes me feel weird that Myrna died the day I entered Partholon. I—I guess I think I might have somehow caused what happened to her, and so the whole issue of Kai finding her stone and then Kegan carving it into what basically amounts to a tombstone for her really does upset me."

"Child, look at me."

Reluctantly, Morrigan turned around so that she could meet Birkita's eyes.

"Listen to me and listen well. You did not cause Myrna's death. She died in childbirth. It was sad and tragic, but it was her fate. Had it not been, I assure you Epona would have found some way to save her life."

"I want to believe you, really I do."

"Believe me, Morrigan. I have listened to Adsagsona's voice for almost sixty complete changes of the seasons. You did not cause this death, Fate did. Now, is that all that happened to you today? You were just upset by coming upon the stone that will be used for Myrna's monument?"

"No, that was only a small part of it. It happened when Kai touched me."

"Touched you! The Stonemaster has been visiting us for decades. Everyone knows of his relationship with Shayla, but he has never before behaved inappropriately with any of the priestesses. Rest assured, child, something will be done about this. He will not—"

"No, no, he didn't touch me like *that*. He was being perfectly respectful. We'd had a really good talk. He explained to me about what it is he does as a Stonemaster, and then he even showed me how to listen for the spirits in the stone myself." Remembering, Morrigan smiled. "The spirits in the marble showed me a garden at the Temple of the Muse—Calliope's garden is what Kai called it."

"Calliope is the Incarnate Muse of Epic Poetry."

"Oh, thanks. I didn't have any idea who she was, and I didn't want to seem so clueless that I had to ask him. Anyway, he said I'd helped him find the right piece of marble to carve for Calliope's bench, and then, just kidding around, he took my hand like he was going to kiss it in formal thanks. That's when it happened." Morrigan stopped and swallowed to clear the sudden dryness in her mouth. "I felt a weird jolt, like I'd been shocked." At Birkita's questioning look she said, "Think of it as a miniature piece of the electricity I told you about."

"Oh, the tamed lightning bolt."

"Right. He must have felt it, too, because his reaction was really weird. He stared at me like I'd turned into a monster or something and then he asked me who I was."

"What did you say?" The worried lines were back in Birkita's forehead.

"I didn't know what to say. I didn't know how to act. He changed so fast. I mean, he'd been so easy to talk to. I really liked him. We'd even talked about Myrna, and he told me that I looked just like her—oh, so did Kegan."

"So it is true. You are, indeed, her mirror."

Morrigan tried not to scowl. "I like to think that she was *my* mirror, but whatever. The end result is the same. Both of them say that I look just like her, except that she didn't have one bit of goddess power."

Birkita nodded slowly. "When it was announced that Myrna would marry a human man we all knew that she would not follow her mother as Epona's Chosen. But what you're saying is she wasn't touched at all by Epona?"

Morrigan shrugged. "That's what Kegan and Kai both said. Actually Kegan said she and I look exactly alike, *except* when I called the crystals to light. He said that Myrna never looked anything like me filled with the power of their light."

Instead of commenting, Birkita told Morrigan to tilt her head back into the stream of warm water so she could rinse her hair. She said little as she helped Morrigan from the bathing pool, wrapped her in thick towels and then situated her in front of the mirror in her chamber and began towel drying and combing through the thick length of her hair. Finally, Morrigan couldn't stand it any longer.

"Why do you think Kai reacted so weirdly to the shock that passed between us? And what the heck was that shock, anyway?"

Birkita met her reflected eyes in the mirror. "Kai hears the spirits within rocks, especially marble. Their spirits tell him the true nature of that object—what they are, where they belong, what is hidden within. It is as if he knows the destiny of the rock he touches."

"Could he have somehow felt the truth about me? That I'm the daughter of the real Rhiannon?"

"I have never known his ability to go beyond the inanimate. I have never even known it to extend beyond stone."

"Well, he sure knew something when he touched me, and that something definitely freaked him out." Birkita's brow wrinkled again and Morrigan sighed. "Freaked out equals shock plus annoyance. Actually, Kai wasn't just freaked. He looked horrified, like he'd just discovered something awful."

"If he believed Epona's Chosen to somehow be a charlatan, the Stonemaster would, indeed, be horrified."

"But how could he really believe that, no matter what he heard or saw or felt or whatever when he touched me? Grandpa and Grandma said Shannon was really Epona's Chosen. You said she's the Goddess's Chosen. Everyone believes it. They've been believing it since before I was born. I can't believe one touch of my hand could make him question that—let alone horrify him."

"Perhaps you were misreading his expression. The fact that you were born in a different world could have caused him to sense something odd about you, something indeterminate he did not understand, and perhaps he was simply surprised."

"I guess you're right," Morrigan said doubtfully. "Whatever happened between us I think the smartest thing for me to do would be to avoid him as much as possible. Anyway, shouldn't he be leaving soon? He did find Myrna's marble, and I helped him find the marble for Calliope's bench. He doesn't have any reason to hang around."

"Kai often comes with several commissions he must fulfill, so it would not be abnormal for him to stay."

"Especially if he wants to watch me."

"Yes," Birkita said.

"So I make that difficult to do, and then he'll leave."

"Let us hope that he doesn't go to Lady Rhiannon and tell her of you."

Morrigan chewed her lip. Then she blurted, "Would that really be so awful? I mean, I can see how it would be bad if the whole world found out about me and started to question whether Epona's Chosen was really Epona's Chosen. But what if it was just Shannon? Would it be so awful if she found out I was here?"

"I cannot imagine losing a child, so it is difficult for me to do more than just guess at an answer to that, but I believe it would cause her great pain to discover you so soon after her daughter's death."

Morrigan fought with the resentment Birkita's words made her feel. "Well, at least that means Kai probably won't run to her and blab about me."

"Let us take one thing at a time."

"So I avoid Kai."

"And come to know Kegan better?"

"Well, I do have a date to go out on the Salt Plains with him tonight at sunset."

"Sunset? It is almost sunset now."

"Oh, jeesh. I had no idea I'd been gone for so long. Okay, help me hurry and get ready. And then can you have one of the priestesses find Kegan and tell him to meet me by the entrance to the cave?"

"Of course, child."

Birkita helped her choose a beautiful piece of material the color of crimson sunsets that looked to Morrigan like it was just one big piece and not a dress at all, but then the older woman draped it around her, fastening it over her right shoulder with a golden brooch and finishing it off by wrapping an intricately tooled golden leather belt around her slim waist. Morrigan chose some very cool golden sandals that laced way up her calves to go with the dress. Then Birkita kissed her, and hurried off to get her message to Kegan. Morrigan took one more look at herself in the mirror and decided the outfit might actually make her look like a goddess, which helped only a little to quiet her nerves as she quickly followed the path to the main entrance of the cave, trying to distract herself from remembering she was meeting a guy who was half horse.

He was already there when she arrived, and he was again carrying a large basket. She saw him before he saw her, so Morrigan had time to slow down, breathe deeply and run her fingers through her hair for the thousandth time. She also was able to see him turn at the sound of her approach, and watch the appreciative look that came over his handsome face as he glimpsed her.

"My Lady, your escort awaits you." He smiled warmly at her and bowed with a well-practiced flourish.

"Thank you, kind sir," she said, and curtsied playfully. "Hey, what's in the basket?"

"Birkita said you spent the day exploring the caves, but she said nothing about you exploring the kitchen. I guessed that you hadn't eaten—again."

"Seems you're getting in the habit of feeding me."

"And this would be a habit that is more enjoyable than most."

"Really?" She fell into step beside him as they walked out of the cave. "Do you have a lot of unsavory habits?"

"Well, I will admit to sneaking into the kitchen late at night—frequently. My mother has told me the habit will cause dark dreams, but so far that hasn't been the case."

"I think it would just cause me to get fat," Morrigan said.

"Well, I can say that tonight I'm glad you haven't made a habit of eating late at night. That would make the next part of the evening decidedly less enjoyable."

They'd exited the cave and were standing just a few feet from its mouth. Morrigan looked up at him and gave him an exaggerated, pretend look of maidenly shock. "Ohmygoodness, you are not implying that you think you're going to see me naked, are you? Because I'll have you know that I might not be that kind of girl."

He smiled and his eyes sparkled. "While the possibility of seeing you unclothed is intriguing, and one that I will admit has not been far from my mind today, it was not to what I was referring."

"Huh?" she said succinctly.

Kegan pointed toward the land in front of them. Below, Morrigan could see the Salt Plains and the shards of giant crystal boulders poking up out of it. "The sun hasn't set, but twilight is not long off. If you want to reach the Salt Plains before twilight, then we will need to hurry."

"Okay, so let's hurry."

He smiled. "I mean faster than your shapely human legs can carry you on those lovely golden sandals."

"So, I'm going to need to ride..." Morrigan started to look around for a horse and then it hit her. Her eyes widened in realization. "You!"

Kegan grinned and nodded. "Me."

"Oh, jeesh, you weren't kidding this morning when you said you'd be my escort and my mount."

"I wasn't kidding."

Morrigan looked up to his tall, totally saddle-free equine back. "I—I don't know about this."

Clearly enjoying himself, Kegan quirked an eyebrow at her. "You cannot ride?"

"Of course I can ride."

"Well, no matter if you're not experienced. I take very little direction."

"Okay, smartie, that's not what I'm worried about and I'm not an inexperienced rider, although my experience with centaurs is limited."

"To me?" he asked with a grin.

"Yeah, limited exclusively to you."

"Exclusively to me…" He moved closer to her and took her hand. "I like the way that sounds, and I give you my word that I shall be gentle with you."

"I don't have any way to get up there." She pointed to his equine back. "I mean, you aren't saddled or anything, so no stirrups."

He laughed. "Rest assured that I can help you mount, my Lady."

Morrigan felt her stupid cheeks getting warm and hated the fact that she couldn't help blushing. "I have a dress on."

"You do. And a lovely dress it is, too."

She sighed. "Thank you. But I'm not exactly dressed for riding."

"Perhaps you aren't dressed for riding an equine mount, but you are dressed perfectly for riding a centaur who adores you."

Morrigan's stomach did a ridiculous little flippity-flop. "And that would be you."

"That would be me," he repeated. "Come." Kegan opened his arms to her and grinned. "Unless you are afraid."

"I am *not* afraid," she said automatically. "I'm just discombobulated."

"Discombobulated? Another Oklahoma word?"

"No." Morrigan's cheeks flamed even hotter. "It's a grandma word."

"We're not going to make it in time."

"Fine. Let's go."

"Come to me then." Morrigan stepped within his arms and he rested one hand on either side of her waist. "Are you ready?"

"Yes," she lied. And then she sucked in a gasp when he lifted her and, as easily as if she weighed no more than the basket he'd dropped at her feet, Kegan twisted at the waist and plopped her unceremoniously onto his back.

Morrigan busied herself with rearranging her dress, desperately glad she wasn't wearing one of her short little jean skirts.

"Hold tight. The descent is steep," Kegan said as he picked up the basket and started forward.

"Hold tight to what? There's no—" Morrigan's words choked off when he surged over the edge of the drop-off and started to slide down the steep incline. Not knowing what else to do, she wrapped her arms around him and tried not to fall off while she peered over his shoulder. Without missing a stride, Kegan glanced back at her and grinned. *A total and utter rake, just like Birkita said,* Morrigan thought. Not that she minded...

17

"That wasn't so bad, was it?"

Scary drop-off and crazy descent behind them, Morrigan had managed to pry her arms from around him. She was sitting up straight, attempting to appear relaxed, with her hands resting lightly on his bare shoulders. Actually, she felt every centimeter of where their bodies met—hers intimately against his. "Oh, yeah, great. I can promise you I'd prefer a saddle," she muttered.

Kegan laughed and looked over his shoulder at her. "You don't need a saddle. You have a lovely seat." The glint in his eyes gave his words a definite double meaning, which Morrigan ignored.

"I'm going to have a sore seat if I don't get down and walk for myself. Aren't we almost there? It's practically sunset."

"Just over this next little hummock," Kegan assured her.

And, sure enough, Kegan climbed up a little knoll and they came out of a little grove of stunted pines to gaze on a vast expanse of water interspersed with enormous, jutting rock.

"Here, let me help you." Kegan swiveled at the waist and hooked his hands around her waist again, lifting her gently from his back to the ground beside him. Morrigan couldn't help smiling at him as he made an obviously reluctant show of releasing her.

"I was probably heavy," Morrigan said, still feeling nervous.

He smiled. "You were perfect."

"Well, do I thank you or give you a good petting?"

His smile widened. "I believe I would enjoy both."

"Let's see how you behave on the way back. I don't want to reward you too soon," she said.

Kegan laughed. "I can see you're going to be one of those difficult riders."

"Oh, so I'm just one in a group. How many women have you given rides to, anyway?"

He was still smiling, but his eyes had gone dark and serious. "I have given my share of rides to women, but they all have become uninteresting shadows of the past in comparison to you, Light Bringer."

"Even Myrna?" Morrigan couldn't stop herself from asking.

"Even Myrna." Kegan gestured out at the Salt Plains. "Better hurry down to lake level, jealous one, or you will miss the sunset."

Morrigan started to say that she wasn't jealous, but bit off that lie before she could speak it. Instead she took what remained of her dignity and walked over to the edge of the little round hill.

"Wow! It's even more incredible-looking down here close to it."

"Then let's get even closer." Kegan took her hand and, leaving the basket on the little hill, they descended the last few feet to reach the level of the Salt Plains.

Morrigan sniffed the air. "Smells like the ocean, minus the fish."

"It is too briny for fish. See how even the scrub plants stop growing well away from the shore?"

She nodded, but Morrigan wasn't really paying attention to him. Her attention had been thoroughly captivated by the jutting hunks of crystal that rose from the shallow, salty water like escaping secrets. The sun was just beginning to nudge the western horizon to her left, changing the sky from the clear blue of a warm autumn day to the passionate colors of fuchsia and saffron and gold. Where the sky touched the crystal boulders it set them alight with the colors of evening.

"I want to go out there." She all but hopped up and down with excitement.

"Your wishes, my Lady, are my commands."

This time when Kegan opened his arms to her Morrigan went eagerly to him, sliding more gracefully onto his back now that her attention wasn't focused on her own embarrassment.

"There!" Morrigan pointed over his shoulder to a crystal boulder that looked fairly flat on top and wide enough for her to stand on. "Take me out to that one."

The centaur entered the lake, breaking the glassy surface and making his way easily to the flat stone several yards from the shoreline. Morrigan noticed that it really was much shallower than it looked. The water sometimes barely covered Kegan's hooves.

"I guess I could have walked out here. You were right, it's not deep at all."

He smiled over his shoulder at her. "You would have ruined those golden sandals. And I like the excuse to get you on my back."

She pushed at his shoulder and pretended to frown at him. "Just put me on that rock over there."

"As you wish, my Lady." And without getting even one of her toes wet, Kegan lifted her off his back and onto the rock.

The instant Morrigan's feet touched the top of the crystal she felt it. Power. It pulsed up from the rock. She crouched, pressing her hands against the jagged surface, and whispered, "Do you know me?"

We know you, Light Bringer.

As in the cave, the answer somehow moved from the crystals through the skin and nerves, muscle and blood of her hands and arms, making its way, currentlike, into her body.

"Do the crystals acknowledge you?" Kegan asked.

She looked up at him, eyes shining. "Yes! They know me. It's a little different from inside the cave. Out here it's more like an echo of a sound, not as exuberant as it is in there. But they still call me Light Bringer."

"Then perhaps you should call forth their light," Kegan said, and then he took several steps back, as if to give her room. He jerked his chin toward the area over her right shoulder. "The timing is perfect. The sun is setting."

Morrigan stood up and turned around. The sun was slowly falling into the western horizon, casting even more flamelike colors into the sky surrounding them. From the section of the Salt Plains that was already in shadow, mist was beginning to curl up from the briny water, white and diaphanous as drifting clouds. Suddenly the brilliant sky and the beauty of the mist and water reminded her of Oklahoma and the many glorious sunsets she had watched with her grandparents, and Morrigan was overwhelmed by a sense of homesickness. *It was your birthplace, but never your world* came the insistent voice in her head that seemed clearer and louder than it had been since she'd entered Partholon.

Cherishing your birthplace does not denigrate your new home...

Morrigan jerked a little in surprise as the voice whispered in the wind around her. Weird that she hadn't heard it in so long. Then she shook her head and drew in a deep, cleansing breath. No. She didn't want to listen to whispers in the wind anymore. She wasn't a nobody who needed to grasp at whispered straws to find her way. She was a Light Bringer, the High Priestess and Chosen of a Goddess.

Morrigan lifted her arms. "Spirits of the crystal, you call me Light Bringer. So I ask that you bring me light!"

Light Bringer! The title echoed eerily around her as the shards of crystal answered her call and blazed. And as the boulders glistened a luminous golden light that seemed to harness the rays of the dying sun, Morrigan gasped with the power that filled her. It was as if the light was shooting through her body and filling her with heat and sensation and joy. She held her arms out in front of her, enthralled by the way her skin glowed, like she was crystal turned flesh, turned fire. And then, on a whim, she held out her hand, palm up, and said, "Light for me." The flame that burst up from her hand was so unlike the furtive little sputtering things she had had to concentrate hard to conjure back in Oklahoma that she gasped in shock, and then the gasp turned into laughter. Flame still glowing from her hand, Morrigan turned toward Kegan.

"Look what I can do!"

"I've never seen anything like it—I've never seen anything like you." Kegan's eyes devoured her, changing the heat and passion and joy that had been building inside Morrigan to pure, raw passion. The centaur read the change within her and began moving toward her. "You are light and flame, so beautiful that it's difficult to gaze fully upon you. You could shine light into any darkness, Morrigan."

He stood in front of her. With a flick of her wrist, she extinguished the flame and then leaned forward and wrapped her glowing arm around his shoulders. Desire was burning so hot within her that she had to calm her breathing before she spoke. Finally, she said, in a voice she barely recognized as her own. "I want you to kiss me, and then make love to me while I'm burning like this."

With a moan that was more like a growl, Kegan bent to possess her mouth, but it was Morrigan who was the pursuer. She met him with a passion that flamed like the crystals surrounding them. Kegan lifted her in his arms and when he would have carried her like that back to the shore she looked into his eyes and said, "No, put me on your back again."

Wordlessly, he changed her position in his arms and turned so that he could place her astride him. Morrigan wrapped her arms around him and pressed her thrumming body into him—breasts, thighs, the very core of her—all the while exploring the strong line of his neck with her lips and teeth.

"Ah, gods! Your body is so warm you feel afire," Kegan moaned.

"Is it too much? Am I hurting you?" she asked breathlessly.

"No, gods no! Don't stop."

Kegan surged out of the water and covered the short distance back up to the top of the little knoll on which he'd left their basket. He lifted Morrigan from his back, holding her close to him and devouring her mouth. When he pulled away she made a frustrated sound and tried to press herself against him again.

"Wait, I must call the Change to me."

What he was saying managed to clear some of the red haze of lust from Morrigan's heated mind and she nodded shakily. "Okay, what do you want me to do?"

"You must remain very quiet. Even if what you see frightens you."

"But—"

"Do you trust me?"

Morrigan didn't hesitate. "I do."

Kegan gave Morrigan a brief, hard kiss, and then moved several paces away from her. With the backdrop of twilight and mist and glowing golden stones silhouetting him, Morrigan watched Kegan bow his head and begin a chant. He spoke low and deep in a language she could not understand, but she could feel the power of his words brushing against her sensitized skin. As he spoke, he began lifting his arms and it seemed to Morrigan that his skin began to vibrate weirdly, like it was moving almost too fast for her eyes to see, and then the vibration became shimmering and, as his chant grew louder and louder, Morrigan's gaze was pulled to his face. She had to press her hand against her mouth to keep from screaming at his expression of agony. And then Kegan's body exploded in light.

Morrigan blinked hard, trying to clear the spots from her eyes. She wanted to call Kegan, but was still too scared to say anything.

"You may speak now," Kegan gasped through gulping breaths.

Her vision cleared and she saw Kegan, naked except for the leather vest he still wore, on his knees—his *human knees.* His head was bowed and he was leaning hard on one of his arms, which was shaking pretty badly. She rushed to him and dropped to her knees, brushing his damp hair out of his face.

"Ohmygod, Kegan! Are you okay? You scared the crap out of me!"

He looked up at her and gave her a crooked grin. "The Change takes some getting used to."

"Some getting used to hell! It was awful. It hurt you."

"Yes. It definitely hurts." His grin widened as his breathing began to return to normal. He stood up only a little shakily, and pulled her up with him.

"You should have told me it would hurt so much." Morrigan rested her arms lightly on his chest, almost afraid to touch him.

"I wasn't thinking of pain when I decided to Change."

She shook her head. "Well, I'll know next time."

"And I am pleased there will be a next time."

Kegan bent to kiss her briefly, then, surprising her, he took Morrigan's hand and walked slowly, though steadily, over to where he'd left their basket. With absolutely no modesty, he peeled off his vest and then opened the basket to pull out a blanket from its depths. As he spread it out on the ground, Morrigan got an eyeful of Kegan as a man. She absolutely liked what she saw, even if his calling the Change to him had allowed rational thought to overshadow raw lust, so that she was beginning to feel nervous. Very nervous.

"Do I pass inspection?"

"Yes," she said quickly, realizing he had been standing there, naked, watching her watch him for several minutes.

"Good. I'm glad the way I look pleases you."

"I like the way you look as a centaur, too." She meant it. He was an excellent-looking male in either form.

"Good," he repeated, smiling slowly. "May I ask a favor of you, my Lady?"

Morrigan looked at him dubiously, but said, "Yes."

Kegan pointed back out at the Salt Plains. Morrigan's eyes followed his hand. The crystals were still glowing, but not with the blaze they'd shone with before. The sky was fading from flame to ash, and the mist was thickening to make everything look surreal.

"Make them light again."

Morrigan looked from the Salt Plains back to Kegan. "You want me to go back out there?"

"No, I want you to stay here with me."

"But I can't do it from here."

"I believe you can." He walked over to the edge of the little knoll and held his hand out to her.

Morrigan came to him and let him turn her so that she was looking out at the softly glowing crystals and he was standing behind her, hands resting on her shoulders. He bent and his warm breath tickled her ear, making her shiver with remembered passion.

"Tell them to light again. They'll hear you."

"I don't know. It's so far away."

"It is, but you are still connected to the spirits. Feel the ground under your feet. Somewhere below us is the cave, and within the cave are more of your crystals. They will connect you to the crystals out there. Concentrate, Light Bringer. Call them. The spirits will answer you."

Use your power… The words filled her mind. Morrigan concentrated, focusing on the ground beneath her feet, just as she had focused earlier when she stood on the crystal boulder. This time she felt farther, searched harder… Yes! Soon there was an answering wave of sensation that lifted from the earth itself. *Light Bringer! We hear you.* It was faint, but it was definitely the jubilant voice of the crystal spirits in the cave. Smiling, Morrigan lifted her arms as she shouted.

"Light the Salt Plains for me again! Light for me!" Morrigan sucked in a gasping breath as the power of light flooded through her and the shards of crystal boulders jutting from the shallow lake lit again with their distinctive sun-kissed light.

"I knew you could do it. You're my flame, my shining one," Kegan said, his voice already deepening with desire.

Morrigan pulled her gaze from the brilliant rocks and turned in his arms. She didn't have to look at her skin to know she was glowing. The light within her pulsed through her blood, heating her and filling her with what was becoming a familiar burning passion that she ached to slake. Her virginity be damned, Morrigan's nervousness evaporated under the heat of her need. She kissed Kegan, long and hard and demandingly. Then she left him to walk over to the blanket he had already spread on the ground. He followed her. She didn't have to look back to know it. She could feel his heat as if it were an extension of her own. Still turned away from him, Morrigan took off her dress, letting it and her underclothes pool in a pile at her feet. When she turned to face him, she was completely naked.

They moved together as if a trap had been sprung. There was no hesitation, no timidity in Morrigan. What she lacked in experience, she made up for in passion. She wanted to taste, touch, experience all of him. It was as if her glowing skin was absorbing his desire. The more she touched the more aroused she became. Kegan was no inexperienced lover. He took his time with her, even though she was pushing him to his limit. He tasted her and readied her before finally positioning himself above her and entering her with one thrust.

Morrigan cried aloud in pain at the sudden intrusion of his hard flesh, causing Kegan's head to jerk back.

"I am your first?" he gasped.

She nodded.

"Ah, gods!" He pressed his forehead to hers and whispered, "You should have told me. I would have been gentler. I would have—"

Her lips stopped his words. She kissed him, letting the delicious heat inside her that had only been temporarily banked begin to flame again. Already her body was accustoming itself to him. Already she moved restlessly, wanting more.

Kegan responded, pulling back only enough so that he could look into her eyes. And when their bodies gathered and then released, she cried his name and he claimed her mouth again, whispering against her lips, "My flame…"

18

Morrigan lay in his arms as Kegan watched the glow of her skin fade. Saying that she fascinated him would be a distinct understatement. What had begun as curiosity, simple physical attraction, and he admitted to himself, an interest in the power she wielded, had shifted into something so alien to what he usually felt for a lover that she had utterly disarmed him.

Kai had been right when he'd needled Kegan about desiring Myrna for the power she could have gained him. Status and power had long been his guiding light. Ironic, really, that he now had a new light. He glanced at Morrigan. Her eyes were closed and her face was relaxed. Kegan flipped more of the edge of the blanket over her and she sighed and snuggled closer to him.

By Epona's sacred chalice, she'd been a virgin! With the un-bridled, passionate way she'd responded to him he would never have guessed it. Morrigan was such a contradiction. She possessed the gifts of a great priestess, yet she seemed utterly sur-prised by those gifts. She burned with desire and passion, yet she had been untouched before he had possessed her.

To possess her... The thought circled around and around his mind. He wanted her, there was no doubt about that. But it was more than a physical lust and more than a base desire for power. Morrigan touched something within him that had lain dormant until he met her. It was true that Myrna had stirred it, but she had been a colorless version of Morrigan, his flame.

Could it be that Epona had fashioned him for Morrigan, and that was why his reaction to her was innate? Kegan frowned. He'd never really considered the ramifications of being the mate of someone's soul. Sure, he'd *appeared* to consider it when he was wooing Myrna. Centaur High Shamans spoke amongst themselves of the responsibility of being destined to mate Epona's Chosen, especially when the current Chosen had a daughter of mating age. They mused about what it would truly be like to love a woman a goddess had fashioned for them. Kegan remembered how he had often been the centaur to make sarcastic comments about the subject, quipping that if a woman had been fashioned for him by a goddess then perhaps she had been made without the typical female gift for nagging.

Kegan closed his eyes and sighed heavily. He had truly been an obnoxious young ass, as the older High Shaman had called him.

"You're sighing," Morrigan murmured.

"Just recalling the mistakes of my past," he said before he considered how the words might sound to Morrigan.

She raised herself on an elbow and lifted a brow at him. "Mistakes of your past? Do tell. Do they involve disgustingly sordid affairs and lots of broken hearts?"

He chuckled. "No, my flame, they do not."

"No broken hearts?" Morrigan snorted. "I find that hard to believe."

"Do you?" He smoothed back the hair that had fallen over one of her blue eyes.

"Well, yeah. I mean, you obviously knew what you were doing, so you must be experienced." He watched with amusement as her cheeks flushed. "Not that I expected you to be a virgin or anything."

"But you were," he said softly.

She nodded. Morrigan didn't say anything, though he could read the depth of her feelings in her eyes. He wanted to pull her closer and hold her and tell her that she couldn't have been more perfect—that he would cherish the gift she'd given him forever, just as he would cherish her. But Kegan sensed Morrigan would find his words condescending. So he simply kissed her softly before saying, "Had you told me I would have chosen a more luxurious spot and a different—"

Her fingers against his mouth stilled his words. "No. I wouldn't have wanted it any other way. This spot was perfect. With the crystals out there and the cave under us I felt safe, like I belong here."

"You do belong here. You belong with me." Kegan put his hand over hers and kissed her fingers. His heart felt so full that he thought it would burst from his chest. How had he believed his life had been complete before he'd met her? And then the realization that without her his life would be dim and empty slammed into his gut. He wrapped his arms around her and pulled her to him, kissing her with newfound tenderness.

She pulled a little back from him after the kiss ended. "What is it?" she asked, studying his face.

Kegan decided that one aspect of being fashioned for one another was the fact that they could read each other perhaps a little too easily.

"In Oklahoma do they have a thing called soul mates?"

Morrigan looked surprised at the question. "I guess so." She thought about her grandparents. "Yeah, I suppose they do. I told you my grandparents raised me, right?"

"Yes."

"Well, I'd say that they're soul mates. I can't imagine one without the other, and they've been married forever."

He nodded, but hesitated, not sure how to frame what it

was he wished to say to her. "Yes, that is one kind of soul mate. A couple who finds one another and spends their lives together. Often when one dies, the other follows soon after."

Morrigan's forehead wrinkled. "Kegan, I don't like to think about anything happening to either of them."

"I'm sorry. I didn't mean—" Kegan broke off and sighed deeply. Then he started anew. "I'm going about this badly. I have no experience in this kind of thing."

Morrigan grinned impishly. "Could have fooled me."

He gave a playful tug to the lock of her hair he had been twining around his finger. "Not *that* kind of thing. What I mean is I have little experience trying to describe what it is when two people are literally fashioned for one another by the gods—when it's preordained at their birth that the two should unite and spend their lives as one. Is that something couples experience in Oklahoma?"

"In books."

"Books?"

"Yeah, people write about it in books and…" Morrigan paused, seemed uncomfortable suddenly, and then, awkwardly, began busying herself with rewrapping the red material of her gown around her. "Uh, it's always happily ever after in books. My friend Gena calls it Romancia Landia. You know, star-crossed lovers, soul mates, made for each other, blah, blah, sob, blah."

"You do not believe it's possible for one person to be solely fashioned for another?"

She must have noticed the change in his tone, because she looked up from fastening her dress. Morrigan shrugged. "I don't know. I've never really thought about it."

"Think about it."

"Huh?"

Kegan rubbed his hand through his hair. The conversation was definitely not going the way he'd intended. He hadn't meant to sound short with her, but the way she was discounting what he was saying made his gut clench. "Morrigan, what I'm trying to tell you is that I think we may have been fashioned for one another." She just stared at him without saying anything, so he hurried on. "You are a powerful priestess, with perhaps as great a gift as Epona's own Chosen. The Goddess always fashions a centaur High Shaman to love Epona's Chosen. I believe Adsagsona may have fashioned me as your mate, as your High Shaman."

Morrigan blinked a couple of times, like she needed to clear her vision. "But I'm not Epona's Chosen."

"I know, but doesn't it make sense that a High Priestess with the great and unusual gift of being a Light Bringer would need a mate who is more her equal, more than a mere man?"

"I guess it might, but you make it sound awful cold. More like a business arrangement than, well, Romancia Landia."

That made him smile. "I said I had little experience in speaking of these things, and that I was doing it badly." He took her hand gently in his, and then pressed it against his bare chest over his heart. "The true reason I believe I was fashioned to love you can be found in here, where my bumbling words cannot make a mess of it."

"Kegan, I don't know what to say." She pulled her hand from his and started going through the basket of food. "I mean, I had a good time tonight and I really do like you, but everything's so confusing for me right now I just can't think long-term about a relationship."

Abruptly he stood and paced several feet away from her. What had just happened? How could she be rejecting him? Had he mistaken what he saw in her eyes? Felt in her touch?

"Kegan? Are you mad at me?"

He spoke over his shoulder to her. "No. I need to call the Change to me, though."

"Okay, I'll be quiet," she said.

He turned his back to her, but he could still feel her eyes on him. Forcing his mind to clear and then focus, he reached into himself and then beyond, to touch and then join that spark of divinity that connects everything in the world—that shifts spirit and matter until one is interchangeable with the other. Kegan breathed in the divine and welcomed the pain as it sliced through him while sinew and bone, muscle, blood and skin shifted and Changed to form centaur.

"That is so amazing."

Still breathing hard, he turned around to find Morrigan watching him.

"*You* are so amazing," Morrigan continued.

Then she dropped the wineskin she had been holding and walked over to him. Kegan felt the tightness in his chest begin to relax as she touched his face and then stepped into his arms.

"You're going to have to give me some time," she said. "So much has changed for me so quickly. I just don't know if I can handle anything else."

Kegan heard himself saying words that just days before would have made him disdain the speaker. "I could help you. You don't have to be alone. You don't have to depend only upon yourself."

Morrigan raised that slim brow at him. "Shouldn't I be depending on my goddess?"

"Perhaps you should consider the possibility that it was your goddess who brought me to you, and that it is her will that we be together." Kegan bent and kissed her, claiming not simply her mouth as his own, but her soul. As Morrigan responded he felt the fierce joy of it beat strong within his chest. She would be his. She must be his.

When the kiss ended he was relieved to see that she was

breathless. Then he really looked at her and realized that her eyes held an odd expression, almost as if she was trying not to weep.

"Kegan, I have to tell you something."

Worry squeezed his chest as he tried to smile. "What is it, my flame?"

"You know how much I look like Myrna?"

Confused, he nodded. "Yes, but I explained that I didn't actually care for her."

"I know. It's not that." She drew a deep breath and Kegan thought she looked like she was readying herself to plunge into cold water. "There was someone in Oklahoma who looked as much like you as I look like Myrna."

Kegan felt as if she had punched him in the stomach. "I don't understand."

"I don't either, not really."

"But you said there were no centaurs in your land."

"There aren't. Kyle looks like you when you're in human form. Exactly like you."

The truth hit him. "You loved this man."

She flushed, which Kegan found more telling than her spoken answer. "No, I didn't love him. I didn't know him that well."

"But you were connected to him."

"Probably about as much as you were connected to Myrna." Kegan snorted.

Morrigan's brow went back up. "Oh, so there was more between you and Myrna than you've admitted."

"We are not talking about Myrna. We are talking about Kyle."

Her gaze was steady. It felt as if she was trying to see within him, and probably being entirely too successful—which should be further proof that the two of them had been divinely fashioned to be together.

"Look, I think we're both more than a little jealous."

Kegan grunted, willing to accede that much.

"But the relationships with Kyle and Myrna are not really bothering me—the fact that they both died the same day is what's freaking me out."

Kegan felt his blood turn cold. "Kyle is dead?"

"The same day Myrna died." Kegan could feel her body trembling. "Which was the same day Adsagsona pulled me from Oklahoma to the Sidetha."

Kegan felt dazed and numb all at once. What was happening here? Then, as if he truly was stuck in the middle of a dream, a desperate voice came to him, carried on the soft evening wind.

"Morrigan! Kegan!"

Morrigan pulled out of his arms. "Birkita?"

The old priestess rushed up over the rise in the knoll. Running, she stumbled up to them, breathing so heavily that Morrigan had to support her as she collapsed.

"Birkita, what's wrong?" Morrigan said as she held the priestess in her arms. Her color was terrible and her body was trembling.

"It is Kai," Birkita gasped as she gulped air.

"Kai! What has happened?" Kegan moved to the priestess to help Morrigan support her.

"An accident." Birkita looked up at him and he could see fear and sadness in her eyes. "Come quickly, Kegan. I believe he is dying."

19

"Are you sure you can carry both of us?" Morrigan said as she slid forward so that Kegan could lift Birkita to his back behind her.

"Of course. Even your combined weight is nothing to me. Just hold tight. I'm going to be moving swiftly." He squeezed her hand before surging off the knoll. At the speed Kegan was going it was impossible for Morrigan to ask Birkita any more questions. She knew she shouldn't let her imagination run wild, but it was hard not to. Birkita had said very little. She hadn't actually had time to fill them in, even if she'd recovered from her rush to them so that she didn't have to gasp words between breaths. Kegan had started hurling them up on his back as soon as he'd realized the gravity of the situation. Morrigan held tight to his newly familiar torso and tried, unsuccessfully, not to feel like a dark cloud of death was following her.

Kegan slid to a halt inside the cave entrance, where Perth was waiting for them, which to Morrigan wasn't a particularly good sign.

"Explain what happened," Kegan snapped as he lifted Birkita and her from his back. When Perth opened his mouth to being the explanation, Kegan said, "Talk while you take us to him."

Morrigan watched the centaur closely as she wrapped her arm around Birkita's waist to help support the old woman while they followed Perth. She'd seen Kegan be playful and flirtatious, romantic and sexy. This was the first glimpse she'd had of another side of him—one that seemed to take on command easily and react with calm leadership in times of crisis.

Perth launched into an explanation of Kai's accident, speaking in short, fast bursts while they rushed after him through the tunnels.

"The Stonemaster was found in the onyx room. He must have climbed up to harvest a piece of the stone. He fell." Perth didn't say anything for several minutes, and Morrigan could see that Kegan was preparing to prod him further, when he went on with his recitation. "He is barely conscious, but he would not allow anyone to move him until he spoke to you."

"The onyx room—that's close to where I saw him earlier today," Morrigan said to fill the tension in the dead air after it was obvious that Perth didn't want to say anything else.

"You saw Kai today?" Kegan asked.

Morrigan could feel the sharp look Birkita shot her. Did Birkita think she had something to do with Kai's accident? Morrigan swallowed back a terrible sickness that threatened to clog her throat and made herself answer Kegan. "Yes, I was exploring the caves. He was in the butter-colored marble room with the stone you're going to carve into Myrna's tomb."

"So he did find the stone."

Morrigan nodded. "Yes, and he was fine when I left him."

Kegan gave her an odd look. "Of course he was." He turned to address Perth. "What are his wounds?"

"He struck his head. His leg is broken." Perth drew a deep

breath before he added, "And one of the shards of onyx disemboweled him."

"Will he live?" Kegan said.

"I believe his insistence that we not move him until you are there answers that question."

Morrigan saw Kegan's jaw tense. "Faster!" he commanded Perth, who broke into a run.

There was no way Birkita could keep up with them, so Morrigan stayed behind to follow more slowly with the priestess. Her stomach clenched into a rigid ball as she tried to put words to the nameless fear that was clinging to her. "Birkita, what did Perth mean when he said that Kai calling for Kegan answered the question of whether he would live or not?"

Birkita spoke through panting breaths. "Kegan can aid Kai's passing into the next world."

She wanted to question Birkita further, but they'd come to the entrance to the onyx room. Birkita drew herself up and entered the room before Morrigan, murmuring to her that she should take a moment to steady herself.

Later, Morrigan realized a lifetime wouldn't have been enough time to steady herself for what waited for her in that room.

The chamber was big, but the glossy black rock that filled it made it seem small, enclosed, almost claustrophobic, even though she'd never been claustrophobic in her life. There was a press of people within. They were clustered in a semicircle around the wall that had the most massive, jagged teeth of stones jutting out of it. Telling herself over and over again *I can do this…I can do this…*Morrigan grabbed Birkita's hand and together they walked forward.

She was taking deep breaths to try to help her stay calm, but when the smell hit her—thick, metallic fresh blood mixed with something foul like diarrhea—Morrigan gagged and shifted to shallow, openmouthed breathing that made her feel light-headed. She'd been keeping her gaze up, trying to ready herself for her first view of Kai, when she noticed that the jagged peaks of onyx she had been staring at weren't just glossy. They were wet. Morrigan tasted bile. Had she not been clinging to Birkita's hand she knew she would have run from the room.

Courage...the Stonemaster has simply met his destiny... The words echoed softly through her mind at almost the same instant Birkita squeezed her hand and whispered, "Courage, child."

Morrigan pulled her gaze away from the blood-coated rocks. The first person she noticed was Shayla. The Sidetha's Mistress was standing completely still. Her back was pressed against the jagged onyx rock and tears were running down her cheeks as she stared down at the man who lay at her feet. Morrigan felt pity for her. Shayla looked completely devastated. Maybe she really did love Kai. Then her eyes found Kegan. He was on his knees. She was looking at him from the side as he bent over a fallen figure. Her eyes shifted to the woman who knelt opposite Kegan. She looked vaguely familiar, and Morrigan realized she must be the Sidetha's doctor. Two younger women stood attentively on either side of her, handing her instruments and strips of linen as the doctor shot commands to them. Finally, Morrigan allowed her gaze to go lower.

Kai was lying on his back. His head was bandaged though red seeped through the white linen. His body was partially covered with blankets, but his right leg stuck out at an odd angle from the knee and, feeling even sicker, Morrigan saw that the white thing she had at first thought was a piece of a bandage or splint was really the broken shard of his tibia. But even as horrible as those wounds were, Morrigan knew that what the doctor was bending over, pressing her hands into and trying to stitch up, was even worse. She looked at Kai's midsection and was relieved that the doctor's hands and implements obscured her view of the wound. She glanced back at Kai's face. He was worse than pale. His skin had an awful grayish tint. His lips were open and he was breathing in shallow pants. His eyes were closed.

Morrigan watched as Kegan gently took Kai's limp hand. The centaur bowed his head over the Stonemaster and began rhythmically speaking words that sounded like they were from the same language he had used to call the Change to him. And then Morrigan jerked with shock when Kai's eyes came abruptly open. She was amazed that his voice sounded so normal and that it carried so easily to her.

"Not yet. Not yet, my friend."

Kegan's chanting stopped immediately and he bent closer to Kai. "You asked for me to come. When you are ready to begin your journey to Epona's meadows simply nod. I will guide you, my old friend."

"You must listen to me, Kegan."

"I am here, Kai."

"She is tainted by darkness."

Morrigan felt Kai's words as if he had slashed a knife into her chest. She let loose Birkita's hand and, as if on its own, her body propelled itself woodenly forward.

"Kai, I don't understand. Who is tainted by darkness?" Kegan was saying.

Kai's eyes, wide and unnaturally bright, searched the circle of people surrounding him until he found Morrigan. "It is she!" The dying man's words were weirdly loud, causing Morrigan to flinch. "The Light Bringer carries darkness within her."

Morrigan's head began shaking back and forth, back and forth. She knew Kegan was staring in shock at her, just as she knew the murmuring crowd was whispering about her. But she had eyes only for Kai.

"No," she said, still shaking her head. "Not me. I'm not like her. Grandpa said I wasn't like her. I am not filled with darkness."

"You are so young." Compassion softened the Stonemaster's pain-racked face. "Your ego blinds you. But darkness is here. And darkness is there." With a shaking, blood-speckled hand Kai raised a finger and pointed at Morrigan. "You should return to the place from which you came and take the darkness with you."

Pain deludes him. Do not allow him to steal your birthright.

"No!" Panic beat furiously inside her, deafening her with the white roar of its wings as she shouted at Kai and the voice in her head. "I am the Light Bringer. I belong here." Morrigan began stumbling back, moving away from Kai.

Birkita was at her side again, grasping her hand and stopping her exit. "You must stay, Priestess." She spoke softly but firmly. "It is your task, along with the High Shaman's, to aid the Stonemaster's spirit journey to Epona."

"You aid him. He doesn't think I belong here." Morrigan pulled her hand from Birkita, turned and ran blindly from the chamber. She didn't once look back. She couldn't. She didn't want to see the doubt and disgust in Kegan's face and the disappointment in Birkita's.

Morrigan didn't have any idea where she was going. The truth was, she didn't care. She just had to get away from their eyes: Kai's, Kegan's, Birkita's, Shayla's. All of them.

She probably should have gone above—back to the surface where she could breathe the night air. But when she came to herself, to rational thought again, she was in her chamber. Morrigan curled up on the fur-lined pallet, drew her knees up to her chest and clasped them with her trembling hands. What was happening to her? What had happened to Kai?

Brina nosed through the leather curtain and leaped up beside her. With a sob of relief, Morrigan put her arms around the big cat. "I couldn't have had anything to do with Kai's death. I didn't do anything. I wasn't even in the cave."

Courage, Precious One...

"No!" With a futile gesture, Morrigan covered her ears with her hands. "I don't want any more of the voice! I don't want to wonder if I'm listening to a goddess or a demon. Can't you just leave me alone and let me fit in somewhere? Let me be just a little bit normal for a change?"

She knew she sounded pathetic—like a whiny baby. G-pa would probably tell her to "suck it up." G-ma would tell her to "settle down and think." She didn't feel like she could do either, but she would give every last piece of goddess power she had to be with her grandparents again—to feel safe and protected and loved.

Brina nosed her face and Morrigan realized her cheeks were wet. She wiped her face with the edge of her dress. What would happen now? Would Birkita turn against her? And what about Kegan? Morrigan kissed Brina's furry face and laid her cheek against the cat's warmth. "He said he was made to love me. Wonder if he still thinks so," she whispered. And, for just an instant, Morrigan considered if she could somehow find her way back through the crystal boulder to Oklahoma.

Exhausted, Morrigan closed her eyes and with Brina curled around her, fell asleep.

She dreamed she was back in Oklahoma. It was one of those autumn days she had always loved when the oppressive heat of summer gave way to cool northern breezes. The leaves in the big pin oak in the front yard were just beginning to turn colors. Morrigan was sitting in one of the rusted metal chairs on the front patio. A glass of her grandma's sweet tea sat on top the huge flat Oklahoma sandstone rock they used as a table.

Morrigan took a deep breath of the cooling air. It smelled of trees and G-pa's butterfly bushes. It felt so good to be home!

Running away is not the answer, child.

Morrigan looked to her right. She was sitting in one of the two other metal chairs. Morrigan's first thought was that she was incredibly beautiful. Her second was that she would have never confused Rhiannon with Shannon. The two women had the same face and form, but she had never seen this expression in any of the multitude of pictures of Shannon—this look of sadness mixed with tenderness.

"You're my mom."

Rhiannon's smile was joyous, but her eyes were luminous with unshed tears. "I am, indeed."

"Is this real? Are you in my dream, or am I just making you up?"

"Sometimes our dreams are the most real aspect of our lives."

"That doesn't sound like a yes or no answer."

"You'll learn that the most important things in life can't be answered with a simple yes or no. They're more complex than that."

"Tell me about it. My life is so complex right now that I don't even understand it, and I sure don't know what to do about it," Morrigan said.

"You will know what to do. When the time comes to make a choice, you will understand what you must do," Rhiannon said.

"But what does that mean? Can't you give me some real help? Tell me what to do?"

"I can't make your decisions for you—no one can. I can tell you that experience taught me decisions made out of negative emotions like anger and jealousy and fear are usually wrong. Instead, trust love and loyalty and honor. Trust yourself, child, and you will find the goddess within. She will lead you to the true goddess and the truth."

"Can't you help me?"

"I have always helped you, Morrigan." Rhiannon reached over to touch her daughter's cheek. "And I always will…"

Rhiannon's body began to fade. "No, wait! I have a zillion questions I need to ask you!"

Rhiannon smiled. "Trust love, and remember, running away is not the answer. It wasn't for me, and it isn't for you."

Morrigan opened her eyes and automatically brushed her fingers against the cave wall. "Light for me, please."

We hear you, Light Bringer!

When the hanging selenite stalactites lit, Morrigan lay on her back petting the sleeping cat curled against her side and stared up at the beauty she was able to call alive. Could she do that if she had been possessed by evil? She didn't think so, or at least she hoped not. Morrigan thought about her dream. It had felt absolutely real, but she hadn't been in Oklahoma. Did that mean her mother hadn't really been there, either?

It seemed like an easy way out—to go to the selenite boulder and see if she could figure out a way to return to Oklahoma.

Running away is not the answer, child.

The words weren't spoken in her mind or even whispered in the air around her, they rose from her memory. So if running away wasn't the answer, what was? Rhiannon, or her subconscious or whatever had said not to make decisions out of negative emotions, but to trust love and loyalty and honor. Easier thought than done, that was for sure.

But wait, maybe it wasn't so hard. She should trust love. Okay, if Kegan's feelings for her were real—if they had actually been made for each other—then he would be the love she should trust. He was a High Shaman. He ought to be able to give her advice about the woo-woo part of what was going on. He'd said she should consider that maybe the Goddess had sent him to her. So if he was still talking to her, versus running screaming in the opposite direction or trying to burn her at the stake, she'd consider it.

Loyalty had to be represented by Birkita. Like Grandma, she was completely loyal, even when it wasn't particularly a good thing. If Birkita still wanted anything to do with her, Morrigan promised herself that she would stop getting pissed off whenever she said something Morrigan didn't particularly want to hear. She'd listen to Birkita. She'd choose loyalty over anger. And she'd choose love over fear. If the two of them would let her.

Morrigan thought about honor. If the other two emotions were symbolized in people, then it would be logical that honor would be, too. Well, G-pa wasn't here, so he (or his mirror image) couldn't fill those shoes. Morrigan's mind drifted, unfortunately, to Kai. Until he'd touched her and then said terrible things about her, she would have guessed that maybe Kai was supposed to represent honor. Great. What if he did and now he was dead?

Overwhelmed, Morrigan pressed her face to Brina's side, trying to let the warm presence of the cat calm her fear.

Fear… No. She was going to choose love, not fear. Morrigan forced her thoughts from the horror that Kai had become to Kegan. She didn't think about him like he'd been when she'd last seen him, kneeling beside Kai's body, staring at her with wide, unreadable eyes. She thought about how he'd looked after they'd made love—how nervous and vulnerable he'd been—how much in love she'd believed him to be. Absently Morrigan's hand went up over her head to rest against the smooth wall of her chamber. With all of the crap that had happened since, she hadn't even had a chance to think about Kegan and, well, the sex.

Jeesh, she wasn't a virgin anymore. And it had been… Morrigan sighed. Kegan had been amazing. She wished he was with her right then and that the horrible thing with Kai hadn't happened. She wanted desperately to see him—to have him reassure her that what he'd said was true. They really were made for each other.

The Master Sculptor is in his chamber.

The words traveled from the crystals, through her fingers, and into her very soul. Morrigan blinked in surprise and sat abruptly up. She pressed her hands firmly against the cave wall. "Can you lead me to Kegan?"

Yes, Light Bringer!

Stomach fluttering nervously, she said, "Then take me to him, please."

20

It was late and, thankfully, Morrigan only met a few people as she let the crystals lead her through the mazelike tunnels of the caves. She didn't know what kind of looks those people gave her. Morrigan kept her eyes on the cave wall, her face turned away from all gawkers. With single-minded determination she made her way to the section of the caves reserved for guests, moving quickly and quietly until the crystal thread of light ended beside a thick leather curtain covering an arched doorway. Morrigan hesitated. Now that she was there she was clueless about what to do. And sick to her stomach.

It would have been nice if she could've knocked or rung a doorbell. For that matter, she would have been ecstatic to chicken out and text message him. Okay, well, none of those things were possible. She should just call his name. Say something like, "Hi, Kegan, it's me, Morrigan. Can I come in?" Or, as G-ma would have corrected her, "*May* I come in?" But what would she do if he yelled back and told her to go away? That would be terrible. Well, shit! *Just go in. He'll either want to see me or he won't.* Quietly, Morrigan pushed aside the leather drape and peeked into the room.

There was only one brazier burning in the large chamber

and the single column of rough marble that stood silent and imposing in the center of the room seemed to pull the white flame to it so that its buttery surface looked luminous. She recognized the marble instantly as the section of stone Kai had chosen for Myrna's tomb.

His back to her, Kegan was standing in front of the marble. His hands were raised and he had them pressed against the surface of the rock. His head was bowed. His shoulders were slumped as if a great weight had settled in the middle of them. Morrigan slid soundlessly into the room, not sure whether to clear her throat or cough or just call his name.

"I know you're there." Head still bowed, Kegan spoke without looking at her. His voice sounded oddly muffled and thick.

Morrigan jumped guiltily. "I didn't mean to sneak up on you. I just..." She hesitated and then decided she might as well be completely honest with him. "I just didn't know if you'd want to see me, so I came on in because I didn't want to hear you tell me to go away."

Kegan straightened. Slowly he took his hands from the marble and then he turned to face her. Morrigan saw that he had been crying and she automatically started toward him, one hand outstretched. But, unable to read the expression on his ravaged face, she stopped just short of touching him and let her arm drop uselessly to her side.

"Did you believe nothing I told you today?"

His words gave her a little sliver of hope, but his expression was still so remote that she hesitated to touch him. "I believe you meant it when you said it, but after what happened with Kai I didn't know if you'd still feel that way."

"Kai is dead."

The words pressed around Morrigan as if they held actual weight. "I'm so sorry, Kegan."

"Do you know why I was crying?"

"Because you're sad about Kai." She glanced at the familiar marble pillar behind him. "And Myrna."

"I was weeping because when I touched the marble and felt Myrna's image within it I was reminded of you and I couldn't bear that you ran from me."

"I didn't run from you. I ran away from what Kai was saying about me."

"You should have stayed. We could have faced it together."

"But don't you think I'm evil?" Morrigan felt herself begin to tremble.

"Of course not," he said angrily. "How could you believe I would think that?"

"What about what Kai said?"

"Perhaps you should tell me what happened between the two of you today."

Morrigan looked into Kegan's eyes and made her decision. She would trust love. "I think what I should tell you is everything, and then maybe you can help me understand what happened with Kai and me today."

"First, come here to me, my flame. If I don't touch you soon I will go mad."

Choking back a sob, Morrigan went into his arms and was enveloped by the scent and heat of him. Loving him didn't fix anything. Loving him didn't change anything. Loving him simply made everything else bearable. She pressed herself against him and inhaled his solid presence. And for the first time really began to believe that they had been made of—and for—each other. He kissed the top of her head and she could feel his warm breath against her scalp when he spoke.

"If the Goddess fashioned us for one another that doesn't mean one of us can run away when things get difficult."

"Well, me being filled with darkness isn't exactly PMS."

"PMS?"

Morrigan laughed against his chest. "Never mind. Let's just say that rampant evil and water-retention grumpiness don't exactly equate."

"You aren't filled with darkness and I already know you can be grumpy."

Morrigan looked up at him. "I'm not grumpy, and how do you know I'm not filled with darkness?"

Kegan held her face in his hands. "You are filled with light, Morrigan, not darkness."

Morrigan stared into his eyes. She wanted to believe him so damn much that it made her chest hurt. And maybe she could, but only after he knew everything. "I need to sit down, and then I have to tell you the truth about me. All of the truth."

He didn't make a jest to try to lighten what she had said. Instead he nodded solemnly and kissed her lightly. Then he pointed to one of the half-a-dozen comfortable raw-leather chairs in the chamber. "Pick any of those. You talk while I pace."

"You're going to pace?"

"I do my best thinking when I pace. You'll get used to it." As if in demonstration he paced over to a wooden table that held a couple pitchers, a bowl of fruit and several goblets. "Wine?" he asked as he poured a red stream from one of the pitchers.

"No, I want to keep a clear head. But some water would be nice," she said as she chose the chair farthest from Myrna's marble.

"Water it is." He filled her goblet from the second pitcher and brought it to her.

She drank deeply, realizing how dry her mouth had been. Then she cleared her throat and began to tell her story.

"First, I want you to know that I've really hated lying, and whenever I could I stuck as close to the truth as possible."

"You sound as if you have been forced to lie."

"I feel like I have. Even Birkita thought it was the only thing we could do, and I agreed with her."

"Birkita knows the truth?"

"Pretty much all of it."

"Tell me," Kegan said.

So Morrigan told him everything, from her birth to her unusual childhood to the day she discovered her powers in the Alabaster Caverns. Then she told him the truth about her mother and father, and about her grandparents, who weren't actually her grandparents, and how they had told her everything the night she freaked out and ran away to the caverns. That was one of the two times he interrupted her.

"By the sacred chalice! You truly are the daughter of Epona's Chosen."

Morrigan thought he looked scarily pale, but she nodded. "Yes. I am the daughter of Rhiannon MacCallan. The *real* Rhiannon MacCallan."

He went over to the table and she saw that his hand was shaking as he poured himself more wine. When he turned back to her, Kegan looked thoroughly shocked, but he smiled at her and his voice was so filled with joy, for an instant it burned away the horror that had happened that day.

"I was fashioned to love you, Morrigan MacCallan, High Priestess and Chosen of a goddess." Then he threw back his head and laughed.

"Well, what the hell is so funny about that?"

He went to her, bent and kissed her soundly. "*I* am what is so funny about that. Someday I'll tell you the story of the ridiculous things I said before I knew you, and I give you my word I will let you berate me for them, even when we are old and gray."

"You're making no sense at all," she said, but she couldn't help smiling at him as she continued her story. With the echo of *running away is not the answer, child* playing through her memory, she explained that final night to him. How she had called alight the spirits of the crystal and how Kyle had found her, and the passion they had discovered together. Until her grandparents, most particularly G-pa, had burst in on them.

At that point Kegan stopped pacing and interrupted her for the second time. "I believe I would like your grandfather," he said.

"Well, he does appreciate good horseflesh," she said.

Kegan snorted.

"*Anyway,* it wasn't long after my grandparents got there that the cave-in started."

Kegan's eyes widened in understanding. "The cave-in—that is how Kyle died. And your grandparents? Did they perish, too?"

"No, no, I don't think so." Morrigan paused and clasped her hands together in her lap. They'd started to tremble. She would not go there. She would never, ever go there. "My grandparents did *not* die. They got out. I made them get out. They thought I would follow them, but I didn't. Even then I knew I wouldn't get out of the cave that way." She looked up from her tightly clasped hands and met his eyes. "Kyle wouldn't leave me. I tried to send him away, but he wouldn't go. It was because of me that he died."

"It was his decision, Morrigan, not yours," Kegan said flatly.

"Promise me you wouldn't make the same decision."

"I will not make such a ridiculous promise."

"Promise me!" she shouted. "Kyle died because of me. Myrna died that same day. Kai died today. I don't think I can stand it if I keep leaving a trail of death wherever I go. I would really run away then—far away where I can't be the cause of anyone else being hurt."

He came to her then and took her hand. "Remember I told you Epona fashions centaur mates for her most powerful priestesses? You believe I was fashioned for you, don't you?"

Morrigan nodded numbly.

"A very powerful priestess needs a centaur mate because she needs someone by her side who is *more* than a man." He gave her his best rakish grin. "Haven't I already proven how much more than a man I am? I'm certainly not so easily gotten rid of."

Her lips tilted up in the barest hint of a smile. "Just promise me you'll be careful and smart. You're not Wolverine, or even Seabiscuit, for that matter."

Kegan's brows drew together in confusion.

"Just more Oklahoma words. I'll explain later. Anyway, when Kyle was covered by a pile of rock from the ceiling I was sure I was going to die, too. Then I heard her voice telling me to go into the crystal and I did. When I came out the other side I was with Birkita in the Usgaran in this world."

"It was Adsagsona's voice that told you to enter the crystal?"

"No," Morrigan said slowly. "It was my mother's voice. The only time I can tell you for sure that I've heard Adsagsona's voice was once during the Dark Moon Ritual I performed the night you and Kai arrived. She spoke out loud and everyone heard her."

"But you said you hear a voice in your mind quite often."

"Yeah, and others in the wind, too. But none of them sound enough like the voice I heard in the Usgaran for me to be completely sure it's Adsagsona talking to me." She paused, gathering her courage. "Kegan, maybe Kai was right. Maybe one of the voices I've been listening to is Pryderi."

"No!" Kegan slashed an intricate pattern in the air with his raised fist while he quickly spoke a series of unintelligible words that sizzled with power against Morrigan's body. "We will not speak that creature's name. Call him the Three-Faced God if you must, but do not name him. There is too much power in a spoken name."

Morrigan shivered. "How do we know Kai wasn't right?"

Kegan began to pace again. "You said your grandfather explained to you that Rhiannon had become tainted by the dark whisperings she listened to?"

"Yes, and she did awful things like run away from this world when it was on the brink of some war with demons." Again Morrigan heard her mother's admonishment, *running away is not the answer, child,* and for the first time she understood that Rhiannon really had been speaking from experience.

Kegan stopped pacing as if he'd hit a glass wall. "She knew of the Fomorian invasion?"

"She knew," Morrigan said miserably.

"You would not do that."

"Do what?"

"You wouldn't leave the Sidetha to face an invader. You'd stay and fight with them, or for them."

Morrigan felt a stirring of hope at his words. "I wouldn't leave. I know I wouldn't leave."

"And that's how you know that you haven't been taken over by evil."

Morrigan frowned at him. "Just because I say I wouldn't run away if some awful scary monsters were attacking us? Hell, Kegan! That's a pretty easy thing for me to say."

He smiled. "Regardless, what you say is the truth." She opened her mouth to argue with him, but he cut her off. "And that's not the only proof. The proof is in your behavior—your actions. Morrigan, listen to me carefully. Your behavior is not evil. Your mother's was, at least before she rejected the darkness and was reconciled with Epona."

"Okay, that does make sense. But we still don't know who belongs to all of these damn voices I can hear."

Kegan went back to pacing. "You didn't mention it, but perhaps we can sift through the voices if we go back to your Ascension Ritual. You said you were sure only once of having heard Adsagsona's voice, but the Goddess had to have spoken to you when you pledged yourself into her service."

"But I didn't have an ascension ceremony. I don't even know what one is."

Morrigan thought he looked at her as if she had lost every bit of her mind. "You have crossed a divide from one world to another. You are the daughter of a great priestess. You are the first Light Bringer in more than three generations of the Sidetha. And you have done all of this without having given a pledge of service to your goddess?"

"Uh, nope," Morrigan said, feeling foolish. Again.

Kegan walked to her and gently touched her cheek. His smile was tender, even though she could see worry lining his handsome face. "My flame, you are the most amazing person I have ever known. How is it you didn't complete an Ascension Ritual?"

"They don't have them in my old world. Or at least if they do, my grandparents and I didn't know anything about them. Not that we didn't honor the gods and goddesses, especially Epona. Grandma made sure we did." Morrigan smiled. "Did I mention she and Birkita are mirror images?"

Kegan smiled back at her. "I am not surprised." He kissed her forehead. "But honoring the gods and pledging yourself to one through a priestess's Ascension Ritual are two very different things."

"So, what should I do?"

"You must pledge yourself to Adsagsona—accept her as your goddess and rebuke serving any other divine being."

"Specifically, anyone dark with three faces?"

"Yes."

"And what if the dark god has been after me?"

"Then it is during the ceremony that he will make himself known to you and attempt to entice you to pledge yourself to him before you pledge yourself to Adsagsona. After that, he will be too late, for unless you formally renounce your goddess, you will belong to her for eternity."

Morrigan drew in a deep breath and attempted a brave smile even though her stomach was churning. "Then it sounds like we need to plan an ascension ceremony."

21

"My stomach really hurts," Morrigan said.

"Breathe, all will be well," Kegan said, putting his arm possessively around her as they walked side by side to the Usgaran.

"What if she's mad at me?"

"You mean as you thought I would be?"

"Yes," she said, ignoring the irony in his voice. "Or worse."

"Morrigan, you need to have more trust in those who love you."

"It's not y'all that I don't trust. It's the depth of my ability to mess things up that I'm worrying about."

He gave the top of her head a quick kiss. "You worry far too much."

"Yeah, well, wait till we've been together for a few years. You'll have more respect for my mess-up ability."

"I like the way that sounds," he said.

"What? My mess-up ability?"

"As endearing as that particular ability of yours is, I was talking about us being together for years. Besides, there are things about me that you may well find somewhat tiresome." He flashed her a mischievous grin. "Though perhaps not many."

She raised her brow at him. "I already know you're a terrible flirt." He widened his eyes innocently and looked offended. She rolled her eyes. "Birkita called you a rake."

"Birkita called me that?" he said, trying not to smile.

"Yep. Not that I needed to be told."

His sigh was long-suffering. "Ugly rumors and exaggeration."

"Oh, please. Whatever with that. But, just so you know. In Oklahoma, modern women do not tolerate their men chasing around after other women."

He grinned. "I've never had to *chase* anyone."

She smiled sweetly back at him. "Okay, let me put it another way. As my grandma would say, what's good for the goose is good for the gander." He narrowed his eyes at her. Morrigan continued to smile angelically. "In other words, if you don't want me messing around with other men or centaurs or whatnot, then I suggest you remember that your nonchasing stopped with me."

"I will never give you reason to question my fidelity," he grumbled.

"Good. Same here," she said smugly.

Then she realized that they had come to the entrance to the Usgaran. The teasing smile left her face and she stopped, tensing automatically at how full the chamber was of busily working priestesses and crafters. She noticed immediately that everyone was much quieter than usual. The amiable chatter was absent and a definite feeling of gloom hung like cloying incense over the large room. Birkita was seated on a ledge close to the crystal boulder, which was dark. In her lap she had a length of half-finished fabric she had been trimming in silver stitching, but her hands were still and her eyes were focused on the boulder. Morrigan thought she looked even paler than usual, and there were dark smudges under her eyes. *Because of me,* she thought guiltily, and promised herself that when this mess with Kai was cleared up and her ascension ceremony over, she was going to insist Birkita do nothing but sleep late and lie around. Morrigan would wait on her for a change, no matter what the old woman said.

Then Birkita looked up and met her eyes. Morrigan tried to read what she saw there, but all she could make out was the priestess's weariness.

"Go to her," Kegan whispered, and then took his arm from around Morrigan.

She knew it was what she needed to do—to walk to Birkita and have the old High Priestess greet her publicly and show that Morrigan had not lost her support, but she was afraid down to her toes that Birkita would yell at her in front of everyone, or worse, ignore her totally.

I've chosen to trust loyalty, Morrigan reminded herself, and stepped into the chamber.

All eyes went to her, but Morrigan ignored them. She looked only at the woman who was the mirror of her grandma. They met in the middle of the room.

"Kegan told me that Kai is dead. I'm sorry. I know the two of you were friends."

Birkita's smile was tired, but filled with warmth. "Thank you, child. I went to your chamber after anointing the body. I should have realized you would be with Kegan." She looked behind Morrigan and included the centaur in her smile.

"So you're not angry with me?" Morrigan hated asking that question in front of all the staring eyes and listening ears, but it had to be done. The Sidetha had to know if Birkita still supported her, and they also had to know the rest of the story.

"Angry with you, Light Bringer? For what?" Birkita raised her voice so that it carried to everyone in the chamber. "For the delusions of a dying man who was so racked with pain that he was seeing darkness everywhere? Of course not!"

Morrigan couldn't stop herself from throwing her arms around the old woman and squeezing her tight. "Oh, thank you," she whispered.

Birkita returned her embrace, and then gently extracted herself. "Now, shall we retire to your chamber to discuss when you will perform Kai's funeral ceremony?"

"No, I—" Morrigan began.

"No!" Shayla exploded into the chamber, striding around Kegan to join the two women in the center of the room. She spoke to Birkita without looking at Morrigan. "She will *not* conduct Kai's funeral. She will not even be there. Her presence would be an insult to the Stonemaster's spirit."

Birkita's face went colorless as the watching room murmured restlessly. "Mistress, we should move this discussion to a more private chamber."

"No. This discussion needs to stay public," Morrigan said firmly, moving so that she was standing directly in front of the Sidetha's Mistress and the woman had to look at her. Morrigan hesitated before continuing, shocked at how drawn and disheveled Shayla looked. Her eyes were puffy and red-rimmed. Her hair was a matted mess and there were nasty-looking stains on her dress. "Actually, I agree with part of what Shayla said. I'm not going to perform Kai's funeral ceremony. It's right that you should do that, Birkita."

"No, Morrigan. You are the Sidetha High Priestess. That is your place now," Birkita said. "The only alternative to you performing the ceremony would be if Kegan would preside. As centaur High Shaman, and Kai's friend, that would be acceptable."

"Kai's funeral rites will adhere to the Sidetha beliefs! This was the Stonemaster's second home. His pyre will be set in accordance with our traditions and he will be honored as one of our own."

Shayla ended on a sob, and Morrigan actually felt sorry for her until, with a snarl, the Mistress added, "But she will not be there."

No one should speak to you like that!

Morrigan tried to ignore the voice in her head, but it so completely mirrored her own anger that she snapped. "Where is your husband, Shayla? Shouldn't he be with you in a time of such grief?"

Shayla drew back as if Morrigan had slapped her. Her cold gaze narrowed. She opened her mouth to spew venom, but Morrigan turned a shoulder to her dismissively and spoke to Birkita. "The reason you need to perform the ceremony is simple. You're still the Sidetha's High Priestess." That shut everybody up. When Morrigan continued speaking everyone in the chamber was focused on her words. "I've been talking with Kegan all morning about this, and, well, you know that in Oklahoma things are a lot different than they are here, right?"

Birkita's gaze went from Morrigan to the centaur who was now standing close beside her. "Yes, you and I have discussed that."

"What you and I didn't talk about, what I didn't even know to tell you, was that I have never gone through an ascension ceremony."

Birkita blinked in surprise. "You have not been formally sworn into the service of Adsagsona?"

"No, never. So you see, I'm not technically a High Priestess."

Birkita's brow wrinkled in confusion. "But you are a Light Bringer, which is a more powerful position than High Priestess."

"Which does not necessarily mean Morrigan is also a High Priestess," Kegan spoke up. "It is true that being a Light Bringer is a great gift. It is also true that a priestess who wields that much divinely given power usually becomes a High Priestess as a natural step in the service of her chosen god or goddess. But Morrigan comes to us from a place where the natural order of things is different."

"Which means she has no right to be a High Priestess." Shayla practically spat the words at Morrigan.

"As High Shaman I can assure you, Mistress, that is not what it means," Kegan said coldly.

Ignoring Shayla, Morrigan spoke to Birkita. "What it means is that I need to go slowly. To start at the beginning and then learn the ways of this world and earn my right to be High Priestess to Adsagsona with you as my teacher." Morrigan was gratified to hear the priestesses in the room murmur their agreement.

"I forbid her to become High Priestess!" Shayla said.

Morrigan rounded on the woman. "You are not Adsagsona." She spoke slowly and distinctly, trying to keep her anger in check. "I realize you have acted like you're a goddess, but acting the part does not make it so. I should know. I've been pretending to be a High Priestess, even though I hadn't earned that right yet. But I promise you that it will be the Goddess who decides if and when I take that title. Not you. It will never be you. Shayla, get this now and get it for good—you're in charge of the day-to-day working of the Sidetha. You are not in charge of their spirits."

"You will not speak to me in this manner!"

Morrigan's temper snapped. With a gesture that was almost automatic, she lifted her arm as she moved forward to Shayla. "Light!" she commanded. From her raised hand white flame shot up into the ceiling of the Usgaran, where it was absorbed and then every selenite crystal in the chamber, including the sacred boulder, blazed alight. The power also blazed through Morrigan, heating her blood and setting her body aglow. Face just inches from Shayla's, body thrumming with power, Morrigan bared her teeth and, in a deceptively soft voice, said, "I will speak to you in any manner I want as long as you stick your sluttly, mercenary nose in the business of the Goddess.

Here's a news flash, bitch. Times are changing, and you better stay out of my way or else I'm going to run right over you."

"Morrigan, enough."

Kegan's voice broke through the wall of heat and anger that surrounded her. Breathing hard, she took a step away from Shayla. Oddly, the Sidetha's Mistress didn't appear shaken in the least by Morrigan's threat. Instead she smiled.

"Thank you for the warning, Light Bringer. I will remember it." Shayla flicked back her untidy hair, turned her back on Morrigan and walked regally from the chamber.

"Anger isn't the way, child," Birkita said softly.

Morrigan looked at the frail old High Priestess whose eyes were filled with wisdom and compassion, and she knew deep within her that Birkita was right. Just as Rhiannon had told her, anger was destructive, and would not lead her down the right path. With a gigantic effort, Morrigan drew long breaths, willing the heat in her body to drain from her and return to the crystals where it belonged. Feeling dizzy, she managed to smile at Birkita. "I guess that's one of the lessons you're going to have to teach me."

"Someone should," Kegan muttered.

Unexpectedly, Morrigan laughed, and the heat remaining within her cooled, leaving her feeling more than a little silly standing there in the middle of the room with everyone staring at her.

She cleared her throat. "So, it's decided that you will perform the funeral for Kai?"

"I will," Birkita said. "And it is also decided that after we finish with the business of funerals *you* will prepare for your ascension ceremony and your formal induction into the service of the Goddess?"

"I will," Morrigan said, smiling.

"There is one more ceremony for which we should prepare," Kegan said.

Morrigan and Birkita looked up at the centaur. "Am I forgetting something, High Shaman?" Birkita said.

Kegan smiled at Morrigan. "Perhaps not. I may have spoken too soon." Then he did something that utterly shocked Morrigan, and, from the gasps of the watching crowd, the Sidetha, too. He took her hand, bowed formally to her and pressed her palm to his chest over his heart. "Morrigan, this day I publicly proclaim my love for you in front of your goddess, High Priestess and your people. I ask that you do me the honor of joining in Handfast with me. To be my mate for this lifetime and, should your goddess and mine will it, an eternity thereafter. Will you have me, Morrigan, Light Bringer of the Sidetha?"

Morrigan thought her heart might beat out of her chest. She stared into Kegan's blue eyes and saw within them a future of love and laughter and happiness. She also saw that, with him, she would never, ever be alone or an outsider again. She saw the mate of her soul.

"Yes, Kegan, I will."

With a shout of joy, Kegan lifted her in his arms and kissed her soundly.

Birkita's laughter mingled with the happy cheers of the priestesses.

"And this is how it should be," Birkita said. "Life balancing death. Joy lighting the darkness of sadness."

Morrigan closed her eyes, kissed Kegan, and wished the moment would never end.

22

"Kai would approve of the setting," Kegan said. "He loved differing color and textures. I know he found the Salt Plains' dramatic landscape and jutting crystals beautiful. His spirit will be pleased."

"I hope so." Morrigan leaned into him as he draped his arm around her. They were standing on the knoll where they had first made love, the one that overlooked the Salt Plains. Kai's pyre had been built in the middle of the hill. The pile of alabaster sap-soaked boughs was massive and lacked only the body and a match. "So this is all going to be okay?"

"All? What do you mean, my flame?"

"It just feels weird, having his funeral here without, you know, *her.*" It was hard for Morrigan to call Shannon Rhiannon, so she'd gotten into the habit of avoiding her name altogether.

"Birkita and I agreed it would be cruel to send word to Rhiannon of her beloved Stonemaster's death while the grief over her daughter is so raw. As we decided I will carry Kai's ashes, along with word of his death, to her when I bring Rhiannon the effigies for the monuments."

"One for Myrna and one for Kai."

Kegan smoothed her hair back and kissed her forehead.

"First you must find the stone that holds Kai's image, then, yes, I will carve it in his likeness."

"I know. I will." But the truth was, Morrigan hadn't found the courage yet to question the spirits of the stones. She told herself it had only been two days since the Stonemaster's death—she had plenty of time to search for the stone that would be carved into his likeness. But in her heart she knew it wasn't an issue of time. Morrigan was afraid, though she didn't understand exactly what it was she feared.

The past two days had been so damn weird. The priestesses talked to her. Actually, they acted fairly normal around her. Birkita was great, as usual, even though Morrigan knew she wasn't getting enough sleep, and she worried about how tired the old priestess looked. Kegan was… Morrigan sighed and snuggled into him. Kegan was amazing. Everyone else either completely ignored her, or they stared at her and did a lot of whispering as soon as she was almost out of earshot. She hadn't seen Shayla since their confrontation in the Usgaran. Birkita told her that the Sidetha's Mistress was keeping vigil over Kai's body and anointing it with spices and oils every day, just as a wife would. Morrigan had wondered aloud about where Perth was during this very public display of his wife's affections for another man. According to Birkita, Perth had disappeared into the bowels of the caves shortly after Kai's death and hadn't been seen since. Her supposition was that Perth would reappear a few days after Kai's funeral and continue the pretense of his marriage as if nothing had happened. Morrigan wasn't so sure. That Shayla had crossed over some kind of edge of reason was obvious. It made sense to Morrigan that the crazy bitch would have bumped off her husband. She figured time would reveal the truth in that.

"Morrigan?"

"Sorry, did you say something?"

"No, no—it's just that people are beginning to arrive." Kegan pointed over her shoulder at the trail that led up the cave side of the knoll. Morrigan looked beyond it to see a line of Sidetha moving out of the cave and making their way toward them.

"That's my cue to move into the shadows."

"Morrigan, what is it? What is bothering you? It was your decision not to participate in Kai's funeral."

"I know," she snapped, and then sighed and gave him an apologetic smile. "I'm just tired of doing nothing," Morrigan said.

"You haven't been doing nothing. You've been readying yourself."

"Feels like a lot of nothing to me," Morrigan said under her breath. Kegan followed her as she moved away from the pyre to the little cluster of scrub pines that had bravely taken root on a raised part of the hill. Morrigan stopped in the shadow of their long, fingerlike limbs. Here she'd be close enough to be a part of the ceremony without being obvious and calling attention to herself. Morrigan's preference would have been to avoid the whole thing, but three things had made her come. One—if she was to be High Priestess after Birkita, as Kegan and Birkita insisted she would be, she needed to observe a funeral ceremony because she would eventually be presiding over them. Two—Shayla couldn't be allowed to tell Morrigan what to do. Three—and the most important to Morrigan— Kegan and Birkita were saying goodbye to a friend and she wanted to be there for them. Ergo her presence at the funeral even though she wished she were almost anywhere else.

"Will you be all right here?" Kegan asked, studying her carefully.

Morrigan gave him a tight smile and waved him away. "Go

ahead. You and Birkita do what you need to do. We'll talk after the funeral."

He kissed her quickly and then went back to wait by the pyre, to be joined by Birkita and the other priestesses who were escorting the litter carrying Kai's body.

Morrigan felt a wet nose nuzzle her hand and smiled as Brina joined her. "I'm glad you're here, pretty girl," she whispered to the big cat and scratched the top of her head, which automatically started Brina's purr motor. Petting the cat, Morrigan tried not to fidget while she watched and waited. Over the past days she had been filled with an increasing sense of restlessness, which was only made all the worse by her inactivity. As per Birkita's instructions, which she repeated ad nauseam, Morrigan was to spend the rest of the days before the next dark moon, which was almost an entire damn month away, meditating. Yep, *meditating*. Morrigan knew she was supposed to be doing some seriously deep mental communing with the Goddess, but nothing was happening. Nada. Zip. Zilch. Nothing. So, basically, she sat in her room most of the day and tried not to fall asleep or die of boredom while she "meditated." When mostly she just wished she could watch some trashy daytime TV.

The voices had even stopped. For the first time in her life, all of them had left her alone. No one spoke to her on the wind. No one spoke in her mind. That should be a good thing, or at least that was what Morrigan told herself, but the absence of the voices made her feel itchy and wrong. Something was getting ready to happen. Something not good.

The Sidetha began filing up the hill, making a wide circle around the pyre until they covered the knoll and all of its sides. Morrigan was glad she'd chosen to watch from the grove. The small incline it was on helped her to see over the heads. The crowd was solemn. There was very little talking, so the sounds of muffled sobs and sniffing seemed amplified in the silence.

Morrigan knew the people weren't putting on a show; Kai had honestly been loved by the Sidetha.

New movement caught her eye and Morrigan saw that the body was approaching. Birkita walked at the head of the procession carrying a long torch that burned steadily in the soft evening light. The body was on a litter being carried by six burly stoneworkers, flanked on each side by six priestesses. At the very end of the procession, walking closest to Kai's head, was a single woman Morrigan knew had to be Shayla. All of the priestesses were wearing long white unadorned robes, as did most of the mourners, including Morrigan. Birkita had explained to her that they chose white for mourning because it symbolized the departing spirit. Birkita's robes were the most voluminous, and were edged in a silver interlocking embroidery pattern of spirals. Shayla wore white, too. Even her face was veiled by a diaphanous piece of material that reached almost to her knees. As the procession passed through the crowd, which parted to make way for them, and drew closer to Morrigan and the pyre, she caught a glimpse of Shayla's face through the veil and thought she looked disturbingly like a zombie bride. She held in front of her the ritualistic sword of the Sidetha. The sword's presence at his funeral meant that the Sidetha were honoring Kai posthumously as one of their own. It was an exquisite long sword with the figure of Adsagsona carved in a hilt encrusted with gemstones, and its sharp, double-edged blade glittered when it caught slivers of Birkita's torchlight.

The procession halted beside the huge pile of boughs near Kegan, who bowed formally to Birkita and then to Kai's body. Without speaking, he helped the men with Kai's litter, and used his height to steady it as they worked as a team to lift it and place it on the flattened, bierlike top of the enormous pile of wood.

The priestesses formed a circle around the pyre, spreading out from where Birkita and Kegan stood beside each other. Shayla didn't join the circle, but she also didn't step into the crowd. Morrigan thought she looked utterly bat-shit crazy standing there with her veil, holding the raised sword and staring with unblinking eyes at Kai's body.

Birkita put the torch in a holder that had been placed in the ground. Then she raised her arms above her and called out to her goddess.

"Adsagsona, I call on you above—" she paused and pulled her arms down to form the open-palmed reverse V "—and below."

Morrigan watched Birkita invoke Adsagsona, and she thought how beautiful the High Priestess looked, how serene and confident. The paleness of her skin that Morrigan had been worrying so much about was mirrored in her cloud-colored robes so that she looked ethereal and goddesslike.

"O Gracious Goddess who gives rest, O Lady of the twilight realms and womb of the earth, we ask you to hear our prayers for the spirit of Epona's Stonemaster Kai, who served the Goddess with his gift as well as his heart. Today we claim him as one of our own, and will, hereafter, call him Sidetha. As one of our people, we ask that you grant him release from this realm, and help speed his spirit into the beautiful meadows of Epona."

Then Birkita and Kegan turned so that they were facing each other and she continued the rite.

"Kegan, High Shaman and Master Sculptor of Partholon, we do call on thee to stand here before us and before our Goddess that we may give honor and love to Kai, whom you have known."

Kegan raised his arms and tilted his head back so that his face was open to the sky, and his voice carried deep and strong all across the knoll. "O Gracious Goddess who gives rest, O Lady of the twilight realms and womb of the earth, I stand here with my face turned to the sky, representative of all who loved him, and I speak of Kai's loyalty and goodness, and the great loss we feel because of his absence."

It was then Birkita's turn to speak again. "But we know that the loss of Kai is only for a time, and we bid you have no sorrow, for surely he is journeying to Epona's verdant meadows where it is always warm and pleasing, where there is no pain or death, sadness or loss, and with all his ills gone he will have youth anew."

Kegan smiled, and Morrigan's breath caught at the expression of utter joy on his face as he spoke jubilantly. "Dying is just a way of rest, a way of going to our Goddess to be renewed and made strong, and then finally to return."

"Great Goddess Adsagsona, you have told us that arrayed in a new flesh someday another mother will give birth, so that with sturdier body and brighter mind the old spirit will take the earthly road again. We wish that journey to be joyous for Kai, who was Stonemaster of Partholon, claimed by the Sidetha, and loved by many." Birkita paused long enough to take the torch from its holder and face the pyre. "And now we release Kai forever from this earthly shell and we rejoice that a new life has begun for him." She held the torch high and cried, "Hail, Adsagsona!"

"No!"

The crowd's echoing response was shattered by Shayla's scream. With a quickness that stunned Morrigan, she dropped the sword and hurled herself at Birkita as she shrieked, "No! I will not let you burn him!" She knocked Birkita to the side and the torch flew from her hands, landing in the middle of the waiting pyre, where it instantly lit. Crazed, Shayla ripped off the white veil that covered her face and began beating at the growing flames with it as if she thought she could put them out.

"No, Shayla, you must stop!" Morrigan heard Birkita cry, and saw the old priestess grab Shayla's arm and try to drag her back.

Not waiting to see what other madness Shayla had planned, Morrigan hurried forward, Brina following her and growling softly as she shoved people out of her way. Gentle sensibilities of the Sidetha who might harbor suspicions that Kai had been right about her be damned, Birkita needed her, so she was going to Birkita.

"Shayla, you desecrate Kai's pyre!"

Kegan's voice carried above the sounds of shock the crowd was making and the growing noise of crackling boughs. Morrigan shoved past a big guy and popped through the crowd in time to see the pyre go up in flames with an enormous *whoosh*.

"No!" Shayla screamed again. She was standing between Birkita and Kegan, who each held on to one of her arms. Brina was crouched in front of the trio, twitching her tail and snarling and looking like she was trying to figure out how to pounce on Shayla without snagging Birkita or Kegan. The other priestesses were staring, rooted into place, which irritated the crap out of Morrigan. She was going to have to instill some backbone into those women. How could they let Birkita, who was older than any of them, wrestle with Shayla?

Morrigan was almost to Birkita when the old woman suddenly dropped Shayla's arm and took a stumbling step back. She was facing her, so Morrigan saw her expression clearly. Her eyes widened in complete surprise, and both of her hands fluttered up in a slow, trembling movement. One pressed against her breast and the other clenched her left arm. Then her mouth opened in a surprised O, her eyes rolled to show their whites, and she collapsed as if all the bones in her body had liquefied.

"Birkita!" The scream tore from her chest, echoing Brina's

snarl as she pounced on Shayla, knocking her to the ground. Morrigan ran to Birkita. Frantically she rolled her over. Birkita wasn't breathing. Morrigan felt for a pulse. There was none. "No! Oh, please, Birkita, no!" Trying to control her body's trembling, Morrigan laid Birkita flat, tilted her head back, clamped her nose and began performing CPR. Between breaths during chest compressions she begged Birkita, "Open your eyes! Breathe!"

She heard the low chanting before she felt the warm, heavy hand on her shoulder. With a surge of anger she looked up into Kegan's face. "No! Stop doing that! She can't die!"

The centaur High Shaman paused in his chanting only long enough to say sadly, "Birkita is already dead, my flame."

I had no clue what time it was or, for that matter, what day it was when I heard Epona's voice.

Beloved, you must come.

I had gotten in the habit of not answering her. I closed my eyes more tightly and snuggled Etain closer to me, inhaling her sweet baby scent and letting her warmth soothe me. If Epona would just leave us alone—if they all would just leave us alone—everything would be fine.

Beloved, you must come, the Goddess repeated. *I have need of you.*

I was too tired to get really pissed off, so I just misquoted Rhett. "Frankly, I don't give a good goddamn."

Enough self-indulgence!

Had I been in my right mind the power that zapped through the air along with Epona's anger would have straightened me right up and made me snap to—but I wasn't in my right mind. Instead I sat up in bed and, keeping my voice low enough not to wake the baby, said, "Self-indulgence? My daughter is dead and you call my grief and pain self-indulgence?"

Epona's form materialized. The Goddess was standing at the

foot of the huge mound of bedding I had in happier days called the marshmallow. Though I have seen her visage many times over the twenty years I had been her Chosen, her beauty was so great, her palpable aura of love and compassion so bright, that it was always hard for me to look directly at her.

And still I couldn't forgive her.

No, Beloved, I do not call your grief and pain self-indulgence. That is what I call your withdrawal from those who love and need you.

I felt a twinge of guilt. ClanFintan. I knew he was suffering, too, and somewhere inside me I understood I needed him desperately and knew he needed me. But I couldn't find my way to his love. I was lost in a foggy maze of pain and anger and the only person I could see through the grayness was Etain.

"I can't be there for anyone right now." I barely recognized the flat, emotionless sound of my own voice.

I would give you more time if I could, Beloved, but I cannot. You must rejoin the world. Your daughter needs you now.

The words *your daughter* hit my body like icy water. "My daughter is dead."

The daughter of your womb is dead. The daughter of your spirit is alive. It is she who needs you.

The icy water turned scalding as the Goddess's words battered me. I had no idea I was crying until the tears washed from my cheeks and fell to soak the silk of my nightgown. Who knew a person could cry so much? I would have thought my eyes would have run dry days ago.

My voice shook and I had to speak slowly to get the words out. "Are you trying to destroy me completely?"

The Goddess moved closer to me. She lifted the hem of her shining golden robe, and with it wiped my face. *No, my most Beloved One, I am trying to save you.*

I gazed up at her and some of the fog in which I'd been lost began to clear. "Morrigan is in trouble?"

She is, and I fear for her soul.

I closed my eyes against a new wave of pain. "Myrna is with you, isn't she?"

You know she is, Beloved.

I opened my eyes and forced myself to meet her brilliant gaze. "I've been very angry at you."

Great anger cannot exist without great love. Then she bent and kissed me gently on the forehead. I trembled under her touch as her love filled me, burning away the last of the sickly fog that had clouded my mind and numbed my heart.

"I'll help Morrigan," I said, lying back on the pillows and beginning to relax my body for the astral projection that I knew was to come. "Let's go to Oklahoma."

The Goddess raised a single golden brow at me, oddly reminding me of myself. *Morrigan is not in Oklahoma, Beloved. The daughter of your spirit is in our world.*

I hardly had time to begin to feel amazement at her announcement, when she hit me with another shock.

Ready yourself, Beloved, you travel to the Realm of the Sidetha.

"Where Kai and Kegan are?" I shook my head, trying to clear the confusion from it.

Kegan is there. Kai is dead, Beloved, killed by the same darkness that stalks Morrigan's soul.

This time my anger was purifying instead of self-indulgent. "The friggin three-faced dark god."

Yes, Beloved, but today my desire is that light banishes Pryderi from both worlds for generations.

"All right. Let's do this, but you're going to have to explain what the hell has been going on." I closed my eyes and I was pulled from my body and catapulted up through the roof of my temple while Epona filled me in...

Kegan's words, "Birkita is already gone, my flame," shocked through Morrigan. All she could do was shake her head back and forth, back and forth in disbelief. Just as she had when Kyle died... Just as she had at Kai's deathbed...

"You did this!" Shayla hissed at Morrigan from where she had collapsed on the ground. Brina crouched between Shayla and Morrigan, growling softly and watching the Sidetha's Mistress through slit eyes while she continued to spew hatred. "You didn't bring light to us. You brought death. You're not a Light Bringer, you're a Death Bringer."

"Shayla!" Kegan's voice was sharp, even though he spoke to her compassionately. "You are not yourself. What you say is caused by your grief. Morrigan had nothing to do with any of these tragic deaths."

Shayla's eyes burned with hatred as she glared at Morrigan. Spittle flew from her bloodless lips as she hurled her words. "I found Kai. He told me that the darkness that follows you caused his death. He said you are being stalked by it and that it would engulf you. All of this is your fault. His death is your fault!" she shrieked.

Morrigan couldn't speak. She couldn't tell Shayla that what

she said wasn't true because she was too afraid the Mistress was right. Morrigan had pulled Birkita's body into her arms. All she could do was hold the dead mirror image of her grandma and stare at Shayla and Kegan. Morrigan felt no grief. She felt no pain. She was detached, observing the events unfolding in front of her as though through a long, telescopic lens.

"Enough, Shayla!" Kegan snapped. "You're wrong. Kai was wrong. I am a High Shaman. I would know if Morrigan trafficked with the dark god. She does not."

Shayla turned her hate-filled gaze onto the centaur, and then suddenly her face crumpled and tears streamed down her pale cheeks. "She has tainted even you."

Morrigan thought Kegan looked sad and a decade older than his years. "I was fashioned to love Morrigan. Think logically, Shayla. You know the Goddess would not fashion my soul mate from darkness."

"Kai was *my* soul mate!" Shayla collapsed. Head bowed, she sobbed her grief.

Morrigan heard Kegan sigh wearily. "Shayla, let the priestesses escort you to your chamber." He bent down, meaning to grasp her arms and help the broken woman to her feet. "I'll send the Healer to you and—"

Shayla grabbed the sword of the Sidetha that until then had lain forgotten where she'd dropped it, and with a movement that was snake quick and driven with unnatural strength, thrust it up into Kegan's chest as he bent to help her. With another blindingly swift movement, she pulled a gleaming dagger from the folds of her dress and hurled it at Morrigan. With a deafening scream Brina leaped, blocking her, and the dagger meant for Morrigan embedded itself in the big cat's throat.

Morrigan's numbness shattered as Kegan and Brina collapsed. She lunged to her feet, screaming. Brina's body was absolutely still and Kegan was trying to raise himself up with one hand, while with the other he plucked uselessly at the sword embedded to the hilt in his chest. "No, stay still, it'll be okay, it'll be okay," Morrigan soothed as she wrapped her arms around his torso, trying to support him and keep him still. "Get the Healer!" she yelled to one of the frozen priestesses.

"It isn't Shayla," Kegan gasped, the words thick with the blood that ran from his mouth.

Panicked, Morrigan looked wildly up, expecting Shayla to launch herself at them. Instead the Sidetha's Mistress was standing in front of the brightly burning pyre, so close that Morrigan could see her white robes were beginning to smolder. Shayla cocked her head, as if listening to a voice in the wind. Then she said in a clear, awful voice, "Yes, yes, you're right. I do want to join Kai." With a terrible smile, Shayla hurled herself onto the burning pyre.

Morrigan had no time for the screams or cries of the people around them. Her world was focused on Kegan. She had managed to prop him against her, and she was holding his torso awkwardly up, trying to wipe up the blood that ran steadily from his mouth and from around the embedded sword.

"Morrigan." Her name was little more than a whisper.

"Shh, don't try to talk. Just concentrate on living."

"You must listen to me." He placed his hand wearily on hers to still her frightened, fluttery movements.

Morrigan looked into his eyes and saw the truth there. Kegan was going to die. She stopped trying to stanch the bleeding and instead took his hand in hers. She would not cry now. There would be time enough for that later. Now she would cherish every second she had left with him.

"I'm listening," she said softly.

"Shayla was under the influence of the dark god. I saw it in her eyes when she stabbed me and killed Brina." He paused to cough painfully and fresh blood gushed down his body.

"The god never meant to kill you. He wanted all your protectors gone." His breathing was labored and his body had begun to tremble. "Do not let him win. He caused all of this—Kai, Birkita, Brina and me. He did this, not you. Remember that, my love, my flame."

"I'll remember, Kegan. I love you and I believe you were fashioned for me," she said in a rush.

He smiled. "Ah, I knew you would come to believe me. So now you must find me again, my flame. In another life…another world…find me…" Kegan's smile faded. He gasped once. His grip on her hand tightened spasmodically, and then the breath left his body in a frothing rush and he breathed no more.

Morrigan dropped her head to his shoulder and rested it there. She couldn't cry. Everything inside her was too broken. She couldn't find the path to tears.

Then one of the priestesses screamed, a sound so filled with terror that it pierced through Morrigan's despair. She lifted her head and saw that Deidre was standing not far from her. The priestess's eyes were round and glassy and fixed on the pyre. Morrigan followed her gaze to see that Shayla's burning body had begun to writhe and as she watched, a shape heaved itself from the dead Mistress and stepped out of the fire. He shook himself, like a dog ridding itself of water, and then he turned to face Morrigan.

He was tall and powerfully built. Thick, dark hair framed a face that was ageless in its classic beauty. His sensuous lips smiled, washing Morrigan in warmth and love. "There you are, my Precious One." His voice was achingly familiar and with a terrible sinking, Morrigan knew she'd been listening to different versions of it all her life.

"Pryderi," she said.

"How easily you know me."

"I would know you anywhere." As she said it, Morrigan

understood it was the absolute truth. Now that she'd seen him—heard him speak—she knew that he would never again be a stranger to her. His whispers would never again be mistaken for anyone except himself.

What a fool she had been.

"I have watched you grow from a precocious child into a beautiful, powerful woman. I am well pleased with you, Precious One. And are you ready now to cast aside lesser things and pledge yourself to me as my Chosen and incarnate?"

Carefully, Morrigan laid Kegan's torso against the ground. She touched his cheek one last time before standing and facing the beautiful dark god.

"You did all of this, didn't you? You caused all of their deaths—first Kyle, then Myrna, Kai, Birkita, Brina, Kegan and Shayla." Her voice was calm and she sounded almost disinterested.

"You are mistaken, Chosen One. Myrna's death was separate from the others. But you are correct that one person caused the deaths of all of the others, though that person was not me."

"Who caused their deaths?" With sickening certainty, Morrigan knew the answer before he spoke it.

"You did, my Precious One. The goddesses you looked to, first Epona and then Adsagsona, did not help you. They allowed your powers to surge unchecked." His laugh was beautiful and deadly cruel. "They call it allowing you free will. I name it more truly as their divine uncaring. Look where it got you. Everyone you love in this world is dead because of you."

"And you can change that?"

"I can change that."

"If I pledge myself to you, you will bring them back to me?"

"No, Morrigan! Don't listen to his lies!" Deidre cried.

With blinding speed Pryderi's hand shot out and the priestess was thrown backward to land in a broken, silent heap. The rest of the priestesses screamed in horror and ran from the knoll, following the Sidetha who had retreated into their caves.

"The priestesses of the cave goddess should learn when it is wise to hold their tongues," he said.

Morrigan didn't allow herself even a glance at the fallen priestess. Instead she repeated her question. "If I pledge myself to you, you will bring them back to me?"

"Unlike the goddesses, I will not lie to you. I cannot bring those who have already died back to you. But I can promise you that no one else you love will be harmed by your un-checked powers. Pledge to me, Morrigan MacCallan, and I will take the burden of controlling your power from you. I will not let you harm any others, and I will cherish you for eternity."

"So it's true. I am a Death Bringer, not a Light Bringer."

"You are both, Precious One."

Morrigan, he's lying to you.

At the sound of her voice, Morrigan's head snapped to the right. She was there, though clearly made entirely of spirit. She smiled at Morrigan, even though tears were falling steadily from her eyes.

"Shannon?" The numbness inside Morrigan that had carried her this far began to fade, leaving behind a pain that pierced her so deeply that it was making it difficult for her to breathe.

Hello, Morrigan.

"Go back to your horse goddess, Chosen One, you have no business here!" Pryderi's voice was venomous with anger.

Oh, shut up, you pathetic creature. I have every right to be here. I've lost one daughter. This one I will not lose.

"You have no say in this! Morrigan has chosen me and not a careless goddess who abandons her to flounder about in the dark. Go back to your temple and leave my priestess to me."

Shannon didn't even glance at the dark god. She had eyes only for Morrigan. *You didn't cause the death of any of these people. Pryderi did. It wasn't your power that was uncontrolled, it was his.*

"That doesn't change the fact that all of this happened because of me," Morrigan said.

Not because of you, honey. Because he *wants you. Don't give him what he wants. Don't make their deaths meaningless. Adsagsona awaits your pledge.*

"Then why isn't the cave goddess here?" Pryderi shouted.

Without looking at the dark god, Shannon said, *He knows that answer as well as I do. Like Epona, the Goddess Adsagsona will not cajole, lie or manipulate you into her service. You must come to her freely, of your own will. Morgie, honey, she has already marked you as her own. All you need to do is take the next step.*

Morrigan looked back at the silent bodies of Kegan and Birkita and Brina. "But if I choose Adsagsona, will she control my powers?"

The goddesses don't control us. They love us and care for us and ask us to make the right choices for ourselves and our people. It is you who must control yourself.

Pryderi's terrible laughter filled the knoll. "I told you how they are—uncaring, distant, too divine to truly love."

Morrigan felt her presence before she spoke.

You must make your own choice, my daughter.

Rhiannon had materialized beside Shannon. Her form was less tangible than even Shannon's ethereally transparent shape, but her voice filled the air—and it was a voice she could now recognize. Morrigan had heard it on the wind, singing lullabies, speaking encouragement, murmuring soft endearments that were almost, but never quite completely, drowned out by Pryderi's more powerful, darkly compelling whispers.

"Mom!" Morrigan gasped the word as if it were a lifeline she was trying to clutch.

Rhiannon smiled her bittersweet smile. *Morrigan, my daughter, you trusted love, you trusted loyalty, now you must find the strength to trust honor.*

"But whose honor do I trust? Adsagsona's? She's not even here," Morrigan cried.

The Goddess is always here, my daughter, Rhiannon said.

And it's yourself who represents honor, Morgie honey, yourself you must trust, Shannon said.

"Show them, Precious One," Pryderi said. "Show them that you have the strength to choose me."

Morrigan bowed her head and the confusion within her cleared. She knew beyond any doubt what she had to do—she also knew she had to get the strength to do it. As she had that wonderful evening with Kegan that seemed forever ago, she reached through her body and down into the earth and the sacred selenite crystals below her.

Light Bringer!

You have to come with me when I call you, all of you. She filled her mind with the thought and sent it back through the connection.

We hear and obey you, Light Bringer.

When Morrigan raised her head she didn't look back at the bodies of the two people she'd loved so much, and the big cat who had been her protector. She didn't look at the glistening forms of her two mothers. Instead Morrigan kept her gaze on the dark god and the crystal boulders that had behind him blazed into a light so brilliant it rivaled the raging fire of the madly burning funeral pyre. Morrigan began to walk slowly to him. By the time she stood before him, he was smiling triumphantly.

"I knew you would be mine, Precious One. Together we will create a new kind of world." He held his arms out to her. "Kiss me, and you will forever be mine."

Everything seemed to happen in slow motion as Morrigan stepped into his arms. Instead of kissing him, she wrapped her arms around him and shouted, "Now light! Come to me! Burn through me!" Instantly, Morrigan was ablaze with the power of the crystals as their white light surged through her body, engulfing Pryderi as well as her. His eyes widened in surprise and he tried to push her away from him, but Morrigan shouted again, "Keep him here! Hold him to me!" And, just as she prayed they would, the power of the crystals obeyed her will.

Morrigan! What are you doing! Shannon was suddenly there. Morrigan could see her over Pryderi's shoulder. Rhiannon was still beside her, only her mom didn't look upset. Her mother nodded slowly at her and, with a voice filled with pride and love, said, *You have chosen well, my daughter. My pride in you is eternal.* Morrigan saw Rhiannon take Shannon's hand. *You must allow Morrigan her destiny, Shannon.* Then her attention was pulled back to Pryderi as the god increased his struggle to break free of her.

"What are you doing!" he yelled. "Release me!"

"No, Pryderi. You see, I've made my choice. I choose Adsagsona and free will. And with my free will I've decided that it's time your evil came to an end."

"No!" Pryderi shrieked. His beautiful face rippled and re-formed as he continued to try to free himself from the burning, white-hot strength of the Light Bringer's power. His sensuous mouth was seared shut. His nose became a grotesque hole. His eyes were no longer smiling and kind. They glowed with an inhuman yellow light. Then, as Morrigan gathered herself for what she knew she had to do, his eyes became dark, empty caverns and the mouth ripped open to show bloody fangs and a slavering maw.

Morrigan looked into that terrible face and smiled grimly. "As of now you are through." With the dark god trapped in her arms, Morrigan MacCallan, Light Bringer and Chosen of Adsagsona, closed her eyes, breathed a last prayer to the Goddess—*Help me to find Kegan again*—and then threw herself into the funeral pyre.

The pain was soul searing and complete, but it lasted only an instant. And Morrigan took the dark god, Pryderi, with her as she died.

EPILOGUE 1

Oklahoma

"Goddammit, I don't care what every knot-headed sheriff in this back-ass-wards county says. I'm not going to quit looking until I find my granddaughter's body!"

"Listen, Mr. Parker, I understand what you're going through but—"

"Like hell you do!" Richard Parker barked at him. "Has your granddaughter ever been buried in a cave-in?"

"Well, sir, I'm twenty-seven. I don't have a granddaughter."

"That's what I said. Like hell you understand. Now either help me or get out of my goddamn way. I could care less if you've officially called off the search for her. I won't call it off till the job's done." Richard shoved past the young sheriff and reentered the cave. "Young pup. Still wet behind his damn ears. Some nerve tryin' to tell me what to do," he mumbled to himself.

"Coach, do we keep digging?"

Richard stopped and looked at the dozen or so men who waited for him inside the cave. They ranged in age from early twenties to late forties and were a mixture of races as well as socioeconomic statuses. But they were all exhausted—all dirty-faced. And they all had one other thing in common besides having at one time played football for Richard Parker. They all would do anything for him.

The old coach smiled grimly at them. "Yep, yep, yep, we keep digging. Mama Parker will be here with some food soon. When the sun sets we'll call it a day and start again tomorrow."

"Got ya, Coach."

Richard grabbed his own pick and shovel and paused to pull the leather gloves out of his pocket and put them on, wincing only a little at the blisters on his palms that had broken open during the past hour. With an air of stubborn resignation, he took his place in the deepest part of the tunnel. It had taken them ten days to clear this far. He knew they were close. They had to be close. He'd find her. She wouldn't be alive. But he'd find his girl and then he'd take her home and bury her.

When his pick hit the boulder he knew by the feel of it what it had to be and carefully, using only his hands, he started to work free the rocks that had fallen against the selenite boulder. He tried not to think too much as he worked. Tried not to remember that the last time he'd seen her Morgie had been standing beside this very boulder.

He found the empty space when he moved the large, flat stone. Tepee-like, two other flat rocks had fallen against the side of the crystal boulder to create a small tent of space. Richard drew a deep, steadying breath and then reached in. His gloved fingers touched something too soft to be rock. Quickly, he pulled the gloves off with his teeth and got on his knees so that he could fit the top part of his body partially into the space. He reached in and touched her. Richard sighed and whispered a prayer to Epona, or whatever god or goddess had guided his digging. He tightened his grip on her and braced himself to pull the body of his girl from the rubble.

Then the old coach froze. Under his bare hand her flesh

wasn't cold and rubbery and dead. She was warm and soft. Carefully and slowly he pulled and she slid easily free of the space. With a steady hand, Richard pressed his fingers against her neck. Her pulse beat steady and strong against his fingers.

With a shout that had the men running to him, he cradled Morrigan carefully in his arms and began striding from the cave.

"Call 911 and Mama Parker! Hell, call that damn wet pup of a sheriff! I found her and my girl's alive!"

When Morrigan opened her eyes her vision was preternaturally clear. She was lying down and covered to her chest with a sheet and thin blanket. Morrigan wasn't in pain and she didn't have a clue where she was. She looked up to see a dim fluorescent light glowing above her head. Beside her bed was an IV tree that held a couple bags of clear stuff. She followed the tubes with her eyes and saw that they were attached to her body. A machine was beeping softly beside the IVs. Wires from it were attached to her chest. Morrigan looked around the hospital room. On a couch next to a draped window Grandpa and Grandma were sound asleep. Morrigan smiled. G-pa's glasses had fallen down on his nose. He'd kicked off his shoes, and his socks were bagging at the toes, as per usual. His arm was wrapped around G-ma, who looked tiny and sweet snuggled into his side, and very, very much alive.

Birkita was dead.

With that single thought her memory gushed back in a painful torrent. Birkita was dead. Kegan was dead. Brina was dead.

For that matter, she was dead.

You are not dead, Morrigan Christine MacCallan Parker, Light Bringer and my Chosen One.

Slowly, Morrigan moved her gaze from her sleeping grandparents to the woman who stood at the foot of her bed. Her beauty was so great that Morrigan had to squint to look at her, and then she realized that it wasn't just her beauty that was so difficult to look upon, it was her divinity, her essence, the awe-inspiring love that she exuded.

"Adsagsona?"

The Goddess smiled. *That is one of my names. I am also called Epona and Modron, Anu and Byanu, as well as countless others. I have many names because mortals have many needs and often it is difficult for them to understand that we are all the Goddess, the embodiment of the forces of the sacred land.*

"I should be dead!" Morrigan blurted, then looked quickly at her peacefully sleeping grandparents.

Worry not, Beloved, they will continue to sleep. We shall not be interrupted. The Goddess looked fondly at the sleeping couple before turning her attention back to Morrigan. *It is quite simple. I could not allow you to die. I had already allowed too much pain and darkness to touch you. I could not let you sacrifice yourself like that.*

Morrigan felt a shiver of fear. "Pryderi? Is he alive, too?"

The goddess's beautiful face darkened. *Pryderi is immortal, and thus he cannot truly die. But what your sacrifice did was to cause him such a wound that you banished him from Partholon and your world for generations and from the Realm of the Sidetha for eternity.*

Morrigan sighed. "So after all of that he's not dead."

Evil can never be utterly destroyed, Beloved. It can be defeated though, again and again. I ask you to forgive me, my Chosen One. Your young life has been difficult. You must understand that I had to let you struggle with the darkness yourself because it is only when evil is seen in its true form by mortals, without the interference of the gods, that the mortal spirit can find the love and loyalty and honor to rise up against it and prevail.

Morrigan thought about Kegan and Birkita and Kai and even Brina, and she knew without any doubt that all of them had looked upon evil and prevailed against it, even though it had caused their deaths. She only wished the Goddess had let her die so that she could join all of them and, according to the Sidetha's funeral rite, begun the journey to a new life.

"I forgive you," she said softly.

The Goddess inclined her head graciously. *I thank you, Beloved, for your forgiveness as well as your many sacrifices.*

"What happens now?" Morrigan asked, feeling the weight of those sacrifices pressing around her heart.

Now you live a full, rich life, my Beloved.

"In Oklahoma?" She wanted to add *without Kegan,* but she couldn't quite make the words come.

This world needs you, Beloved. They have forgotten what it is to revere the land and the Goddess who embodies it. As my High Priestess, you shall help them to remember.

"But what about the Sidetha? Their High Priestess is dead." Morrigan blinked hard, willing herself not to cry.

Now that the darkness that has been influencing and leading so many of them is gone, they will begin to appreciate the gifts I have already given them.

Morrigan nodded slowly. "Deidre isn't dead."

She lives, as does my favor within her.

"She'll make a good High Priestess."

And Arland will make an excellent Master, especially with Raelin as his Mistress.

"Arland's the guy who was so respectful to me in the amethyst room." She smiled at the Goddess. "And Raelin will be a great Mistress. Looks like the priorities of the Sidetha will be changing."

That is my intention, Beloved, as it is my intention that the people of the modern world begin to know the return of the Great Goddess.

Morrigan's smile faltered. "But I don't know what I'm doing. I need a High Priestess to help me."

The Goddess nodded toward Morrigan's sleeping grandmother. *You have a High Priestess who will guide you. Did you think I would allow all of my Beloved Birkita to perish? Much of her essence has always been here in this world with the mate of her soul, Richard Parker.*

Morrigan's eyes filled with tears. "I didn't know—I didn't understand."

There is much yet for you to learn and to understand. Remember, my blessing goes with you wherever you are. You will hear no more voices in the wind. Pryderi can no longer touch you.

"But what about my mom, Rhiannon? I know that sometimes I heard her voice. Won't I hear her anymore?"

The Goddess's smile was luminous. *Rhiannon has finally journeyed to my verdant meadows. Her task here is done—her atonement complete. But should you need to hear a mother's voice, listen to your heart. You will always find a part of Rhiannon, and Shannon, there.*

"I'll remember," Morrigan said through her tears.

Know that I am well pleased with you, my Beloved. You chose to trust love and loyalty and honor. But I ask you to remember one more emotion—one more truth.

"What is it?"

Hope, my Beloved. I want you to remember to trust hope.

"I'll remember hope." Morrigan thought of Kegan and felt a stab of painful loss. "Or at least I'll try," she said.

To try is all I can ask of any of my Beloved Chosen. And also remember how much I love you, Chosen One, and that my love will last for an eternity...

The Goddess raised her hands in blessing, and then with a shimmering of light, disappeared.

Morrigan was wiping her eyes and blowing her nose when her grandparents opened their eyes.

"Morgie old girl!" her grandpa cried, coming off the couch quickly, if a little stiffly, and taking her hand. "You're awake! Mama Parker, look, our girl's awake."

"Oh, hon!" Grandma hurried around to the opposite side of the bed to take Morrigan's other hand. "Are you okay? We've been so worried about you."

Morrigan squeezed their hands and smiled at them through a flood of new tears. "I'm fine! Really."

"You're home now, Morgie. Everything will be fine." G-pa kissed her hand roughly and wiped quickly at his eyes. Then he smiled across the bed at his wife. "I told your grandma that I'd find you. She was the only one who really believed me."

Grandma sniffled and brushed Morrigan's hair out of her face. "I knew that between your grandpa and the Goddess, a miracle was bound to happen."

"You found me, G-pa?" Morrigan asked.

"Yep, yep, yep. No way I wasn't going to. Everyone called it a miracle when I pulled that boy from the rubble." He snorted. "That was no damn miracle. I was already there and I've known CPR for a coon's age. It was you, Morgie old girl, you were my miracle."

Morrigan grinned at his familiar, craggy old face. Then all of what he said registered. "Wait, what boy?"

"Well, hon, that nice Kyle. The young man you were in the cave with that night," Grandma said.

"Shouldn't have had his hands all over you," Grandpa grumbled. "But it is a damn shame what happened to him. I could have liked him—if he'd learned to keep his hands to himself."

Morrigan shook her head. "I don't understand what y'all are talking about. Kyle died. I saw him buried by the cave-in."

"Nope. The boy was knocked out. I ran back in to get you after I made sure your grandma was safe. I couldn't get to you, Morgie, but I found Kyle and pulled him out."

"He wasn't breathing and he didn't even have a pulse, but your grandpa worked on him until the paramedics got there."

"He's alive?" Morrigan said, pushing herself up and trying to stop the shaking that had begun in her body.

"Steady, Morgie old girl. He's not really alive," her grandpa said gruffly.

"What do you mean? He's either alive or dead."

"What your grandpa means is that he never regained consciousness. He's been in a coma for almost two weeks now."

"Brain dead as a cabbage. They took the tubes out yesterday. It'll only be a few days and his body will follow the rest of him."

Morrigan wrapped her arms around herself and closed her eyes so that she could listen to her heart and hope flared in her like a burning crystal.

"Morgie, hon, we're so sorry," Grandma said gently, touching her shoulder. "We shouldn't have told her like that," she said to her husband.

Morrigan opened her eyes. "Take me to him."

"Oh, no, hon. You need to rest and it's late. Tomorrow will be soon enough."

Morrigan grabbed her grandma's hand and looked into her eyes. "Please. I have to see him. Now."

"You're too weak to walk," Grandpa said. "Besides, you have all that stuff hooked up to you."

Before he could stop her, Morrigan reached down and yanked both IVs out of her arm and the sticky things from her chest. "The stuff is gone, and I'm not too weak to walk." Morrigan swung her legs over the side of the bed and stood up, steady and straight, to prove it to him.

"Hon, let's show Morgie to Kyle's room," Grandma said, watching Morrigan closely.

"All right, but you two are going to have to explain what happened with those tubes and plugs to the nurse in the morning. And I don't want to hear a word from anyone if Morgie falls and hurts herself."

"I won't fall. I'm going to hang on to you, G-pa," Morrigan said, wrapping her arm through his.

"Huh," he snorted, but patted her hand gently where it rested on his arm.

Morrigan tried not to think. Her entire being was focused on one thing—hope. Her grandparents led her quietly from her room, down the short hall, and to another room almost identical to hers. They pushed open the door for her and she let loose her grandpa's arm. "I need to go in by myself, okay?"

"Of course, Morgie old girl. Your grandma and I will wait right out here for you."

Morrigan went up on her tiptoes and kissed his cheek. Then after they left the room she made her way slowly to Kyle's bedside.

He had a lot less stuff around his bed than she had had around hers. Morrigan studied his face. Even though he was too pale, and his cheeks were hollow and his eyes sunken, he looked so much like Kegan that she couldn't stop her tears. She sat on the edge of his bed and took his hand in both of hers.

"I know you're not Kegan, but you're all I have left of him and I was hoping that he might somehow be able to hear me because I know the two of you are connected. I didn't really get to tell you goodbye. Everything happened too fast. Kegan, it wasn't all for nothing. Our light beat the darkness, at least for a while—the Goddess said a good long while. I wanted you to know that." Her breath caught on a sob, and she wiped her eyes with her sleeve. "And I'll remember my promise. I'll trust hope and believe that somehow I'll find you. It might take another lifetime, but I'll find you, Kegan." She bent and pressed his limp hand to her lips. Then she lay his hand back on the bed, put her face in her hands to muffle her sobs and cried out her broken heart.

"Am I lost, my flame?"

Morrigan gasped and wiped frantically at her face to clear her vision.

Color was already beginning to return to his cheeks and he was smiling at her—that familiar, amazing, wonderful smile Birkita had called rakish.

"Kegan?"

"Morrigan, my flame, you will have to explain to me what has happened to the sword that not long ago pierced my chest and killed me," he said as he felt around his chest and didn't find a protruding hilt. Then he glanced down at his body and frowned. "And where is the rest of my body?"

"Kegan!" Laughing and crying at the same time, Morrigan hurled herself into his arms as her grandparents rushed into the room.

"Morgie, is everything—" her grandpa began, and then he snorted. "Boy has his hands all over her again."

In Kegan's arms Morrigan began to laugh, and echoing the sound of her happiness, the air around them in that room in Tulsa's very proper, very modern Saint Frances Hospital was filled with a cloud of glistening, golden-winged butterflies that circled the bed jubilantly before changing into yellow rose petals and falling all around them.

"Looks like Epona's been busy again. I do believe she's made another miracle," Richard Parker said as he put his arm around his beloved wife and watched his granddaughter, his girl, laugh in the man's arms who was supposed to be thoroughly dead.

"Oh, hon, I never doubted it."

EPILOGUE II

Partholon

I leaned back against ClanFintan and sighed contentedly as his arms came around me. Together we gazed down at our granddaughter, who was sleeping peacefully.

"I've missed you, my love," he said into my ear, careful to speak low so that Etain wouldn't wake up.

"I've missed you, too," I told him. "I'm sorry. I just couldn't find my way out of the pain to you."

His arms tightened around me. "I was here all along, waiting for you to come back to me."

"Thank you for loving me like you do."

I could feel the rumble of his familiar chuckle. "It has little to do with me. It is your goddess's doing, though I am heartily pleased she fashioned me for you."

"And me for you," I said. Then I paused and had to swallow several times before I said the rest of it. "Myrna's not really gone, you know. There's a part of her living here, in her beautiful daughter. There's a part of her living on in Epona's meadows with the Goddess. And there's a part of her—a magical part of her—that's living in Oklahoma with my parents and the man the Goddess fashioned to love her." I turned to look into his dark, familiar eyes then. "I can bear it now, and go on to find joy in this life."

"Shannon my girl, we will go on to find joy in many lives to come, may your goddess be willing."

As ClanFintan bent to claim my mouth I heard the whisper of Epona's loving voice in my heart and knew my spirit and my daughter's spirit and her daughter's spirit were truly at peace.

Well done, my Beloved One…well done…

The story continues in

ELPHAME'S CHOICE

Book Four of the
GODDESS OF PARTHOLON *series*

P.C. CAST

Read on for an exciting preview...

POWER. NOTHING WAS that good. Not Partholon's finest chocolate. Not the beauty of a perfect sunrise. Not even...no, she wouldn't know about *that*. She shook her head, purposefully changing the pattern of her thoughts. The wind whistled sharply through her hair, and some of the long strands blew into her face making her wish she had tied it back out of the way. She usually did, but today she had wanted to feel its heavy weight, and she admitted to herself that she liked the way it flowed behind her when she ran, like the flame-colored tail of a shooting star.

Her stride faltered as her concentration wavered and Elphame quickly regained control of her stray thoughts. Maintaining speed took focus. The field she ran in was relatively flat and free of most rocks and obstructions, but it wouldn't be wise to let her thoughts wander. One misstep could snap a leg all too easily; it would be foolish to believe otherwise. For all her life, Elphame had made it a point to shun foolish beliefs and behavior. Foolishness and folly were for people who could afford everyday, normal mistakes. Not for her, for someone whose very design said that she had been touched by the Goddess, and was, therefore, held apart from what was accepted as normal and everyday.

Elphame deepened her breathing and forced herself to relax her upper body. *Keep the tension in your lower body,* she reminded herself. *Keep everything else loose and relaxed. Let the most powerful part of your body do the work.* Her teeth glinted in an almost feral grin as she felt her body regather and shoot forward. Elphame loved the way the corded muscles in her legs responded. Her arms pumped effortlessly as her hooves bit into the soft green carpet of the young field.

She was faster than any human. Much faster.

Elphame demanded more of herself, and her body responded with inhuman strength. She may not have been as fast as a centaur over long distances, but few could outdistance her in a sprint, as her brothers liked to frequently boast. With a little more hard work, perhaps none would be able to best her. The thought was almost as satisfying as the wind on her face.

When the burning started she ignored it, knowing that she had to push herself beyond the point of simple muscle fatigue, but she did begin to angle her strides so that her run would take her in a huge spherical path. She would end up back where she had begun.

But not forever, she promised herself. Not forever. And she pushed herself harder.

"Oh, Goddess." Watching her daughter, Etain whispered reverently, "Will I ever get used to her beauty?"

She is special, Beloved. Epona's voice shimmered familiarly through her Chosen One's mind.

She pulled the horse to a halt well within the stand of trees that flanked one end of the field. The silver mare stopped and twisted her head around, cocking her ears at her rider in the horse's version of a question. And Etain knew that her mare, the equine incarnation of the Goddess Epona, really *was* asking a question.

"I just want to sit here and watch her."

The Goddess blew imperiously through her nose.

"I am not spying!" Etain said indignantly. "I am her mother. It is well within my right to watch her run."

The Goddess tossed her head in a reply that proclaimed she wasn't so sure.

"Behave with the proper respect." She jangled the mare's reigns. "Or I shall leave you at the temple next trip."

The Goddess didn't dignify the comment with so much as a snort. Etain ignored the mare who was now ignoring her, and muttered something about grumpy old creatures, but not loud enough for the mare to hear. Then she squinted her eyes and held her hand up to block the setting sun from interfering with her view.

Her daughter was running with a speed that caused her lower body to blur, so that it appeared that she flew above the brilliant green shoots of new wheat. She ran bent forward slightly at the waist, with a grace that always amazed her mother.

"She is the prefect blending of centaur and human," Etain whispered to the mare, who swiveled her ears to catch the words. "Goddess, you are so wise."

Elphame had completed the long loop in her imaginary track, and she was beginning to turn toward the grove in which her mother waited. The setting sun framed her running body, catching the girl's dark auburn hair on fire. It glowed and snapped around her in long, heavy strands.

"She certainly didn't get that lovely straight hair from me,"

Etain told the mare as she tried to tuck one of her ever-escaping curls behind her ear. The mare cocked an ear back attentively. "The red lights that streak her hair, yes, but the rest of it she can thank her father for." She could also thank him for the color of those amazingly dark eyes. The shape was hers—large and round, resting above high delicate cheekbones that were also copies of her mother's, but where Etain's eyes were mossy green, her daughter's eyes were the entrancing sable of her centaur father's. Even if Elphame's physical form hadn't been completely unique, her beauty would have been unusual—coupled with a body that only the Goddess could have created, the effect was breathtaking.

Elphame's pace began to slow, and she changed direction so that she was heading directly for the stand of trees in which her mother and the mare waited.

"We should make ourselves known so that she doesn't think we were lurking around in the shadows watching her."

They emerged from the tree line, and Etain saw her daughter's head snap in their direction in an instinctively defensive gesture, but almost immediately Elphame recognized them and raised her arm to wave hello at the same time the mare trumpeted a shrill greeting.

"Mama!" Elphame called happily. "Why don't you two join me for my cooldown?"

"Of course, my darling," Etain shouted back. "But slowly, you know the mare is getting old and—"

Before she could finish the sentence the "old mare" in question sprang forward and caught up with the young woman, where she pranced spryly sideways before easily matching her gentle canter with Elphame's gait.

"The two of you will never be old, Mama." Elphame laughed.

"She's just a putting on a show for you," Etain told her

daughter, but she reached down and affectionately ruffled the mare's silky mane.

"Oh, Mama, please. *She's* putting on a show…" Elphame let the sentence trail suggestively off as she quirked her eyebrow and gave her mother a knowing look that took in her glittering jewelry and the seductive wrap of her buttery leather riding outfit that fitted snuggly over her still shapely body.

"El, you know wearing jewelry is a spiritual experience for me," she said in her Beloved of the Goddess voice.

"I know, Mama." Elphame grinned.

The mare's snort was decidedly sarcastic, and Etain's laughter mingled with her daughter's as they continued compatibly around the field.

"Where did I leave my wrap?" Elphame muttered half to her mother, half to herself as she searched the edge of the tree line. "I thought I put it on this log."

Etain watched her daughter scramble over a fallen limb as she searched for the rest of her clothing. She wore only a sleeveless leather top, which was wrapped tightly around her full breasts, and a small strip of linen that hugged her muscular buttocks, and was cut high up on her hips, before it dipped down to a triangle to cover her in the front. Etain had designed it herself.

The problem was that although the girl's muscular body was covered with a sleek coat of horsehair from the waist down, and she had hooves instead of feet, except for the extraordinary muscles in her lower body she was otherwise built very much like a human female. So she needed a garment that would allow her the freedom to exercise the inhuman speed with which she had been gifted, as well as keep her decently covered. Etain and her daughter had experimented with many different styles before happening upon one that successfully accomplished both needs.

The result had worked well, except that it left so much of Elphame's body visible. It mattered little that the women of Partholon had always been free to proudly display their bodies. Etain regularly bared her breasts during blessing rituals to signify Epona's love of the female form. When Elphame uncovered her hoofed legs, people stared in outright shock and awe at the sight of the Chosen's so obviously Goddess-touched body.

Elphame loathed being the recipient of the stares.

So it had become habit for Elphame to dress conservatively in public, only shedding her flowing robes when she ran, which was almost always alone and well away from the temple.

"Oh, I found it!" El cried, and trotted over to a log not far from where they stood.

She picked up the length of fine linen that had been dyed the color of emeralds and began winding it around her slim waist. Her breathing had already returned to normal; the fine sheen of sweat that had caused the downy hair on her bare arms to glisten had already dried.

She was in spectacular shape. Her body was sleek, athletic and perfectly honed, but there was nothing harsh or masculine about its casing. Her lovely brown skin looked silky and seductively touchable; it was only after actually touching her that the finely wrapped strength of the muscles beneath the skin could be fully realized.

But few people dared to touch the young goddess.

She was tall, towering several inches over her mother's five-foot-seven-inch frame. During early puberty she had been thin and a little awkward, but soon the curves and fullness of womanhood had replaced that coltishness. Her lower body was a perfect mixture of human and centaur. She had the beauty and allure of a woman, and the strength and grace of a centaur.

Etain smiled at her daughter. As from the moment of her

birth, she had embraced Elphame's uniqueness with a fierce, protective love. "You don't have to wear that wrap, El." She hadn't realized she had spoken her thought aloud until her daughter looked quickly up at her.

"I know you do not think I need to." Her voice, usually so like her mother's, suddenly hardened with suppressed emotion. "But I have to. It is not the same for me. They do not look upon me as they do you."

"Has someone said something to hurt you? Tell me who it is and he will know the wrath of a goddess!" Green fire flashed in Etain's eyes.

Elphame's voice lost all expression as she answered her mother. "They do not need to say anything, Mama."

"Precious one—" the anger melted from Etain's eyes "—you know the people love you."

"No, Mama." She held up her hand to stop her mother from interrupting. "They love *you*. They idolize and worship me. It is not the same thing."

"Of course they worship you, El. You are the eldest daughter of the Beloved of Epona, and you have been blessed by the Goddess in a very special way. They should worship you."

The mare moved forward until her muzzle lipped the young woman's shoulder. Before she answered, El reached around the mare's head to stroke her gleaming neck.

She looked up at her mother and said with a conviction that made her sound older than her years, "I am different. And no matter how badly you want to believe that I fit in, it's just not the same for me. That is why I must leave."